How Enchanting,
How Utterly Enchanting Noelle
Was, Simon Thought . . .

He watched as she sat dabbling her bare feet in the mountain pool. It was maddening to think there was no way she could have plunged into the pool with him, both of them stark naked, to disport themselves to their hearts' content, and then to make love on a bed of ferns as nature must have intended since the inception of time.

Noelle drew her feet out of the pool, and bent to dry them as well as she could on the hem of her petticoat. He went to kneel in front of her, to help her draw on her shoes, and the feel of her slender, high-arched foot in his hands sent a new wave of madness flowing through him. He laced the ribbons around her ankles and tied them, and then he stood and drew her into his arms, and he was kissing her at last . . .

Dear Reader,

We, the editors of Tapestry Romances, are committed to bringing you two outstanding original romantic historical novels each and every month.

From Kentucky in the 1850s to the court of Louis XIII, from the deck of a pirate ship within sight of Gibraltar to a mining camp high in the Sierra Nevadas, our heroines experience life and love, romance and adventure.

Our aim is to give you the kind of historical romances that you want to read. We would enjoy hearing your thoughts about this book and all future Tapestry Romances. Please write to us at the address below.

The Editors
Tapestry Romances
POCKET BOOKS
1230 Avenue of the Americas
Box TAP
New York, N.Y. 10020

False Paradise

Lydia Lancaster

A TAPESTRY BOOK

PUBLISHED BY POCKET BOOKS NEW YORK

Books by Lydia Lancaster

The Arms of a Stranger
False Paradise

Published by TAPESTRY BOOKS

An *Original* publication of TAPESTRY BOOKS

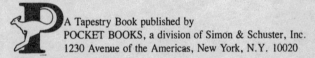

A Tapestry Book published by
POCKET BOOKS, a division of Simon & Schuster, Inc.
1230 Avenue of the Americas, New York, N.Y. 10020

ISBN: 0-671-54607-4

First Tapestry Books printing July, 1986

10 9 8 7 6 5 4 3 2 1

POCKET and colophon are registered trademarks
of Simon & Schuster, Inc.

TAPESTRY is a registered trademark of Simon & Schuster, Inc.

Printed in the U.S.A.

False
Paradise

Chapter One

THERE WAS NOTHING THAT NOELLE MAYNARD FELT LESS like doing than attending Brenda Cottswood's eighteenth birthday celebration. As fond as she was of Brenda, who had been her friend since childhood, Noelle wouldn't have made the journey into Kingston from Maynard Penn, and agreed to spend at least a week away from the plantation, if her half sister Vanessa hadn't virtually driven her to go.

"I'm sick and tired of looking at your face! You're driving me out of my mind, hovering over Father day and night and acting like a ghost at the feast! It isn't as if you can do anything for him, the house is filled with servants who attend to his every need, and he's hardly aware that you're here. The Cottswoods will be mortally offended if you don't put in an appearance, and goodness knows you have few enough friends left as it is, isolating yourself here in the country as you've done ever since Father was stricken."

1

There was enough truth in Vanessa's words to make them sting, even though Noelle knew that it wasn't out of consideration for her that Vanessa was so determined to send her away for several days. Vanessa had her hooks into another man. This time it was Jonathan Farnsworth, whose wife was sweet and trusting, and who had three small children. Noelle herself would rather have died than come between a man and his wife, enticing the man to betray not only the one who loved and trusted him, but his own moral code, but Vanessa had no such inhibitions. When Vanessa had an itch, she scratched it, it was as simple as that, and if lives were ruined in the process, it was no concern of Vanessa's.

Noelle was certain that she herself was the only person on the island of Jamaica who knew that her sister wasn't what she seemed to be. In appearance Vanessa was an angel, her golden hair and melting blue eyes adding to the impression she gave of total goodness. But appearances were deceiving. Vanessa's beauty concealed a total lack of morals or conscience.

Noelle knew that Daniel Maynard, their father, had never had an inkling of Vanessa's true character. She herself had only begun to suspect a little more than a year ago, but she had been horrified at her suspicions, even wondering if jealousy of the far more beautiful girl prompted her to try to find some flaw in her half sister's character. But then her younger brother Kenneth had come storming into the house late one afternoon, his face white with shock, and trembling with fury.

"Noelle, it isn't a proper subject for me to talk to you about. You're a girl and you shouldn't even know about such things. But as soon as Father gets back from Spanish Town, all hell is going to break loose, and you have a right to be forewarned. It's going to just about kill Father, but I have to tell him. We can't let Van go on as she is, and only he can put a stop to it."

"Ken, what on earth are you raving about?" Noelle had felt her blood go cold, and she had a feeling that

2

something dreadful was about to happen, that would tear their family apart. "What has Vanessa done?"

"She's having an affair with a married man, that's what she's done! I saw them with my own eyes, Van and Mr. Gorden, Andrew Gorden! They were in the foothills, by that waterfall where we've picnicked so often. They were so wrapped up in each other that they didn't even hear my horse when I approached them."

Kenneth's laugh had been bitter. "When I say wrapped up, I mean that literally! They were making love, Van's hair was down around her shoulders and that's the only thing that covered her, she was stark naked, and so was Mr. Gorden, and they were rutting like . . . like . . ."

Noelle's face had lost every trace of color, and then flamed with a shock that matched Kenneth's own. On several different occasions, she had thought that she had seen something pass between her sister and one or another of the neighboring men, but she had never dreamed that it had gone as far as this! She had figured it was harmless flirtation, no more than that, although harmless flirtations were frowned upon even in this year of 1832.

"Kennie, not Mr. Gorden! Why, Sarah Gorden is the sweetest woman in Jamaica, and they have children! A married man, she wouldn't, she couldn't!"

"She could, and she would, and she did. I've suspected something like this for months now, only I never caught her in the act before. There's a certain way a woman looks at a man, a man always knows." At sixteen, Kenneth considered himself a man, with all a man's knowledge of women. In any other circumstances his sureness of his masculine perspicacity would have been amusing, but there was nothing amusing about this.

"Noelle, you should have seen Van's face when I shouted at them! You never saw such fury! I think she would have killed me with her bare hands if she could have. But of course she couldn't. Andrew Gorden wasn't angry, he was horrified, I swear I thought he was going to cry! He kept stammering and stuttering and trying to tell

Van that I wouldn't betray them, but I set them both straight about that in short order, I can tell you! I'm not going to bruit it about, of course, our family would never be able to live down the disgrace. But I told Mr. Gorden what I thought of him, and Vanessa, too. I told him that I'd find some pretext to call him out if I ever saw him anywhere near Vanessa again. He was still trying to pull on his trousers when I left, assuring me that he would remove himself from the island if only I would promise that no word of his indiscretion reached his wife's ears.''

"Are you really going to tell Father? It will all but kill him! Wouldn't it serve for Mr. Gorden just to leave Jamaica and never come back?''

"No, it wouldn't.'' Kenneth's face had been set. "I'm certain that this kind of thing has taken place before. I've told you that I've seen Van look at this man or that, always married men. I suspect she thinks married men are safer, you see. They're not in any position to make a fuss when Van throws them over, and they have even more reason to keep their affair a secret than she does. Don't you remember how George Hunnicutt left the island a few months ago, taking his pregnant wife with him? He looked like death warmed over, and I'd seen Van looking at him with that hotness in her eyes on more than one occasion. She looked like a cat that had a bird in its power, just waiting to pounce and rend it limb from limb. Hunnicutt used to get so nervous that he was shaking in his boots, and my guess is that he couldn't bear it any more, and so he left.''

Pacing up and down Noelle's room, with its louvered windows and the mosquito guard around the tester bed, Kenneth's face had been set. The honor of the family was at stake; Vanessa had to be stopped before she brought disgrace down on all of them. He was certain that his older half sister was as immoral as an alley cat, that no one man could ever satisfy her, and sooner or later everything would come crashing down around their heads because some poor fool of a man would lose his head and blab the whole story of their illicit affair.

"I need a drink. Finding Van like that shook me up more than a little. I just wanted to warn you what to expect when Father gets home." Kenneth was not a drinker. Daniel Maynard was abstemious in his own consumption, taking a glass only on social occasions, and his son was following in his footsteps, but he was proud of having attained the age when his father left his consumption up to his own discretion. Being allowed to choose what and how much and when to drink was a mark of manhood.

Their father was in Spanish Town consulting with the governor about the Emancipation Act, which would free the slaves, about how best to offset the financial repercussions that were sure to follow. He was also concerned about the welfare of the slaves once they were set free, and wanted steps outlined to assure that they would not suffer undue hardship once their livelihood was not provided for by their owners.

There was also concern over the numerous slave uprisings on the island, caused by the mistaken belief among the slaves that the act had already been passed and that the fact was being withheld from them, so that they were still being held in bondage when they should be free. The uprisings, although small and fairly isolated, were worrisome, and caused a good deal of uneasiness among the whites on the island. The future of the Jamaican planters did not look bright, and like all of the other wealthy whites of Jamaica, Daniel was trying to salvage whatever could be salvaged from the debacle that was sure to come.

Fortunately, Daniel had been wiser than most of his fellow planters. A farsighted man, he had seen the inevitable emancipation coming, he had not overextended himself, and he had made large and prudent investments outside of Jamaica. Where his contemporaries would be ruined, he would be left with a considerable fortune no matter what befell, but still he felt that it was his duty to do everything possible to bring the emancipation about with as little suffering to both whites and blacks as men of integrity could devise.

It would be several days before Daniel returned to

Maynard Penn. Noelle dreaded having to face Vanessa when her sister returned from her shameful rendezvous with Andrew Gorden. As dreadful as the scene was bound to be when her father was confronted with his older daughter's immorality, it would have been a relief to have gotten it over with immediately, instead of letting the tension hover over them all like a dark cloud.

How could she bear to look at Vanessa, what could she find to say to her? The very foundations of her life were shaking. For a gently born, young unmarried lady to indulge in affairs of the flesh with any man, let alone with married men, was so unthinkable that if Vanessa's behavior were to be discovered by the general public the very fabric of their lives would be rent into a thousand tattered pieces.

As it happened, Noelle did not see Vanessa at all that day, or for several days to follow. Vanessa returned to the plantation house, but only long enough to pack some boxes, and then she left without seeing either Noelle or Kenneth.

"Do you suppose she's making a run for it, now that she's been caught out?" Kenneth had wondered as he and Noelle shared their evening meal. "She could manage it, I suppose, she has her mother's jewels, you know that Father gave them to her on her eighteenth birthday. And no doubt she could persuade her former lovers to give her all they could scrape up on short notice, with a promise of more to follow. There's always some ship sailing from Kingston, she could go anywhere, lose herself completely so that she would never have to face Father's wrath."

Noelle had been presented with her own mother's jewels on the advent of her eighteenth birthday, which had taken place only two months before, but the pieces were nowhere near as numerous or as valuable as those that Daniel had lavished on his first wife, Michelle. Daniel had worshiped the ground Michelle walked on, just as he worshiped Vanessa, who was the exact image of her dead mother. Michelle had died when Vanessa had been only two, and Daniel had never loved another woman. He had

6

married Laura, Noelle and Kenneth's mother, a year later, only because he had needed a mother for Vanessa and a mistress for his plantation, and because of his urgent need for a male heir.

Noelle had no quarrel with the way Daniel had treated her mother. Laura had been small and dark, gentle and rather plain of face except for the sweetness of her smile, and Daniel had never been anything but the personification of kindness to her. If he could not love her as he had loved Michelle, he had been genuinely fond of her, he had respected her and treated her with gentleness that had never wavered. He had been grateful to her for giving him first Noelle, and then Kenneth, the boy he needed to walk in his footsteps when the time came.

But Laura had cared little for jewels and such. She had been content to run the plantation house, to supplement her husband's care of the slaves with her own compassion and gentleness. Shy and retiring, she had cared little for society, and she had never ventured to try to compete with Daniel's first wife, whose beauty had become a legend. She had loved Daniel with her whole heart, and never demanded that he love her as he had loved Michelle.

Laura had been a contented woman. If her husband felt less passion for her than she for him, still she was secure in the knowledge that he loved her in his own way. He had given her two children, whom she had raised with discipline tempered with adoration, and when she died, when Noelle was fifteen, she left this life without complaint.

Like her mother, Noelle had little use for the trappings of wealth, and she had loved and admired her beautiful older sister until Vanessa's indifference to her had made her turn to her brother for companionship, a companionship that had grown and flowered until they had become like two halves of a whole. She and Kenneth were confidants and friends; their loyalty to and love for each other had remained unshaken even through childhood disagreements and the difficult period when Kenneth had taken up purely male pursuits in which she could not share.

7

"She didn't take Chloe with her, so maybe she is running." Noelle had looked at Kenneth, and the hope in his eyes was echoed in her own. Chloe had been Vanessa's nursemaid since the day Vanessa had been born, and the huge black woman was never left behind when Vanessa visited Kingston or Spanish Town or other plantations.

They both went to bed that night with hope in their hearts that Vanessa had gone. In the morning, when Vanessa had not reappeared, their hope soared. Chloe professed to know nothing, only that her charge had decided to visit Kingston and had refused to take her with her.

"Said she wouldn't need me, said she ain't goin' be gone that long." Chloe said, her face impassive. "Said that long's Massa Daniel's away, I'm needed here, to keep the slaves in hand."

There was no doubt that Chloe was a great influence in keeping the other slaves in hand, even though there was little danger of an uprising on a plantation where the master always treated them fairly. The other slaves were terrified of Chloe, because the black woman was that rarity in Jamaica, an obeah woman. On the island, it was men who nearly always held such a position of power, the power of magic, of being able to work charms and lay curses on their enemies, the power of life and death. Chloe had only to speak, and her orders were obeyed. Daniel had always frowned on the woman's pretentions to magic powers, and he would have sold her long ago, disliking the fear she aroused in his people, except that Vanessa had wept and begged, and he could never bear to deny Vanessa anything.

It had sounded more and more as if Vanessa were gone for good. Daniel would grieve, but they would do everything they could to ease his grief. He would probably search for her, but they had confidence that if Vanessa did not choose to be found, she would not be found. They might even hint that she had eloped with a man not wealthy or aristocratic enough to meet with Daniel's

8

approval, and try to convince him that wherever she was, she was well and happy and she would get in touch with him eventually.

It was that afternoon that Kenneth came down with a slight indisposition. It had seemed trivial at first, but the next day his condition had worsened, and Doctor Eastlake had been sent for. The doctor had said that it appeared to be an infection of some sort, although he had had no idea of its source.

On the third day Kenneth had gone into delirium, and then lapsed into a coma, and he had died that evening just as the sun was going down. His death had come so suddenly that Daniel Maynard had not been sent for. Noelle, and Doctor Eastlake as well, had thought that the young man would be well on the road to recovery before Daniel returned.

The doctor had shaken his head and said that it was one of those unaccountable things, a tragedy that could not have been prevented. Daniel arrived home to find his house a house of mourning.

And Vanessa had been with him. Vanessa, weeping, seemingly devastated with the same grief that was tearing her father apart, Vanessa clinging to him for comfort just as he clung to her, inconsolable in their grief.

It had been impossible for Noelle to go to Daniel with her story of Vanessa's wicked affairs. Not only impossible, but it would have been inhuman. And even through her own grief, which came near to threatening her sanity, Noelle had realized that without Kenneth to tell his story, she had no proof, and there was no doubt whose word her father would believe when it was a choice between her and Vanessa. She could only hope and pray that having had such a narrow escape, Vanessa would be frightened into changing her ways, and there would be no more affairs.

But she determined to watch Vanessa carefully, and if the affairs did resume, she would attempt to get proof so that she could warn her father about what was going on, in time for him to put a stop to it before scandal compounded the grief that was already devastating him.

To Noelle's already grief-stricken horror, Daniel's grief over Kenneth had affected him to such an extent that his health had begun to deteriorate. Special diets, doses prescribed by Doctor Eastlake, had little or no effect. Little by little, Daniel's once robust body had weakened, his hands developed a tremor so that he spilled his coffee when he lifted his cup to his lips, his strength seemed to seep away day by day. Every day, he rested more and attended to the affairs of the plantation a little less. He lost weight, until he was reduced to skin and bones.

Doctor Eastlake was at a loss. "Grief sometimes has lethal effects on the human body. I feared for him when he lost Vanessa's mother, but he pulled out of it then and we can only hope that he will pull out of this."

"It can't be just grief! He must have some disease!" Noelle cried out to the doctor in her agony as she watched her father dying before her eyes.

"My dear girl, it is no disease that I have ever come across. Believe me, I have researched every available source on strange and exotic diseases, and I have consulted my colleagues. We have come to the conclusion that this is a sickness of the spirit against which only love and care and prayer can be effective. It isn't to be wondered at that two such losses as your father has suffered should have affected his health. There is still hope. Go on as you are doing, tending him with loving care. Sooner or later he will come to the realization that although he has lost his son, he still has you and Vanessa, and he will make the effort to get well."

But so far, it had not happened. And little by little, over the intervening months, Vanessa had taken over the reins of the plantation, until now she was the acting mistress of Maynard Penn. With Chloe one step behind her, as was proper and respectful for a slave, she issued her orders, and she was obeyed.

When George Martin, who had been at Maynard Penn for so long that he had grown old in his position as the head white overseer, decided that it was time to retire and spend the remainder of his life with one of his sons and his

10

daughter-in-law, enjoying watching his grandchildren grow up, Vanessa had not replaced him. They still had Michael Martin. But then Mr. Martin had become ill, and Doctor Eastlake had told him that it was essential for him to return to the more invigorating climate of England if he were to regain his health, and Vanessa had not replaced him either.

Now only black overseers remained on the plantation. When concerned planters remonstrated with Vanessa, she pointed out that with the emancipation so near it was hardly worthwhile to find replacements. Her black overseers were competent and trustworthy, and there had never been any trouble at Maynard Penn. When her father recovered sufficiently to take over its management again, it would be up to him to choose replacements if he thought that it was worthwhile. In the meantime, things were running smoothly, and she was saving the plantation money by getting along without white overseers.

Vanessa had no fear that there would be a slackening off of work because of the lack of white overseers. Chloe saw to that. The slaves' fear of her made them work to the limit of their capacity with no overseers set over them at all. Indeed, they worked even harder now that the white overseers were gone, in terror that Chloe would put a curse on them if they did not. Their master was sick and not able to protect them from being worked too hard, just as the white overseers had not driven them beyond their limit.

Noelle was so heartsick that she might have fallen into complete despair except for Dicey. Even as Chloe was loyal to Vanessa, Dicey, who was Noelle's age, was devoted to Noelle to the death.

Living on the plantation as they did, where the only companionship with other white girls of her own age came from infrequent visits, it was inevitable that Noelle and Dicey would become friends. As children they'd played together, and when Kenneth had begun to spend a good deal of his time at pursuits in which Noelle could not join him, the two girls had become even closer. And when the recent troubles had come, Noelle felt that if she hadn't had Dicey, she would have perished from loneliness.

Vanessa was once again carrying on her illicit affairs. Although no one outside of the plantation was aware of it, she was often away for a day or an evening, and returned with that smug, satisfied look on her face that told Noelle, with her new awareness, that she had sated herself with sex. Noelle had no doubt that all of these affairs were conducted with married men. What Kenneth had told her about married men being safer made sense. A married man was in no position to betray her.

Driven beyond endurance, sickened that Vanessa would behave in such a way while their father was so ill, she had at last confronted her sister with what she knew.

"How can you do it, how can you bring yourself to be so base, so low?" Noelle cried. "And how can you dare?"

"My sweet, innocent little sister, there is no danger involved. Every man I grant my favors is under the impression that I am madly in love with him, that only such deep and compelling love would have led me to give myself to him. And when I tire of him, I weep and tell him that I can no longer live with my guilt, that it tears me apart to think that I have betrayed his wife, his innocent children. I beg him to forgive me, I tell him that my love for him is so deep that I will never love anyone else, that I will never marry, but that our affair must end for the sake of my immortal soul, and his. They go away more deeply in love with me than ever, convinced that I'm a saint. It's all in knowing how to handle them, dear Noelle. If ever you should find yourself in need of such diversion, I will be happy to instruct you."

"You admit it, you admit it all!" Even though she had already known how debased her sister was, Vanessa's shameless admission shocked her to the core.

"But only to you, dear sister." Vanessa's laugh was mocking. "Who would believe you, if you were to carry tales? No one, my dear! I have already taken care to plant seeds of doubt on your credibility. How it grieves me to have my plainer, younger sister so jealous of me! I've done everything to make you love me, but still your resentment of me festers in your heart, until I weep and pray that some day your heart will soften toward me and you will love me as a sister should love a sister. No, dear Noelle, no one would believe you, your tales would be put down as still more of the jealous spite that I have made sure everyone believes of you!''

"You are a devil!'' Her face white with shock and rage, Noelle had made to strike her sister, but suddenly Chloe was standing between them, her dark, fathomless eyes filled with warning. Chloe, who was only a fraction under six feet tall, who must weigh well over two hundred pounds, none of it soft, but hard, as hard as iron. There was no way Noelle could reach Vanessa to punish her, there was no hurt she could do her, as long as Chloe was there, always on guard.

And even if Chloe were not there, for Noelle to lash out at and strike and beat and claw her sister would only prove to everyone that everything Vanessa said about her was true. Vanessa was too intelligent to fight back, she would suffer the beating, and then make sure that all of their friends saw the marks and bruises. Vanessa would sigh, her eyes melting with compassion, and make excuses for Noelle while holding back her tears, and her reputation as a living saint would be enhanced a hundredfold.

Sick with frustration, sick to her soul, Noelle understood much now that she had not understood in the past. It was inevitable that a good many young and eligible young men should have come courting the Maynard sisters, and even though Noelle lacked Vanessa's spectacular beauty, she had attracted a few admirers. But in every case the young man who had been so attentive at first had cooled toward her, and turned his hopeful affections toward Vanessa. Vanessa had poisoned their minds with her hints and insinuations and given them second thoughts about marrying a girl who was mean and spiteful.

Even Henry Cottswood, one of Brenda's two brothers, who had been the most persistent of Noelle's admirers, had turned from her, so infatuated with Vanessa and so determined to win her that it had seemed for a while that he might succeed in persuading her to marry him. When Vanessa gently disabused him of the notion, his infatuation for her had remained undiminished.

Noelle had not harbored any romantic notions about Henry even when he had been courting her. Squarely and solidly built, overbearing and having an inflated opinion of himself, he was not Noelle's idea of a husband and lover, even though she was fond of him because she had known him all her life, and because he was Brenda's brother. Still, she had been bewildered and hurt when he had proved as faithless as all the others.

Now she knew what had happened. Vanessa had made him believe, as she had made all of the others believe, that she was a spiteful little cat who was jealous of her sister. Vanessa's patient grief had touched their hearts, and their hearts had promptly been handed to Vanessa on a silver platter.

It wasn't that Vanessa had wanted those green young men, who might have proved unmanageable if she had allowed them the privileges as her lover that she allowed married men. It was simply that she enjoyed taking them away from Noelle and watching her squirm.

And there wasn't a thing that Noelle could do about it. For the first time, she felt a surge of pure hatred rise in her heart. Before, she had been saddened and horrified at Vanessa's lack of morals, but now it was hate she felt, so overwhelming that it made her feel physically ill.

"You want me away from the plantation so that you can keep trysts with Jonathan Farnsworth," she threw at Vanessa. "No doubt you plan to bring him into this house, to carry on your affair with him under our father's roof! Father will never know, he's too sick to know what's going on in his own home, and none of the servants will dare to talk. He probably refused to come here, if I were here."

Vanessa was amused. "One point for you. I'm weary of meeting my lovers under the open sky, a bed will be a deal more comfortable, and the outside meetings carried an element of risk, as I learned when Kenneth stumbled over Andrew Gorden and me. So off you go. And if you think to tattle to Brenda, you had better think twice. I have already convinced Doctor Eastlake that I fear for your sanity, and dropped hints in a few other ears. The stage is set to take steps to keep you under control if you should prove troublesome . . . well out of the way of any more ears to listen to you.''

Noelle turned away from her sister blindly, convinced that if she stayed for one more moment she would try to kill Vanessa, even with Chloe there.

"You go," Dicey told her later, in the sanctuary of her own room. "You are looking mighty peaked these days, you need a change. Take Julie instead of me, I'll be right here watching over the master, I'll care for him as good as you, you know I will. You go along, and don't worry your head. I promise I won't take my eyes off your father till you get back."

Noelle was up against a stone wall, and there was no way out. She couldn't climb over it, or tunnel under it, or walk around it, and all of her cries for help went unheeded. Beating her hands against it only bruised and bloodied them. And all the time, Vanessa and Chloe watched, and smiled, their eyes filled with mockery, knowing her helplessness.

Vanessa had won, for now. But Noelle vowed that it would only be for now. Some day, some way, she would find a way to bring her sister down, and then she and her father could gather up the broken threads of their lives and begin to weave them into something new.

Chapter Two

THE COTTSWOOD HOUSE IN KINGSTON REFLECTED THE wealth of the family. Bertram Cottswood had made his fortune in trade, his warehouses were bursting with all the products of Jamaica. Sugar, coffee, indigo, rum, all that could be wrested from the fertile island passed through his hands, to be sold abroad at profits that had made him a very wealthy man.

The current hard times had not affected Bertram as much as they had the plantation families. Like Daniel Maynard, he had guarded his assets and invested wisely, although many other of Kingston's leading families were feeling the pinch.

For all the family's wealth and the fact that she was the pampered only daughter, Brenda was singularly unspoiled. A trifle plump, her round face lacking any real claim to beauty, she was so sunny-natured that she had no lack of young men eager for her company, and now she

16

was engaged to Bryce Lynford, and the betrothal was to be announced at her birthday fête.

In spite of her worry over her father, Noelle had enjoyed the drive in to Kingston. It had been too long since she had left the plantation, and the beauty of her surroundings had made her spirits lift in spite of herself.

The day was hot, but the striped awning of the open curricle provided shade against Jamaica's relentless sun, and a parasol further protected her complexion. As the curricle wended its way through the streets of the harbor town, she drew in a deep breath and smiled at the natives in their colorful costumes, carefree as they vended their wares or went about their unhurried errands for their masters.

Like all of the female slaves on the island, the young woman Julie wore a cashmere handkerchief draped over her shoulders, and a silk turban covered her hair, while gold hoop earrings glittered in the sunlight every time she moved her head. She wore the regulation striped dress, and she preened herself as she caught the eye of more than one young buck who grinned at her impudently, to Noelle's amusement. The men in their pink and white trousers and their pink or yellow shirts and their broad straw hats cut dashing figures, and she didn't blame Julie for being pleased. She'd see that the girl had ample freedom to wander while they were here, goodness knew that there was little enough pleasure at Maynard Penn for the slaves anymore.

The curricle no sooner had drawn up in front of the Cottswood residence than Brenda came flying with her hands outstretched, to throw her arms around her friend as soon as Noelle alighted.

"You came! I was so afraid you wouldn't, and I just couldn't have borne it! You'll never believe the surprise I have in store for you! A new man, and what a man! Two new men, actually, but Doctor Macintyre doesn't count, although he's personable enough and attractive in a sort of long-faced, homely way. But he hasn't two shillings to rub against each other even though he's so intelligent and

17

obviously of good family that he's beginning to be invited everywhere. It's the other man you must set your cap for. I declare that I'm having second thoughts about Bryce, I just might tell Papa not to announce our engagement until I have time to decide whether or not I might be able to snare Captain Spencer!

"Of course, I wouldn't care much for living in Boston, I've heard that everyone there is terribly dull and staid and I'd be bored to death. All the same I'm glad that Vanessa didn't come, because if she were here neither of us would have a chance, but as long as she isn't here you might as well see if you can be the lucky one, unless I tell you not to because I just might want him for myself!"

Brenda stopped talking only because she had run out of breath. In spite of the heaviness of her heart, Noelle had to laugh.

"How you run on! Who is this phenomenal Captain Spencer, who can make you have second thoughts about Bryce? You know you're madly in love with Bryce, and besides it would break his heart if you didn't marry him."

"I know, and I could never do that to Bryce, but I can't help thinking how exciting it would be if I weren't in love with him so I could set my cap for Captain Spencer! If Captain Spencer had come here before I fell in love with Bryce, I wouldn't have let him get away, I can tell you! Papa's done business with the Spencer Line for ages and ages, but Captain Spencer has never been here before. It just isn't fair that I should be in love with Bryce, and then have Captain Spencer show up when it's too late for anything to come of it, but I suppose that letting you have him will be almost as good because we're best friends, only I warn you that I'm going to flirt with him anyway even if my engagement to Bryce is going to be announced tomorrow night at the stroke of midnight!"

Brenda's chatter, as silly as most of it was, kept Noelle's mind off her worries about her father. Concern for him was still there just under the surface, but Brenda went from one subject to the next so rapidly that it was necessary to give all of your attention to what she was saying or you'd lose the thread. And gaiety like Brenda's was contagious, it was impossible to brood when she was around, making you laugh at her every other sentence.

Although the days in Jamaica were very hot, it almost always turned cool in the evening, when breezes from the mountains and the sea chased the heat away. It was going to be a lovely night for the birthday and engagement celebration, and Noelle could not help but feel a tingle of excitement as she surveyed herself in Brenda's cheval glass after Julie had finished dressing her and doing her hair. Noelle had told her that she was free the rest of the evening, much to the girl's delight. She had gone hurrying off to find excitement of her own, and now Noelle's anticipation grew as she heard carriages arriving, and she found herself wishing that she'd had a new gown made up.

She wasn't going to worry about her father tonight, she tried to assure herself. Dicey was with him, and she trusted Dicey. Besides, there was nothing she could do about it, here in Kingston, so she might as well enjoy herself, because she was determined that she would not leave Maynard Penn again until her father was well.

She confessed to herself that she was agog with curiosity to see this Captain Spencer whom Brenda had never ceased raving about. He had been off on an expedition to Spanish Town when Noelle had arrived yesterday, and had been gone all day today as well, with Henry and Claude Cottswood with him as companions and guides. No doubt the three men had been anxious to escape the hectic last-minute preparations for the party. But he would be here this evening, and Noelle would see at last just what it was about him that had put Brenda in such a state.

Giving herself one last look in the glass, she decided that she looked as well as it was possible for her to look considering the faint shadows under her eyes, brought on by countless days of worry and sleepless nights, and she turned to join the festivities that were already getting under way. Her heart was beating a little faster than normal, and there was a flush on her cheeks. A party without Vanessa there to overshadow her completely was enough to bring the flush of excitement to her cheeks and the sparkle to her eyes. It had never happened before, in all her life. And so she had better make the most of it, because it might never happen again.

Simon Spencer, too, was determined to enjoy this evening to the fullest. As long as he was compelled to spend a good deal more time in Jamaica than he had planned, since a storm at sea had damaged his ship, the *Maid of Boston*, he might as well enjoy himself. He had been brought up never to let an opportunity pass without making the most of it, his father holding that one lifetime was not enough to encompass everything a man needed to learn and to experience.

Simon enjoyed Claude and Henry's company. Claude was as jolly and easygoing as his sister, and when Henry put himself out to be affable he was good company.

The Governor's Palace in Spanish Town had been a surprise to him, not resembling in the least the other great houses he had already seen on the island. While these other houses were glaringly white and airy looking, the governor's house had been built in the mode of an English manor house, alien to its surroundings, a dark and gloomy edifice that Simon could not say he cared for.

Situated in Governor's Square, it was made even more incongruous by the statue of Lord Rodney which stood nearby. Flanked by two brass cannon, Lord Rodney was attired in Roman costume, so out of place here that Simon couldn't help wondering what the native Jamaicans thought of it. Not much, he was willing to wager, any more than he did himself.

To his gratification, the governor had been in residence, and Claude and Henry had been able to gain him an audience. Simon's father would be pleased at that, although he would be displeased at the delay that would put the *Maid of Boston* behind schedule.

But it was the countryside itself that Simon was most interested in. Nothing could be more different from

Massachusetts. The vegetation was so rank and lush that its impact fairly stunned him. There was color everywhere, so vivid that it was hard for the eye to credit it. Even the fences along the roads were festooned with exotic flowers, Pride of Barbados with its orange and scarlet bells trembling in the heat, forget-me-nots growing wild, and lilac sorrel.

Groves of tamerind trees with fernlike foliage intrigued him, as did the clouds of white and blue butterflies that flew in and out among the drooping branches of cabbage trees. Ebony trees were spectacular with blooms that his companions told him burst out after every shower. Hibiscus flamed, along with countless other blossoms that he could not put a name to. The dodder plants, with their leafless, tangled stems that looked for all the world like giant spiderwebs, left him speechless.

But for all the beauty that surrounded him, Simon was disturbed by the rot that underlay everything. Even the brilliant flowers showed black rot on their undersides when you investigated them closely, the decay shocking senses that only moments ago had thought that this paradise was perfect.

The paradise was imperfect in other ways, as well. Simon had already learned that there were two hundred thousand slaves on the island, and twenty thousand free blacks, born of a white father and a quadroon mother, who were considered white.

In comparison, there were only forty thousand whites. It was no wonder that there was an undercurrent of uneasiness all throughout Jamaica, although the white men he had met here did their best to discount it to outsiders like himself. To Simon, with his keen observation, it seemed that the island was a powder keg with its fuse already glowing, and he was glad that he was not a permanent resident here.

The three young men had returned to Kingston only in time to dress for Brenda's party. Simon was staying at the Cottswood house. Bertram Cottswood had pressed his hospitality on him when the *Maid of Boston* had come limping into port, her sails bedraggled, spars smashed and splintered, with Simon fuming at himself because he wasn't sure that an older, more experienced captain could not have brought the ship through with less damage. He had confidence in his own ability, but it didn't pay for a man to believe that he knew everything there was to know, and close his mind to the value of experience.

"It's going to be a perfect night for the party," Henry remarked. "There'll be a good breeze, and there isn't a hint of rain." Simon had already been impressed at the way the evenings turned cool no matter how hot the day had been, just as he'd been astonished at the fact that it never got really dark here, the way it got dark in Massachusetts, after the sun had set. Even the middle of the night was as light as twilight, light enough so that print could be read by starlight with no additional illumination.

"The weather wouldn't dare not be perfect!" Claude grinned. "Brenda wouldn't allow it!" He turned to smile at Simon. "Our sister came along after we two boys were born, and girls always having been as scarce as hen's teeth in our family, she's been spoiled rotten. If she commanded the sun not to rise so that she could sleep later in the morning, she would expect to be obeyed."

"She doesn't seem in the least spoiled to me," Simon protested, although he figuratively kept his fingers crossed. Compared to Boston girls, he had to admit that Brenda was spoiled, but all in all she was so sunny tempered that it scarcely showed.

All the same, he was glad that Brenda was already spoken for. He had an idea that if she had decided that she was interested in him, he would have had a hard time getting away. He had already aroused far too much attention from other unattached females here, and he had an uneasy feeling that, because of the financial situation, even the most aristocratic of families might be willing to marry off a younger daughter into a Boston family of good standing, so that they would have one less to provide for, along with the assurance that she would spend the rest of her life in security. As Simon had no intention of marrying any time in the near future, he would have to walk a thin line.

As for the celebration this evening, he would as soon that there wasn't going to be one. He'd never been one for large parties, and most certainly not for large parties where there would be a number of girls who would be uncomfortably interested in him. He would be hard put to be attentive and polite without giving a false impression of an interest that he did not feel. It promised to be ticklish, and he would be glad when it was over.

"I wonder if Noelle has arrived?" Henry mused, as they parted to go to their rooms to dress. "I hope that she managed to tear herself away from Maynard Penn. It's time she had a breathing spell."

Claude cocked a mocking eyebrow at his brother. "Are you planning on taking up your courtship where you left it off when you decided that her sister was the better catch? Not that I would blame you, Noelle's a good enough catch in her own right, even if she can't hold a candle to Vanessa. If you set your mind to it, you might be able to get her back; she isn't likely to have many offers as long as Vanessa is single and available."

"And what if I am?" Henry's voice was belligerent. Being reminded that Vanessa Maynard had spurned him did not set well with him, it still smarted. His pride had suffered as much as his heart. He no longer fancied himself in love with Vanessa, but he would have enjoyed owning her and being the envy of every other man on the island. If he were to marry Noelle, there would be no more derisive smiles when his friends and acquaintances thought that he wasn't looking. Henry did not take kindly to being made to look a fool, and if he married Noelle, who could be certain that he didn't prefer her to her sister?

Noelle would suit Henry very well. She was shy and retiring, even tempered, and would be easily led and dominated, and she was an attractive girl in her own right when her sister wasn't standing beside her. His family would be delighted, and she would bring a considerable dowry with her. Now that Kenneth Maynard was dead, everything that Daniel Maynard had would be divided equally between his two daughters when he died, and Noelle's share would be a fortune not to be sneezed at.

"Noelle?" Simon's interest was caught. "What a pretty name! Is she as pretty as she should be, to live up to it?"

"She certainly is, although her older sister is the real beauty. Vanessa is like a goddess, all golden and shining, while Noelle is small and dark. But there's no use in trying to describe Vanessa to you, you have to see her to believe her, and you'll meet Noelle this evening, if she has put in an appearance."

Interesting, to say the least! Maybe it was just as well that this paragon among women, Vanessa Maynard, was not to be a guest at the gala. One attractive, unattached close friend of the Cottswood family would be enough to cope with, without a second who was reputed to be irresistible! As long as one of them would be here, it was as well that it was the younger one, who would pose less of a threat.

Still, he couldn't help smiling at the thought of the sensation it would cause in Boston if he were to arrive home with a bride as beautiful as Vanessa Maynard was reputed to be. The New Englanders would look at her with suspicion, certain that no morally sound woman could be so lovely.

Shaking off the amusing notion, Simon turned his attention to bathing and changing into a fresh uniform for the party. He had no intention of returning to Massachusetts with a Jamaican bride, so speculation on the matter was idle.

In spite of her uneasiness at being here instead of at home watching over her father, Noelle's breath caught as she surveyed the scene that met her eyes when she joined the other guests. The gardens were strung with dozens of paper lanterns, glowing like fireflies among the trees and flowering bushes, making it look like a fairyland.

Everyone who was anyone in Kingston was here this evening, as well as many families from outlying plantations. The gentlemen were handsome in their evening clothes, the ladies were so many brilliant birds of paradise, flaunting themselves in the latest fashions. The evening had already turned mild, cool enough so that it could be enjoyed to the fullest. Music made a soft backdrop, there would be dancing, and enough food and drink to satisfy the most jaded of appetites, along with opportunities among the unmarried to make new conquests.

Now Brenda was coming toward her, with Bryce Lynford sticking so close to her that it was as if they were joined by an invisible cord. Brenda was towing a man Noelle had never seen before along with her, her hand on his arm urging him along.

"Noelle, there you are! I want to present Doctor Ian Macintyre to you, he has only been in Jamaica for a short time. Doctor Macintyre comes from Scotland, and he has the most outlandish accent, I vow I can scarcely understand him half of the time!"

The long, plain face was made intriguingly interesting by the twinkle in Ian Macintyre's eye, and Noelle had to stifle a giggle as he drew out his acknowledgment of the introduction with an exaggerated burring of his r's. She was certain that he was underlining his accent for Brenda's benefit, and the twinkle in his eyes told Noelle that he knew that she knew it, too. They were fellow conspirators at an instant's notice, and Noelle felt her heart warming to this young doctor who, according to Brenda, did not have two shillings to rub together. His lack of fortune certainly did not faze him; he was completely at ease here among the wealthy.

"Miss Maynard, it is an honor to meet you, a true honor!" Ian Macintyre said, taking her hand. He made to release it immediately, as convention demanded, and then he changed his mind and held onto it, his clasp warm and strong, as he studied her with the light of admiration in his eyes. The admiration was not feigned, it had nothing to do with the light flirtation that was expected at an affair like this, and Noelle's cheeks flushed.

"I am happy to meet you, as well. Brenda has spoken so highly of you that I've been anxious to see you in the flesh."

"There's not much to see, I'm afraid. I never took any prizes for my looks." The exaggerated burr was gone, but the voice was cheerful. "What there is of me is at your service, Miss Maynard. Have you a fever, a headache? No? Then I will have to content myself with dancing with you, rather than attending you on your sickbed, with the opportunity to hold your hand and lay my fingers on your brow. You will dance with me, will you not? More than once?"

He made the question sound so anxious that Noelle laughed. What a nice man Ian Macintyre was! She couldn't have cared less that he didn't have two shillings to rub together, he was the nicest and most interesting man she had ever met.

"Of course I'll dance with you, and more than once," she said. All of a sudden it didn't matter that she didn't have a new gown; Ian had never seen the one she was wearing before anyway, and even if he had, he wouldn't have noticed. It was her he was interested in, not any finery she could deck herself out in. And she'd lay her last penny that he was no fortune hunter, either. There was a look of dedication about him that told her that money meant very little to him. His evening clothes were clean and well pressed, but also well worn, yet he wore them without the least trace of self-consciousness, as though such trifles could not matter less.

"You mustn't monopolize her, Doctor Macintyre. She hasn't been in Kingston for a long time, and she'll want to circulate and renew acquaintances," Brenda told him.

"I'm sorry, but I have every intention of monopolizing her, if she will permit it." The words were spoken firmly, brooking no argument.

"And I am sorry, but you will have to relinquish her for

at least a few moments.'' Brenda's voice was just as firm. Noelle's friend had no intention of letting Ian Macintyre monopolize her, as nice as he was and as much as she liked him. Ian was suitable as a friend, but as a suitor he would not do at all. And there was another man whom Noelle must meet, who would do very well indeed.

Brenda nodded toward where her two brothers were standing just a short distance away, as at ease in their evening clothes as though they were second skins, and much more elegant than those that Ian was wearing. Noelle smiled at them, and then her eyes came to rest on a third young man who was standing with them, and her eyes widened and her heart began to beat a wild tattoo in her breast. He must be Simon Spencer, the man Brenda had been raving about ever since she had arrived, he couldn't be anyone else.

There was no reason for her heart to be beating so wildly. If this was Simon Spencer, he wasn't nearly the Adonis Brenda had led her to expect. It was true that he was tall, but he was no taller than Ian. His shoulders were broader, but he looked more rugged than handsome. His face was deeply browned from being exposed to wind and weather, his jaw was strong, the planes of his face were clearly defined, hard and firm. Even at this distance she could see that his eyes were the most piercing blue she had ever seen, and his hair was dark brown, thick, and curling just a little where it met his collar. A strand of it had fallen across his forehead, making him look as though he had just stepped in out of the wind.

Brenda veered away from her, making for her brothers and their guest, with Bryce still glued to her side looking as proud as a small boy with a new drum. Brenda belonged to him, and even a personable new face could not challenge his ownership. Noelle found his air of proprietorship touching. Brenda was lucky in her choice: Bryce would adore her as long as they lived as man and wife, never annoyed by her prattle or her bossiness, firm in his belief that she could do no wrong.

For a moment, Noelle wondered if she herself were not

making a mistake in not taking Henry Cottswood more seriously. He had called at Maynard Penn several times after Vanessa had let him down, in her gentle way, and made him realize that there was no hope for him as far as she was concerned. He had been obvious in his intention of wanting to make it up with Noelle. It must be wonderful to belong to someone, to know that your happiness was assured.

But Henry was not the man to assure her future happiness, no matter how determined he was. Noelle did not love him, she could not imagine herself in love with him, and for her, marriage without being ragingly in love was unthinkable. Her mother had been content with less, but Noelle was made of different stuff. If fate decreed that she could not have the best, then she would never marry at all.

They were coming toward her now, and as the stranger drew closer, she sensed a vibrant aliveness in him that made her catch her breath all over again. Against the darkness of his skin, his eyes seemed to glow with an inner light of their own, and to be able to see through her skin and bones straight to her soul.

"Miss Maynard," Simon said. "It is a pleasure to meet you. Miss Cottswood has talked of nothing but you ever since my arrival, fretting that you wouldn't come. I'm happy that you didn't disappoint her." His voice had a timbre that made Noelle shiver. She had an idea that this man never had to shout, that the authority of his voice would make other men jump to do his bidding.

"Thank you," she murmured. She had been brought up ingrained with all the social graces; there wasn't any reason in the world she should feel tongue-tied, as though she were an ill-at-ease child attending her first social function. "I'm happy that you happened to be here in Kingston, so that you too can enjoy Brenda's party."

"Are you a native of Jamaica, a Creole?" Simon asked her. He already knew that whites who were born on the island were called Creoles, even if their forebears had come from other countries. He bent his head a trifle, so that he could look at her intently out of those compelling eyes. Noelle's head felt light. His eyes were hypnotizing, and she knew now why Brenda had been so impressed with this man.

"Indeed I am. My father emigrated here from England, but I was born here, although my sister Vanessa was born in England. So you can see that I am a Creole, but she is not. Do you find that confusing?"

She put a curb on her tongue just in time, appalled because she'd been on the verge of nattering on about her father, about Kenneth and his sudden, mysterious death, and about how Daniel Maynard had been so stricken with grief that she feared for his life as well.

What would Mr. Spencer have thought of her if she had gone running on to someone she had only this moment met? In another moment she would have made a complete fool of herself. To burden a stranger with your intimate problems was the worst breach of etiquette. Brenda would have been aghast, and so would Mr. and Mrs. Cottswood. As for Captain Spencer, he would without any doubt never want to lay eyes on her again.

The thought of not seeing Captain Spencer again was like a knife in her heart. All thoughts of cutting her visit short so that she could return to Maynard Penn flew from her mind. Another two or three days could make no difference in her father's condition; Dicey was completely reliable and would see that a message was sent to her if there was any change in Daniel's condition.

How long was Captain Spencer going to remain in Jamaica? She had no idea how long it would take to repair his ship. That, at least, was an acceptable subject of conversation.

"How are the repairs to your ship progressing, Captain? Was the damage extensive, or something easily remedied?"

"The *Maid of Boston* took more of a beating than I like to dwell on," Simon told her ruefully. "It will be at least another ten days to two weeks before she will be seaworthy again. However, there are compensations. I find that I am enjoying my stay on your island more with every day that passes."

Standing beside them, Brenda was beaming, her matchmaking soul delighted because her best friend and this wonderful, exciting man were hitting it off. Dear Noelle needed a distraction from her troubles, and wouldn't it be wonderful if she and the captain should fall in love? If they were married, Noelle would have to go and live in Massachusetts, and although it would break Brenda's heart to lose her, it wasn't as if they would never see each other again. With a ship's captain as a husband, Noelle could come back to visit Jamaica any time she chose, and she would certainly want to see her father as often as possible.

Noelle seemed to be drowning in Simon's eyes, those piercing, hypnotic eyes that held her own with such an intensity that she could not glance away. As far as she was concerned, she and Simon were the only two people in the room. Ten days to two weeks! She began revising the length of her own visit to Kingston in her mind. The Cottswoods would be happy to send one of their servants to Maynard Penn to bring back a report on how her father was faring. She would make sure that the servant understood that he was to talk to Dicey in person, and bring back a word for word report of what Dicey said.

The music had started, and Simon proffered his arm.

"Would you do me the honor of indulging me?" He was bemused as Noelle stepped into his arms for the dreamy strains of the waltz. What was there about this girl that made such an impact on him? Granted she was pretty enough, but she wasn't a raving beauty; he had seen prettier girls many times in his life and had been much less impressed with them. At twenty-four, he had been tempted at least three or four times to ask one of those enchantresses to become his wife, but in each case he had had second thoughts.

Simon had the same appetites as any healthy young man, and the same need for romantic companionship, but his life just as it was was so satisfactory that the need to take the plunge into matrimony was not compelling. There was plenty of time, there would always be another girl, and in the meantime he enjoyed his freedom and the exacting hours he spent in learning everything there was to learn about running the Spencer Line, so that when the time came for him to take over he would be prepared. And then there were the weeks and months he spent at sea, visiting foreign ports, a life filled with variety and excitement.

But now a little wisp of a girl was in his arms, her piquant face looking up at him, her dark eyes seeming to hold a thousand questions. And something else, some underlying, dark current of sadness and trouble that disturbed him. What trouble could a girl so young, the daughter of a wealthy plantation owner, possibly have here in this island paradise? He was imagining things, he must have a touch of the sun, he wouldn't be surprised if he were a little feverish. He'd have to take care or his hostess would call in that pompous old physician, Doctor Eastlake, and he'd dose him with Glauber's salts and cream of tartar and Peruvian bark, the island's cure for such a malady.

Holding Noelle was like holding a moonbeam, she seemed to have no more weight or substance. Her dark hair, dressed in the ringlets of latest fashion, had a fragrance of its own that he couldn't define, but it seemed to get into his blood and make it run fast and hot. Her chin was just a trifle pointed, her nose just barely upturned at the tip, intriguing in themselves, but her eyes were her chief claim to beauty. Large and dark, they were framed by lashes that made him marvel that they were real. If it hadn't been essential that he get the *Maid of Boston* back on the high seas as soon as possible, he would be strongly tempted to extend his stay in Jamaica.

That was nonsense, of course. He had to get back to sea, the Spencer Line was proud of its time schedule and nothing must delay him longer than absolutely necessary.

His inner mind warned him to be careful, to take his time, to be completely sure before he did something that he might regret. The girl was young, and there wasn't a fiancé in the offing, or Brenda, with her unstoppable tongue, would have told him.

If he still felt this way about Noelle in a year's time, he could return to the island to see if she was still free. If she married someone else in the meantime, so be it. It would only mean that it hadn't been meant to be.

Simon wasn't the only one at this gala who was bemused by the small, dark-haired girl who was looking up into Simon's face as though no one else in the world existed for her. From the sidelines, not yet having asked any other lady to dance, Ian Macintyre watched her, and put down the regret in his heart. The impact she had made on him was one that had never happened to him before.

Small wonder, that! Ian told himself, smiling wryly. Up until the time he had left Scotland, he had had no time to go courting, and no money for it, either. Not that he was in much better case now. It would be a long time before he was in a position to offer any girl anything, much less a girl like Noelle Maynard.

His family was comfortably off, but Ian had no intention of asking them for any more than they had already done for him. He was not the oldest son in his family; they had stretched themselves to help him through his medical studies, even though he had earned part of the fees himself, and allowed himself no luxuries.

Still Noelle intrigued him as no other girl had ever done. Her delicate little face, with the dark shadows of sorrow in her eyes, had touched a chord in his heart. If circumstances had been different, if he had been well established and prosperous enough, he would have tried to give the captain from Massachusetts a run for his money.

That thought, too, made Ian smile with self-mockery that held more than a little humor. If a miracle happened and he was able to step into Phinneas Eastlake's shoes tomorrow, if some unknown relative died and left him a fortune, it would still not change the way Noelle and Captain Spencer were looking at each other. Ian had lost any chance he might have had the moment those two had met.

Probably it was just as well. The young Scotsman was inclined to spend all his waking hours with his nose in a book, increasing his knowledge, and here in Jamaica he spent a good share of his days ranging the countryside, searching out native plants with an eye to unraveling their mysteries as pertained to beneficial effects for humankind. Any wife of his would be a lonesome wife, no matter how much he might love her.

All the same, he felt a regret that stabbed him to his heart.

Chapter Three

To Noelle, the entire evening of Brenda's birthday gala was enchanted. At times it seemed that she was moving in a dream, that at any moment she would awaken and weep because none of this magical time had happened.

Yet she knew that she was awake, and that it was all true. She danced with Simon again and again, each time more wonderful than the last. The other guests smiled at them approvingly, and for the most part left them alone, their romantic hearts warmed by this new romance that was blossoming among them. Only Ian claimed her for three or four dances, with a good-natured insistence that she could not turn down.

"You remind me of Cinderella," Ian told Noelle, during one of the times he had claimed her. "There's that glow about you that nothing else can match. Are you certain that you won't find yourself in rags at the stroke of midnight, and your coach horses changed back into mice, and with only one slipper?''

"Compared to the other ladies, I am already in rags!'' Noelle dimpled at him, her eyes laughing. How different she looked when she smiled, and when the sadness fled from her eyes! "This dress is two years old. I hadn't planned on coming until the last moment and so I didn't have a new one made up. And my slippers aren't glass, for which I'm profoundly thankful! Can you imagine how uncomfortable glass slippers would be? By now my feet would be covered with blisters, and I wouldn't be able to dance at all!''

"In that case, I'm as thankful as you are that your slippers aren't glass, although I wouldn't care at all if you were dressed in rags.''

Noelle looked at him, her eyes thoughtful. "Do you know, I had that very impression about you when we were introduced. I was fretting a little about my dress, and I thought, here is at least one person who wouldn't care! I think that you are a very nice man, Doctor Macintyre.''

Ian steeled himself against flinching. Girls did not fall in love with very nice men, they fell in love with dashing, handsome men like Simon Spencer. Still, his heart was warmed by what Noelle had said. She liked him, and that in itself was something to cherish.

On her part, Noelle found herself talking to Ian as though she had known him all her life. She was actually startled to realize that she was telling him all the things she had wanted to tell Simon, and prevented herself from confiding, such a short time ago.

"Kenneth shouldn't have died. Even after all this time I can't convince myself that there was any logical reason for him to die. He was only sixteen, Doctor Macintyre, and he'd always enjoyed the best of health! And then he was gone, almost overnight, and I can't reconcile myself to it no matter how I try. It makes it worse to have my father ill, Kenneth's death devastated him, and now it seems as if I'll lose him, too, although Doctor Eastlake assures me that he will improve with time. Can someone as strong and vital as my father used to be actually die of grief? It seems that if that were true, I would have died when Kenneth did, but I didn't, I'm still here and I'm still healthy, although I have never left off grieving for him.''

Ian was cautious about his reply, although he held Noelle a little more closely, his heart going out to her. He would like to see Daniel Maynard himself, to evaluate his illness and his chances for recovery, but there was no way that one doctor could infringe on another doctor's case, especially the case of a doctor as pompous and certain of his own infallible knowledge as Phinneas Eastlake.

"I expect that it depends on the person, although I myself would be surprised if a strong man, in the prime of life, should fade away from grief. You must have faith that he will recover, Miss Maynard. Sometimes these things take a great deal of time."

Noelle's face lighted up, so radiant that Ian felt his throat tighten. "Then you think that he will recover, even though it takes a long time?"

"I should think that we would have every reason to think so." Ian wished desperately that he could say more to relieve Noelle's mind, but he had no business at all giving an opinion about a man he had never seen, much less an opinion about another doctor's patient.

Then Simon claimed Noelle again, and Ian turned his attention to doing his duty as a proper guest, and asked other ladies to dance, not all of them young. The young, pretty ones could fend for themselves, it was the older ones, with their beauty fading, who needed the reassurance that they still had value. Ian had always been one to take the part of the underdog. He even tried to keep his eyes from searching out Noelle and Simon as they danced, but he had only indifferent success about that. His eyes were drawn to them like magnets, and every time, he felt that stab of regret that he could not be the man at whom Noelle looked with her heart on her sleeve.

"What is it like, your Massachusetts?" Noelle asked Simon. She had an aching need to know everything there was to know about this man.

"It's hard to describe it to someone who has never been off this island," Simon told her. "You certainly can't imagine what snowdrifts six or eight feet high are like, or the cold in the winter that bites right through to your bones. All the same, it's exhilarating. And ice skating! You'd love to skate. It's almost like flying, with your blood racing and the world around you like a white fairyland."

Noelle's eyes were shining. "I know I'd love it! But it isn't always winter there, is it?" Her voice was so anxious that Simon laughed, drawing her a little closer in his arms.

"Of course it isn't! Spring is like the world being reborn, with everything soft and tender and new. Our summers are lush and green, although not as lush and green as your Jamaica, and they can be hot, although not as hot as it is here. But of all the seasons, I like autumn the best. The air is as crisp as a chilled apple, there's the smell of burning leaves in the air, and the foliage turns scarlet and orange and yellow and brown, as though you were looking at a canvas by a master artist."

"Here, it is always much the same, except that we get more rain in the fall than at other times." Noelle's voice was wistful. "And your ship, Captain Spencer. How wonderful it must be to have a ship of your own, to be able to sail anywhere in the world!"

"Would you like to see her?" Simon asked.

Her face looked as if he had offered her the crown jewels of England. "Oh, yes! Would it be possible?"

"Tomorrow, then," Simon told her. "I will give you the grand tour."

The music had stopped, and all around them other couples had stopped dancing and were leaving the floor, but neither of them were aware of it. They still moved in the pattern of the waltz, the music in their ears as though it were still playing. It wasn't until Brenda, her face flaming, touched Noelle's arm that they realized what had happened and that the other guests were laughing, and even as they realized it, applause broke out, along with indulgent smiles.

Simon's natural self-possession came to their rescue. He bowed, and led Noelle from the floor as though they had been performers to whom the applause was no more than their due. Noelle burst out laughing, and he laughed with her, and her heart soared. With any other man, she would have wanted to sink through the floor and disappear, but Simon made it seem like an adventure.

When Brenda's betrothal was announced at midnight, Noelle no longer had the faintest twinge of envy. For her, there was only one man in the world, and he was the one who stood beside her as they raised their glasses in a toast to the engaged couple, he was the one who smiled down into her eyes. And he was the one who shared the last dance of the evening with her, with them waltzing as though they were in a dream.

Their moments together could not be prolonged any longer. Most of the guests had left, and it was time to say good night.

"We'll leave for the docks immediately after breakfast." Simon told her. "It will be cool enough then so that you can enjoy inspecting my ship. Good night, Noelle. I'll see you in the morning."

The lack of formal address sent Noelle's heart to soaring. It had been an oversight, but it filled her with elation. Noelle! Simon. Simon and Noelle. She fell asleep holding the names close to her heart, and nearly forgot to pray for her father. But her father would understand, and so, she hoped, would God.

There was a soft breeze across the water the next morning, and Noelle marveled at the perfection of the *Maid of Boston,* even though her untutored eyes could see that the ship had suffered a great deal of damage. The mainmast had been splintered, yardarms destroyed, sails torn to shreds. As she realized the extent of the damage, her face paled. What if the ship had gone down with all hands, what if Simon Spencer had been plunged into a watery grave? Simon dead before she had ever known him!

"It must have been a dreadful storm!" she said. "It's a miracle that you were able to weather it at all."

"It gave us a battering," Simon admitted. "But I have a good crew, none better, and the *Maid of Boston* was built in our own shipyards. A less seaworthy craft would have been in real trouble."

In spite of the clutter caused by the repair work that was going on, the deck itself was holystoned to an immaculate cleanness, the brasses gleamed in the sun from diligent polishing. Noelle noted that every member of the crew, as well as artisans from the island, held Simon in respect, and evidenced a genuine liking for him as well. Her father would have liked Simon, and Kenneth would have held him up as a model.

She pushed away the stab of grief that these thoughts engendered. There was no place for sadness in her life today. She was alive, and she was young, and she was falling in love. And after today, there would be tomorrow, and another tomorrow after that, there would be a week or ten days of tomorrows, and she refused to think how it would be when the tomorrows ran out and Simon would be gone.

Looking at her, her face glowing with pleasure and excitement as she exclaimed over the beauty of his ship, Simon's thoughts followed much the same lines.

It was unthinkable to propose to the girl now, only the second day he had known her. It would be just as unthinkable to propose to her immediately before he sailed. His New England upbringing urged him toward caution. It was not the way of Massachusetts men to jump into any situation feet first, without examining every facet. All the same, the urge to propose to her was so strong that he was shaken.

"Have you seen enough?" he asked, wrenching his mind away from such fanciful thoughts. "What shall we do for the rest of the day? I suggest that you take me on a tour of Kingston and the near countryside. I'm sure that the Cottswoods will spare us their curricle, as they are still recovering from last night's party."

He approved the fact that Noelle showed no signs of fatigue, although both Brenda and her mother had still been in bed when they had left the house. New Englanders were a hardy breed, and if Noelle had been tired and languid today simply because she had danced until nearly dawn the night before, his interest in her would have waned.

"If Brenda doesn't feel up to coming with us, Julie will have to," Noelle warned him, a teasing light in her eyes even though Simon sensed that, like himself, she would rather that they could have been alone. It was just as well that convention demanded that they be chaperoned, it would serve to force him to keep these disturbing urges of his under control. He held out his arm so that she could place her fingertips on it as he escorted her down the gangplank, correctness personified. If his blood was racing in a way it had never raced before, only he knew it.

Vanessa Maynard was bored. Jonathan Farnsworth had turned out to be a disappointment to her. Here at Maynard Penn, with nobody on the place except the slaves and her father, who hadn't the remotest idea of what was going on outside of his own bedroom, still Jonathan had been filled with trepidation and a sense of guilt that had made him inept, so that he had fumbled and sweated, so clumsy and apologetic that she had wanted to scream at him to get out of her sight.

Brief, clandestine trysts in the countryside, with no eyes for miles around to observe them, had been one thing for Jonathan, but here where every slave on the place knew what was going on was something entirely different. While Vanessa thrived on taking risks, Jonathan cringed at the thought.

In the end, after only three days of Vanessa's anticipated idyll with him, she had decided that it was time for her to suffer her own pangs of conscience and tell him that there was no way she could go on with their affair. Only her passion for him had made her forget decency, but now that she realized the enormity of their sin there was nothing she could do but send him away even though her heart was breaking.

Vanessa was a past mistress of scenes such as this. She could bring tears flooding to her eyes at will, she could make her lips tremble, and it did not fail her this time. Jonathan, professing undying love for her, vowing that he would never have another happy moment as long as he lived, left her, more under her spell than ever, but secretly relieved that he would be taking no more chances.

One of the Cottswoods' house men had just left Maynard Penn, sent by Noelle to check up on their father's condition. He had insisted on speaking to Dicey, and his conversation with her, repeated word for word by Chloe, was still turning around in Vanessa's mind.

A stranger was a guest of the Cottswoods, a sea captain from Boston. He was young, and already all the Cottswoods' servants as well as nearly everyone in Kingston were conjuring up a romance between him and Noelle. All of the young, unattached ladies of Kingston were all aflutter about the captain, but Noelle had walked off with the prize.

The situation had possibilities. Granted they weren't great, but Vanessa was in need of a new distraction. She had known every possible lover in Jamaica all of her life, she was weary of the same faces, she needed a new and exciting flirtation even though nothing could come of it. The Cottswoods' servant had said that this Captain Spencer was unmarried, so Vanessa could not have a physical affair with him, but it would be amusing to bring him under her spell and take him away from Noelle at the same time.

Any possibility of marriage for her younger half sister was not in Vanessa's plans. It was essential that Noelle should not acquire a husband who would take her away and keep her under his protection, who would make sure that Noelle received her full share of the Maynard fortune when Daniel died. Even without the prospect of making a new conquest to relieve her boredom, Vanessa would have had to go to Kingston and nip the romance between her sister and the captain from Boston in the bud.

Chloe was set to packing Vanessa's most becoming gowns, and she attired herself in her newest traveling costume, its moss green color selected to make her golden hair and translucent complexion more ravishing than ever, its cut calculated to show off every curve to its full advantage.

She had no compunctions about leaving Maynard Penn without a master or mistress. There would be no trouble during her absence. Chloe would stay, and the slaves were too terrified of the obeah woman to commit the smallest infraction.

During the long drive to Kingston on the following day, Vanessa toyed with the possibility that she might have an actual affair with Captain Simon Spencer, even though he was unmarried. If he were as handsome and personable as the Cottswoods' slave had told Dicey, an affair with him would bring her the excitement of which she was in such sore need on this dull, boring, provincial island.

The more she thought about it, the better she liked the idea. Someone new, someone strong and virile to satisfy the unquenchable lusts of her body, the burning that never gave her any peace. The *Maid of Boston* would be ready to sail in just a few days, the captain would leave the island, and long before he returned, Vanessa would be gone. The danger was minimal, the prospects of such excitement enticing.

She made up her mind. If this sea captain were as handsome and desirable as he was reputed to be, she would take him. At least she would have something worthwhile to remember while she waited for her father to die and give her the fortune and the freedom she had dreamed of all of her life.

The day was growing late, there was only time to return to the carriage and get back to Kingston before the evening meal. They must not be tardy, it would be a breach of manners. Still, it was hard for them to break away from this idyllic spot, in the low foothills, where a crystal clear pool was surrounded by ferns and all the exotic growth of the island.

Julie was already in the carriage waiting for them, while the coachman dozed, oblivious to the beauty around him. A man took his rest when he could, and Raphael had taken full advantage of many such periods of rest in the last several days.

Julie was impatient. The coachman was past middle age and of no interest to her, but a younger, handsomer Cottswood servant would be waiting for her when they returned, and they had plans of their own for the evening as soon as they were excused from their duties, plans that made Julie itch with anticipation. Still, she did not resent the delay, because romance was exciting and sweet and Julie wanted her young mistress to have the full advantage of the captain's company for whatever little time remained to them.

How enchanting, how utterly enchanting Noelle was, Simon thought, looking at her as she still sat dabbling her bare feet in the water. It was maddening to think that there was no way she could have shed every stitch of her clothing and plunged into the pool with him, both of them stark naked, to disport themselves to their hearts' content and then to make love on a bed of ferns as nature must have intended since the inception of time.

Noelle drew her feet out of the pool at last and bent to dry them as well as she could on the hem of her petticoat. Leaning over made the neckline of her gown gap so that the tops of her breasts were visible almost to her small rosy nipples, and Simon felt a flood of heat that was almost his undoing.

Gathering up her stockings, Noelle stepped behind a growth of bushes to put them on.

"Bother!" Simon heard her say. "My feet are still damp enough so that my slippers don't want to go on. Help me, Simon."

He went to kneel in front of her, and the feel of that

43

slender, high-arched foot in his hands sent a new wave of madness flowing through him. He laced the ribbons around her ankles and tied them, and then he stood and drew her into his arms, and he was kissing her at last, their first kiss and one that made his head swim. The kiss went on and on, until it seemed that their bodies were melting into each other's, that they would never be two separate people again, to walk their own ways. Only when it became unendurable, when some last faint trace of sanity told him that he must release her immediately or it would be too late, did he let her go.

Noelle's cheeks were flaming, her lips still parted, her eyes filled with a glow that would put a sunset to shame. "Oh, my goodness!" she said. "Oh, dear me, my goodness gracious! We must go, Simon, we're going to be late." But when she made to take a step away from him, her legs were trembling so badly that he had to reach out to steady her, and a new wave of feeling flooded over her.

This had to stop! It was going beyond the bounds of decency! It was only God's sweet mercy that Julie and the coachman were there in the carriage, within sight of them, or who knew what might have happened. Why, she and Simon weren't even betrothed, they scarcely knew each other, and for them to kiss like this, to press their bodies so close together that not even a sheet of paper could be inserted between them, was so outrageous that her face flamed even hotter at the thought of it. Whatever had she been thinking, to allow it?

She knew what she had been thinking. She had been thinking that she wanted the kiss to go on forever, that she never wanted Simon's arms to release her, that this was what love was all about, and that nothing but that love mattered.

She loved Simon, and she knew with no trace of doubt that she would go on loving him for as long as she lived. And looking at him, remembering the miracle of that kiss, she was certain that he loved her.

If only her father weren't so ill, if only things had been different, who knew what might not happen in the very near future? The thought of what might have been, if things had only been different, if only Simon didn't have to sail so soon! It was unbearable that they should have only these few days, that there was no time for events to evolve in their natural course before they would be torn apart, perhaps forever.

How was she to know what girl might be waiting for Simon to return to Boston even now, some girl who had as high hopes as her own? A girl he had known for years, with a bond between them that she had not had time to weave in the short time she had known him? But she herself had no one. When Simon left her life would be empty, with only the prospect of seeing her father die by inches before her, and with Vanessa making her life a torment.

Simon was alarmed by the shadow of sadness that had come over her face. "Noelle, what is it?" he demanded, taking her into his arms again.

He felt a tremor pass through her body. "It's nothing. I was only thinking of how soon you must sail, and how much I will miss you." Noelle made an effort to smile, but her lips trembled, and the darkness was still in her eyes.

"I'll be coming back, perhaps sooner than you think." Simon told her. He smoothed her hair back off her forehead, his fingers gentle and lingering, and then he kissed her forehead and the corners of her eyes where tears that she was trying to fight back were gathering. "You know I'll come back, Noelle, and when I do we shall see each other again."

Now the shadows left her eyes and they began once more to glow. Simon kissed her again, tenderly this time and, at first, without the passion of that earlier kiss. Then his kiss deepened, and they were clinging together as lovers have clung since the beginning of time when they were about to be parted, trying to drain the last drop of being together before they were torn apart.

Slowly, hand in hand, loath to leave this place of enchantment, they returned to the carriage, but now

Noelle's heart was singing and Simon couldn't have cared less that he had all but committed himself. He would be sure to come back to Jamaica as soon as it could be arranged, because this girl would draw him like a lodestar until he had returned to her. Looking at them, Julie smiled and hummed to herself. Her mistress was happy, and so Julie was happy.

Brenda came running to meet them as soon as the curricle drew up in front of the house.

"Noelle, there's the most wonderful surprise! Come along in, do, we've all been waiting for you, whatever kept you so long?"

Noelle paid little heed to Brenda's words. Brenda thought that every trivial thing was a wonderful surprise, and that must be a wonderful way to be, but right now Noelle had other, more important things on her mind. She was in love, deliriously, soaringly in love, her heart and her body burned with it until she wondered that she wasn't consumed where she stood.

Simon had promised her that he would come back, Simon had promised her that they would see each other again. Simon had kissed her, and looked at her with love in his eyes!

It was almost more than she could assimilate. During these last, dark months, with Kenneth's death tearing at her heart and then her grief from watching her father fade away, she had all but given up any hope of ever being happy again.

But now a miracle had happened. Simon had come into her life, and even though he had to go away so soon he would come back, he had promised. Maybe her father would be well by then, maybe he would lead her down the aisle when she became Simon's wife, and give her away to the only man in the world for her.

If the worst happened, but she wouldn't let herself consider that possibility, if her father died, still Simon would come back, and she would not be alone. She had thought that when her father died she herself would have no more reason to go on living, but instead life would just be beginning for her. She would never forget her father and Kenneth, she would hold them dear in her heart in all the years that were left to her, but they would want her to be happy, and she would be happy, beyond all the imagining of her dreams.

She was smiling as she and Simon followed Brenda into the Cottswoods' drawing room. And then her footsteps stopped on the threshold as though a barrier had suddenly appeared out of thin air, and she stared at her sister, Brenda's wonderful surprise.

Vanessa stood in a shaft of sunlight so that her hair was haloed in its light, she seemed to glow, her beauty was so enhanced that even Noelle's breath was taken away. Beside her, Simon had also stopped, and she heard the sharp intake of his breath.

A moment ago Noelle's heart had been filled with radiance. Now, in a matter of seconds, it was filled with darkness.

Vanessa had no right to be here. Vanessa was supposed to be at Maynard Penn, carrying on her affair with Jonathan Farnsworth. But she was here, smiling at Simon, and Noelle had seen that look in her sister's eyes before. Seeing that look on Vanessa's face, hearing Simon's stilled breath, Noelle felt as though she were dying.

Chapter Four

BRENDA LOST NO TIME IN PRACTICALLY DRAGGING Noelle to her room, urging her to bathe and change after the
day-long picnic that had left her dusty and rumpled. The
plump girl was spilling over with sympathy for her friend.

"Goodness gracious, it's been just ages since Vanessa
has honored us with a visit, and of all the times for her to
pick, just when Captain Spencer was getting so interested
in you! I would have sworn that there was a romance
blossoming between you, but now of course the captain
won't have eyes for anybody but your sister. I declare, you
do have the worst luck! I'm glad that Bryce never had eyes
for anyone but me! If he looked at Vanessa the way
Captain Spencer looked at Vanessa just now, I'd scratch
his eyes out!"

Noelle struggled to hide the wince on her face. Simon
had looked thunderstruck, there wasn't any doubt that

Vanessa's beauty had struck him full force, just as it always happened with any man seeing her for the first time. She pressed her lips closely together to keep from reminding Brenda that there had been a time when Bryce had looked at Vanessa like a starving child pressing his nose against a bakery shop window. He'd made as great an effort to win Vanessa as all the other young men who had become smitten with her, he'd come riding out to the plantation almost every day to try to court her.

It was Brenda's good fortune that the not very handsome, not overly tall, and very slightly stocky Bryce had realized that Vanessa was out of his reach, and turned back to Brenda before she had had any inkling of his passion for the beautiful girl he could never hope to win. If Brenda hadn't been so besotted with him that she'd accepted his lame excuses of visiting Maynard Penn to see Daniel Maynard, she would have seen his infatuation for Vanessa herself. But Brenda lived in a little glass bubble all her own, a perfect world where no unhappiness or unpleasantness would dare to intrude.

Noelle dressed with care, having Julie use all the skill at her command with her hair. Julie, who was aware that Vanessa's arrival was a threat to her younger mistress, needed no urging. Julie, like all of the other slaves at Maynard Penn, disliked the older mistress, and right at the moment she wished that she knew a voodoo woman or a gangan here in Kingston whom she could persuade to cast a spell on the bad mistress so that she wouldn't take Captain Spencer away from Noelle.

But Julie didn't know of any magicmaker in Kingston, and even if she had, Chloe's spells probably would be stronger so it wouldn't have done any good. If the older mistress wanted Captain Spencer, Chloe would see that she got him.

Satisfied with her appearance at last, Noelle went to join the others. She held her head high, her pride refusing to let her show any hint of the turmoil inside her. At least nothing had been settled between her and Simon, she wouldn't have to suffer the humiliation of being publicly jilted! Pride was a bitter thing to have to live on, but it was better than nothing.

Her heart leaped as Simon crossed the drawing room to meet her, his eyes lighting up. "What an amazing transformation in such a short time!" he said. "This afternoon you were a gamin, wading in a pool, and now you're a grown up young lady again and altogether too lovely for comfort!"

Across the room, Vanessa looked at her younger sister and smiled. Noelle, her heart singing, smiled back at her. Simon still liked her, he liked her better than Vanessa, nothing had changed, everything was going to be all right!

"Captain Spencer has been telling me about your outing. I'm glad that you had such a pleasant time, it's been far too long since you've had any diversion." Both Vanessa's face and her voice spoke of nothing but the fondest concern for Noelle. Her host and hostess beamed at her with approval, but they weren't surprised. Vanessa was nothing but good, she was an angel, of course she was happy that Noelle was enjoying herself and receiving the attentions of such a personable young man.

There were guests for dinner that evening, and Vanessa was the center of attention. Everyone made much of her, praising her for her devotion to her father and the plantation, and expressing delight that she had been able to come into town. But although Simon's eyes reflected his appreciation of her beauty every time he looked at her, they always returned to Noelle, and it was to Noelle that he gave the largest share of his attention.

Simon had indeed been stunned by Vanessa's beauty. He thought that he had never seen such pure, unadulterated loveliness before in his life. But her very perfection made him wary. She would be a hard woman to live up to, she was so lovely that it was almost uncomfortable to be in her company. Noelle, although lacking as classic and stunning a beauty, had a sweet and simple nature, a vulnerability, that still touched his heart and filled him with dreams of keeping her by his side for all the rest of his life, of protecting her and cherishing her and devoting himself to her happiness.

Noelle, he thought, was warm and soft and very human, with none of her sister's untouchable air about her. A man didn't want a saint for his wife, he wanted a woman of flesh and blood, one who would return passion for passion, a woman he would never be afraid to touch.

Brenda was flabbergasted. It was almost impossible for her to believe that Captain Spencer still preferred Noelle after he had seen Vanessa. And Noelle was acutely aware that the other guests were just as surprised. By the time the evening was over, she was glowing with such happiness that she felt as beautiful as Vanessa. It had happened at last, she had found the only man she could ever love, and he loved her in return, not spurning her the moment he saw her more beautiful sister!

"Noelle, come and sit with me while I get ready for bed," Vanessa said, after the guests had left. "You can brush my hair, you're the only one besides Chloe who can do it without pulling and making my head ache. Captain Spencer, I'm sorry to take my sister away from you, but it is late, and we haven't seen each other for days, and we have a lot to catch up on. I'm sure you'll forgive me this once. Tomorrow you can have her back."

There was no way Noelle could get out of going with Vanessa, although her heart sank. Van certainly hadn't asked for her company out of sisterly love, she had something else in mind, and Noelle was certain she wasn't going to like it. Once out of earshot of the others, she would revert to her usual hateful self, every word she uttered calculated to hurt and sting. But this time Noelle determined to hold her ground, and she prepared to give battle at the first sneering word.

Vanessa sat down in front of the dressing table and took the pins out of her hair, letting it fall in all its golden glory around her shoulders and down to her waist. Instead of handing Noelle the hairbrush, she began to stroke the silken strands herself, turning to look at her sister with speculative eyes.

"Is there anything serious between you and Captain Spencer?" Vanessa asked.

Noelle's eyes didn't waver as she gazed back at her sister. "There might be. Would it concern you if there were?"

"Noelle, we haven't always gotten along. I know that you don't approve of me. But I am as I am, and I can't help it, and there's no way I can change. And yes, it does concern me, if you and this Yankee captain are in love. I'd like to see you married, and away from Jamaica, if you want to know the truth. I have nothing against you personally, but you're a constant thorn in my side. And there's always the danger that someone might listen to you, if you chose to tell what you know about me. So you see, if you were to marry this sea captain and go to live in his Massachusetts, it would be to my advantage as much as it would be to yours."

Noelle was so surprised that for a moment she couldn't speak. But what Vanessa said made a great deal of sense. There was no doubt that Vanessa would be happy to be rid of her. Once again, her heart leaped.

"Does that mean that you won't do anything to spoil things between Simon and me? You won't persuade Father that I'm too young, you won't try to make Simon turn from me in favor of you, just to spite me, even though you don't want him for yourself?"

"It means exactly that." Vanessa's voice was flat. And then she laughed. "Noelle, your mouth is hanging open! Don't look so stupidly surprised! Of course I won't throw any obstacles in your path. The sooner you marry your captain and sail away from this island, the happier I will be! Go on, go to bed, and if you can't think of any way to bring Captain Spencer around to popping the question before he sails, just come to me and I'll be happy to instruct you in how to make any man do exactly as you wish!"

This was more like the Vanessa Noelle knew: hard, spiteful, delighting in shocking and hurting. And for that very reason, Noelle's heart began to sing. Vanessa meant what she said, Simon was safe from her, she wanted Noelle to marry him! If only Father were well, if only she could bear to think of leaving him . . .

But she didn't have to think about that tonight. Simon would have to sail and then return to Jamaica before they could be married, and by that time Daniel might be well, and she would walk down the aisle of the church on his arm, and he'd give her away to Simon, and she would enter through the gates of paradise never to leave.

Nothing she could do, no influence she could bring to bear, would ever change Vanessa. Telling her father about her sister's true nature would gain her nothing, and only bring him pain. Van would persuade him that none of it was true, that Noelle said such things against her through jealousy and spite.

But sooner or later, Vanessa would make a mistake, and her true nature would become known. It would break their father's heart, but his heart would be just as broken whether Noelle were there or not. And after the emancipation had gone through and her father's affairs had been settled, he would come to her and Simon in Boston and make his home there, and she would give him grandchildren to fill the empty and aching places in his heart.

In the morning Vanessa expressed a desire to see Simon's ship, and for the first time since she had been old enough to realize Vanessa's effect on men, Noelle's heart wasn't twisted as she saw how the crew and the artisans stared at her sister with awe-stricken eyes. She was the one on Simon's arm, she was the one he looked at with love in his eyes. And when Vanessa, during an instant when nobody was looking at them, smiled at her and winked and nodded, Noelle's cup of happiness ran over. Vanessa had reconfirmed, by that gesture, that Simon was all hers.

One of Kingston's leading families, the Albrights, gave a gala that evening in honor of the engaged couple, although Vanessa's unexpected presence rather stole the show.

Once again, Noelle didn't mind in the least all the

attention that was lavished on her older sister. Simon had to dance with Brenda, of course, as a matter of courtesy, and he had to dance with Mrs. Albright because she was his hostess, and with Faith Cottswood because he was a guest in her home. And he danced with Vanessa, because she was a newly arrived guest of the Cottswoods, and Noelle's sister. But Simon was safe from Van, Van didn't want him. He could dance a dozen times with Van, and Noelle still wouldn't mind, just as long as he always returned to her with that eager look in his eyes.

"Here you are!" Henry was speaking into her ear. "You haven't danced with me all evening. You aren't sulking because Vanessa is dancing with Captain Spencer, are you? Personally, I'm glad that she showed up here in Kingston, you haven't had time for anybody but Simon ever since you arrived. I hoped that we would become closer during your visit. You can't possibly still be angry because of that short period such a long time ago when I fancied myself enamored of Van? It hardly lasted any time at all, but I'm beginning to think that you're never going to forgive me!"

"Of course I'm not angry with you. I was never angry with you in the first place," Noelle told him, exasperation in her voice. "After all, why should you be the exception, and not fall in love with Vanessa?"

"But I'm not in love with her now. Oh, I still admire her tremendously, no one could help doing that, but it's you I'm interested in with matrimony in mind. Before I lost my head that one time and strayed, it was all but settled that we'd be married someday, and I'm still hoping that you'll see your way to accepting me. We're suited to each other, we could have a good life together, and both our families would be pleased."

Just for a moment, Noelle's heart softened toward him, even though he was taking a great deal for granted in saying that it had been all but settled between them. It had never been all but settled between them: Henry had been attentive to her, but the interest had been all on his part.

And he seemed so sincere now that it was a pity that she would have to dash his hopes.

And then Henry spoiled it all by adding, with a tactlessness that was so much like Brenda's, "It isn't as if you have any chance with Captain Spencer now that he's met Vanessa, so you might as well be sensible and settle for what you can get. Me, I mean."

"Henry, I'm very fond of you. I've always been fond of you. And I know it would please our families. But I don't love you, and I have no intention of marrying anyone I don't love. Even if it were true that I would have no chance with Simon now that he's seen Vanessa, I would never entertain any notion of marrying you. If I have to settle for Vanessa's cast-offs, then I'll never marry at all!"

"Temper, temper!" Henry reproved her. "You sound more than a little spiteful, Noelle. It isn't becoming to you, either. But then I never had to contend with a brother who put me in the shade, so I suppose I have no right to pass judgment on you. I still think you should give serious consideration toward our getting married in the near future. I may not measure up to the captain, but I'm not all that bad, and I can provide a very comfortable life for you. You don't want to end up an old maid."

Noelle gave him a look that was half withering and half laughing. "That's just the trouble between you and me, Henry. You treat me and talk to me more as if I were your sister than a girl you're in love with! And that's the way I feel about you, as if you were my brother. If I married you, I'd always have a nagging feeling that we were committing incest!"

"Noelle!" For once in his life, Henry's stolid face registered shock. "For heaven's sake don't let anyone else hear you say such things, it's downright indecent!"

The number ended at that moment, and Ian Macintyre loomed up beside them. "I'm putting in my claim for the next dance before Simon can get back to you," he told Noelle, grinning that impish grin that made him so attractive. "Sorry, Henry, but I'm cutting in. You get to see a lot more of her than I do because she's staying at your house, so it's only fair that I should get to snatch her out from under your nose for one dance."

Settling herself into the curve of Ian's arm as they stepped out onto the floor was like coming home to a safe harbor. Just being with him had a soothing effect on her, and her anger at Henry's assumption that she would fall into his arms now that Simon had met Vanessa vanished, and she could even laugh at herself for letting it get under her skin. Although she had met Ian only a few days before, she felt as though she had known him all her life. It didn't matter that he didn't dance as well as Simon, or that he wasn't anywhere near as handsome. She felt comfortable with him, he could make her laugh, and they never lacked for conversation.

"When I came to Jamaica, I had no idea that I would spend so much time dancing, much less with a girl as lovely as you," Ian told her now. "I'm afraid that I'm lacking in social graces, I've always been too busy to make the round of parties and balls. But now that I've had a taste of it, I find that I like it."

"You don't have to flatter me, Ian," Noelle teased him. "A good share of what you call the social graces is sheer hypocrisy. I know that I'm not repulsive to look at, but I know that I'm no raving beauty, either."

"Beauty . . ." Ian told her, holding her a little closer, ". . . is in the eye of the beholder. I read that somewhere, I just can't remember where. But whoever said it was dead right. I like looking at you, you please my eyes. And I like dancing with you. I know that I'm as clumsy as an ox, but you never let me know it."

"You are not clumsy." Noelle couldn't help laughing. "You just aren't very graceful." It was wonderful to be able to talk so naturally with someone, with no nervousness or fear of saying the wrong thing. "You'll improve with practice, I've no doubt. In the meantime, I'm satisfied as long as you don't mutilate my feet."

Their banter was light, their smiles showed how much

they enjoyed each other's company. By the time the number ended, the last of Noelle's annoyance with Henry had disappeared.

"I'll dance with you again, if you ask me," she said. There! It would have been unthinkable for her to say that to any other man without appearing to be a brazen hussy. She liked dancing with Ian, and with him it was perfectly all right to say it.

"I'll hold you to that promise." Ian's eyes smiled down into hers, and she felt warmth spread through her, sweet and comforting. And for the first time, she realized that Ian had not been dazzled by Vanessa's beauty, that he, like Simon, preferred her, and she experienced a sense of self-assurance that she had never felt before.

Simon gave her a half-apologetic, half-humorous look as he passed them on his way to bow in front of a venerable lady of at least seventy. He had received the message that his hostess's aunt wished to trip the light fantastic, and she wanted to trip it with that sinfully attractive Yankee sea captain. As a guest in the Albright home, Simon was obliged to oblige her, although he was certain to enjoy it immensely even though it was a duty. He had a deep-seated liking for old ladies who were feisty and full of wit.

Ian, too, had left her to do his duty toward one of the older ladies, and so it was Henry who claimed Noelle again. There was a scowl on his face as he led her out.

"I should have thought that you had better sense than to waste your time on young Macintyre. The man is a nonentity, he has no fortune, no practice to speak of, no real social standing. If your purpose is to try to make Captain Spencer jealous, then you would do better to give your attention to me. I, at least, am eligible husband material, and I have already given Simon to understand that there's an understanding between us."

Noelle had to bite her lip to keep from laughing. Henry sounded so ridiculously pompous! Simon had particularly asked her, early in their acquaintanceship, if she and Henry were engaged or had any thoughts in that direction.

That rock-hard New England conscience of his had made him make sure before he started to pursue her himself. A gentleman does not infringe on another gentleman's territory. Men! Noelle thought. There was no understanding them, but the world would certainly be a boring place without them!

"Henry, I am not trying to make Captain Spencer jealous. I happen to like Ian Macintyre a great deal."

"Then you had better stop liking him, because I have no intention of being made to look a fool in front of the whole of Kingston! No fiancée of mine is going to flirt with another man."

"I am not your fiancée. And I am not flirting with Doctor Macintyre. And even if I were, isn't your accusation a little like the pot calling the kettle black? How about the time you pushed me aside in favor of Vanessa, without as much as a by-your-leave?"

"Don't be petty. That's over and done with. This is now, and as of now it's the general understanding that our engagement is in the immediate offing, so it behooves you to act accordingly. I was about to speak very firmly to Captain Spencer about monopolizing your time, guest or no guest, but that won't be necessary now that Vanessa is on the scene. But I shall certainly make young Macintyre aware that his attentions to you are not welcome."

"Henry, you are an ass!" Noelle said, exasperated. It was fortunate that the music came to a stop at that moment, because Henry's face turned a mottled red, and for a moment she was afraid that he was going to explode with anger right here in public. She smiled at him sweetly and let him escort her from the floor, still too angry to get a word past his strangling throat.

Henry's mood was not improved when she danced four more times with Simon before the evening was over, and twice with Ian.

"Henry looks like a thundercloud," Ian told her, grinning, as they stood outside with some of the others. "I wouldn't be surprised if he called me out, I only wonder whether he will call me out first, or Simon."

"You needn't be afraid of that. Henry has too high a regard for his own skin to risk having it punctured, even if the puncturer is a doctor who could patch him up on the spot." Noelle's laughter rang out, and Ian's heart twisted. He could almost hate Simon Spencer for allowing the *Maid of Boston* to become disabled, at this particular time, so that he had been thrown into contact with this girl to whom Ian had been so strongly drawn since the first time he had seen her. But the young doctor was a practical man. Love abided by no rules, it settled where it willed, and as long as Simon and Noelle had met and to all appearances were already deeply in love, then he must accept it and make the best of it. He had no intention of trying to supersede Simon in Noelle's affections. In his present circumstances, he had nothing to offer her, and he had enough common sense to know that he couldn't compete with the Yankee sea captain in any case. He looked up from his thoughts to see that their host and hostess had already gone inside, and now Vanessa linked arms with both Brenda and Ian and spoke to Henry.

"Henry, will you be a darling and pour me a sherry? The evening was so exciting that I believe a little wine will help me relax so that I'll be able to sleep well." Before they had time to think, Henry, Brenda and Ian were already inside, leaving Noelle and Simon to themselves, and a second smile in their direction assured them that she would keep the other two young people occupied so that they could have a few moments alone.

Simon drew Noelle into the garden. "I have a feeling that your sister did that on purpose," he chuckled. "What a discerning young lady she is! Remember to thank her for me, darling. I've been aching to do this all evening, and I'd all but given up hope that there'd be any opportunity."

Then she was in his arms, and he was holding her close in the scented evening air, the half-twilight giving the scene a magical dimension that Noelle knew she would never forget. She returned his kisses with all the ardor any man could have wished for, clinging to him with her entire body trembling against his. Simon had to take care not to crush her as his own passions flamed nearly out of control. She was so fragile, she was so precious to him! Seeing Henry pursue her tonight, and seeing her laugh up into Ian Macintyre's face when they had danced together, he had felt the first searing pangs of jealousy ever to bedevil him. This girl was his, and all of his former caution about waiting to make sure, all his former concern that she was too young and he had no right to sweep such an innocent child off her feet, vanished into the starlit night.

The magic moment was shattered by Henry's voice, filled with annoyance, reaching them from the doorway.

"Noelle, where are you? Oh, there you are! Captain Spencer, don't you realize that she will be eaten alive by mosquitoes if you keep her out here, she isn't protected by coat sleeves as you are! Come along inside, I vow that some people are completely devoid of common sense!"

Noelle had to stifle a giggle. No doubt Henry would find his opportunity to let Simon know, once again, that he had a prior claim on her, and she wondered what Simon's reply would be. One thing was certain, Henry wasn't likely to appreciate Simon's answer. The pressure of Simon's hand on her own before he released it told her that. As to the mosquitoes, she hadn't even realized until Henry had pointed it out to her that she had been bitten. She'd itch like fury after she got to bed, but if the itching kept her awake it would be all to the good, because it would give her more time to relive those few precious moments before they had been so rudely disturbed.

For once, Brenda's nonstop chatter failed to annoy her after they had gone to their room, she simply tuned it out and reveled in her own euphoric thoughts until the girl had run down and finally went to sleep. She herself slept shortly afterward, hugging her pillow and pretending that it was Simon she was holding in her arms.

The following day, Simon returned from a before-breakfast inspection of his ship with a satisfied smile on his face.

"From all appearances, the repairs will be completed in

about ten days. They took longer than I had anticipated, but now at last things are looking good.''

It was time that he was getting away. His enjoyment of this island paradise had all but undermined his sense of responsibility. One thing was certain: his father would not be pleased with him if he stayed on in Jamaica one day more than was necessary. Before he left, he would ask Noelle to wait for him, and when he got back to Boston he would prepare his family for the advent of the loveliest daughter-in-law that they could ever have hoped for.

''What a pity that you must leave our island so soon!'' Vanessa said. ''But you still have a few days. Captain Spencer, I must return to Maynard Penn tomorrow, it doesn't do to leave a large holding like ours without supervision for more than a day or two, especially in view of all the unrest on the island. But I was wondering if you wouldn't like to visit the plantation? It would do my father a world of good to have your company, he's too much alone, and he has always taken an intense interest in America. And you might be interested in learning the running of a plantation, there's a good more to it than you might think.''

Simon's eyes lighted up. He would like to see Noelle's home, it would be a delight to be at the plantation with her, away from all the demands that were made on their time here in Kingston. And it would give him the opportunity to speak to Daniel Maynard about Noelle. He would leave the island in a much happier frame of mind if he took with him Noelle's father's consent to marry his daughter.

''If you're certain it won't be too much trouble, I'd enjoy nothing more.''

''We'll be leaving the first thing in the morning?'' Noelle asked, her cheeks flushed with pleasure that matched Simon's, and for the same reasons. ''I'll see to my packing right away!''

Vanessa's voice was filled with sisterly consternation. ''Oh, no, Noelle darling! You mustn't dream of curtailing your visit with Brenda! She has all sorts of galas and outings planned, you mustn't miss them, it's been far too long since you've enjoyed any gaiety! It isn't as if you're needed at Maynard Penn, I can get along without you very well, so you must certainly stay on here and not disappoint Brenda.''

Now Brenda raised her voice, almost wailing. ''Of course you can't go back so soon, you've only just got here! I'll never forgive you if you don't stay! Henry, tell her! Mama, Papa, don't let her go! Noelle, you just can't go!''

Whether Brenda was her dearest friend or not, Noelle felt like choking her. But Brenda's mother added her voice to the persuasion.

''Do stay on, Noelle dear! I've made all sorts of plans with you in mind, and Brenda depends on you to help her in the selection of her trousseau. As sensible as my daughter is in all other matters, she hasn't the sense of style that you have, and I confess that I have no sense of style at all! We are really counting on your help in the selection of patterns and materials!''

Noelle wavered, but Brenda was starting to cry. Reluctantly, looking at Simon with her heart in her eyes, she rose to put her arms around her friend.

Although he was as disappointed as Noelle, Simon chided himself that Vanessa was right. Noelle had had a grim time of it these last few months, first losing her brother, and then seeing her father stricken with such a severe illness. This time in Kingston was something that she sorely needed; a young girl has a right to parties and laughter and gaiety.

''It would be a pity to cut your visit short. But I believe that I will go, I have a particular interest in talking to your father. And I'll see you again when I return to Kingston, before I sail.'' His glance at Noelle spoke volumes, and Noelle's heart lightened. She knew why he wanted to see her father, and it would only be for a few days, after all. And Simon confirmed her hopes when he managed to draw her aside after breakfast was over.

"I hate leaving you for even so short a time, but it would be a shame for you to disappoint Brenda, and miss out on all the fun. I want you to make the most of every moment, and dance the hours away, just so long as you don't allow Henry to persuade you that you should announce your betrothal to him while I'm gone!"

Noelle blinked back tears. "Don't be so silly! I shall avoid Henry like the plague! Simon, how can I enjoy myself when you aren't here?"

"You'll be too busy to miss me," Simon assured her. "If Brenda and Mrs. Cottswood give you a minute alone that you don't know how to fill, let Ian squire you around. Ian's good company, and it will keep you away from Henry."

Speaking of the devil, Henry loomed up behind them. Casting a laughing-eyed glance at Simon, Noelle eluded her would-be suitor by exclaiming that she had to go into conference with Brenda and Mrs. Cottswood immediately, before Brenda chose all the wrong patterns from the pattern books. Henry had at least the satisfaction of knowing that in the morning Simon would be gone, and after his return he would be sailing almost immediately. And just about time! It was deucedly difficult to court a girl when she gave all of her time and attention to another man!

They all attended another gala that evening, and Noelle and Simon weren't able to snatch any time alone. And Henry wasn't to be caught short on their return home, as he had been the evening before. He had a firm grip on Noelle's arm and propelled her inside the house. Simon's eyes were filled with amusement, and Noelle had to exercise all her control not to let her own amusement show. By tacit agreement, they went along with Henry's wishes because there was no point in fomenting a quarrel when there was so short a time before Simon would sail. But once inside the house, Noelle circumvented Henry by pleading fatigue and retiring immediately to bed.

"Now she's done it! I just knew she'd be up to something, even though she's doing it in all innocence!"

Brenda exclaimed, as she followed along. "I just didn't think how it would affect you when I begged you to stay on here, and now Simon will be alone with Vanessa for days and days. He's sure to fall in love with her! It's all my fault and you'll probably never forgive me!"

"I'm sure everything will be all right." Noelle assured her.

"Well, I'm not sure at all! I should think you'd be worried to death! I won't blame you if you never speak to me again, if anything happens!"

Brenda went right on nattering, long after they were in bed with the mosquito bar protecting them. Noelle wondered if poor Bryce would ever have a chance to make love to her, after they were married, before she wore him out with her never-ending chatter, and he fell asleep while he was waiting for her to close her mouth long enough for him to kiss her.

Everything was going to be all right. Simon was going to Maynard Penn to speak to her father, and she didn't have to worry about Vanessa. Vanessa never indulged in an affair with an unmarried man, and Noelle believed her statement that nothing would make her happier than for her to marry Simon and leave Jamaica.

In just a few more days, Noelle would be betrothed. She whispered the words to herself, and felt a warm glow envelop her body.

". . . not that Simon could be blamed. Men just naturally fall in love with Vanessa, they can't help themselves, but still it's just a dreadful shame . . ." Noelle heard the words droning on.

"Good night, Brenda." Noelle said firmly. "I'm going to sleep now, so if you go on talking you'll just be talking to yourself."

Chapter Five

BRENDA AND NOELLE STOOD ARM IN ARM, BIDDING Vanessa and Simon good-bye. They were already in the open curricle, and Vanessa was leaning toward them.

"Mind now, I want you to enjoy yourself!" she admonished Noelle. "You are to buy whatever you want, the shopkeepers will accept your signature, I sent word to them. I want you to come back to Maynard Penn blooming like a rose, so that we will be swamped with young gentlemen calling to court you, unless Henry beats them all out before you return!"

How clever Van was, Noelle admitted to herself ruefully. No doubt this was one of her subtle little ploys, giving Simon the idea that he would have competition unless he made haste to ask for her hand! As underhanded as it was, and as unnecessary, still she had to admire her sister's knowledge of men and how to manipulate them. It was not a trait she would admire in herself, but it still must come in mightily handy to girls who would not hesitate to stoop to use such tactics!

"I will if I can, you can depend on it!" Henry was jovial this morning, happy to see the last of his rival for a few days, but there was a glint of determination in his eyes. "And you can depend on Brenda to see that she buys out the shops. Captain Spencer, we'll see you again before you sail. Enjoy your visit to Maynard Penn, and be sure to remember to tell Mr. Maynard that we send him our best regards."

Filled with the self-assurance that his sense of self-importance gave him, Henry turned to Noelle as the curricle drove away. "Now there's a match if I ever saw one! I don't have the least doubt that by the time Simon comes back, there'll be an understanding between those two! Simon Spencer is the only man I've ever known who's a fit match for Vanessa, they'll make a striking couple. Well now, they're gone, and now we'll have plenty of time for each other, and that's the way it should be."

"Now Henry, if Van and Captain Spencer do make a match of it, then you'll have the inside track with Noelle and you'll have her all to yourself all the years you'll be married, so you mustn't be selfish now and monopolize her while she's visiting me!" Brenda scolded her brother.

Noelle's jaw ached with the effort not to grit her teeth. Like Henry, Brenda already had Simon and Vanessa married in her mind. What a surprise they'd get, when Simon came back and they announced that they were engaged, with her father's approval! It would almost be worth the days she'd have to wait just to see the expressions on their faces, especially on Henry's. Brenda, she admitted, would be happy for her even though she'd bemoan the fact that now they would never be sisters.

It was wildly exciting to go through the shops, choosing whatever took her fancy. She took Vanessa at her word and didn't stint herself. After all, the things she was buying would go to make up her trousseau. She not only wanted to be beautiful for Simon, but she wanted to make the best possible impression on his family when the time came.

In the afternoon the ladies always rested through the hottest part of the day, and that evening the Cottswoods had guests, older people of their own generation, and to Henry's chagrin Brenda plotted with Noelle to escape early to their room, pleading that they were still fatigued from their shopping. They spent their evening in Brenda's chamber to good advantage, going over pattern books, both for Brenda and for herself.

She was almost beside herself with relief and delight when Ian Macintyre called at an unseemly early hour the next morning and asked her to ride out with him. Ian, his eyes twinkling, told her that Simon had found the time the day before to tell him that he was leaving, and that any time he could spare for Noelle would be appreciated, so that she wouldn't be driven to distraction with a steady diet of Henry's company.

"Change into something suitable for riding," Ian told her. "I don't own a curricle, but I borrowed an extra horse. You can come plant hunting with me, and maybe you'll have a better idea of what I'm looking at than I do. Papa Emile has been instructing me, but I have an idea that he's holding back more than he's telling."

"Papa Emile? But he's a gangan!" Noelle exclaimed. "However did you happen to meet him? He doesn't have much to do with white people, since he isn't a slave."

"I sought him out, not the other way around. Fortunately, he took a liking to me and didn't slip poison into the rum he offered me."

"Papa Emile doesn't poison people!" Noelle told him severely. "He only makes good charms and spells. He used to come to Maynard Penn until Chloe took exception to him and made Vanessa ask Father not to let him come anymore. All the slaves looked up to him, and I think he helped them a great deal with his cures."

"I'm sure he did." Ian said. "But the wily old man still isn't letting me in on his innermost secrets. So far, all he's given me is a cure for stomachache and some plant you can use to ease childbirth. As most ladies prefer mid-wives, and the rest of them swear by Doctor Eastlake instead of at him, that last isn't going to be of much help to me."

Noelle laughed with pure delight that Ian had the temerity to mention such a thing as childbirth to her, when polite society refused to acknowledge that there was such a thing as pregnancy. Babies simply appeared out of nowhere, and everyone expressed amazement, as though they had had no idea at all that one had been in the offing.

If she laughed at Ian's audacity in the subject matter suitable for a young lady's ears, she laughed twice as hard when she saw the horse he had borrowed for her to ride. It was a sorry-looking animal, its coat moth-eaten, its head hanging with dejection.

"It's my fee for curing a man's stomachache with the herbs Papa Emile gave me." Ian's eyes were twinkling more merrily than ever. "The gentleman had no money, else he would have called in Eastlake, so I told him that the loan of his horse for the day would even the score. And you shouldn't hurt the creature's feelings by laughing at him, it isn't kind."

"He's a lovely horse!" Noelle declared, stroking its nose. "I'll be as proud as a queen to ride him!"

As if the animal had understood her, it lifted its head and whinnied, nuzzling against her hand. They both laughed harder as Ian helped her into the saddle, and Ian told her that he had borrowed the sidesaddle from the Cottswoods' stable, although Henry had no idea that he had done it.

"We have to stop at my place first. Beggar always goes with me on my jaunts, but I didn't bring him to the Cottswoods' because he would have tripped me up trying to get inside with me, and I'm afraid that he wouldn't be very trustworthy around elegant furnishings if he managed to run between my legs and get in. We'd better get started, I don't know how long Brenda will be able to keep that brother of hers busy." Brenda, still contrite for having forced Noelle to stay, had volunteered to keep Henry occupied until Noelle and Ian could get well away.

They were already four miles out of town before she clapped her hand over her mouth with an exclamation of dismay.

"I forgot to bring Julie with me! I was so excited at escaping from Henry that it flew right out of my mind! There'll be a scandal, Ian."

"Do you really mind? At least it will shake Henry up," Ian said cheerfully.

Noelle was overtaken by mirth again. She didn't mind a bit. She had an idea that she had forgotten Julie halfway on purpose, because having the slave girl tagging along behind them on one of the donkeys the Cottswoods kept for the use of their slaves would have detracted from her sense of freedom. And shaking Henry up would be good for him, and the opinion of anyone who thought that Ian would take advantage of her simply because she was unchaperoned wasn't worth having. Anyway, the excitement of the announcement of her engagement to Simon, when he returned, would sweep today's little escapade right out of everyone's mind.

If Ian had thought that she would have a more restful day with him than by shopping with Brenda and Faith Cottswood, Noelle couldn't fathom what his idea of restfulness was. Ian was tireless, and he took it for granted that she could keep up with him when they tethered the horses and walked and climbed in search of his elusive plants and herbs. By the time he produced the picnic lunch of bread and cheese and a bottle of inferior wine from his saddlebags, she was ready to sit down and rest, and so ravenous and thirsty that the simple fare was a feast.

When they got back to Kingston, she was disheveled, her face and hands were dirty, and her hair had come loose from its moorings, but it had been one of the most enjoyable days of her life.

"We'll have to do this again sometime soon." Ian told her when he left her at the Cottswoods' door. He was inordinately pleased with himself for having shown her such a good time.

"We certainly will! Ian, thank you. I don't know when I've enjoyed myself as much, even if I wasn't any help at all in identifying the medicinal properties of plants for you."

"No matter. I'll show the lot I brought back to Papa Emile, and he'll either tell me what they are or he won't," Ian said.

Henry was livid with anger when he confronted her as she entered the house. And in the background, Brenda and Claude and their parents made no effort to conceal their shock.

"How could you have done such a thing, what were you thinking of? By now the story is all over Kingston, everyone knows that you spent the entire day with Ian Macintyre without a chaperone! If you have no thought for your own reputation, you should at least have taken ours into consideration, we're responsible for you while you're visiting us, your actions will reflect on us!"

"I'm afraid that I just didn't think. A ride in the country appealed to me, so I simply went." Noelle braced herself to weather the storm with as much dignity as she could muster, considering the state she was in.

"Oh, my glory, just look at you!" Brenda's eyes were wide. "You look as if . . . you look as if you've been . . ." For once the plump girl was at a loss for words.

"Is ravished the word you're groping for?" Noelle asked her innocently, and Faith Cottswoods' gasp was all but drowned out by Brenda's and by Henry's. "I assure you that I was not. Ian Macintyre is a gentleman. I look like this because we did a lot of walking and climbing. If you will excuse me, I will repair the damages so that I'll be fit to sit at table with you. And as far as my reputation is concerned, I'm sure that everyone in Kingston knows both Ian and me well enough not to assume the worst."

"Just the same, it was completely thoughtless of you, not to say actually reprehensible!" Henry was not in the least mollified. "For the rest of your visit, you're not to be allowed out of our sight, is that understood?"

Noelle nodded. It was the easiest way out. But she hadn't said that she would obey the command, she had only indicated that she understood it.

To her chagrin, she had no opportunity to disobey in the immediate future. Ian sent word by a ragged boy that he was attending a dying woman and would not leave her side until it was over, in case he could ease her passing simply by being there. And after that, Papa Emile had promised that he would ride out with him personally, and give him firsthand instruction in the native flora, an opportunity that he had to grasp before the old gangan changed his mind. Noelle understood, but her disappointment was acute all the same.

Henry had appointed himself her shadow, keeping his promise that he would not let her out of his sight. His constant attendance on her drove her to distraction, her hostess's pained expression that reproached her for her unseemly conduct drove her to distraction, Brenda's complaints that she wasn't paying strict enough attention to her chatter drove her to distraction.

At least her reputation was not damaged beyond repair. To back up their belief in her innocence and their loyalty to the Cottswoods, the Binghams, one of Kingston's leading families, gave a hastily planned party on the second evening following the incident that had raised so many eyebrows.

For such short notice, it was a fairly large gathering; Kingston at large seemed to think that the Cottswoods needed their moral support in view of their young guest's behavior. Noelle was as annoyed as she was amused, but she was a good deal more concerned with wondering if Simon would return to the city on the following day or at least on the next. It already seemed as if he had been gone for weeks; how was she going to be able to bear it, after they were married, and he went to sea on long voyages that might keep him away for months?

Doctor Eastlake was among the Binghams's guests,

although Ian was not there. Noelle wondered if he had not been invited, the omission a reproof. If that were the case, she wondered if Ian would even realize why his name had not been on the invitation list, or if he would be aware that there had been a party at all.

Doctor Eastlake, however, was very much in evidence, and Noelle took her courage in her hands and asked to speak to him in confidence. The doctor was clearly annoyed when she took him away from the lively discussion he had been having about the effects on the island's economy once the emancipation had gone through.

"Is it about your father, my dear?" he asked her with what show of patience he could muster. "I assure you that his condition remains the same. There is no cause for alarm. Men in a great deal worse case than his have recovered, although it does seem to be taking him a rather uncommonly long time. Still, his shock and grief were severe, and time itself is the great healer. You must be patient, he's bound to take a turn for the better any day now."

"It isn't about Father, it's about Kenneth. I still can't understand how he could have died. I know that you assured me that it was natural, but a great deal of time has passed, and I wondered if you have given it any further thought. Something, some detail, might have come to you that you missed at the time."

Now the doctor made no attempt to hide his annoyance. "My dear young lady, there was nothing to come to mind! Your brother contracted some obscure tropical infection, and while his death was tragic there was nothing unnatural about it."

"But what if someone wished him ill? He and Vanessa quarreled violently shortly before he became ill."

"I have listened to quite enough of this nonsense! Are you trying to insinuate that your sister had anything to do with Kenneth's death? She wasn't even at Maynard Penn when it happened, she was in Spanish Town with your father! Whatever the quarrel was about, if there was indeed a quarrel, and you haven't blown a few cross words up out of all proportion, Vanessa could have had nothing to do with Kenneth's becoming ill!''

The doctor's scowl would have intimidated someone less determined, but Noelle had been puzzling over Kenneth's death for too long to back off now.

"I know that Vanessa wasn't at home, but Chloe was! And everybody knows that Chloe has powers, she knows all sorts of herbs and drugs, and there's nothing she wouldn't do for Vanessa.''

"Even to the point of murdering her young master? Really, Noelle! I'm beginning to think that your sister is right, that your mind is unstable! She has said as much to me before, but I discounted it, putting it down to your grief. Now it appears that it may be a more deep-seated malady, that you are in need of care until your mind clears and you can be sensible about things!''

Henry spoke directly behind Noelle's shoulder, making her start. He had come searching for her, and he had overheard more than Noelle would have liked.

"Noelle, what nonsense is this? I wouldn't have thought it of you!" Henry's face was red with anger. "I know you've always been jealous of Vanessa, but this surpasses the bounds of decency! Just because Vanessa walked off with Captain Spencer doesn't give you a license to malign her! Your sister is the sweetest, kindest young woman ever to walk on this earth, and for you to try to spread malicious stories about her speaks poorly of your character!''

He glared at her. "If you keep on, I'll have second thoughts about you! Cattiness and malice are not desirable traits in any woman, much less in a woman a man is considering making his wife! Doctor Eastlake, I'm sorry that you were subjected to this blatant nonsense! Come along, Noelle, come away this minute, and for heaven's sake smile! People are beginning to look at us, wondering what's going on, and I'm hanged if I want our friends to get any inkling of your nonsense! You will try my patience too sorely one day, and then you will have to face the consequences!''

"Not only maligning her sister, but maligning my professional ability as well!" Doctor Eastlake was clearly outraged. "I don't want to hear another word, Noelle, or I might be tempted to forget my long-standing friendship with your father, and be forced to give my considered and *professional* opinion that you are suffering from a mental aberration that we can only hope will be of short duration! I hope I have made myself clear. Henry, dear boy, talk some sense into her head, make her understand that no good can come of such insinuations, she is only making a fool of herself."

"I'm humiliated!" Henry hissed in her ear as he drew her away. "Thank God that nobody but myself and the doctor heard your outrageous accusations! I would be made a laughingstock forever having considered making you my wife!"

Noelle's face flamed with fury. The gall of him! Why couldn't he get it through his head that she wasn't going to marry him, that she wouldn't marry him if he were the only man who ever asked her!

From across the room, she saw a pair of bright, interested eyes, and her heart leapt. Ian had come after all, he had just been late. As much to annoy Henry as to follow her own inclinations, she drew away from Henry and met Ian as he crossed the room to her, both of them ignoring the other man's indignation at this further proof of her intractableness.

"Ian, I'm so angry I could spit! No one takes the slightest heed of me when I tell them that I'm not satisfied about Kenneth's death. Doctor Eastlake even had the temerity to tell me that I'm suffering from an aberration of the mind! And then there's my father, he isn't getting any better and he should have been fully recovered by now. Please, Ian, will you go to Maynard Penn and examine him? I need you to do it. I won't rest until I have heard another opinion."

"Noelle, there's nothing I'd rather do, but it's impossible," Ian told her, for once with no trace of laughter in his eyes. They were serious, and she could tell that he was concerned for her, and even more important, that he at least was willing to listen to her doubts and suspicions. "Unless Doctor Eastlake himself were to ask me for a consultation, there is no way I can barge in on his patient. The rules of medical ethics are very strict in that regard, and to break them would finish me as a doctor."

Noelle's heart plummeted. Ian had been her last hope, and now that was gone. Doctor Eastlake would never ask the younger man to examine his patient. He had supreme confidence in his own judgment and he would consider Ian an upstart.

"Don't look at me as if the world has come to an end!" Ian entreated her. "I'm sure that Eastlake is competent enough. At least he is in attendance, and although the possibility exists that your brother might have met with foul play, Chloe could hardly get away with tampering with your father's treatment while a qualified doctor is keeping close tabs on him."

"But couldn't you come to the plantation after I've returned, just as a guest? I would take you in to see my father, and maybe you could tell something just by looking at him."

"It would be just as effective to have Papa Emile look at him, I'm afraid," Ian told her ruefully. "I would need to make a thorough examination, and there's no way I could do that."

At the look of despair that came into Noelle's eyes, Ian made a last effort to make her feel better.

"There's one thing I can do," he said. "I'll ask Papa Emile if there's anything in his experience with drugs and herbs that could induce your father's condition. If he were able to give me some clue, I'd have a better idea of what to look for during my casual visit."

"Oh, Ian, would you do that?" The light came back into Noelle's eyes. She was desperate for any hope to cling to, and Ian had at least held out a straw.

Henry reclaimed her, glaring at Ian with a barely

perceptible nod. Noelle had to let him draw her away, or else create a scene, but although her feet were reluctant to move away from Ian, her heart felt lighter. She'd get Ian in to see her father somehow, in spite of Vanessa, in spite of Chloe. Ian had promised that he would come, and she knew that he would keep his promise.

Chapter Six

Simon was entranced by the countryside during the journey to Maynard Penn. They had traveled beside the Rio Cobre for some distance, the banks of the river covered with ferns and reeds and smaller growth, the river itself flowing through rocky gorges, tumbling and foaming, the road shaded by coco palms and bamboo. Lushness and beauty such as this were so alien to him that he marveled that they could exist, but Vanessa took it for granted, laughing at him gently when he exclaimed over some vista or other.

"I expect that it's very different from your Massachusetts," she had said. "And I expect that your Massachusetts would seem as strange to me as our Jamaica does to you."

Maynard Penn was larger and more self-contained than Simon had imagined. The endless acres of cane, the broad leaves rustling in the breeze, awed him. Vanessa told him that they grew only Bourbon, which was the choicest, and it seemed to Simon that a man could get lost in those fields with the cane far taller than a tall man's head. It took two years for a crop to mature, but the fortunes that had been made from it made it well worthwhile.

Besides the fields, some of which were planted with indigo instead of cane, the plantation had so many outbuildings that Simon lost count. The boiler house stood out from them all, and the sugar mill. The huts occupied by the slaves were made of wattle, and formed streets, a sizable town in itself, and each hut had its own vegetable garden, all nestled here in the clearing with forest all around.

There was a palisade around the plantation house itself, for protection in case of an uprising. The logs of which it was constructed were covered by long-thorned leaves of penguin pineapple, making a formidable barrier in case of trouble, although Vanessa assured him that at Maynard Penn there was no danger.

The house was constructed of white plaster, with double staircases with wrought-iron railings leading from the outside to the living quarters on what Simon would have called the second story, because the space below was used for storage.

Because of the warmth of the climate, plantation houses had a peculiar design in order to take full advantage of every breeze. The hallways formed a cross, with windows at each point so that the wind would have full sweep. The bedrooms were in the arms, each with two outside windows covered with netting to keep out mosquitoes and other flying insects, and light curtains billowed in them to give an impression of coolness.

When Simon and Vanessa entered the house, two housegirls were polishing the parquet floors by shuffling back and forth with cloths held between their toes. Simon suppressed a chuckle, speculating about what his mother or any other New England housewife would have to say about that. She would have ordered the girls down on their hands and knees to do a proper job, and demonstrated exactly how it should be done, if need be! The floors themselves were a marvel of intricate design, made up of mahogany, greenheart, graynut, and blood nut, the names of the woods exotic to Simon's ears.

Dicey appeared in the doorway of the drawing room, out of breath from running, her face lighted up with anticipation of seeing Noelle. Her expression changed to one of disappointment when she saw that her younger mistress had not returned with Vanessa.

"Come now, Dicey! You wouldn't want Noelle to miss all the festivities in Kingston, now would you? She will only be away for a few more days. Captain Spencer, Dicey is Noelle's girl, and she has been keeping a close watch over my father while I was away. How is Father, Dicey? Has there been any change? I must go up to him at once."

"None at all, Mistress Vanessa," Dicey said.

"But we aren't going to give up hope!" Vanessa's voice was firm. "He's going to get well, Dicey. Doctor Eastlake assures me that he is. He'll be out later in the week to see him, and just as likely he'll see a change for the better that our untrained eyes have missed."

"Yes, ma'am." Dicey lowered her eyes. Simon thought that there was a lack of conviction in the girl's voice, and something else that was not as easy to determine. Handling men as he did, for long weeks and months at a time, Simon had become expert at hearing even subtle nuances in voices that might spell discontentment or trouble, so dangerous on shipboard that they must be guarded against at all times.

"I do hope that Father will be up to seeing you, Captain Spencer. I'll see how he is, and if it's possible, you can meet him this evening."

Another woman had entered the room, walking so silently in spite of her size that Simon wasn't aware of her presence until she spoke.

"Welcome home, Mistress Vanessa. Everything is as it should be here."

"Chloe! Simon, this is Chloe. She has been with me since I was a little girl, and she's my good right hand."

Inscrutable eyes studied Simon, revealing nothing, and in spite of the warmth of the room he felt a chill creep down his back. What a mountain of a woman Chloe was! Man or not, Simon wouldn't have relished meeting her in some dark alley if she had a grudge against him. Disgusted with himself for his feeling of instant revulsion, he reminded himself that he had little experience with blacks, and that although those he had seen so far here in Jamaica had been friendly and smiling it did not mean that there could not be an exception to the rule. Chloe was probably naturally impassive. Vanessa certainly held her in high esteem.

"Chloe, show Captain Spencer to his room and make sure that he has everything he needs. I'm going to look in on Father now. Dinner will be at the usual time."

"Yes, ma'am." Chloe said. But there was no servility in her voice, she might have called Vanessa by her given name, as an equal. Once again, Simon felt a chill. He was not usually wrong in his first impressions of anyone, and something about this woman struck a false note.

A manservant was already unpacking Simon's luggage when he entered the room that had been assigned to him. "This is Jacob. He will care for you while you stay with us," Chloe told him.

If Simon hadn't already suspected that something here at Maynard Penn was wrong, he might have missed the faint hint of fear that emanated from the man Jacob as Chloe fixed her eyes on him. Simon would have sworn that Jacob was terrified of the woman.

Even after Chloe left the room, something still struck Simon as being wrong, and then he put his finger on it. Jacob was not talkative, the way the Cottswoods' servants had been. There was no beaming smile on his face, no gleam of white teeth against dark skin, no eagerness to please. Jacob went about his duties efficiently, but with none of the friendliness that Simon had found so enchanting in the other blacks on the island.

He tried to draw Jacob out, but his questions about whether or not Jacob liked his work at Maynard Penn and how often he was able to go into Kingston to enjoy the festivities the slaves put on there brought only the briefest of replies.

Abraham, at the Cottswoods' house, had chattered on a mile a minute, interspersing everything he said with questions of his own about Massachusetts, about life aboard a sailing ship, or whether or not Simon wanted his drink freshened, or would care for a bite to eat to stay him until dinner time.

Things might be done differently on a plantation than they were in town, Simon pointed out to himself. On a plantation, with only a handful of whites among hundreds of blacks, and miles from help, strict discipline might be needed where it was not in town. Still, he missed the friendliness that he had become used to, and he wished that he could bring a smile to Jacob's face.

There was only he and Vanessa at dinner. Candlelight flickered behind the glass globes of hurricane lamps, the food was exotic and highly spiced, as all of the food in Jamaica seemed to be. Simon liked it, but he had a momentary longing for a slice of his mother's apple pie, or a crock of baked beans, or a piece of good, honest, unadorned codfish. And the service was a little too perfect for his liking. At home, the hired girls clattered dishes and weren't above shuffling their feet or spilling something on occasion, but here the service was silent, executed so efficiently that you were hardly aware that the servants were there at all.

"More wine, Captain Spencer? Then I think you might spend a few minutes with my father before he is settled for the night. You must remember that it must be only a few minutes, we must be sure not to tire him, but a new face will do him worlds of good."

The room Vanessa led him into was dim, with only a single candle casting a circle of light from a table. But there was enough light falling on the ailing man's face for Simon to feel shock. He'd known that Daniel Maynard was ill, but the man in this bed was a living skeleton. The hand that lay outside the sheet was clawlike in its thinness, his cheeks were sunken, his eyes dull, set in deep sockets that were bereft of the flesh that must once have covered them. There was a grayish cast to his skin, with no trace of the faint color of fever that Simon had expected.

Simon had seen that look on men's faces before, it was the look of death, but in almost every other case the men had been old, their span on earth used up, and ready to go. But Daniel Maynard was only in his late forties, certainly he had not yet passed his fiftieth birthday.

"Spencer? Captain Spencer?" The voice was only a thread, so weak that Simon had to bend close in order to make out the words. "And your ship is . . ." Daniel groped for the name, distressed because he could not remember it although his daughter had told it to him only an hour or two ago.

"The *Maid of Boston*, Mr. Maynard. I am very glad to be able to meet you, and I hope that you will be feeling better soon."

"Yes, yes, I am ill. But I will be better soon. They take good care of me. Where is Noelle?"

"Father, I explained to you that Noelle will be staying in Kingston a little longer." Vanessa took her father's hand and pressed it against her cheek, and Simon saw that her lips were trembling and his heart went out to her.

"Kingston. It has been long since I have been in Kingston. How long has it been, daughter? I can't seem to remember."

"It hasn't been so very long." Vanessa lied, her voice gentle. "And you will go there again soon."

"The last time . . . Kenneth was with me." To Simon's consternation, the man in the bed began to tremble, and tears came into his eyes. Vanessa looked distressed.

"I think you had better go now, Captain Spencer. Father is tired, he needs to rest."

Simon left Vanessa to soothe her father, and stepped out into the gardens to enjoy the cooler air that had already settled over the plantation now that the sun had gone down. He paced up and down, pausing every now and then to examine some exotic flower or shrub in the strange twilight that would last throughout the night. The beauty of the tropical evening did little to calm the uneasiness that seemed to have pervaded him. What a tragedy it was for a man to be struck down in his prime!

And that in itself struck a jarring note in Simon's mind. A strong man, a vital man such as he had been told Daniel Maynard had been before his son had died, might have grieved, and his grief might have lasted for a long time, but surely it should not have left this man an empty husk of himself. Death and grief were as much a part of life as birth and joy. Men accepted it, often unwillingly, but still they accepted it because it had to be accepted, and they went on with their lives because that was also something that they had to do. This sickness of Daniel Maynard's seemed unnatural, and he thought of Ian Macintyre, and wished that the young doctor could see Daniel soon. Eastlake might have years more experience, but if Simon were ill he wouldn't let the pompous man near him if Ian were available.

Vanessa joined him in just a few moments. Her face in the half light was pale, her eyes dark with distress.

"I'm sorry that my father is having a bad night, Captain Spencer. It must have been unpleasant for you. But perhaps he will be more himself tomorrow, and then you can visit him again."

Her voice was brave, but Simon saw the glitter of tears in her eyes, and this time he followed his natural instincts and drew her into his arms, her head cradled on his shoulder. It was a gesture of comfort he would have given his sister, if she had been in such sorrow as this girl whose father was so gravely ill.

In his arms, Vanessa trembled, but not from the grief that Simon imagined she was feeling for her father. Desire spread all through her body like a tidal wave, hot and demanding.

She was going to have this man, even though up until

now she had never risked having an affair with a man who was not safely married. Simon made all those other men seem colorless and unexciting. Simon was strong and vital, vital as no other man she had ever met. Every atom in her body cried out in an agony of desire for him. Here, at last, was the man who could satisfy her completely, who would leave her sated and content, knowing that she had at last achieved the ultimate in sexual fulfillment.

But it wasn't because Simon would be leaving Jamaica so soon, making the risk of having an affair with him small, that Vanessa had invited him to Maynard Penn. There was another, even more important motive for her seduction of him. It would not suit her purpose at all to have Noelle marry Simon, for Noelle to leave Jamaica, far beyond her reach. Noelle, like her father, must die. Noelle married, and to as strong and intelligent a man as Simon, would be a threat to her, and Simon would make sure that she received her full share of Daniel Maynard's estate after Daniel died.

Knowing her younger sister as she did, Vanessa was certain that Noelle would refuse to marry Simon once she knew that Simon had gone to Vanessa's bed. Noelle was proud, she had made it clear in the past that she would not accept her sister's leavings. Their romance would be nipped in the bud, Noelle would send Simon away with the understanding that she would never have anything to do with him again.

Then Vanessa would be safe, her plans could be carried out just as she had laid them out so long ago. Daniel would die, and Vanessa would make sure that her sister met with an accident on shipboard while they were voyaging to England. Chloe would see to the drowning, and Vanessa would give every appearance of being devastated with grief because Noelle had committed suicide. Vanessa would make sure that the captain of the ship knew that Noelle was not stable in her mind, that the death of their father so soon after the death of their brother had been too much for her to handle, so that Vanessa was afraid that she was taking leave of her senses. And here in Jamaica, Vanessa had already planted enough seeds of doubt about Noelle's lack of stability that no one would be surprised that she had taken her own life.

Vanessa had the utmost confidence that she would make a brilliant marriage in the very near future, a marriage that would bring her the title she wanted, and another fortune to add to the fortune she would already have. And then, within a few months, her husband would die, and then there would be Paris, her ultimate goal.

Paris! She would make her home a showplace, her salons would be glittering, all of French society would beat a path to her door. In Paris, there would be little need to be discreet, she would be able to carry on as many affairs as she chose quite openly, and be admired rather than condemned for it. She would be lavished with gifts worth a king's ransom, her carriage would bear her own crest, her gowns would bedazzle all beholders. Her name would be a household word, and she would revel in it!

If word of her notoriety sifted back to Jamaica, it would only increase her enjoyment of her new state. How they would squirm, those former lovers of hers, how they would writhe with secret shame that they had allowed themselves to be bewitched by her! They would be ashamed to look at their own faces in the mirror when they arose in the morning, and in Paris, Vanessa would laugh and mock them even as she made more conquests that would put their mild little affairs to shame.

It was just as well that Simon couldn't see Vanessa's face as she nestled it more closely against his shoulder. Her expression was one of triumph. Simon was here at Maynard Penn. Tonight she would sleep alone, tossing and burning with frustrated desire, but tomorrow night it would be an entirely different story. By tomorrow night, her beauty and her nearness to him would have inflamed Simon with a passion he would not be able to control, just as had happened with every other man she had ever wanted.

She slept at last, smiling in spite of the fires that raged within her. And in Kingston, Noelle also slept, although not nearly as happily, because of her frustration over having the mystery of Kenneth's death still unresolved, and the mystery of her father's lingering illness equally unsolved.

But she had the comfort of knowing that Simon was at Maynard Penn, that he might be able to persuade her father to ask for Ian to examine him. If that failed, she herself would manage to get Ian in to see Daniel. She would have to be content with that for the moment, and hope for the best.

Vanessa paced her bedchamber, fury and frustration in every line of her body. She had never before encountered a man who was so hard to seduce. Simon had been at Maynard Penn for three days now, and she was no closer to getting him into her bed than she had been on the first day.

That damned morality of his, that damned, rock-hard New England morality! She had done everything but strip herself naked and throw herself on him, and still he held himself back. He didn't even seem to realize that she was his for the taking, he went on treating her like a sister, the sister-in-law he hoped that she would soon become! Any other man she had ever known would have taken her, even if he was promised to someone else.

She couldn't waste any more time. It had to be tonight. She was determined to sate herself with him, sate herself so fully that the memory of it would last her for her lifetime, and then throw it in Noelle's face that she had had him!

Chloe entered the room on those silent feet of hers, so that Vanessa started as she turned in her pacing and saw the woman standing there, watching her with her inscrutable eyes. "You wanted me?"

"Yes, I want you! Damn it, isn't it obvious that I want you? Something has to be done about Simon Spencer."

There was a flicker of a smile in Chloe's eyes, gone so

quickly that Vanessa couldn't be sure that it had been there.

"Tonight, then. In his wine. Mind you take sherry, Mistress. You won't be needing what he'll be taking."

Insolence! Vanessa wanted to slap her, but she didn't dare. She needed Chloe, she had always needed her, none of her plans could have come to fruition without her and the drugs and potions she was so expert at concocting. Without Chloe, Kenneth would still be alive, and he would have brought her father's wrath down on her; without Chloe, Daniel Maynard would be well and in full possession of his faculties, and she could have said good-bye to all her dreams.

"Do it, then," she said curtly, dismissing the woman. In the back of her mind, there was a ghost of a thought. Some day, in the not too far future, she wouldn't need Chloe anymore.

The thought died even as it was being born. She would always need Chloe to serve as a counterpoint to her own fair beauty, to add to her fame, to be handy with her potions in case some desired man should prove reluctant, and in case some discarded lover should seek to cause her trouble. And to make sure, and this was the most important of all, that her beautiful body would never be distorted by pregnancy.

Not only that, but Chloe would know if she thought of getting rid of her. Chloe always knew what Vanessa was thinking. Sometimes Vanessa had an uneasy, almost frightened feeling that her slave could read minds. As loyal as Chloe was to her, Vanessa was wary of her. To anger the obeah woman would be taking her life in her hands. Chloe's fortunes hinged on Vanessa's, and Chloe had no intention of letting Vanessa slip through her fingers.

Never mind that now. All that mattered was tonight.

She dressed with care that evening, wearing a gown that appeared to be modest but that was cut and shaped so subtly that every curve of her body was suggested in a tantalizing manner calculated to inflame any man who beheld her. For this evening, she wore no jewels. The line of her throat was virginal, the gestures of her lovely hands were not distracted from by the flash of diamonds or emeralds.

Simon was not a heavy drinker. When social etiquette demanded it, he had a head as hard as the rocky coast of New England. But tonight the wine he took at dinner seemed to have a strange effect on him, and he felt a stirring in his loins that was both embarrassing and distracting.

Perhaps he had had too much of the hot Jamaica sun today. In the morning, he had visited Daniel, a brief visit that had left him distressed that the man had been no clearer in his mind than he had been on the first occasion. After that, he had visited the fields and the slave quarters.

The conch shell that had called the slaves to work had brought him up from an uneasy sleep. The shells were blown every morning, and soon afterward the slaves would file to the fields. They returned to their huts for the midday and evening meals. Their diet consisted of bananas, scraps of meat and fish, plantains and yams. There was not much variety, but the food was plentiful, because a slave must be fed in order to work.

The thing that had struck Simon the most forcefully as he had watched the slaves as they tended the cane was their quietness, the lack of chatter and laughter. Once Simon had visited a plantation in North Carolina, and there the slaves had laughed and smiled, and broken into song, the improvised words and cadence pacing their work and making it more bearable.

Here at Maynard Penn, the slaves worked in silence, their eyes never lifted from the ground as they battled the weeds that would have taken nourishment from the cane. No man called softly to a woman, no woman responded with a flirtatious giggle. They worked with a will, but they were more like automatons than living people. Simon wondered if it were so on every plantation on the island, or if their master's illness had a subduing effect on them.

There was something disquieting about it, and it troubled him, even though Vanessa had told him that the slaves had changed since they had known that their freedom was not far away, and that they were inclined to be sullen now because it had not already been granted them.

He had visited the sugar mill again, and the boiler houses, fascinated by their mule-driven machinery. Some plantations used water power or the wind, but here at Maynard Penn mules were favored. A mule was always ready to work, while other power sources might fail.

With an effort, Simon forced himself to concentrate on what he had just been about to say to Vanessa.

"I met Ian Macintyre in Kingston, as you know. I also became acquainted with Doctor Eastlake. Eastlake may have been a fine physician in his day, but he had his training a long time ago. To put it bluntly, I think he's too old and set in his ways to be trusted with a case like your father's. I think that a younger man, such as Ian Macintyre, should be called in."

"We've always had Doctor Eastlake. Father would not tolerate anyone else," Vanessa told him, her eyes clouding with that sadness that wrenched at Simon's heart. "He's considered the finest physician Jamaica ever had."

"But he's over seventy, and he certainly isn't open to suggestion that he might have overlooked something in your father's case! If I were you, I shouldn't let any more time go by without calling Ian in."

"It's worth considering. Not that I don't trust Doctor Eastlake implicitly, but it would be comforting to know that every possibility had been explored. As soon as Father has one of his lucid moments, I'll ask him if he will consent to it."

Simon was not satisfied with that. What if Daniel did not have a moment that was lucid enough for him to make the decision? He was in no condition to decide something of this importance for himself. But the stirring in his loins distracted him, and Vanessa's beauty, as she sat with the candlelight making a halo of her hair and giving a translucent quality to her skin swept his arguments from his mind.

"Let's go outside, Simon." It was the first time she had used his given name, and Simon felt a glow of pleasure. "It's a beautiful evening, and we should enjoy it while we can."

If there had ever been a night made for romance, this was the night. The sky was alive with stars like millions of candles, the breeze caressed them with soft, seductive fingers, the ethereal quality of the half-light made Vanessa seem to glow with an inner light of her own, so beautiful that Simon's throat tightened just to look at her. They strolled through the gardens, and Vanessa laid her fingertips on his arm, and her touch burned through the cloth of his coat sleeve and set him afire.

He didn't know what was wrong with himself. In all his life, he had never felt such a compulsion to take a woman with all the passion in his body, to own her, to revel in her, to make every inch of her his own. He no longer seemed to be in command of his own body or his own emotions.

The island had enchanted him, this girl had enchanted him, he was powerless to fight it, and when Vanessa paused in her pacing and turned to him, her face upraised in the starlight, the last of his control was swept away. He drew her into his arms, his mouth covered hers, tasting, savoring, as he crushed her body to his.

"Oh, Simon, I need you so, I need you so much!" Vanessa murmured, the words torn from her. "I've been so alone, you can never know how alone I've been! Kiss me, hold me, love me!"

He lifted her in his arms without being aware of her weight and carried her inside. There was no other human being in evidence, the house was deserted except for them and the sick man in his own chamber, with either Chloe or a slave called Joseph to watch over him.

The door to her bedroom stood open and inviting, and he carried her inside, his hands already working at her gown. Trembling, she helped him, achingly, she arched her body into his, and all the fire of the universe descended on them, enveloping them and consuming them as at last they came together.

Simon was appalled at what he had done. Not only did he love Noelle, not only had he had every intention of marrying Vanessa's younger sister, but Vanessa was a sweet and innocent girl, a virginal young woman, and he had taken advantage of her. Nothing could mitigate the enormity of his guilt, seducing her, virtually raping her in her own father's house where she should have been safe, where no decent man would have dreamed of doing such a thing!

His face pale, he looked at the weeping girl and tried to express his abhorrence of his actions.

"Vanessa, I can't say how sorry I am. If your father were well he would have every right to shoot me like a dog. But it will be all right. We'll simply have to be married, as soon as it can possibly be arranged." The words were wrenched from him with unbelievable pain. Noelle! By this one, utterly insane action, he had forfeited his right to Noelle forever. How would he be able to live without her, how would he ever be able to forget what might have been if he hadn't let his baser emotions erase every vestige of common sense he had ever had?

But what was done was done. He had compromised Vanessa's honor, and he had no choice but to marry her. His remorse was all the more bitter when he reflected that nearly every man he would ever know would envy his having Vanessa for a wife, while all the while, down through all the years remaining to him, he would remember a small, delicate, merry girl whose eyes had laughed into his and who had implanted herself in his heart too firmly ever to be removed.

Inside, Vanessa was purring. Chloe's potion had worked beyond her wildest expectations. The memory of this night would remain with her forever. Now nothing remained but for her to tell Noelle that her sweetheart had feet of clay, and to tell Simon that she would never, under any circumstances, marry him. Even if he were relieved to the point of elation that she would not have him, it would do him no good to turn back to Noelle, because she was sure that Noelle would repudiate him even if it tore her heart to shreds.

All had gone just as Vanessa had planned, and she was fully satisfied.

Chapter Seven

Aaron Godbehere stood in the Cottswoods' drawing room, his cap in his hands, his weather-beaten face looking embarrassed to find himself in such elegant surroundings. But the message he had brought was important, and the sooner he related it the sooner he could leave.

"If you could get word to the captain, I'd be much obliged. Tell him that the damage isn't serious, but it will be several more days before the *Maid of Boston* will be seaworthy. On the other hand, there's no need for him to come rushing back to Kingston, it's nothing that I can't take care of myself. The fire got a pretty good hold before it was discovered, but we got it out before any vital damage was done. It's only a matter of repairs and it should be taken care of in say, six or seven days."

No one knew exactly how the fire on the *Maid of Boston* had started. Sheer carelessness on someone's part, or it might have been set with malicious intent. Aaron had had words with one of the local craftsmen only two days ago, and had dismissed him for shoddy workmanship. The man had been angry, insisting that his work was good, but Aaron's standards were those of New England shipyards and he had ordered the carpenter off the ship and told him not to return.

There was no way to prove that the carpenter had been the one who had set the fire, and Aaron knew that an investigation would take more time than Simon would be willing to spare, as far behind schedule as they already were. Although it galled the first mate to let someone get away with arson, prudence indicated that he should go full speed ahead with the repairs, and set double guards, and let it go at that. One thing was sure: it would not happen again.

"I'll go myself," Noelle said. "I've stayed in Kingston too long as it is." A servant could be sent with the message just as well, but Noelle's position here had become intolerable. Henry was making her life a misery, and all of the Cottswoods' objections to her insistence on spending all the time she could with Ian was a bone of contention between them. Except for Henry, all of them liked and respected Ian, but still they held to the position that she and Henry were all but engaged, and so it wasn't seemly for her to see so much of another man.

Not only that, but she ached to see her father again, and to be held in Simon's arms. Perhaps Daniel was better, perhaps Simon had persuaded him to call in Ian to examine him. She couldn't bear to wait one more day to find out.

Aaron had come to the house as early as he could expect anyone to be up and about, even in this climate where people made it a practice to rise early so that they could rest in the heat of the afternoon, and within an hour, in spite of all the protests she had to override, her luggage was stowed in the Cottswoods' curricle and a sulking Julie was letting her know exactly how she felt to be snatched from the pleasures of Kingston.

"Julie, that is enough! You've been here for days and days, and if I could have spared Dicey from nursing my father you wouldn't have got to come at all. Be satisfied with what you have had, and stop grumbling!"

Noelle seldom spoke so sharply to any slave, but she had more important things on her mind than listening to a disgruntled girl whose only interests were decking herself out in finery and flirting with every man she saw. Julie would be free soon enough, and then she could do as she pleased, but for now she was still a Maynard Penn servant and it was her duty to behave as such.

The journey from Kingston to Maynard Penn had never seemed so long, but she was there at last, and she flew into the house on feet as light as air. Simon and Vanessa were in the drawing room, and Simon came to his feet when he saw her, his face strained and white.

Noelle stopped in her tracks, and her heart seemed to stop beating, and for a moment she was afraid that the worst had happened and that her father had died and a messenger was already on the way to Kingston to tell her of his passing.

What Simon told her was just as bad. His voice was filled with agony. He had never found anything so hard to say in his life, and to have to hurt this girl who was so dear to him that losing her was like having his heart wrenched out of his body was almost more than he could bear.

"Noelle, Vanessa and I have something to tell you. We have decided to be married before I sail."

For a moment, Noelle thought that she was going to die, and then she was afraid that she wouldn't. It was all there written on both their faces, Simon's so pale and filled with shame, and Vanessa's so gloating behind its seeming innocence.

She had no doubt that this was entirely of Vanessa's engineering. Her sister had seduced Simon, and now he felt that he had to marry her to set things right. But although the seduction had been of Vanessa's engineering, Simon had still fallen victim to her beauty, he had still allowed himself to be seduced, and that hurt so badly that it was all she could do to stand her ground instead of running blindly to the sanctuary of her room to lock herself in and never face another human being as long as she lived.

If you have any pride at all, she told herself, bring it out now and make it sit up and dance! She had to bear Simon's loss, but there was no way that she could bear his pity!

Simon would suffer when he found out that Vanessa had only used him to satisfy her lust, when he found out, as he must sooner or later, her true character. But it would be too late for him by then, just as it was already too late for Noelle.

She was proud of the way she delivered Aaron Godbehere's message, proud of accepting Vanessa's sisterly kiss on her cheek without flinching, and even more proud of the steadiness of her voice as she congratulated Simon as custom demanded, and wished Vanessa happiness.

"If you will excuse me, I'll go to Father now," she said. She didn't look at Simon, she couldn't bear to, but at least her voice was still steady.

"Little mother hen!" Vanessa laughed fondly. "You will find no change, I'm sorry to say, but at least he isn't any worse."

Noelle would judge that for herself. She wouldn't be satisfied until she had seen him, and until she had talked to Dicey.

But Dicey was nowhere in evidence when she reached her father's room. Instead, Joseph was there watching over the stricken man, his face grave and impassive, revealing nothing as Noelle questioned him. The master was just the same, and no, Mistress, he didn't know where Dicey was, he only knew that he had been told to sit with the master.

Noelle bent to kiss her father's forehead, and to take his hand in hers. How wasted his hand was, a skeleton of a hand, surely he was worse, in spite of what Vanessa had said to the contrary!

Daniel opened his eyes at her touch and tried to smile. "Noelle?" His voice, too, was wasted, every word costing him more than he could afford. "You're back from Kingston? Or did I just imagine that you've been away? I can't seem to remember things these days, everything gets confused."

Noelle's heart was wrung with pity for him, this man whose mind had always been so clear, who had never forgotten any detail, no matter how trivial.

"Yes, Father, I am back. I had a very enjoyable time, but I missed you terribly. Is there anything you want, anything I can bring you?"

But his eyes had already closed again, and he did not answer her. Noelle's last, desperate gamble, one she had thought about all during her journey back, to ask her father for permission to send for Ian, in case Simon had not already obtained it, flew away.

Tomorrow then. Surely he would be alert enough for a long enough time tomorrow! She would ask him at the first sign of clarity in his eyes, and then Ian would come, he could come immediately and he would examine Daniel and he would know whether or not this was a natural illness, or something else.

She went to her own room and laid aside her broad-brimmed hat and her gloves, she removed her dress and bathed in the fresh water that one of the housegirls had already brought, wondering all the time where Dicey was. But of course Dicey hadn't known that she was coming today, she might simply be taking half an hour to bathe, or to get herself something to eat.

Wearily, because it had been a long journey in Jamaica's heat, she changed into a fresh gown and did what she could with her hair. Not that it mattered what kind of an appearance she made, it would never matter again. Steeling herself, she forced herself to leave her room and face Simon and Vanessa again.

"Where is Dicey?" she asked, directing her question to Vanessa, once again avoiding looking at Simon. "She doesn't seem to be anywhere in the house."

Vanessa's face was a picture of sympathy. "I'm sorry, Noelle darling. I had to send Dicey to the quarters. Young

Adele is ailing, she gave birth two days ago and it didn't go well, she has fever. Dicey is the best nurse we have, outside of Chloe, and of course I couldn't spare Chloe, so Dicey had to be sent. But until Dicey can return to the house, you can have Julie. You should have called her to dress your hair, but of course you look perfectly lovely even though you did it yourself. Kingston must have agreed with you, you're positively blooming.''

She looked, Noelle knew perfectly well, like some poor relation who had crept into the drawing room to sit in a corner, hoping that she wouldn't be noticed and sent away. She felt Simon's eyes on her, and involuntarily, she glanced at him. He was suffering too, it was written all over him, but still she felt a surge of wild anger at him because he had allowed himself to come under Vanessa's spell.

After all that had passed between them, after the enchanted evenings of dancing in each other's arms, after the passions of the kisses they had exchanged that day of their first picnic, when they had known they were falling in love, he had still succumbed to Vanessa, and she would never forgive him for it. She would weep for him, she knew that she would spend untold nights soaking her pillow with her tears, but still she would not be able to forgive him.

She had lost her brother, she was losing her father, and now she had lost Simon. It was the end of her world, of her life.

"I'll go to the quarters and see her now, if you'll excuse me," she said, wrenching her eyes away from Simon's face.

Vanessa raised a protesting hand, her face filled with consternation. "My dear, you cannot do that! Adele is very ill, you must under no circumstances expose yourself to her fever!"

"If it's childbed fever, I'm in no danger of contracting it," Noelle said, her voice heavy with irony. "I assure you that I haven't just given birth!" Ian's frankness was catching, she would never have dreamed of saying such a

98

thing in front of a man before she had been exposed to it. But why shouldn't she say what she meant? She couldn't care less whom she shocked or what artificial rules of etiquette she broke. She would probably become an eccentric, and people would shake their heads and hesitate to invite her to their balls and galas for fear of what she might say.

"It may not be childbed fever, but something that could be spread. That's why Adele isn't in the slaves' hospital, we have to take every precaution. Not that she won't be all right in a few days." This to Simon, who was attending to the conversation with interest. "The blacks are surprisingly resilient. They manage to survive fevers and illnesses that would kill a white person."

And that, Noelle thought viciously, was a blatant lie. The slaves were particularly vulnerable to illnesses and diseases, but there was no use in contradicting her sister. Instead, she left the room again to return to her father.

"Poor Noelle!" Vanessa took a delicate sip of her wine. "I'm afraid that she had entertained hopes in your direction, while you were in Kingston, and the news of your determination to marry me instead has upset her. She's had singularly poor luck with suitors, I'm afraid. If only she weren't so prickly, taking offense at the slightest thing, and showing such an unforgiving nature! However, Henry still seems to want her in spite of her less attractive traits, and I expect that she'll settle for him in the end."

"It seems to me that she could make a wiser choice. Ian Macintyre is more than a little taken with her, and I know that she feels the highest regard for him."

Vanessa looked thoughtful. "You may be right, Simon. In Noelle's case, it wouldn't matter that Doctor Macintyre has no fortune of his own, she'll have a generous dowry when she marries, and her half of the Maynard assets when Father dies. I only hope that if she and Ian Macintyre make a match of it, people won't say that he married her for her money, but I'm sure most of them will do just that."

"Then they'll be mistaken," Simon said, his voice

definite. "Ian Macintyre would never marry for money. And he's man enough not to let such remarks bother him."

"I hope that he's man enough to cope with Noelle's tempers, as well," Vanessa said, sighing. "But we don't have to worry about such things now. She will make her own choice, and I certainly hope that she'll find the right man one day, one who will make her happy at last."

She couldn't have hoped it anywhere near as much as Simon hoped it. If Noelle were to turn to Ian, and eventually find happiness with him, at least his conscience would find that much solace, although his own happiness was forever shattered.

In one of the wattle huts that made up the slave village, Dicey raised her head to listen to footsteps as she sat beside the new mother, Adele. She was holding the infant on her lap, humming in a soft, low tone that soothed the infant, who was hungry. It was a boy child, and Dicey thought that it would live and thrive.

She thought it was Miranda who was coming into the hut. Miranda had had a girl child three months ago, the first for her and her man Elisha, even though they had been mated for seven years, and she was the one who was feeding this new baby, by Vanessa's orders, although Dicey was certain that Adele could have nursed him herself.

As a matter of fact, Dicey didn't think that Adele was sick at all. Before Master Daniel had been stricken, new mothers had been allowed a full week before they were sent back to the fields, but Vanessa had changed that rule. Now, at Maynard Penn, as at most of the other plantations in Jamaica, twenty-four hours was considered sufficient, forty-eight at the most. But Vanessa said that Adele was sick and Chloe said that she was sick, and they had sent Dicey to tend her, and Dicey hadn't dared to say a word. As she sat and rocked and hummed to the baby, she was the one who was sick, sick with fear.

She was almost certain that Chloe had seen her when the powerful black woman had dropped something into the tonic that Doctor Eastlake had left for Master Daniel. Dicey had just opened a new bottle, the doctor had left several of them, a tablespoonful to be taken three times a day, to strengthen him. Chloe had come to the master's room and sent Dicey to get herself something to eat, but Dicey had darted back as soon as she'd left the room, thinking that she might as well collect up the dirty spoons and glasses and take them along to be washed. Mistress Noelle was particular that everything the master used should be sparkling clean.

Some sudden caution had made Dicey stop before she had reentered the room. A few feet from the partially opened door, she had seen Chloe dripping some liquid from a little vial into the newly opened bottle. Her instinct had made her turn and run, as silently as possible, praying that Chloe hadn't seen her. Dicey, like every other slave at Maynard Penn, was terrified of the obeah woman, and she had known that she had seen something that she hadn't been supposed to see.

Dicey knew that Noelle wasn't satisfied with the master's progress, that she didn't believe that a man who had been so strong should be wasting away. The two girls had no secrets from each other, Dicey was the only person at Maynard Penn whom Noelle could talk to, and she shared all of her fears and worries with her.

No matter how silently Dicey had moved when she had returned to the master's room, and how quickly and silently she had run away again, she knew that Chloe had ears like a cat and she believed that she had the ability to see things that were behind her. And so Dicey was afraid.

Her terror made her tremble and her stomach knot up so that she could hardly eat. She was afraid to eat in any case. How did she know what Chloe might put into her food? Sharing her fear, Cuffie had been sneaking her food from his own meals, from his own plate, although his punishment if he were caught entering Adele's hut would probably be the same death that Dicey was convinced Chloe had in store for her. Fear for Cuffie intensified Dicey's fear for herself.

It wasn't Miranda who entered the hut, but Cuffie. In spite of her worry, Dicey's eyes lighted up at the sight of the young black. Cuffie was tall and strong, the firm planes of his face bespoke intelligence, and Dicey loved him more than life. They would already have mated, except that both he and Dicey were determined that their children should not be born as slaves, but would enter the world free.

Slaves in Jamaica were branded, and since Vanessa had taken over the management of the plantation Chloe had ordered that even newborn babies must be branded in spite of the fact that all of the slaves were supposed to be set free in the near future. Chloe liked to cause pain, she liked to see people suffer, it added to her sense of power. It particularly pleased her to see the pain and suffering of the parents for their children, powerless to prevent it. This boy child Dicey was holding and rocking would be branded, and Dicey cringed at the thought of his wails of agony as the hot iron burned into his flesh.

"Mistress Noelle is back," Cuffie said, touching the baby's face with gentle fingers. "She got here late this afternoon."

"I know that." Every black on the plantation knew of all arrivals and departures, and Dicey had heard talk of Noelle's return when other slaves had passed Adele's hut. Although none of them had dared to stop to tell her, Dicey knew that they had walked slowly and talked loudly to make sure that she would hear.

"You going to tell her what you saw?" Cuffie asked her, his eyes filled with concern. "You got to tell her, Dicey."

"Ain't no way I can tell her. I dare not go near the house. I cannot set foot there till Chloe tells me."

If she ever got to set foot in the house again! That fear was stark on both their faces as they looked at each other.

102

Adele wasn't sick, Dicey had been sent here to get her out of the way. If Adele had been sick, the lazar house, the slaves' hospital here at Maynard Penn, with its own doctor, Doctor Dupree, would be where she would have been sent. All of the large plantations had their own slave hospitals and a doctor to care for the blacks, because there were always children ailing or dying from the yaws, and slaves who had contracted the dread coco bay, a form of leprosy, and fevers were always prevalent, as well as lesser ailments and the numerous injuries that were always cropping up.

"Ain't no way I can get to Mistress Noelle, either," Cuffie said. As a field slave, he was never allowed beyond the palisade that protected the plantation house. There was no way out of their dilemma, and they could only wait, with dread, for what would happen.

"Might be I could get word to one of the house slaves, have him tell Mistress Noelle that I got to talk to her. Or tell Captain Spencer that I got to see him, private. Captain Spencer comes to the fields to watch, some man might be close enough to tell him without being seen."

"No!" Dicey's voice was sharp. "Not Captain Spencer! We can't trust him, Cuffie. He's *her* man. She's had him in her bed, and he's under her spell. He'd tell her and then it would be all up with us for sure. You'd be killed as well as me."

Dicey would simply die of what would appear to be the fever Adele was supposed to have, a sickness she had come down with from contact with the new mother. But the way Cuffie would die did not bear thinking about. Chloe might decide to make him suffer, to make him writhe with pain, as she had other slaves she had had something against, or had simply afflicted in order to keep the rest of the slaves in terror of her. Limbs twisted, faces contorted, they had screamed their lives away, thankful for the relief of death when it finally came.

"The day we are free, I ain't so sure I want to stay on at Maynard Penn," Cuffie told Dicey. There was the gleam of perspiration on his face, and his eyes were filled with worry. "Not so long as Mistress Vanessa and Chloe are still here. Mistress Vanessa is an evil woman, Dicey, she's pure evil. I know it and you know it. Chloe helps her in her evil."

"That's all the more reason we got to stay. If you won't stay, then you'll have to go without me." The words tore at Dicey's heart. All the same, she meant them. "Long's Mistress Noelle's here, I got to stay. She ain't got nobody but me."

"I reckon that's so." Cuffie reached out to touch her, his touch on her face as gentle as it had been on the infant's. And then his face twisted in a grimace of pure hatred. "I wish she'd drop dead, that beautiful one! I wish she'd drop dead tonight, and Chloe with her! Then maybe the master would get well."

"You don't wish it no harder than I do, Cuffie." Dicey's voice was soft, so as not to disturb the sleeping girl she was tending. Not that Adele would tell what she had overheard, but it wasn't safe anywhere on this plantation to say anything against Mistress Vanessa or Chloe. "I wishes it and I wishes it, but it ain't going to happen. Not lessen something happens to make it. We might leastwise be rid of Chloe, if what she put in the master's medicine is bad and we could prove it, but even that ain't got no chance of happening unless I can git to Mistress Noelle. And if Chloe's certain sure that I saw her put something in the master's tonic, then I ain't never going to git to Mistress Noelle."

"She ain't certain. Was she certain, you'd be dead by now." Cuffie tried to inject a note of confidence into his voice that he was far from feeling.

"She's sure. Even if she wasn't, she wouldn't take no chances," Dicey said.

She began to cry, silently, no sound at all escaping from her. Wordlessly, Cuffie took the baby from her and laid it on the pallet beside its mother, and took Dicey into his arms.

"Ain't nothing going to happen to you!" he said fiercely. "Not if I have to kill Chloe myself to keep it from happening!"

But as before, there was fright beneath his brave words, and the two of them clung together, trapped in a situation from which there was no escape.

Chapter Eight

THINGS WEREN'T GOING AT ALL THE WAY VANESSA HAD planned, and it had thrown her into a fury. Simon had been supposed to sail in just two or three days, and if he had harbored the notion that she would be waiting to marry him when he returned, it would have made no difference, because she would be in England long before that. Her plan had been to satiate herself with this incredibly vital man, making sure at the same time that Noelle would turn her back on him, and that was all.

But now the fire on the *Maid of Boston* had ruined everything. Simon was a far cry from the pliant men she had always before been able to manipulate, and all of her sad, sweet talk of being unable to leave her father, of her horrible guilt for having sinned, of having hurt her sister so much that she would never be able to forgive herself, that she could never bring herself to marry the man her sister loved, fell on deaf ears. Simon overrode every word as if she had not spoken at all. They had loved each other, they had committed themselves, and nothing would make it right except being married. He had wronged Vanessa, and however much both of them might regret it, it changed nothing. Marriage was the only answer.

Now he had taken it into his head that they must be married before he sailed. The few extra days before the sailing date, because of the fire, would make it possible.

"Even if you can't sail with me because of your father's illness, we must still be married. What if something were to happen, what if there should be consequences from our actions? And the life of a seafaring man is far from certain. I wouldn't have been in Jamaica at all if it hadn't been for a storm that all but foundered my ship. There isn't any guarantee that I will make the voyage back to Boston, and then back here, without meeting my end in another such storm. I don't believe that such a thing will happen, but there is always the possibility. Think of being left unwed, and with a baby on the way! I cannot take that chance."

Vanessa could hardly tell him that there was no possibility that a baby was on the way, that Chloe would see to that. And now Simon was pacing, laying plans as he paced, and it set her teeth on edge.

"I'll go into Kingston tomorrow. You shall come with me, and we'll arrange for a special license, Bertram Cottswood will know how to go about it. It won't be the wedding you deserve, but it will have to do. And we'll see Doctor Eastlake, and insist that he calls Ian Macintyre in on your father's case at once. I'm not satisfied at all that your father's illness is being treated properly. Ian is making a specialty of obscure island diseases, he's young and highly intelligent, as well as highly trained, and having a fresh mind bear on the case might make all the difference."

"Father would never allow it. He has complete faith in Doctor Eastlake," Vanessa tried to tell him, but he brushed her words away as though they were of no consequence.

"Your father is in no condition to make such a decision. It's up to you to do what we think best for him. Eastlake can hardly refuse, if you ask him, and as your husband, I will be able to use my authority."

"Simon, you're rushing things! You don't give me time to think!" Vanessa protested, pressing her fingertips against her forehead in a gesture that would have melted any other man's heart. To her fury, it had no effect on Simon at all.

"There isn't anything to think about. It's what we have to do, both get married before I sail, and see that your father has every possible chance of recovery by getting Ian Macintyre on his case. You don't have to worry about leaving your father for a few days, Noelle is here now and she seems perfectly competent to nurse him, and it's obvious that your woman Chloe is capable of handling any plantation problem that might arise. I've seen army officers less capable than she! Get your packing done this evening, Vanessa. We'll want to leave for Kingston the first thing in the morning."

Damn the man, Vanessa thought. Damn him to hell! There was no way she was going to go into Kingston with him, no way she was going to marry him or allow this young Doctor Macintyre to examine her father! Eastlake was all but senile, so dodderingly set in his ways that he was as easy to manipulate as any of Vanessa's love-stricken, married lovers. But Ian Macintyre was an entirely different matter. With Simon urging him on, his examination would be thorough, and that must not happen at any cost!

Damn all the fates that had made events take these unexpected turns! It had been bad enough when Noelle had returned to Maynard Penn, even without her news that the sailing of the *Maid of Boston* would be delayed. With Noelle in the house, Vanessa had not been able to entice Simon into her bed again. And since that first time, he had refused wine or any other spirits, putting his aberration down to overindulgence, so that because he ate exactly what she and Noelle ate, Chloe hadn't been able yet to devise a way to drug him.

Another man would have reasoned that because they had committed the act once, there was no reason not to repeat it, especially since he thought they were to be married. But not Simon! For Simon, one such lapse was entirely enough, and he had no intention of repeating it.

She could have survived that, someday lived to laugh about it. But to go along with these new, outrageous demands of Simon's was unthinkable. Something must be done, or everything she had ever dreamed about would come down around her head in ashes.

Noelle paused on the threshold of the drawing room. Simon thought that she looked pale and wan, and he wished there were something he could do to make things easier for her.

"Vanessa, how is Adele? Isn't it possible that she's recovered enough so that I could see Dicey?"

"My dear, I wish that that were true! But Adele's condition hasn't changed, you must on no account go near the slave village. We have to make sure that no infection is carried to Father."

Noelle looked so crestfallen that Simon had to make an effort to tell her of their new plans, hurting her even further.

"Noelle, your sister and I are leaving for Kingston in the morning. We are going to be married before I sail." There was no way to soften the blow, she had to know. Not that she had given any indication that her heart was broken, but he knew her pride, and it made him hate what he had done to her even more.

But his other piece of news was sure to be welcome to her, and so he hurried on.

"Vanessa and I have decided that we will ask Ian Macintyre to examine your father. He struck me as a most capable man, as I am sure you will agree."

Noelle, whose breath had been knocked out of her by Simon's announcing his immediate marriage to Vanessa, managed to draw a breath again. Her heart still felt as though it had been lacerated, but it probably wouldn't bleed to death even though it felt as though it would. She would survive, no matter how she felt right now. What Simon had said about having Ian treat her father was something to cling to as a drowning person clings to a lifeline.

But then her tentative smile of pleasure faded. "It would be wonderful if it were possible, but Ian has already told me that there is no way he can interfere between another doctor and his patient. Apparently it's something that isn't done."

"It will be different this time," Simon assured her. "As Vanessa's husband, I will be the head of the household as long as your father is incapable of making decisions. Eastlake can't refuse if we demand a consultation with Ian."

"Poor Noelle!" Vanessa cried. "It is a pity that there won't be balls and parties to celebrate my wedding, you're being intolerably cheated! Simon, one extra day won't make any difference. We simply must spend tomorrow with Noelle, get her out of the sickroom. There's a wonderful place in the foothills, beautiful beyond imagining, and we will picnic there together tomorrow."

The plan, a plan that could not possibly fail, had come to Vanessa full-blown, her mind racing because of her need.

As much as Simon disliked any delay at all, he couldn't resist doing something that would please Noelle. An outing would do her good, she was far too pale.

"I can't leave Father," Noelle tried to say, but Vanessa would have none of it.

"Nonsense! Chloe will be with him. I want the three of us to have this one day before Simon has to sail."

Noelle wavered, her heart torn in two. It would be agony to watch Simon and Vanessa together, Vanessa smugly triumphant and Simon looking as miserable as she herself felt. On the other hand it would be her last opportunity to spend any time in Simon's company, he would return from Kingston to Maynard Penn very briefly, to hear Ian's opinion about her father, and then he would rush off again to board the *Maid of Boston,* and sail. And he would be Vanessa's husband, and she wouldn't be able to ever again be in the same room with him.

"Do you ride, Simon?" Vanessa asked. "I'm afraid a carriage won't take us where we're going."

"Sailors aren't noted for their abilities on horseback, but I rode as a boy. I doubt I'll fall off and have to be carted back on a shutter."

"Then it's settled. I'll see that you have a tractable mount. Noelle is quite a competent rider, but I promise that we won't set too fast a pace for you."

"I'll take Nero, and leave Pilot for Captain Spencer," Noelle said. And to forestall any argument, she went to her father.

Vanessa's face was filled with consternation when Simon and Noelle joined her for breakfast the next morning, Simon looking forward to the day's outing with enjoyment and Noelle with dread, wondering how she could bear to spend a whole day watching Simon doting on her sister, and Vanessa's well-concealed gloating.

"It's such a disappointment! A message came this morning, before daylight. Mr. Ellsworth, you know him, Noelle, Father's banker, sent word that he is going to call, he'll be here before nine at the latest, with some papers it's essential that I read and sign. And his wife, dear Beulah, is coming with him, and it would be the worst discourtesy for me not to be here when she is making such an effort. But there is no reason you two can't start out without me. They won't stay for more than an hour at the most, and I'll be able to catch up with you easily, on Orion."

"You can't go galloping over the countryside alone!" Simon expostulated. "I won't hear of it!"

"I won't be alone, Simon. I'll take two of the grooms with me as escort, and of course I'll bring Julie along. It is a bother, but it needn't spoil our day. And Noelle, I have the most wonderful news for you! Adele has taken a decided turn for the better, and Dicey needn't stay with her any longer, so she will be going with you, she's already getting ready, so happy at the prospect of seeing you again that it will make your heart sing just to see her! There, it's all settled! I'm sending Elisha and Hector with you as guides, and the picnic lunch is already packed.''

Simon was still unhappy about the deviation in their plans, but he didn't have the heart to disappoint Noelle. And Noelle's heart leapt. Not only was she to have Dicey back again, but she would have an hour or two, at least, alone with Simon, without Vanessa!

Now that there was this new development, this opportunity to talk to Simon alone, she debated with herself whether or not to tell Simon of Vanessa's true character. It would be the only chance she would have, and shouldn't Simon know what he was getting himself into by marrying Van?

And then she decided against it. Simon wouldn't believe her, it was as simple as that. Like everyone else Vanessa had ever charmed, he would believe that Noelle was only maligning her sister out of jealousy and spite. At least, by keeping silent, she would still have her pride. It was heart-wrenching to think how disillusioned and furious Simon would be when he did find out Vanessa's true nature, but it was something he would have to find out for himself. His life would be ruined, but it would be ruined whether or not she told him something that he would refuse to believe.

Let it be! she told herself. Enjoy today as much as you can, because it will be the last you will ever see of Simon.

Being with him would be a mixed blessing, because what on earth could she find to say to Simon, what could they talk about, after he had turned his back on her after showing such interest in her, and gone running after Vanessa as though he were a dog after a bitch in heat? As uncouth as it sounded, she thought that the expression was apt. Simon had proved to be as unreliable and gullible, where Vanessa was concerned, as all the other men who had turned from Noelle when they had come under her sister's spell. That thought helped her to harden her heart, and to resolve at least to keep her pride.

She would appear as lighthearted and gay as she could force herself to be, never giving this man who had played havoc with her emotions an inkling of her true feelings. It was small recompense for losing the only man she would ever love, but it would have to serve.

Simon looked at Pilot doubtfully when the horses were led out to the mounting block, but the name was a good omen, it had a seafaring sense to it and the horse was big enough to carry him without trouble. But his alarm when he saw Nero prancing and pawing at the ground was evident on his face, and his voice was filled with protest.

"You aren't going to attempt to ride that creature, Noelle, surely!"

Noelle laughed, and swung into the sidesaddle, gathering up the reins. Nero began to plunge around, tossing his head, his ears flattened, but she brought him under control seemingly without effort.

"He's only lacking exercise. He'll settle down once we're on our way. Dicey, I just can't believe that you're coming with us! I was beginning to think I'd never see you again!"

Dicey tried to smile as she sat her mule, but the smile didn't reach her eyes. Even if *she,* that she-demon Vanessa, wasn't with them, she wouldn't have any chance to tell Noelle what she had to tell her, because Captain Spencer was here, and Captain Spencer belonged to Vanessa now, he was the enemy, and she daren't speak in front of him.

"I'm surely happy to be back with you, Mistress Noelle," Dicey managed. If Noelle had despaired of ever seeing her again, Dicey knew just how true that might have been! She didn't understand why Vanessa had allowed her to go on this picnic, it didn't make sense. Her foreboding showed in her face, but Noelle didn't notice in her happiness at their reunion.

Elisha and Hector, both of them strapping men, their muscles rippling in the early morning sunlight, were also on mules, and Elisha had the leading rein of another mule in his hand, a pack animal carrying the picnic baskets and rugs and cushions. Neither he nor Hector looked at either Simon or Noelle, but kept their eyes straight ahead, their faces unsmiling.

Simon had heard that in the South, back in America, many slaves never looked directly at a white person, fearing that it would be taken for insolence. It was just as well that in Jamaica, at least, slavery was coming to an end. No human being should be so degraded, forced to behave as though he were less than human.

But the inequities of one man holding another man slave had no part in today's outing. He put it from his mind, something to be mulled over during his days at sea. As had happened every time he had traveled through the Jamaican countryside, he marveled at the beauty all around him. Their way led gradually upward, toward the Blue Mountains, and on all sides the lushness, the greenness and the splashes of brilliant color made this seem like some alien planet.

Nero was still acting up, he had a razor edge on him, what he needed was a good gallop to dull it a little. "Keep Pilot on a tight rein, Captain Spencer. I'm going to let Nero out, and you don't want him making it a race," Noelle said.

Nero seemed to sprout wings. Noelle rode him like a Valkyrie, her laughter floating back to Simon as she reveled in the racing hooves and the wind in her face, every inch and muscle of her body working as one with the horse under her. He must have misheard Vanessa, Simon thought, when she'd indicated that Noelle was less than an accomplished horsewoman. He had never seen anything like this before. If Vanessa were a better rider, she must be phenomenal!

For a moment he had the impulse to take out after her, to try to halt her wild gallop before she was thrown or before Nero stumbled and broke a leg. How could any girl still in her teens control such an animal?

His common sense told him that he would have no chance of overtaking her, however, and so he held Pilot to an easy trot. But by the time Noelle checked Nero's run and wheeled him around to ride back and join him, he had broken out into a cold sweat.

He could see Noelle laughing as she approached him, and he marveled at the change in her face. She was radiant, her cheeks flushed and her eyes sparkling, and once again he felt an overwhelming despair that he had lost her through his own weakness, his own failure to control his baser instincts. Noelle might not have Vanessa's classic and flawless beauty, but no man in his right mind would have preferred the older sister.

Nero pranced sideways, tossing his head and throwing foam from his mouth, when Noelle reined in beside him. The animal's muscles were quivering and he looked as though he would like nothing better than to start running all over again.

"There! Now he'll behave himself. It's a shame that you're more at home on a quarterdeck than in a saddle, or I would have challenged you to a race. Kenneth and I used to race all the time. Of course he always won, except for the times he let me ride Nero. I'm afraid that you wouldn't have had any chance at all, so I didn't embarrass you by challenging you."

It was the first time that Simon had heard her mention her brother without a look of terrible sadness in her eyes. How close the two of them must have been! With Kenneth, at least, Noelle had come first, but now that he was gone there was no one who did not hold Vanessa in higher regard, no one but Simon himself, and now he could not even tell her how he felt.

Fearing a return of her melancholy, he thought it would be wise to change the subject.

"I ought to take you over my knee and paddle you!" he said. "You scared the britches off me, taking off like that!"

Imps of mischief danced in Noelle's eyes. "You'd have to go through Elisha and Hector to get to me. They wouldn't take it kindly if they thought you were threatening me. Not that I would need their help. I'm quite capable of defending myself!"

She touched Nero with her heel and lifted the reins, and the horse reared, pawing at the air, apparently all too willing to knock Simon from his saddle and trample him. Pilot shied sideways to avoid the flailing hooves, and Simon flinched.

"Truce! Bring that beast under control!"

"He never was out of control, Captain Spencer," Noelle said, her voice mocking. Captain Spencer! A few days ago she had called him Simon, her voice warm and eager, and now she spoke formally, as though they were no more than casual acquaintances. "Shall we continue on, if you have quite lost your desire to paddle me?"

"By all means, let's go on. Dicey, does your mistress always behave in such an outrageous fashion?"

There was no response from Dicey to his friendly smile. Her face was stolid as she answered.

"Mistress Noelle has always been kind to me, and I have never known her to misbehave." Did Simon imagine it, or was there a look of dislike in the girl's eyes as she regarded him, almost but not completely concealed?

That was blatant nonsense. Dicey had no reason to dislike him. She couldn't even know that he had shown an interest in her mistress in Kingston, because she and Noelle had had no contact with each other since Noelle had returned to Maynard Penn. Still, his sense of uneasiness persisted. Dicey should have shown more pleasure at her reunion with Noelle, if Noelle's attitude toward her personal slave girl was anything to go by.

He shook the mood off. He mustn't let anything interfere with doing his utmost to see that Noelle enjoyed this outing. It was the last time he would ever see her alone, and he had memories of her to store up for all the years that lay ahead of him.

The distance to their destination was a great deal farther than he had thought it would be. He hoped that they would reach the picnic spot early enough so that he would have time to rest his aching muscles and bones before they had to start back. He had a wry picture of himself being boosted onto Pilot's back, unable to mount without the help of Hector or Elisha, and what a sorry impression that would make on two girls who had been born to the saddle!

They had been climbing steadily, and all around them the scenery became more rugged and spectacular. Trees pressed in around them on every side, and the path they were following had petered out into no more than a faint track. If he had been alone, he would have been lost by now, and would have had to rely on the position of the sun to find his way back. But their guides pressed on steadily, never hesitating.

Nevertheless, Simon's uneasiness grew. Surely Vanessa should have caught up with them by now? Orion was reputed to be the fastest horse on the plantation, and she would not have been slowed down by his inferior horsemanship.

There was one last, very steep climb, so that the riders had to lean forward in their saddles to help the horses maintain their balance, and then Noelle cried out "We're here!" and a vista so beautiful was revealed to him that he was all but struck dumb.

This must be what Eden had been like, before Adam and Eve had been cast out. A waterfall fell from a rocky crag somewhere high above them, to fall foaming into a crystal clear limestone pool that was fringed with ferns so thick and lush that it was hard to credit that they were growing, natural plants. It was cooler here in the mountains, and the shade from the trees that crowded in around them added to the coolness. The perspiration that he had worked up from this last climb dried on his skin, and he drew in deep breaths of air as clear and pure as the water in the pool.

"It's as if a part of heaven had been transplanted to earth!" he said, when he could find his voice. "It was worth the ride, and a great deal more. I wouldn't have missed this for the world."

Elisha and Hector dismounted from their mules and began to unpack the picnic basket and rugs and cushions. To Simon, it looked as if there were enough supplies for a dozen people, not just for one outing for himself and Noelle and Vanessa and the three slaves.

These Jamaicans knew how to live lavishly, he thought. Everything he had seen on the island had been rife with luxury. Exotic, highly spiced foods, servants to serve your every need, even orchids on the dinner table, as commonplace here as daisies were in the fields of Massachusetts.

Vanessa was like an orchid, he thought, a creature of such beauty that men were awed to look at her. But Noelle was like a daisy, a black-eyed Susan, fresh and crisp and wholesome, someone a man wouldn't be afraid to touch for fear that she would wilt and turn brown at the edges, too delicate to bear contact with human hands.

When he left Jamaica, after he and Vanessa were married, he hoped that Noelle and Ian would be drawn together. If he couldn't have Noelle for himself, he could think of no one he would rather bring her happiness than Ian. And he desperately wanted Noelle to be happy, to have all the happiness she deserved, even though he couldn't be the one to bring it to her himself. Ian was a good man, he would cherish her and love her all the days of her life, and if she were to learn to love him in return, it was as much as Simon could ask. Simon himself would never forget his loss, but Noelle must be happy!

He groaned, keeping the sound as unobtrusive as possible, as he eased himself down off Pilot's back, but Noelle heard him and she laughed.

"Are you feeling a little sore, Captain Spencer? I think that before you attempt the ride back, we ladies had better take a stroll so that you can swim in the pool. The waterfall will massage your aching muscles and take the stiffness out. We promise that we won't peek, don't we, Dicey?''

Dicey made no answer, only nodding as she spread out a cloth to place the food and dishes on. She did not look at Simon, and once again he had the uncomfortable feeling that she held something against him.

''I wonder what's happened to your sister,'' Simon wanted to know. ''I thought that she would surely have caught up with us by now.''

Noelle didn't care if Vanessa never caught up with them. She supposed that it was too much to hope for that Vanessa had come a cropper on the way, that Orion would have thrown her, that her neck might have been broken. What a horrible thought! She was becoming vicious, as vicious as her sister. It disturbed her deeply, and she had to fight to keep her voice light.

''Oh, Mr. Ellsworth is a real fussbudget when it comes to matters of business. He'll hem and haw, and make Van read every paper three times before he allows her to sign it, and spend a lot of time explaining what's already down in black and white. And his wife, as dear as she is, doesn't know when to stop when she gets to talking, she'll want to catch Vanessa up on every scrap of island gossip. But Van will be along any moment now, you'll see. She's quite expert at cutting people off and getting rid of them once they've become tiresome, without their even realizing that they've been pushed out the door.''

Simon was watching Dicey as the girl moved to the pool to submerge jugs of fruit juice to cool them. How gracefully she moved, how gracefully all of the island women moved. It hurt him to think that these people were enslaved. Dicey had been born to be free, free and proud. At least this girl bore her slavery lightly, as Noelle's personal servant and friend.

''Dicey must be just about your age, isn't she?'' he asked.

''Almost exactly. She's always been more like my sister than a servant.''

Simon raised his left eyebrow, and Noelle's heart

119

fluttered. She wished that he wouldn't do that, it still had the most devastating effect on her, making her blood race through her veins and her body tremble.

"She hasn't given much evidence of being overjoyed to see you, so far today." The words were more a question than a statement.

"She's shy in front of a stranger, that's all. When we're back at home, alone in my room, she chatters like a magpie, and I'm just as bad."

"I expect you wouldn't ever want to part with her?" This was more a statement than a question.

"Good heavens, I'll never part with her! Whatever put such a ridiculous notion in your head? I know that the emancipation is coming, but Dicey will never leave me, she'll always have a home with me."

Simon hoped and prayed that by the time he returned to Jamaica, that if Daniel Maynard had died, Noelle and Ian would have things settled between them, be at least betrothed if not actually married. If things didn't work out between them, he would have no choice but to take Noelle back to Massachusetts. A girl of such tender years could not be left alone, she would have to make her home with Simon and Vanessa, and being so close but forever held apart would be unbearable for both of them. Unless, of course, Noelle hated him so much that their closeness would only inflame her hatred still more, and that would be equally hard to bear.

At least she would have Dicey. But Simon did not care to contemplate what his parents would think of the overwhelming Chloe. At least he was certain that the huge black woman would not intimidate his mother, even though Sarah was only a whisper more than five feet tall and weighed not quite a hundred pounds. If it came to a showdown between them, Simon would put all his money on his mother.

Another thing was also certain, and this caused him even more pain. His mother would like Noelle better than Vanessa, and wonder if he had taken leave of his senses, choosing the wrong girl to be his wife.

Noelle sank down on the cushions and arched her back, stretching her arms over her head. She removed the wide-brimmed hat she had worn to protect her complexion from the sun, and peeled her riding gloves from her hands and tossed them aside.

"Someday I'd like to ride out without being so constricted," she said, exasperation in her voice. "The world wouldn't come to an end if I rode out hatless, and nobody would drop dead if my hands got a little brown because of the lack of gloves! Are ladies subjected to such stupid rules in Massachusetts, Captain Spencer?"

"To a degree, I suppose they are, but nowhere nearly the degree that prevails in Jamaica," Simon told her, glad of a subject that wasn't painful. "Our conventions are inclined to be moral, not esthetic. A hint of tan would not decrease a girl's value in our eyes, where one flirtatious look in the wrong direction might damn her. You might find the one set of conventions as restrictive as the other, I'm afraid."

"Not I! I'm not inclined toward casual flirtation."

Simon flinched at her words, feeling that they had been directed at him with mocking irony, because he had paid court to Noelle, and no matter how much he regretted it, he had betrayed her.

To his relief, Noelle qualified her statement. "But I am certainly inclined toward having more freedom of movement and body than I'm allowed here. I want to be a person in my own right, with my own rights, not just a delicate object that must be preserved and protected against the day some man may want me as his wife, an object who must conform to every rule of convention and beauty, shown off as an ornament he could afford. Every man should have to spend at least a year playing the role of a woman, and then perhaps we would be allowed at least a modicum of the freedom men enjoy!"

Kneeling beside the pool only a few feet away, Dicey glanced back at her mistress, praying that she would have an opportunity to get Noelle alone before this picnic was over and tell her about the mysterious liquid she'd seen

Chloe add to Daniel Maynard's bottle of tonic. For all Dicey knew, once they got back to Maynard Penn, Vanessa might pretend that Adele had taken a turn for the worse again, and once again banish her to nurse her, with no access to Noelle at all.

Dicey was still puzzled over having been allowed to come with Noelle on this picnic. It didn't make sense. But she was sure of one thing. Vanessa never did anything without a reason. She would know that Dicey would tell Noelle what Chloe had done, so Vanessa must be up to something, but for the life of her, Dicey couldn't figure out what it was.

For a period of not more than a second or two, Dicey's mind failed to register what she saw as she looked over her shoulder, and by then it was almost too late. For a moment, her throat was paralyzed, and she had to struggle to get the scream out.

"Watch out! Captain Spencer, watch out!" Her scream seemed to hang suspended in the air, long enough for her to come to her feet, not screaming now but saving her strength to do what she had to do, else Noelle would be dead in one more second, and Captain Spencer with her.

Dicey's scream stopped Simon in the middle of the act of following Noelle's example and sitting down. From his half-crouch, he turned, just in time to throw himself aside a fraction of an instant before Elisha's knife would have been plunged into his back.

Moving with all the sureness that his life aboard pitching sailing ships had ingrained in him, Simon came to his feet and grasped Elisha's knife hand with both of his, at the same time thrusting out his foot to trip the muscular slave.

Dicey had no time to see what happened next. She herself had leapt upon Hector's back, her hands clawing at his throat in a grip that Hector could not shake off. The knife thrust he had aimed at Noelle's back was deflected, so that the blade caught on her upper arm, cutting through the fabric of her sleeve and leaving a thin line that began to well with blood. Paralyzed with the impossibility of what could not be happening, Noelle was scarcely aware that she had been cut. Wide-eyed, wild-eyed, she jumped to her feet, her screams of horror seeming to overlap Dicey's scream that was still echoing from the hillsides.

Dicey was like a madwoman, her love for Noelle giving her a strength that was far beyond normal. Hector struggled, trying to dislodge her, but she clung to his back like a cat, biting the back of his neck now, drawing blood and a chunk of flesh with it.

Now Hector's scream, of fear and pain, overlapped Noelle's. With one last gigantic effort he managed to throw Dicey off, but she was on him again in an instant, and this time Noelle was helping her, the pure instinct for survival making her fight as hard as Dicey. She struck out at Hector's face, her fingers clawing at his eyes, catapulting herself against him with such force that he went down with both Noelle and Dicey on top of him.

Only a few feet away, Simon and Elisha were locked in a life and death struggle. The slave was more heavily built than Simon, but Simon had a lithe and rock-hard strength that he had inherited from his New England forebears and that had been further toughened by his life of physical activity.

The cords of Elisha's neck stood out as he heaved and strained against Simon's weight on top of him, the muscles in his arms bulged, his eyes were screwed up with his efforts to free his knife hand and send Simon's lifeblood flowing out onto the ground.

Slowly, exerting all his strength, Simon's grip forced Elisha's hand to open, and the knife dropped to the ground. Both men reached for it, but Elisha grasped it first, raised it, and thrust. It caught Simon in his shoulder, sinking deep.

Hector's frantic heaving had thrown Noelle off him, although Dicey was still astride him, punishing him with both her fists and her teeth. Even in that desperate moment, Noelle's eyes took in what was happening between the two men. Without thinking, she threw herself on Elisha, her attack so sudden and so unexpected that it gave Simon the slender thread of advantage that could save his life. With the last of his strength, he wrenched the knife from his shoulder and lunged upward with it, and the blood from his body mingled with the blood from Elisha's, one indistinguishable from the other, both hot and red.

Elisha collapsed, his eyes wide and filled with terror. His life was draining away, and he knew it.

Hector had thrown Dicey off at last. Bleeding himself, and seeing that Elisha was done for, he panicked and bolted. With one quick sprint he was on Pilot's back, jerking the tethering reins loose. He pounded his heels against Pilot's sides, and the horse took off at full gallop. Tethered close by, Nero, driven into a frenzy by the fighting men and the smell of blood, jerked his own lines free and set off at a blind, terror-stricken gallop after Pilot.

Simon clutched at his shoulder, wondering how much blood he was going to lose before he managed to stop the flow, and knelt beside Elisha. He had never killed a man before. He had been in fights, no man can come to adulthood without getting into at least one vicious battle, but no man had ever died at his hand before. Sickened, bewildered, not understanding any of this, he demanded, "Why? Elisha, in the name of God, why?"

"She said . . ." Elisha's voice came with a supreme effort ". . . Chloe said kill them. Kill them all. And then come back and say the Maroons did it, but they let you and Hector go because you're black, and killed Dicey because she tried to help her mistress."

"But why? Why would Chloe tell you to kill us?"

"Don't know. But when Chloe say, we does it. Got to, else we'll die from her spells. Not only Hector and me, but my Mandy, and our baby . . ."

There was a gurgling in Elisha's throat, and his eyes rolled back in his head.

"Didn't want to," he managed. "Never wanted to.

Only 'cause of Mandy and little Annie, and Hector's woman and their three babies . . .''

His head fell to one side, his eyes open and staring. His throat tight, fighting nausea, Simon put his ear against the black man's chest. There was no heartbeat. Elisha was dead.

Chapter Nine

SIMON ROSE TO HIS FEET, STILL FIGHTING AGAINST THE weakness that threatened to overwhelm him, but his knees buckled and he went down on them, everything swimming in front of his eyes.

Noelle was pushing against him, urging him to lie down. He tried to deny that it was necessary, tried to say that he would be all right in a moment, but when he was stretched full length, with a cushion under his head, he had to admit that it was better than being on his feet.

Dicey was ripping the tablecloth into strips. She handed a tightly folded strip to Noelle. "Hold it against his cut, press down good and hard," she ordered.

"I know." Noelle's mouth was compressed into a hard line to still its trembling. She had seen wounds before, and she knew that this was a bad one. Every so often two of the young male slaves at Maynard Penn got into a fight over a woman or over a throw of the gaming bones, and one of them was injured. Although Doctor Dupree treated them, Noelle usually went to the lazar house to make sure that they were progressing satisfactorily. It was not a duty that Vanessa cared for, she had little feeling for the slaves, but Noelle, like Daniel, was always concerned for their well-being, and it was the duty of a mistress to make sure that they had the best of care.

Her hands shook as she pressed the wad of cloth against Simon's injury, and then she cried out, her voice filled with alarm.

"Dicey, I think he's fainted! Oh, God in heaven, I think he's dead!"

Dicey hurried to kneel beside the white man. She pressed her fingers against the side of his throat, and felt a pulse.

"Ain't dead, but he's lost a heap of blood, he ain't going be traveling for a spell. Mistress, you'd best go see if them mules is tethered good and tight. They're all we got now, and we'll be needing them, once the captain can manage to stay on one. I'll get him bandaged up, and that's all we can do right now, 'cepting pray."

Her face set, Dicey eased Simon's shirt off of him as gently as she could. She knew now what Vanessa's motive had been when she'd recalled her from her duties of nursing Adele and told her to attend Noelle on this outing. Just as Elisha had said, they had been meant to die, all three of them, and by blaming it on the Maroons, Vanessa would have received nothing but sympathy and compassion, above suspicion, because who would dream of suspecting Vanessa Maynard of having had a hand in the murders of her half sister and Captain Spencer and a harmless slave girl?

Even if Dicey had already told Noelle and Captain Spencer of what she had seen, it wouldn't have made any difference then, because none of them would have been alive to tell anyone else. That was why Vanessa had made an excuse not to come with them, she would have been at home while the murders were taking place. Everyone would say what a miracle it was that she had not gone with them, or else she would have been dead as well, one more tragedy to add to all the other tragedies that Maynard Penn had suffered.

In spite of her brush with death, Dicey was sorry for Elisha. Elisha had been a good man, he'd loved Miranda deeply and he'd loved his new child even if it was only a girl and not the son he'd hoped for. He never would have lent himself to such a scheme if Chloe hadn't so terrified him with her threats that he'd had to agree in order to save the lives of Miranda and his child. Hector too would have been terrified into obeying, in order to save his woman and children from deaths of unspeakable agony.

Dicey worked efficiently, securing a fresh pad over Simon's wound and strapping it firmly in place with strips of the tablecloth that she wound around and around his chest. The wound had bled freely, and that was a good thing. It had cleaned itself. But Dicey had no way of judging how much blood Simon had lost, and that was a bad thing. She hoped that it hadn't been too much.

Noelle came back just as Dicey was finishing. "He isn't going to die, is he?" she asked, her voice ragged with worry. "He can't die! I won't let him, I love him, if he dies I'll want to die too! Why does everyone I love have to die? Kenneth, and my father is dying, and now Simon!"

"I don't think he's going to die. Hold out your arm, mistress. We got to take off your jacket and roll up your sleeve, you're all over blood."

Noelle looked at her arm stupidly while Dicey bathed it with water from the pool and bandaged it. She hadn't even realized that she'd been cut. It didn't matter anyway, even though it had begun to hurt. It was only superficial, it was Simon who was desperately hurt, Simon she had to think of, not herself.

"It just doesn't make sense!" she said, her voice filled with all the bewilderment she felt. "I can't believe that it happened!"

"You heard Elisha, same as me," Dicey told her. "Chloe told 'em to do it."

"But why? There simply isn't any reason!"

"She had reason." Dicey's voice was flat. Her eyes were filled with misery as she looked at Noelle. "Chloe's been putting something into your father's medicine. I think she's been doing it right along. While you were away, I caught her at it. And then she sent me to tend Adele, and I figured she was going to poison me or spell me, and say I'd caught Adele's fever and died of it. Then I wouldn't have been able to tell."

Simon's voice made both girls start. Noelle had been so intent on what Dicey was telling her that she had taken her eyes off him, and Dicey had been looking at her mistress, so neither of them had noticed that he had opened his eyes.

"But you could have told us as soon as we started out today. Chloe wasn't anywhere around then. Why didn't you tell us, Dicey?"

Dicey's eyes were filled with agonized apology, and her voice was filled with shame.

"I didn't trust you," she said. "You are Mistress Vanessa's. I mean, you and Mistress Vanessa . . ." her glance at Noelle was stricken.

"You can say it." Noelle's voice was flat as she struggled not to show any emotion. "Captain Spencer was Vanessa's lover, that's why you didn't feel that you could trust him."

Dicey hung her head. "Yes, Mistress," she whispered.

Simon didn't dare to look at Noelle. Waves of shame washed over him, hearing it put so bluntly. "But that still doesn't explain why Chloe would order all three of us killed! Dicey, yes, but why didn't she do that before we came on this picnic? Then there would have been no reason to kill us!"

"Mistress Vanessa told her." This time Dicey looked directly at him, her eyes clear and filled with conviction. "Chloe would do anything for Mistress Vanessa, even kill. She's killed before, she's killed slaves with her spells, and for Mistress Vanessa she'd kill without even thinking."

"But she wouldn't have any reason to kill me! Vanessa would never wish me harm!" Simon was fighting to believe what he said, unwilling, unable, to accept that it could be any other way. "She was going to be my wife, she loves me! And why would she want any harm to come to Noelle? You must be wrong, Dicey!"

Dicey shook her head, but it was Noelle who answered him.

"Vanessa would never have married you, Simon. Vanessa has had many men, many lovers, but, other than you, all of them were already married. She preferred it that way, because they wouldn't have dared to cause her any trouble when she tired of them and refused to see them anymore. She wanted you, but I doubt that she would have taken you as her lover if she hadn't known that you were going to sail very soon."

Her eyes met and held Simon's, filled with conviction. "My sister isn't like other women, Simon. She has to have a great many different men. Kenneth knew it, he caught her with one of them, exactly in this spot, and he was going to tell our father, only Father was in Spanish Town at the time, and Vanessa went to join him, and before they came home Kenneth had been taken sick with some infection, and died."

Noelle's face was very white, and her eyes were filled with a torment greater than any he had ever seen on any other girl's face before.

"My brother died, Simon. And there wasn't any reason for it, it didn't make sense! I tried and tried to convince Doctor Eastlake that it wasn't natural, but he wouldn't listen, nobody would listen, nobody will ever believe a word against Vanessa. Kenneth was never sick, except for trifling childhood ailments, and he even escaped most of those. But he died, and he was going to tell Father about Vanessa, and Chloe was at Maynard Penn, she didn't go to Spanish Town with Vanessa."

Noelle choked, but she recovered herself, her eyes darker with tragedy than ever. "And there's Father. He was a strong man, Simon, strong and hearty, he was never sick either, any more than Kenneth. I know how hard

Kenneth's death hit him, but it still isn't natural that he should be wasting away inch by inch! I've begged Vanessa to have another doctor look at him, and I asked Ian to examine him, but I've already told you about that. Ian said that he couldn't unless Doctor Eastlake asked him, and Doctor Eastlake never would.''

Noelle's face hardened, her eyes still holding Simon's. "I think that my father is being drugged. I think that he's being poisoned with some slow poison. I think that Chloe is doing it, at Vanessa's orders.

"As to why Vanessa would want you dead, it's because you were the one man strong enough to thwart her plans. You insisted that she must marry you, you were going to bring Ian to Maynard Penn to examine my father. She couldn't stop you, and so the only thing left for her to do was kill you.''

Simon felt sick with horror. Vanessa, beautiful, angelic Vanessa! How could these things be true? But reluctantly as the admission to himself was made, he remembered how Vanessa had done her utmost to turn his suggestion of bringing Ian to Maynard Penn aside. And he remembered, writhing with shame, how easy it had been for him to seduce her, how willingly she had come into his arms, how eagerly she had taken him to her bed! She had feigned feeling pain, she must have feigned it, but he had been so mad with passion for her that he hadn't noticed.

But now, in retrospect, he remembered how Vanessa had matched passion with passion, how she had responded to him with a fire and a wildness that surely no virgin could have experienced the first time she had known a man! Only he'd been too blind to see it, too infatuated with Vanessa's beauty, with her angelic reputation, to entertain the least suspicion. In his eyes, Vanessa had been the saint she was reputed to be, and he had despised himself for having taken advantage of her!

Another thought came into his mind, an ugly suspicion that refused to retreat even while he tried to ignore it. He had been astonished that his passion for Vanessa had been

131

so out of bounds, so impossible for him to control. He had always been able to control himself, control was ingrained in him.

Chloe, drugs, potions . . . he shuddered violently, making Noelle cry out with alarm.

He had been used. There was no other explanation for it. He had been drugged, given something to arouse his passions to such an extent that he would not be able to control them.

Anger rose in him, anger such as he had never known. Used, duped, treated as a fool, a toy, a woman's plaything! He would never be able to face himself in a mirror again without feeling shame. Every drop of New England blood in his body rebelled at having been so used, he felt unclean, but worst of all, he felt like a fool. A stupid, idiotic fool, to be taken in by a beautiful face and an innocent manner that had hidden a true nature that made him recoil with horror.

He didn't want to believe any of this. With all his heart, he wanted to reject it, to say that it wasn't true. But Simon had been raised to face facts, no matter how unpleasant they were, and the facts were here.

Fact. Kenneth had died, of an unknown cause, in spite of always having enjoyed perfect health.

Fact. Daniel had been stricken down, seemingly by grief, but a grief he should have mastered long since rather than going into a further decline that had brought him close to death.

Fact. Dicey had been banished from the house after she had seen Chloe tamper with Daniel's medicine, and sent to nurse a girl who wasn't ill, with the distinct possibility that she would be murdered and the death put down to the fever she had contracted from the girl Adele.

And the most irrevocable fact of all. Elisha and Hector had tried to kill them, all three of them, and it was only because of Dicey's warning cry that they were still alive. Elisha had confessed, with his dying breath, that Chloe had given them the order to commit the murders. Simon knew, as well as he knew that he was still alive, that Elisha had not lied. Even as the man had been dying, there had been shame in his eyes, and a mute begging for forgiveness.

It was Dicey who jerked him back to reality.

"We can't stay here. When Hector gets back to Maynard Penn, Mistress Vanessa will send other men looking for us."

Simon felt a chill that had nothing to do with his weakened state. He was the man, it was his duty to protect these two girls, but in the press of the fast-moving events he had not thought of something that obvious. He looked at Noelle, and saw that her face was as white as the bandage Chloe had wrapped around her arm.

He rose to his feet, but the dizziness that overtook him on reaching a standing position almost felled him. The ground tilted, and he all but lost consciousness.

Noelle was beside him in an instant, crying out in protest. She supported his weight to keep him from falling. "You can't travel, you're far too badly hurt! Simon, what are we going to do?"

That was a good question. The only weapon they possessed was the knife Elisha had tried to kill him with. Hailing from Massachusetts, where any man could walk abroad in the daylight hours without being armed, it had never occurred to him to bring along his pistol for a picnic outing, even though he remembered now that Claude and Henry Cottswood had gone armed when they had taken him to Spanish Town, and even Ian had told him that he carried a pistol when he went searching for plants and herbs in the countryside, laughingly wondering if he would be able to hit anything he aimed at if it should become necessary for him to defend himself.

"Simon, if Dicey and I can help you onto one of the mules, do you think you can hang on?"

"I can try. We must get to Kingston." Simon's voice sounded far away in his own ears.

"We can't go to Kingston." Dicey's voice was sharp.

"We would be waylaid long before we got there. Mistress Vanessa will send men out to watch as soon as Hector gets back."

"But we have to get there! This attempt on our lives must be reported, Vanessa must be taken into custody!"

"Simon, we have no proof that my sister has done anything wrong," Noelle told him. "All she would have to do would be to say that Elisha and Hector had tried to kill us in an attempt to escape and join the Maroons who live in these mountains."

"But Elisha confessed! You and Dicey both heard him, as well as I!"

"Vanessa has already destroyed any credibility I might have." Noelle's face was still far too white, her eyes dark with banked fires of anger. "She has convinced everyone we know that I am so jealous of her, so spiteful against her, that I would say anything to discredit her. You were wounded, you might have misunderstood Elisha, or he would have lied, not knowing that he was going to die, and trying to exonerate himself by blaming Chloe."

"But there are the other things! Dicey saw Chloe tamper with your father's medicine, for one."

"Dicey would not be allowed to testify. No slave can testify against a white person here in Jamaica. Someone might listen to her story about Chloe, but Dicey is my girl, her loyalty to me is well known, she would not be believed. No one in all of Jamaica would believe us, Simon. You have no idea of the regard in which Vanessa is held. Can you imagine any man believing anything against her, can you, honestly?"

No, Simon had to admit, grinding his teeth against the pain that was fanning out from his wound and threatening to strike him down. Noelle was right, they hadn't a shred of solid proof. People would believe what was easier to believe, that Noelle was striking out against the sister who had taken him from her, that Dicey was lying out of loyalty to her, that he himself was a stranger who knew little of the problems Jamaicans had with slaves, that it was Noelle who had persuaded him that Vanessa was behind the attempt on their lives.

Simon had faced many difficult situations in his life. There was always one crisis or another on shipboard, there were storms to battle, occasionally some member of the crew would become disgruntled and attempt to foment a rebellion. Foreign ports often presented hazards that had to be faced and overcome. But he had never found himself in a situation like this.

"As I see it . . ." his words were widely spaced, difficult to articulate in his weakened condition when his mind did not want to function ". . . our best chance is to get your father away from Maynard Penn to some place of safety. Then, if he makes a miraculous recovery, our story would have some credibility. He himself could not help but see that he had been drugged, and that only Chloe, under Vanessa's instigation, could have done it."

The absurdity of his words struck him so forcibly that he almost laughed, a laugh of such bitterness that it nearly choked him. Wounded, not even able to stand on his feet without a girl supporting him, unarmed except for a knife, how was he to gain entrance to Maynard Penn and spirit Daniel Maynard away, against all the forces Vanessa could muster against him? As soon as Hector got back and she knew that her plan had failed she would order the plantation and every approach to it guarded.

"We got to hurry," Dicey urged them. "We got to find some place to hide."

It took the full strength of both of the girls to boost Simon onto the largest and strongest of the mules, and once there he swayed so dangerously that Noelle was forced to climb up behind him and hold him so that he would not fall off. Dicey rode the second mule and led the third. She had packed up everything for the pack mule to carry; they would need every scrap of food before this was over. When that was gone, they would have to live off the land. Something edible could always be found, and most important, there was plentiful water in the mountain streams and pools.

They had no plans beyond finding some safe place and staying there until Simon regained some of his strength. It was time they needed, time for Simon to recover, time to think and to plan.

If Simon was too near unconsciousness and too unfamiliar with this island to realize the danger, Noelle and Dicey were not. They might be successful in hiding from pursuers from Maynard Penn, but there was an equal danger from the Maroons now that they no longer had Elisha and Hector as bodyguards, and they would have to climb higher and deeper into the mountains in order to avoid their pursuers. A white man to be killed and robbed, two young and attractive girls to be taken prisoner, even the mules were valuable. Renegade slaves would not be inclined to show mercy, there had been too many atrocities against them.

Dicey tried to choose paths that would not leave traces, but she was a housegirl, untrained in the ways of the mountains. Often she dismounted and, using a branch, swept away their tracks, but that was all she could think of to do. There was no time to be more careful, even if she had known how. They had only the few remaining hours of daylight to find a place of concealment, because by first light tomorrow, they would become as hunted animals.

And there was always the possibility that the Maroons would find them first.

Vanessa was restless, her nerves as jumpy as a cat's. Waiting was never easy, especially waiting for news of such importance. It seemed to her that she had been waiting all of her life that mattered, ever since she had been a young girl barely entering her teens, when she had first dreamed her dreams and known that it would be years before they could be realized.

That was when she had first become aware of her burning, bodily urgings, of her raging hunger for men, and for a life far more exciting and fulfilling than life on this island could ever be.

Her father had had no right to marry again, to sire first a sister, and then a brother, cutting by two-thirds the inheritance that should have been hers alone. Her father, doting on her as he did, would have denied her nothing, and that would have made the waiting easier. Knowing that when her father died she would receive only one-third of his estate had made even the prospect of complete freedom less attractive.

Actually, her share would be less than a full third, because Kenneth would be the one to inherit the plantation itself, so that Vanessa could not sell it to add to the fortune that she had planned on. But the biggest obstacle of all had been her father's robust health, which promised that by the time he died, Vanessa's beauty would have faded and she would be too old to embrace all of the things that made life worth living.

If it hadn't been for Chloe, she might have given up hope. But Chloe understood her dark passions, and Chloe was powerful, so powerful that everything might still be salvaged when the time was ripe.

Daniel's and Noelle's deaths had already been fated, as well as Kenneth's, at the time Kenneth had discovered her with Andrew Gorden. His discovery had only moved Vanessa's plans ahead by a little while. Plans for their deaths had already been formulated. Everything she had always wanted was close to fruition, the waiting time so short now that even she could wait a little longer with patience.

Her only mistake had been in allowing herself to be so impressed with Simon Spencer that she hadn't been able to resist taking him for her lover. It was her insatiable lust that had betrayed her, her burning need to have this captain from New England, the most virile, attractive man she had ever seen. A short affair, very short, but the most satisfying one she had ever had.

But she had underestimated Simon's strength of character. In the end, he had posed a real threat to her with his insistence that they be married before he sailed, his insistence on bringing Ian Macintyre to examine her father. He was the only man she had ever encountered whose will was as strong as her own.

Dicey's discovery of Chloe tampering with her father's tonic had catapulted everything into the necessity for immediate action. Dicey had been intended to die before Noelle returned from Kingston, but her sister had returned unexpectedly, making it imperative that something be done to prevent Dicey talking to her. And Simon too must be disposed of before he brought down everything around her head.

Noelle's death, when Daniel was already dying of grief over losing Kenneth, would send him into his final decline, and nobody on the island would be surprised when this last, stunning tragedy carried him off. In one quick stroke, all of them would be disposed of, and Vanessa's freedom would be hers.

Within three months, she would be in London. Within a year, she would have a title and be widowed and make her home in Paris. So soon, so soon! All she had to do now was wait for Elisha and Hector to return to the plantation with the news that Noelle and Simon and Dicey had been murdered by the Maroons. Her father's demise would take no time at all, the shock would carry him off almost instantly, needing only a little push from Chloe.

The minutes and the hours dragged on while she waited. When Julie loomed up behind her, having entered the room in that maddeningly silent way these people had, and spoke her name, Vanessa almost jumped out of her skin. And then a wave of elation flooded through her. Elisha and Hector were back, and her time of waiting was over!

Her elation turned to a disappointed annoyance that turned her face ugly before she brought herself under control when Julie said, "You have a caller, Mistress. A gentleman from Kingston."

Who the devil could be calling on her at this time of the afternoon? It would be a coincidence beyond believing if it were Mr. Ellsworth, and he was the only one she could think of who might have occasion to drop in on her unannounced. Her story to Simon and Noelle, that she could not start out with them because the banker and his wife were going to call, had been pure fabrication, concocted so that she would be at home at Maynard Penn when her sister and her lover were murdered.

It wasn't Mr. Ellsworth who was waiting for her in the drawing room when she entered, her face smoothed out to its usual beauty, a smile forming on her lips as though this were the one person on all the island she was the most delighted to see.

"Mr. Macintyre! Forgive me, it's Doctor Macintyre, isn't it? It's so nice to see you, we have so few visitors these days that you are doubly welcome! Julie, bring refreshments immediately. Doctor Macintyre, what do you prefer, rum or brandy, or perhaps a light wine?"

This was perfect, and something that she couldn't have planned. If Ian Macintyre were here when the news of the triple killing arrived, he would be a witness that she had been at home, he would testify that her shock had been so great that she had collapsed, that her grief had been without bounds.

"I have no need of anything at all, Miss Maynard. I happened to be near Maynard Penn, and I only thought to stop in for a moment to pay my respects." Ian felt his face flush at such a blatant lie.

Ian had come, with no other destination in mind, to call on Noelle. The ridiculousness of his situation was not lost on him. It was generally understood in Kingston that Noelle had made it up with Henry Cottswood, and their engagement would be announced at any moment. Henry himself had assured him of this, when Ian had called at the Cottswood home to see Noelle only yesterday, and been told that she had returned to the plantation. Henry had made it very clear that Ian could have no hopes in Noelle's direction at all.

But Noelle hadn't told him that she was engaged to Henry, the last time Ian had seen her. Quite the contrary, she had complained that Henry was driving her to distraction. So unless she had had a change of heart at the last moment, Henry was whistling through his hat. That was what he was here to find out.

Not only that, but Ian hoped to get a look at Daniel Maynard while he was here. If the man was up to a short visit, at least he would have seen him at firsthand even though no examination of any kind could take place. It was doubtful that Ian could tell much just by looking at him, but you could never tell. And if he could talk to him, if he could lead him into describing how he felt, Ian might get a better idea of what was wrong with him. As far as medical ethics were concerned, he was walking a very fine line, but Noelle had seemed so desperate when she had begged him to see her father that he had felt compelled to come.

"How nice of you, Doctor Macintyre! People don't call nearly as often as I would like. Now that you are here, you must stay for supper! It's a long ride back to Kingston, you'll feel the need of sustenance before you can get back."

"A cup of coffee, then, no more," Ian said. "This is a beautiful home. Captain Spencer must be enjoying his visit. Is he around, by any chance? I'd enjoy seeing him again, and your sister, as well."

"What a shame! They aren't here, Doctor Macintyre, they went off on a jaunt into the mountains this morning, to spend the day. But they should be back at any time, which is all the more reason you should stay. They would be sorry to miss you, I know."

Ian's eyebrows contracted. "A picnic? Isn't that a bit risky, with all the unrest on the island?"

Vanessa laughed, the sound so musical that Ian was entranced until he jerked his mind back to more important matters.

"They took an escort with them, of course. I assure you that they'll be quite safe. But the picnic spot is quite a distance away, and they might be late in getting back if they misjudge the time. Why don't you spend the night? We can put you up with no trouble at all, and I'd like for you to stay. Then you and Captain Spencer could spend the entire evening talking about whatever gentlemen find to talk about.''

"No, no. I wouldn't dream of imposing on you. But I would like to see your father, if only for a moment. Everyone in Kingston holds him in such high regard that I'd be honored to meet him.''

"I know that he'd be pleased to meet you, as well,'' Vanessa assured him. "If you will wait for just a moment, I'll see how he feels.''

She was back in less than a minute, looking truly sorry.

"It's a pity, but my father is sleeping. I'd wake him, except that Doctor Eastlake is so adamant that his rest must not be disturbed on any account. But you can visit us another time, you will always be welcome. Or he may be awake and alert later this evening, if you will only change your mind and stay.''

Ian was tempted, but he had a patient in Kingston on whom he wanted to check, and there was Beggar as well, who would be waiting to be fed, and the goat had to be milked.

Thwarted at every turn, he resolved to return to Maynard Penn tomorrow. He would see Noelle and find out if Henry's insistence that he and Noelle were all but betrothed had even a grain of truth in it, and he would make another attempt to see Daniel Maynard. Noelle would help him there, so he would not be so easily put off.

He whistled a tuneless tune as he turned his horse's head back toward Kingston, but then his whistling broke off. Hadn't Vanessa Maynard been just a wee bit too insistent that he stay? She certainly had no interest in him, and with Simon's company you would think that she wouldn't want an extra man around to distract him from giving her all of his attention. Something in the beautiful girl's manner struck him as false, even though she had only acted in accordance with Jamaica's rules of hospitality.

He shrugged. There was nothing he could do about it

141

tonight, but he would most certainly return to Maynard Penn tomorrow!

It had taken Hector a long time to make up his mind. His first inclination, after he had escaped from the scene of the aborted massacre, had been to head for the higher reaches of the mountains to seek out the Maroons and join them, where he would be safe from Chloe's retaliation for having failed to carry out his mission.

But there was his family, his wife and children. If he didn't return and report what had happened, they would suffer for it. They would die, and their deaths would be slow and tormenting, Chloe had left no doubt of that in his mind.

And so, although at first he had ridden farther up into the mountains, he had turned Pilot's head and made his way down again, his heart filled with dread but knowing that he had no choice.

It was late, far later than it would have been if he had headed directly back to Maynard Penn after he had seen that the sea captain had overcome Elisha and he had panicked and run. Although the Jamaica night was as light as twilight, he knew that the other slaves would have been asleep for hours, and only Chloe and Mistress Vanessa would be waiting for him.

He was mistaken about that. One other person at Maynard Penn was awake and waiting. Cuffie had left his bed, and his hut, some time ago, filled with trepidation because the picnic party had not returned. Dicey was with them, and until she was back safely there would be no sleep for him.

Now Cuffie lay flat on his stomach only a short distance from the palisade that protected the plantation house, watching for the party to return. If he were discovered here where he had no business to be, the punishment would be something that he did not dare to think about else he would skulk back to his hut and safety. At the least every inch of skin would be taken off his back by the whip, at the most Vanessa and Chloe would claim that he was a would-be assassin who had been creeping up on the house to kill the mistress in her bed. In that case he would be killed out of hand. In these days, no plantation owner had to worry that his action would be frowned upon, with them all jumpy and taking every precaution against being butchered.

Cuffie did not move as he lay there, not as much as by a twitch of a muscle. Now, when the waiting had become unbearable, he heard the sound of a horse approaching. There was only one horse, and his heart sank. Something had happened, and he knew instinctively that whatever it was, it wasn't good.

He recognized Pilot, and the man on Pilot's back. It was Hector. And almost before he had made the identification, two figures approached the rider from the house, the evil mistress and Chloe.

Vanessa's voice was scarcely more than a whisper, but Cuffie heard her clearly.

"Well? Is it over? Are they dead? Where is Elisha?"

Hector slid down off Pilot's back and fell to his knees in front of his mistress.

"They ain't dead. Elisha, he's dead by now, I think. The captain killed him. And I had to run, wasn't nothing else I could do or I'd have been killed too."

"You fool! You miserable, worthless fool! How dare you fail!" Vanessa's rage made her voice shrill, and cold rivers of fear washed up and down Cuffie's body.

"The captain's hurt bad. But Elisha was hurt even worse. Maybe the captain'll die, like Elisha," Hector stammered, his terror making him all but unintelligible.

"Noelle, Dicey?" Vanessa demanded, her voice deadly.

"I cut the young mistress, but Dicey jumped on my back and my knife only got her arm. Dicey hurt me, biting an' clawing like a wildcat. And with Elisha down, it was three to one and I had to run else I'd of been killed too, and there'd have been nobody to come back and tell you that they's still alive. Had to come tell you, knowed that's what you'd want me to do."

The desperate hope that his mistress and Chloe would realize that he had done the right thing was dashed by Vanessa's next words.

"Kill him," Vanessa told Chloe. "Do it now."

The large woman took Hector's knife from his belt and brought it down in one powerful thrust that felled him as he remained on his knees. He would not have dared to try to resist her in any case.

"Bury him." The words were crisp. "Do it yourself, put him where nobody will find his grave." All the rage she felt was expressed in her voice. Simon Spencer and Noelle were still alive, as well as Dicey, and beyond any doubt they realized by now that it had been she who had ordered their deaths. Elisha might have confessed, but even if he hadn't, neither Simon nor Noelle were stupid. Combined with what Dicey would have told them, they could come to no other conclusion.

She would not be thwarted now! She had waited too long, she had dreamed her dreams for too long, no one and no turn of fate would be allowed to stand in the way of their completion!

"You are to arouse enough of our best men to guard every approach from the mountains. If Simon and Noelle try to reach Kingston or another plantation, they are to be stopped and killed. I don't have to tell you how to make the men obey."

Vanessa paced, her brow marred by a frown. She could guard against her sister and Simon reaching civilization, but what if, with Simon wounded, they didn't try to come down out of the mountains until Simon had had time to recover some of his strength? What if they took refuge in some hiding place? There was no telling how long they could hold out, and no telling whether Simon's intelligence and desperation wouldn't let him find some way to reach the authorities without being stopped and taken. Every day that passed would make Vanessa's danger more acute.

Her brow smoothed out as she smiled, a smile that froze Cuffie's blood.

"I'll send for the chasseurs," Vanessa said. "They'll find them and bring them back to where we can dispose of them. It can still be laid to the Maroons, we will dispose of the chasseurs at the same time so they will have no chance to talk."

"Yes, Mistress." Chloe stooped and lifted Hector's dead body in her arms, holding him as if he weighed no more than a child, in spite of his size and weight. "That plan will work. The chasseurs will bring them back."

The chasseurs! Dicey and Noelle and the captain were done for. Once the chasseurs got on their trail nothing could save them. Cuffie's stomach roiled, and his supper of breadfruit and a piece of salt meat started to come up, even though he had eaten it so many hours before. Sweat ran into his eyes and blinded him. He pressed his face into the ground, choking back his sickness. The slightest sound and he, too, would die, just as Hector had died, and as Dicey and Noelle and Captain Spencer were going to die.

Chapter Ten

THEY HAD TO STOP FOR THE NIGHT BEFORE DICEY WOULD
have wished, because Simon had become a dead weight as
Noelle's arms tried to support him. He had lost even more
blood than they had feared, and now he was so weak that
he could no longer make any effort to hold himself upright
on the mule.

The spot Dicey chose was well concealed, even though
she had hoped to find something even better. It would
have to do, Simon could not go on. She helped Noelle
ease him down from the mule's back, and it took their
combined strength to lead him to a flat spot where he
could lie down at last. Dicey brought one of the cushions
from the pack mule, and Noelle slipped it under his head.

Simon opened his eyes as the pain of being moved
subsided. He tried to smile, but it was a futile effort. The
result was more like a grimace.

146

"I'm about as much use as a newborn babe," he croaked.

"Never mind. You'll be stronger tomorrow." Noelle made her voice firm, although she wondered whether Simon would be stronger or weaker when the sun rose again. She pushed panic from her mind; they had enough trouble without indulging in such negative speculations. Simon would be stronger in the morning, a night's rest would do wonders.

Dicey led the mules more than half a mile away, and concealed them in a dense growth of thicket after she had let them drink from a stream. She gathered armfuls of grass and other growing things to feed them; mules were strong and hardy, they could survive and keep on going on less than this.

Noelle was sitting beside Simon, holding his hand, when Dicey got back.

"Where have you been? I was worried, you were so long. I'd begun to think that the Maroons had captured you."

"Had to hide them mules far enough away so's if any Maroons are around, the noise they make won't lead 'em to us," Dicey explained. "No way to keep 'em quiet, was they near by."

Noelle's already wan face paled even more. She didn't want to think about the Maroons, but she knew that they were somewhere in these mountains, an ever-present danger on top of all the other dangers they faced.

She hadn't heard of any recent raids by the renegade slaves. Usually they struck at isolated plantations, to pillage and carry away anything of use to them, striking without warning and making a quick retreat before forces could be marshaled against them. A raid now and then was tolerated by the government, it was only when white people were killed that the militia penetrated into the mountains in search of them to bring them to justice. There would be no searching militiamen now, who might rescue them from their plight, they had only their own strength and their own wits to rely on if they were to go on living.

Noelle and Dicey carried nothing of value, unless they might be stripped of their clothing to be given to the women among the Maroons, but they might think that Simon had weapons and kill him out of hand in order to obtain them. She would rather not dwell on how she and Dicey would be disposed of. Dicey was an extraordinarily beautiful girl. It was almost certain that they would take her prisoner and force her to become the woman of one of them. Dicey would never be able to bear it. She would kill herself rather than let any man but Cuffie touch her.

As for Noelle herself, she had scant doubt that she, like Simon, would be killed. The Maroons would not dare to leave her alive, and they would not risk taking her prisoner. For a captured white girl to be found among them would bring down the gravest of punishments on their heads.

Noelle looked at Dicey and saw the same fear in Dicey's eyes, but Dicey only compressed her lips before she spoke.

"The captain's got to eat something. He can't get no strength back unless he eats. There's plenty for a long time. See if you can get some of this chicken down him. I'll fetch some water, I never thought to fish the jugs of juice out of the pool so water will have to do. You got to eat too, we're going to need our strength."

Noelle fed Simon first, breaking off tiny bits of chicken breast and feeding him with her fingers, as if he'd been an infant. Simon made a valiant effort to chew and swallow, trying to smile at her between bites, but soon he turned his head away. He could take no more, he had to sleep, his weariness pressed down on him like a mountain of granite.

Every bite Noelle ate choked her, but she forced it down because Dicey was right. At every least sound of bird or small animal she started, ready to leap to her feet and give battle with all the determination that was in her before she was overcome. But nothing disturbed them in their hiding place, and soon her own weariness overcame her fear, and she too lay down on a bed of ferns and closed her eyes.

What a fool she'd been to insist on taking Nero today, instead of her own Psyche! Psyche wouldn't have panicked and run off as Nero had done, there would be one good, fast horse, because Psyche was fast in spite of having a placid nature. Then when Simon became stronger, he could have taken Psyche and made a run for Kingston, or in case his strength returned too slowly, Noelle could have gone, riding like the wind, to bring back help to the two who remained hidden here in the mountains. On Psyche, either of them would have a chance, however slender it was, while now they seemed to have no chance at all.

It was cold in the mountains after the sun went down. In his sleep, Simon shivered, his teeth chattering. His stirring woke Noelle, and she went to lie down beside him, pressing her body against his, her arms around him in an attempt to warm him with her own body heat.

She found herself babbling, unable to stop the flow of words. "You're not going to die. I won't let you die. I don't care if you loved Vanessa, you're just a blind, impressionable man after all, you didn't know any better, but that's no reason you should have to die.

"Men are so stupid! Just downright stupid, they all fall in love with Vanessa, she could turn into a demon right in front of their eyes and they'd still see only how beautiful she is, and go right on loving her. I ought to hate you, you and all the other idiots who let Vanessa take them in. If we ever get out of this mess, I'll never speak to you again, I'll never as much as look at you, but I'm not going to let you die, because I love you, damn you!"

She stemmed her hysterical words at last, thankful that Simon still slept and would never know what a fool she had made of herself. She held him even more closely, her tears staining her cheeks and dampening his shoulder, the one that wasn't hurt, which was a mercy, because she didn't know what effect salt tears would have on a wound.

Although she would have sworn that it would be impossible, she dozed off, and soon she slept. Dicey sat a short distance from them, her arms wrapped around her knees, her eyes wide open, watching for any movement in the eerie half-light of the Jamaica night, her ears straining for any sound that was not natural to their surroundings. It wasn't until dawn was less than two hours away that she, too, lay down and closed her eyes, sleeping the sleep of exhaustion.

Sometime during the night, Simon's and Noelle's positions shifted. Now it was he who held her in his arms, warming her, holding her head against his shoulder. He held her tenderly and protectively even in his sleep, and once, when he roused a little, raging with thirst, he brushed her cheek with his fingertips, and then kissed her forehead. Even only half awake he realized that he had no right, he had forfeited any such right when he had turned his back on her in favor of Vanessa, and he despised himself, and muttered, before he calmed down again, still holding the girl he had betrayed in his arms.

He awakened at the first full light, and thought that he had been dreaming. He could remember snatches of his dream, he'd thought that Noelle had been talking to him, she'd called him an idiotic fool for falling in love with Vanessa, she'd said that she'd never speak to him again or even look at him. But she'd said something else, and it hadn't seemed like a dream at all. She'd said that she loved him, that she still loved him even if he'd been the world's worst fool.

He was still holding Noelle close, and her sleeping face looked so pure and innocent in her sleep that he castigated himself all over again. If she had really said what he had thought he'd heard her say, he didn't blame her for vowing never to have anything to do with him again. Nothing he could ever do could make up to her for the pain he'd caused her. Already burdened by having a sister who was evil incarnate, already suspecting that her brother had been murdered and that her father was being killed by some slow poison, having to bear the fact that nobody would listen to her or believe her, he had had to come along and let her fall in love with him, and then add to her suffering until it was a wonder that she hadn't broken down under her burden of grief.

Dicey came, soft-footed, and spoke in a low voice. "Let her sleep while I fetch the mules and get the gear packed up. Then we'll eat something, and get started again."

Simon nodded, his arm tightening more protectively around Noelle. He felt so useless, so utterly, ridiculously useless! He should be the one to fetch the mules, to pack things up, to lead them higher into the mountains and keep them safe, not Dicey, a slip of a girl still in her teens, and frightened half to death as well. But he knew that he didn't have the strength, and so he had to suffer through letting Dicey do it.

God, how he wished that he had a gun, something to defend them with besides the knife he had taken from Elisha! If they were set upon, he wouldn't even be able to get on his feet to make any attempt to wield it, they'd be overwhelmed in a matter of seconds. He thought of the arms that were on the *Maid of Boston*, and the thought tormented him as pictures of food torment a starving man. He thought of Aaron Godbehere, his first mate, a crack shot and a good man in a fight, and of the others of his crew who could hold their own in any melee ever imagined. Tough, hard New Englanders, the lot of them, men he'd trust to fight back to back with him, men who would make all the difference in the world if only they were here.

But they weren't here, and there wasn't any way to get them here. Simon was on his own, the sole protection for two young girls who had done nothing to deserve being hunted down and killed in these mountains.

He had no illusions that they would not be hunted. One man had already died, proving the ruthlessness of the woman who wanted them dead. Elisha had been a good man, and Simon winced to think that he had had to leave his body unburied. If he had had the strength, he would at least have covered it with stones so that no predatory animals could ravage it.

Noelle's eyelids fluttered, and she opened her eyes and looked, with dawning consternation, at Simon, her eyes darkening with some emotion he couldn't read when she realized how closely he was holding her against him.

She removed his arm from around her and sat up, although he tried to pull her back down again.

"You can sleep a little longer. Dicey's gone for the mules, but it will take her a while to get back."

Noelle shook her head. "No. I have to wash, and try to straighten my hair." Her face was still flushed with sleep, and it made her look younger and more vulnerable than ever.

A trickle of brook was close by, Dicey had chosen the spot well, and Noelle knelt and splashed water over her face and neck. Used to bathing every day, which was essential in the tropics, she wished that she could strip off all of her clothing and scrub the dust of yesterday's travels away, but with Simon so near there was no way she could do that.

The thought made her face flame. Hastily, she sacrificed a ruffle from her petticoat and soaked it in the water and carried it back to Simon and bathed his face and his throat. There was already a stubble of beard on his face, making her wonder what he would look like if he wore a full beard.

Simon ran his thumb over the stubble, rather unhappily. "It'll itch, by tomorrow," he said. "I've never wanted to put up with a beard, even though some of my crew wear them for protection in the northern winters. For myself, I'd rather be frostbitten."

"Frostbitten?" Noelle had no idea what Simon meant. "I have to loosen your bandage and look at your wound. I'm afraid that it might hurt."

The bandage had stuck, and Simon bit down on his lip as Noelle eased it away as gently as she could. To take his mind off the pain, he tried to tell her what frostbite was.

But she wasn't listening. Instead, she tried to stifle a cry of dismay when she had uncovered the wound. The area around the stab wound was inflamed, puffy, and swollen.

She made another trip to the brook to resoak the cloth and bring it back to try to cleanse the area, wincing when Simon winced.

"I wouldn't worry about it. It doesn't look good, but I'm tough," he told her. "I've been hurt worse than this many times, and recovered. On shipboard, we learn to fend for ourselves."

But wounds tended to heal themselves on shipboard, on the open sea. Simon didn't understand why, but doctors he knew testified to the fact, as baffled by it as he was. And Simon wasn't on shipboard now, and he knew that he had an infection that could cause him no end of trouble.

Dicey came back with the mules, and together the two girls rebandaged his arm, Dicey's eyes as filled with worry as Noelle's when she saw the inflammation, but she didn't voice her fears.

"We better eat, and get moving," she said. "Captain Spencer won't be able to travel fast, so we'll need all the time we got. If he could walk, we'd be better off without the mules, but there ain't no way he kin do that, weak as he still is."

Dicey was right. They did not make good time. Not only did they have to make frequent stops so that Simon could rest, but the way was rougher now, as they continued to climb. Once again, Dicey tried to brush away traces of their passage, although she did not want to take the time to do a thorough job of it.

As they kept moving ahead and upward, their eyes darted from side to side and strained to see what was in front of them. Once, around noon, they stiffened and froze in their positions, certain that they had been overtaken either by men from Maynard Penn, or by a party of Maroons. Simon laughed a weak laugh of relief when an old boar and two sows crossed their path only a little way ahead of them, but Dicey frowned at him and indicated that they must be silent and not move a muscle. When the three animals crashed away through the brush, Dicey sighed with relief.

"Them ain't just pigs, Captain Spencer. They're wild, and they're dangerous! If they'd rushed us, we'd have been in real trouble. Their tusks can cut a man to pieces, and they're vicious. Gentlemen hunt them for sport, and the Maroons hunt them for food, but us folk had better steer a clear path around them."

That evening, as on the night before, Dicey tethered the mules a good distance from their camping place. All three of the fugitives were much more tired than they had been the night before. The effort of the climb, and the additional hours of worry, had taken their toll.

They finished what was left of the chicken and the fruit, leaving some bread and ham for another day, because the salt meat would keep better. Simon would have given a year of his life for a pipeful of tobacco, but he had brought none with him. A gentleman did not smoke in the presence of ladies, even out of doors. Now he wondered if being a gentleman was all it was cracked up to be.

He fingered the stubble on his face. It was longer now, and he wondered if he could try to shave it off with Elisha's knife. He decided against trying it. With no soap and no mirror, and in his shaky state, he'd probably end up cutting his own throat and then the girls would be entirely alone.

Even Dicey wasn't able to keep her eyes open for long that night, in spite of her determination to watch over her mistress. All three of them were cold, but Dicey suffered the most because once again Noelle and Simon slept close together to share their body heat. Dicey was invited to join them, but she declined, wanting to sleep nearer the track they had been following so that she would awaken if anyone came near. They dared not build a fire even if they had had any means of building one. Its light would be seen a long way, a sure giveaway of their whereabouts.

And so they shivered, and dozed, and wakened to shiver again. It was during one of those periods of dozing that Dicey was startled out of her skin, and tried to jerk awake already fighting.

A hand clamped over her mouth. "Don't scream, Dicey, don't you go ascreaming! It's me, Cuffie."

Dicey collapsed against him, shaking and stifling her sobs. "But how? I don't understand . . ."

"I had me a good idea where you was going to picnic. And it wasn't so hard from there. You can't keep mules from dropping, and you missed little bitty traces of it."

Simon had come awake; the constant alertness, even in sleep, that was required on shipboard warning him that something wasn't right. "Dicey?"

Her whisper calmed him as he struggled to his feet. "It's all right. It's Cuffie. He's a friend."

"Don't whisper, Dicey. Whispers carry farther than just talking in a soft voice," Cuffie cautioned her. "Is you all right, Captain Spencer? And Mistress Noelle, is she all right?"

"Noelle is fine, she was only scratched and it's healing nicely. I'm afraid I can't say as much for myself." Simon's voice held a wry dryness, but he was careful not to whisper, as Cuffie had warned them. "Elisha got me pretty good. Did I hear you say that you'd found where we went to picnic? You must have seen Elisha, then, and known you were on the right track."

"Knowed you'd picnicked there, there was some signs. Didn't see Elisha, he wasn't there. Didn't see no signs that he walked away, neither."

They looked at each other in the strange half-twilight, and recognition was on all of their faces. If Cuffie hadn't seen Elisha's body, then someone had taken the body away. It wouldn't have been anyone from Maynard Penn, they wouldn't have stopped to remove it. Therefore it had to have been Maroons.

"If you could find us, they certainly could," Simon said, struggling to keep his voice steady. "I wonder why they haven't fallen on us before now."

"Can't tell, with them. They knows you're here, all right. Maybeso they just don't want to be bothered, right

155

now, maybeso they just took Elisha to bury him. Might be they had other business, or they just don't want to go messing with any white folks and bringing the militia down on 'em.''

"Let's hope that it's that!" Simon said fervently. "I'm glad you're here, Cuffie. We certainly can use a man's strength, I wouldn't be of much use if anything happened, at least for another day or two.''

As low as their voices were, they disturbed Noelle, and she too came fully awake and came to join them. She threw her arms around Cuffie and hugged him, crying with delight and relief.

"Cuffie, how did you ever find us? I can't believe that you're really here!''

"Had to find you. Had to find Dicey, and you and the captain. Mistress Vanessa, she's set guards to watching so's you can't git noplace without being caught. And Mistress Vanessa, she said she was going send for the chasseurs, they'll be on your trail any time now, if they ain't already.''

Noelle's and Dicey's gasps of terror made the short hairs on the nape of Simon's neck stand up. "Chasseurs?'' He frowned, trying to remember what he had heard about them, but except that they were employed to track down runaway slaves, it eluded him.

"We better get moving,'' Cuffie told them. "It'll be full day before we knows it. We got to get higher in the mountains, find a place even the dogs can't find us. There's a place I've heared tell of, a place the slaves talk about when they's thinking of running. If we can get there we might have a chance. Not much of a chance, but better'n anywhere else.''

Cuffie brought the mules, and it was he who now led the way. He took them by torturous paths that only he could see, and sometimes there was no path at all. He seemed to be watching for landmarks, although how he could be sure if they were the right ones or not, Simon had no idea. The weakness brought on by his wound must be making his brain weak, he thought, just when he needed every iota of brainpower he possessed to help keep them alive.

Daylight came, and noon, and late afternoon, and still they climbed, traveling through areas that Simon would have sworn could not be traversed. Cuffie urged them on, not allowing a stop to eat at midday, but late in the afternoon Simon reeled on his mule and would have fallen if Cuffie hadn't jumped to support him. They had to make camp where they were, because Simon could go no farther that day.

Noelle cried out in alarm when she started to unwind his bandage to look at his injury. His body was hot, and his eyes were dull with fever. And when she had uncovered his shoulder, she felt pure terror sweep over her.

Simon managed to focus his eyes on his shoulder as well. "We'll have to risk a fire," he said. "A small fire, just a few coals will do. The infection is spreading, and it isn't going to get any better unless something is done about it. The only thing I know to do is cut it out, and then cauterize the wound. I've seen it done, in places where nothing else would avail, and sometimes it worked."

Noelle caught the word "sometimes" and felt dread like a living weight descend on her. The implication was clear. Sometimes it worked, but sometimes it didn't.

But even through her dread, she knew that there was nothing else to be done. They were miles from civilization and medical aid, and it might be days before they could come down out of the mountains, if they lived to come down at all.

If the primitive surgery that Simon proposed didn't work, and the infection continued to spread and he died, she wouldn't care whether or not she was overtaken and killed. It didn't matter that Simon was no longer hers, that in actual fact he had never been hers, it didn't matter that he didn't love her. A world without Simon, alive and vital and well, in it, would be too dark a place for her to want to survive.

She found courage from some deep place inside her that

157

she had never known existed. She would survive, she had to survive. There was Dicey and Cuffie, who must not be caught and killed. And there was another reason so compelling that she would walk through the fires of hell to accomplish. Vanessa must be punished, for Kenneth's death, for Simon's death, for the impending death of Noelle's father. If Noelle lived for only one more day after seeing Vanessa brought down, she would be content.

The fire was a small one, the smallest possible, but even so the kindling of it took well over an hour that seemed as long as an eternity. Here on this lush island, tinder was not something that was easily come by. It took Cuffie a long time to find bits of twigs and dry, dead leaves and grasses that might possibly be ignited.

They had no flint and steel. Attempts to produce sparks by striking stones together proved futile, as did their efforts to make a fire as Simon had sometimes done when he had been a boy, playing at Indians, by twirling a pointed stick into the hollow of another dry piece of wood.

So much for Indian lore, Simon thought grimly, his frustration making him want to rave and curse. Only the fact that he had been brought up to realize that nothing was gained by anger or blasphemy kept him from venting his rage on these inanimate objects that refused to obey his will. That, and the presence of Noelle, who was already frightened enough without his adding to her fear by a show of brute temper.

Sitting back on his heels, he cursed himself for a fool. The fever must have affected his mind! The means of kindling a fire had been here all along, right in his pocket.

The watch his father had given him on his eighteenth birthday, the occasion when he had first taken over the bridge of one of the family ships for a coastal voyage, had stopped because he hadn't remembered to wind it since their misadventure had begun. There would have been no point in winding it anyway. Time had no meaning now, only daylight and dark, and climbing higher into the vastness of the mountains.

But the face of the watch was covered with glass, and there was still hot sunlight. Grimly, Simon moved the little pile of tinder into a patch of sun. His hand shook as he attempted to remove the glass with the tip of Elisha's knife, and again he felt like cursing, and had to clamp his lips tightly together to hold the words back.

"Cuffie, can you get this glass out?"

Cuffie took the watch and the knife, not understanding at all, but so used to doing any white man's bidding that he set about the task without asking questions. Neither Noelle nor Dicey understood either, but watched, perplexed, the grimness of Simon's face keeping Noelle from asking the purpose.

A silent question in his eyes, one that his training did not allow him to voice, Cuffie handed the glass to Simon.

At last! Now, at last, perhaps they were getting somewhere! Simon knelt by the pile of tinder and held the curved piece of glass directly above it. Come on, come on! his mind raged. I know it will work, it has to, every law of nature says that it has to!

Cuffie's eyes widened with comprehension when a tiny wisp of smoke rose from the tinder. Instantly, he threw himself full length on the ground, and at the first flicker of flame, almost too small for the eye to see, he began to blow on it.

"Gently, gently, don't blow it out!" Simon cautioned him.

All of them looked at the little heap of glowing coals, when the larger sticks that Simon had piled on the fire had burned down, with dread in their eyes. Then Simon squared his jaw and handed Cuffie the knife.

"Noelle, walk a little way away and turn your back. You might want to hold your nose as well, you aren't going to like the smell. Cuffie, do it now. Cut out all the infected part, and then get the blade red hot and hold it against where you've cut."

Noelle's lips were white, but she stood her ground. "If you can bear it, I can."

"I might scream loudly enough to break your ear-drums," Simon warned her.

"You don't dast. It would echo all through these hills," Cuffie told him. The rest of them didn't need to be reminded that there might be ears to hear, that they had no idea how close to them the Maroons who had taken Elisha's body away might be. And they had no idea how fast the chasseurs might have traveled.

Simon lay down flat on the ground and braced himself. He'd never been a coward where pain was concerned, but he knew that this was going to be worse than anything he had ever experienced before. Shamefaced, he realized that he didn't want to give a poor showing of himself in front of Noelle. It would be humiliating if he screamed.

Noelle reached for Dicey's hand and held onto it with painful force, but Dicey gave no indication of discomfort. Both of the girls winced as Cuffie brought the point of the knife in contact with the inflamed flesh. A shudder passed through his body, and it was echoed in those of each of the girls.

As sickened as he was at the prospect of what lay before him, Simon thought, wonderingly, that he had never realized that a black person could turn pale. But Cuffie's face was pale, it had taken on a grayish tinge, even though his hand did not tremble.

"Do it," Simon said.

The knife broke the flesh, and Cuffie cut. Beads of perspiration soaked his forehead, and he bit his lower lip until it bled, but he did what he had to do. Simon held himself rigid, using every ounce of his determination not to cry out, but there was no trace of color left in his face when Cuffie had finished, and he averted his eyes as the slave laid the blade of the knife in the coals.

When Cuffie brought the flat of the blade down on his quivering flesh, Simon's body arched and his eyes opened wide. Then they rolled back in his head, and he fainted.

Noelle clapped her free hand over her mouth, doubling over as the odor of charred flesh assailed her nostrils. Dicey supported her as she fought against retching.

By the time Simon stirred, Noelle had herself under control. She was kneeling beside Simon when he opened his eyes, her fingers pressed against his lips to keep him from moaning.

"Done the best I could, Captain Spencer," Cuffie said. "How you feeling?"

"Like I'd like to be unconscious again," Simon said. His shoulder was on fire, sending pain radiating out until his whole body seemed to cringe and writhe with it, although he lay still, not moving as much as a muscle.

"Don't reckon you can ride, even with Mistress Noelle or Dicey holding you on," Cuffie said. He wasn't satisfied with this place, he wanted to reach his ultimate goal, the place he had heard about through rumor, but he had no idea how far it was and it would be insane to try to go on before morning. "You just lay easy and rest. I'm going to move the mules, and Dicey and me will bring back something to eat."

They settled down to sleep before the light was gone, leaving Simon thinking that if he lived out the rest of his life here he would never get used to the lack of real darkness. Nothing on this island was as it should be, and he felt an aching longing to be on the high seas again, or better still, at home in Boston, with his family gathered around him and no pain tearing at him making sleep almost impossible.

He was delirious with fever during the night, and Noelle held him close, talking to him and trying to soothe him.

"You'll be all right. You have to be all right! I'll help you. If I could bear your pain for you, I'd do it without flinching. Oh, Simon, Simon! If only things had been different, if only you had never seen Vanessa! I'll never love anyone else, I'll never want anyone else as I want you!"

There in the lonely mountains, with no assurance that they would live for another twenty-four hours, Noelle wanted Simon as she had never dreamed that she could want a man. To die without ever having known the joy of giving herself to the man she loved seemed harder than death itself. To be one with him, to know the ultimate oneness that only such a mating could bring! Once again, tears streaked her face as she held Simon close, and her sense of loss and frustration was bitter.

Dicey took the first watch, leaving the more dangerous hours later in the night for Cuffie. She was able to sleep well tonight, because Cuffie was here. No matter what happened, they would be together when they had to face it.

Cuffie's face was grim when he confronted them at the first real light of morning.

"The mules are gone," he said.

Noelle's throat constricted, so that Dicey found her voice before she did.

"The chasseurs?"

Cuffie shook his head. "If it had been the chasseurs, they would have taken us. It wasn't them. It was Maroons."

"Thank God you left the mules so far from our camp, else they would have found us too!" Simon's voice was fervent.

"They knows we're here, all right. They just didn't see fit to kill us, yet. We'd better get moving, unless they change their minds and come back."

Chapter Eleven

IAN SAW THE CHASSEURS AS HE WAS COMING DOWN FROM the foothills, one of his frequent expeditions in search of more specimens to add to his collection of native plants. He paused in his descent to watch them, reining in his horse and sitting still in the saddle, his hand firm on the reins to keep the animal from shying by the sight and scent of the strangers and their dogs.

There were two of them, and each of them was accompanied by three dogs—large, fierce animals, capable of tearing a man apart—muzzled now, as they were always kept muzzled until it was time for them to bring down their quarry. And in addition to these terrifying animals, there were two smaller dogs, their noses to the ground, dogs that Ian knew were adept at tracking, perhaps the best tracking dogs ever bred and trained anywhere in the world.

The sight made him shiver in spite of the warmth of the

day. It was obvious that they were following a trail, but Ian had thought that the day of the chasseur was past. With the emancipation so near, it was hardly worthwhile to hire these slave catchers to bring back any escaped black. The last and most reliable word Ian had heard was that the planters would be compensated only twenty pounds or less for every freed slave. As most of the prime field hands had been bought for eighty pounds, the loss of one or two now was only a drop in the bucket.

The chasseurs were Spanish, imported from Cuba for the sole purpose of tracking and capturing escaped slaves. They were tall men and wiry, and possessed of legendary strength and endurance. Even their manner of dress inspired fear. Their shirts were worn open at the throat to expose the crucifixes they wore, their feet were thrust into boots that were nothing more than the entire hides of pigs' legs, put on when the hide was green and allowed to dry on the chasseurs' legs.

They were temperate men, never touching alcohol in any form. Their diet was spartan, they ate only vegetables with a little salt. Their only indulgence was the slim black cigars they smoked, and they forebore even this while they were on a hunt. Their endurance was incredible, and they seldom failed in their mission.

The chasseurs gave him only one glance, their faces showing indifference to him. Still Ian sat on his horse and watched them until they were almost out of sight, puzzling over whom they could be after.

Once he had left the foothills behind, Ian hesitated again, pondering which direction to take. It was still reasonably early, and he had no pressing business waiting for him back in Kingston.

It took him only a moment to make up his mind. He had missed Noelle and Simon on his first visit to Maynard Penn, and had failed to get a glimpse of Daniel Maynard. He would make a return visit now. At least he would see Noelle and Simon, even if it was not possible to see Daniel.

Vanessa greeted him in the drawing room as she had

before, as beautiful as he remembered her and just as charming. But his disappointment when he learned that once again neither Noelle nor Simon was at home was acute.

"I'm sorry that you've made the trip for nothing, Doctor Macintyre. If you had let us know you were coming, I'm sure that they would have stayed at home. But they went jaunting off somewhere, Captain Spencer is eager to see everything he can while he's still here, and Noelle is the one who is free to accompany him."

Ian resisted the temptation to raise his eyebrows. Something wasn't right here. Everyone in Kingston knew that Simon had been smitten by Vanessa, that his interest in Noelle had cooled the moment he had seen her sister. But here he was, spending all his time with Noelle rather than Vanessa.

Once again Ian made a bid to be allowed a short visit to Daniel, and once again he was circumvented. Daniel was not having a good day, he must not be disturbed, seeing a stranger would tire him.

Ian was annoyed, but there was no way he could force himself into the sickroom. Eastlake, the pompous ass, would probably be incensed if he should find out that Ian had even asked to see his patient, even if only to pass the time of day with him.

"I saw something strange while I was coming down from the foothills," Ian said. "There were two chasseurs, and they gave every appearance of being on a trail. Have you heard of any escaped slaves, Miss Maynard?"

Vanessa's eyes were guileless. "No, I haven't heard of any trouble. But then I'm confined to the plantation these days, as you know. Perhaps Noelle and Captain Spencer will hear something, on their ramblings. It does seem odd, but perhaps whoever escaped is held to be dangerous, so that it would be essential to get him back before he could incite others into an uprising."

Ian stayed for only a few minutes. It didn't occur to him until he was well on his way back toward Kingston that Vanessa hadn't offered him any refreshment, nor urged him to stay longer. Now the breach of hospitality struck a false note, especially after the way Vanessa had done her utmost to keep him on the occasion of his first visit.

Beggar was frenetic with joy at the sight of his master, leaping on him, barking, licking his face and hands. Ian bent to fondle his ears and rough up his coat.

"So you missed me, did you? Were you afraid that you'd have to go without your supper, or could it be that you simply like me?"

Beggar snuggled against him, his stump of a tail wagging so fast that it was a blur. Ian had no envy of men who owned thoroughbred dogs with pedigrees as long as his arm. This bedraggled stray he had given a home was all the dog he wanted.

"I have to rub Explorer down first, you know, and feed him. He's been working while you've been sleeping." How his contemporaries back in Scotland would laugh if they could hear him talking to a dumb beast! But when a dog and a horse and a goat were all you had, they became important, more friends than pets.

Simon Spencer, Ian thought, was a fool. He could have had Noelle, it was obvious that she had fallen head over heels in love with him, but he had turned from her in favor of Vanessa. His only consolation was that as long as Simon was no longer in the running, the day might come when he would be in a position to ask Noelle to be his wife. He did not consider Henry Cottswood seriously as a rival. Noelle would never settle for him, even on the rebound.

So there was hope, even if it was slender. He gave Beggar a loving cuff and rose to his feet. Hope was what men lived on, and as long as Noelle was free, he would cling to his.

"The important thing is not to panic," Simon told his companions. "The chasseurs may be professional trackers, but they're only human beings, they have no supernatural powers that can't be overcome. I have almost my full strength back"—this was an exaggeration, but he strove to put conviction in his voice—"and Cuffie is a young and powerful man. Together there is every chance that we will be able to outmaneuver and outthink them."

"The dogs," Cuffie said. "Them dogs can track anything, and you left clothes at the plantation, and they'll have been given a good sniff of my hut. Ain't nothing going to keep them from tracking us, and them big dogs is vicious."

"Vicious, but still dogs. If we can't outwit a few dogs we don't deserve to be called men. I was concerned about our lack of weapons, but as long as you're sure that the chasseurs are armed only with knives, the odds have been cut down to our size. I'd give my next voyage's profits for a pistol, but there are other alternatives. Cuffie, how would you like to make a couple of spears?"

Cuffie looked at him, bewildered. "Spears, Captain Spencer?"

"Spears." Simon's voice was firm. "More than two, as a matter of fact. It's to be hoped that the chasseurs won't get close enough to us so that the girls might have to defend themselves, but as a last resort they could do it. Since we have a very good knife, all we need is long, straight branches."

Noelle tried to picture herself lunging at a chasseur with such an improvised weapon, and her mind boggled. The chances were that one of those fierce dogs would be at her throat, tearing it out, before she could lift it. And she knew that Simon wasn't anywhere near as strong as he was making out to be. Even under the thick stubble that now covered the lower part of his face, she could see how pale he was under his natural deep color caused by sun and wind on the open seas. Also, she did not believe that Simon realized just how invincible the chasseurs were.

Simon had warmed to his subject. "I can make a bow," he said. "Or more than one."

A look at Cuffie's face made him change his mind about more than one. Of the four of them, he was the only one who had ever used a bow. There would be no time to explain to them about point of aim, about deviations of wind, let alone time for them to stop and practice. Provided that he could make a usable bow at all!

Finding reasonably straight branches from which to fashion spears wasn't the easy task that Simon had thought it would be, but finding a branch springy and strong enough for fashioning a bow was even more difficult. Still, Simon persevered.

Cuffie looked at the "spear" that Simon handed him, his eyes filled with doubt. But he took it, and drew back his arm, and made a practice cast. It fell far short of the mark he had set for himself.

"Go on practicing, but take care not to splinter it on a rock," Simon advised him.

Cuffie went on practicing. Simon completed another spear, and then two more, clumsy-looking things, the stone spearheads set into notches and bound on with strips of cloth. Any cave man would have laughed himself sick at the sight of them.

Making a bow proved to be as futile as his first attempts at kindling a fire. Three branches split when he tested their elasticity. The fourth passed the test, but there was still a matter of a bowstring.

"Would the string of one of my petticoats do?" Noelle asked. She flushed, shamed at mentioning an undergarment, and then she had to laugh, thinking how amused Ian Macintyre would be at her embarrassment. Association with him had gone a long way toward wiping out such false and stupid modesty, and he would not think much of her lapse.

Thinking of false modesty, she cast aside the petticoat once she had removed the drawstring. Now she would have more freedom of movement and not be so weighted down.

If the completed bow was a sorry-looking weapon, the arrows were even sorrier. There was no perfectly straight branch from which to fashion them and, lacking feathers, Simon had to fletch them with the stiffest leaves that could be found.

"Let's hope that our lives won't depend on this thing,"

Simon said, rising. He was cramped from having squatted on his heels for so long, and he stretched, and that made his shoulder protest with pain that radiated all through his body. In spite of himself he gasped, and Noelle was beside him instantly, reaching out to support him.

"I'm all right. We'd better get moving," he said.

Carrying the improvised weapons, only too cognizant of their inadequacy, they started to climb again. Cuffie led the way, agile and surefooted, with Dicey close behind him. Noelle came next, and Simon brought up the rear. There was no discernible path, Cuffie seemed to be choosing their way by instinct alone. The way was so precipitous that soon Simon was gasping for breath, his shoulder one burning fire of agony, his face and body soaked with perspiration. He was mortified when Noelle dropped back to reach out a supporting hand to help him up some of the steepest places, but this was neither the time nor the place for pride, their only concern was to reach their destination.

Once again, Simon was struck with the impossibility of the situation. This couldn't be happening, not in the civilized world of 1832. It was beyond comprehension that he, a sea captain from Boston, should be running for his life in the mountains of Jamaica, with some fabulous creatures called chasseurs hot on his trail. Not only on his trail, but on the trail of a delicate girl who should have been sipping tea in her father's plantation parlor, and two slaves who had turned out to be the best friends he had ever had and for whom he felt the warmest feelings of a friendship that would last for a lifetime, however long or short that lifetime might be.

Dicey had hiked her skirt up to her knees, knotting the remainder of the tablecloth around her waist to hold it in place. Everything else had had to be left behind, but the linen might be needed, for bandages if for nothing else.

The slave girl's dress was light and virtually weightless, while in contrast, Noelle's riding habit was heavy and weighed her down. Her boots chafed her feet; they had been designed for riding, not for walking, and the soles slipped on the rocks, and there were painful blisters on her heels. Her physical discomfort hindered her progress and left her gasping and panting for breath. She was slowing the others down, all because of what she was wearing.

She slipped again. Drat and darnation! Angrily, she regained her balance, and thinking of Ian she called out, "Dicey, wait! Help me out of this dratted thing! We'll never get anywhere as long as it's dragging me down at every step!"

Simon couldn't control the grin that twitched at his lips as she stepped free of the cumbersome garments. What a gamin she looked, clad only in her camisole and petticoat, her hair tangled around her face in a dark cloud, her face streaked with dirt.

Noelle glared at him. "If you think it's funny, you don't have to look at me! If you were a gentleman you wouldn't look at me anyway! I'd like to see you climb and keep up, dressed in that thing!"

Simon picked up her discarded garments and, emulating Dicey's example, he fastened them around his waist. All he said, mildly, was, "You might need these later . . ."

What a picture they must make, he thought, the four of them, toiling ever upward, exhausted, filthy, he with his ridiculous arsenal of weapons, Noelle in her camisole and petticoat, with riding boots incongruously completing her outfit, and Dicey with her skirts hiked to her knees and the tablecloth wrapped around her waist! If those chasseurs had any sense of humor at all, they'd laugh themselves into immobility when they came up with them, and be easy captives, taken while they were doubled over with mirth!

But no such thing would happen. From what the others had told him, the chasseurs were humorless as well as lacking any human emotion except the drive to do what they were paid to do.

How much farther could the girls go on, how much farther would their strength hold out? Simon worried about them, denying to himself that his own strength was ebbing, strength he had had little enough of in the first place. They were all exhausted, they were hungry, their bodies ached, his shoulder was a mass of searing pain that he had to grit his teeth against at every step.

Cuffie paused, pointing. "There," he said.

They looked where he pointed, and felt their hearts plunge into despair. Surely no human being could scale that cliff. But Cuffie was moving forward, his toes digging in with superhuman strength, reaching back to help Dicey with one hand wherever he could find a handhold with the other.

In turn, Dicey reached back to help Noelle, and Noelle, hanging on by sheer willpower and her splintered fingernails, reached back to steady Simon. Single file, a human chain of four people, they inched their way upward, inch by torturous inch, each step gained by an expenditure of human endurance that they would have thought impossible.

If one of them slipped and fell, it would be all over with them. Just as likely they would all go plummeting to their deaths in a futile attempt to arrest the fall of the one who had slipped. And if they didn't follow that one to death, they would lose all heart to go on.

Every breath, now, was searing agony as their lungs labored to draw in oxygen that was depleted faster than it could be replenished. Their muscles cried out in protest at the strain that was inflicted on them. It seemed as if their very tendons were being torn, that they were separating, to leave them crippled and helpless.

Noelle was blinded by the hair that blew into her eyes and by the perspiration that ran into them from her forehead. It seemed to her that they had been climbing for hours, that they had been climbing forever, that there had never been anything in the world but the side of this mountain. She reached ahead, groping for another handhold, and just as she found it, her foot in her unyielding boot slipped, and she felt herself begin to fall.

Directly behind her, Simon dug his own feet into their precarious holds, and reached out and grasped her around her waist. "Easy, don't struggle, find a foothold, find a handhold. You can do it."

He wasn't sure that she could. He was even less sure that he could hold her for even a few more seconds. He had caught her with the arm on the side of his wounded shoulder, and every grain of strength was draining out of it. The cords in his neck stood out in his effort to hold onto her, and his breath tore at his throat.

And then, like a miracle, Cuffie was there, one hand directing Noelle's foot to a hold, and then her hand to a hold, and most of her weight was taken from Simon's straining arm. "Up, up!" Cuffie implored. "It's only another few yards. Dicey is already there. Captain, hang on, I'll come back to help you as soon as I get the mistress up."

Miraculously, Noelle was up, Dicey was pulling her, and she sprawled in a heap on a narrow ledge. She lay there on her stomach, her hands clutching at the solid earth.

Dicey knelt beside her and wiped her forehead with a corner of her skirt. "You're safe," she said. "We're here."

They were all there, all four of them. But if they had managed to climb the cliff, the chasseurs would certainly be able to climb it. Their only hope was that the dogs would not be able to.

"Can't stay here," Cuffie urged. "Got to go on. But it'll be easier now."

"Just where the devil are you taking us?" Simon wanted to know, his voice a croak. He felt as if his throat were cracking, and every breath he took seared his lungs.

"Wish I knowed," Cuffie said. "But it's there. Had to climb the cliff first, and we climbed it, so we know we're on the right track. All we got to do is go on."

Wearily, feeling that the effort was beyond her, Noelle got to her feet. Scratched, cut, scraped, her petticoat and camisole in tatters, her hands and face and arms filthy, her hair a tangled mass around her shoulders, Simon's heart was torn as he looked at her. He wanted to take her into his arms and hold her close, to comfort and protect her. But there was no time for that. They had to go on.

Somewhere in the world, there were houses, there were soft, clean beds to rest in, there were long, cold drinks to ease their parched throats. Boston still existed, where there were no chasseurs to pursue them through treacherous mountains, where there was no beautiful, evil woman determined to destroy them.

Simon brought himself back to the present. There was no time for dreaming. As his head cleared as he gulped great lungfuls of air, he took stock of their situation.

The spears that had been made with such labor had been lost in the climb. Only the bow and the arrows, secured to his back, remained, and the knife that he had thrust into his belt.

They went on, moving as fast as their exhausted bodies would allow. Their way still led upward, zigzagging, making hairpin turns over terrain that was virtually impassable. They paused after scaling a particularly steep stretch, again gasping for breath. Simon and Noelle and Dicey sank to the ground immediately, but Cuffie turned to look back and down across the direction they had come. He stiffened, shading his eyes with his hand, and then he said, his voice choked, "Look there, Captain Spencer."

In the clear mountain air, they could see the cliff that had seemed so insurmountable while they had been scaling it. And, halfway up the cliff, they could see two figures, tiny in the distance but still clearly distinguishable. But what brought a chill to their hearts was the impossible fact that two of the huge dogs were also making the ascent. Scrambling, clawing, slipping back, still they gained ground as their masters moved behind them to steady them and boost them upward over spots where their claws could not find a purchase.

"I don't believe it!" Simon breathed. In spite of the peril the sight engendered, he couldn't keep his awe out of his voice. "I would have sworn that it was impossible!"

For the first time, Cuffie's face reflected despair.

"Ain't no use now. They're going to catch us. We

might as well save what strength we got left, only it won't do us no good, once those dogs jump us." His face was anguished as he looked at Dicey and his mistress. "I thought that coming this way we'd have a chance, but we ain't, not no more."

"Will the chasseurs send the dogs ranging ahead of them?" Simon's voice was sharp. They weren't caught yet, and while they were still uncaptured he refused to give up hope. There must be a way, there had to be! A terrified, exhausted slave might give up, but as long as he had strength in his body and the will to make his mind function, Simon would not.

It might be that they would have to go down fighting. If that happened, he would give as good an account of himself as possible, and he knew that Cuffie would do the same. Thank God for Cuffie! Without him and his loyalty and his strength, there would have been no chance at all.

He considered the bow he was carrying, but discarded the idea of using it except as a last resort. He doubted that one of the makeshift arrows would kill a man, and it had been years since he had used a bow, let alone one as clumsy and unreliable as this. Maybe, when they were sure of being overtaken, he would be able to put one of their pursuers out of action, but he wouldn't have time to try for the second before the dogs were upon them.

His eyes searched the terrain immediately around them, his mind working with the keenness and speed of desperation. There, only a few feet from where they were looking down, might be the place. Could he take advantage of the overhang that dropped off steeply to plunge hundreds of feet in a sheer drop? Just opposite it there was a ledge, difficult to jump to, but it might be possible for an agile man.

A pitfall, he thought. As insane as the idea seemed, it also seemed to be their only chance.

The climbing figures were hidden from them now, but Simon knew that they would be coming on. There was no way the chasseurs were going to fail. If the girls had been able to make it, they would make it, and even get their dogs up the cliff.

But there was still a little time, no matter how fast the dogs would be able to cover the intervening distance.

"Cuffie, I want branches, a lot of them, to extend that overhang. We'll have to anchor them any way we can, they don't want to be anchored firmly, but they must stay in place for as long as necessary. Noelle, Dicey, help Cuffie gather the branches, and then go on ahead of us until you can find a place to keep well out of sight. After we have the platform made, I'm going to jump across to that ledge and stay in plain sight."

Cuffie understood, and there was a flash of hope in his eyes. "Know what you got in mind. Them dogs hit that platform, they's going to drop straight down, and then there'll only be the men."

"Dogs are intelligent animals. They may not be fooled by the trick," Simon warned him.

"If they ain't, then we ain't lost nothing by trying," Cuffie said.

No man, unless he were blind, would have set one foot on the flimsy network of branches that Simon and Cuffie constructed at full speed. But dogs cannot see as well as men, Simon remembered one of his uncles, who raised hunting dogs, telling him. They relied on their sense of smell, and seeing movement. These dogs would be in hot pursuit, and Simon would be on the other side, waving his arms to make sure that they saw him. With any luck at all, he would be the one they would go for, if Cuffie kept himself concealed.

"That will have to do. Get back with the girls, Cuffie. I'm going to jump now," Simon said. His stomach turned over when he looked down and he felt an attack of vertigo.

And then Cuffie pushed him out of the way, and leapt, leaving Simon with his mouth hanging open. There was no way to call him back, he wouldn't come. Cuffie had made the leap because he knew that he was better able to do it, as weakened as Simon was. And the return leap, if the ploy worked, would be even more dangerous. From this side, there was room to get a few feet of space to make a running jump, but on the other there was a sheer wall directly at the jumper's back. The leap would have to be made from a standing position, a feat that would take all of the most agile man's powers.

Simon raised his hand in a silent salute as Cuffie landed on the other side and turned to look back at him. Cuffie had given them their best chance, and now it was up to Simon to take the fullest possible advantage of it.

He chose his spot carefully, well away from where Noelle and Dicey were hiding. He would be concealed from the chasseurs until they were almost upon them. He would have just time to try to take one of them out with the bow and arrow, and if he succeeded, there would be only hand to hand combat, with knives, between himself and the one that was left. Calculating his chances against a chasseur with a knife, Simon sent up a silent prayer that Cuffie would be able to make the return leap. There were times when a man had to admit that he needed a little help.

If he lost his life, but either killed or put the second chasseur out of action, then Noelle and Dicey and Cuffie would have to try to make their way alone out of the mountains. He refused to let himself think about what their chances would be. They'd have to do it, if they were to survive.

As short as time was, he left his hiding place and went to Noelle. Putting his hands on her shoulders, he looked deep into her eyes.

"Noelle, if by some chance I don't make it and you do, and you can get to Kingston, go to the *Maid of Boston* and tell Aaron Godbehere, my first mate, what has happened. Stay on the ship, don't leave it unless he and other armed members of the crew are with you. If you fail to convince the authorities of the truth of what you tell them, tell Aaron that my orders are for him to take an armed group of our crew to Maynard Penn and remove your father by force, and sail for America with both of you. My family will welcome you and care for you, and my father is not without influence. He will find a means of getting to the truth, and bringing Vanessa to justice.''

Noelle's face paled, but she nodded her head. If Simon were to die today, and she were to live, her first duty would be to her father. She must get him to safety before she could indulge herself in the grief that would never leave her for as long as she lived.

"Take Dicey and Cuffie with you. They must not be left behind,'' Simon said. "You can set them free in America, although I am sure that neither of them will ever leave you.''

Noelle nodded again. Simon's arms went around her and held her close, so close that he could feel every curve of her body through her camisole and petticoat. Banked fires raged up in him, and he could have wept at all he had lost when he had been foolish enough to let this girl get away from him. He could feel her trembling against him as her arms fastened themselves around his neck. Fool, fool, and now it was too late, it might always be too late, he might never have the chance to possess her as he longed to possess her, to make her his wife, to hold her and love her with all the passion that his body and his heart possessed!

"You told me you loved me, one night while you were holding me to keep me warm. You thought that I was sleeping, but I heard you. Say it again, Noelle. Say my name the way you said it then!''

"Simon, I love you,'' she said.

His head came down, and he kissed her, holding her cruelly fast, his mouth hard and demanding, kissing her as he had wanted to kiss her ever since this mad adventure had begun.

When he let her go at last, her face was still pale, but two flags of color flamed in her cheeks, and her eyes were swimming with tears.

There was no more time. He had to regain his place of concealment. Even then, he risked raising his head so that he could watch the track to where the ridiculously inadequate deadfall waited, with Cuffie waiting on the other side of the chasm.

The dogs came fast, eerily silent, simply running with deadly purpose. Simon's breath stilled in his throat as they ran toward the deadfall, attracted by the waving of Cuffie's arms and the hoarse shout he sent echoing across to reach their ears.

For one agonizing moment, Simon was afraid that he and Cuffie had done their work too well, that the dogs' very momentum would carry them across. But then the structure collapsed.

For the rest of his life, Simon would hear the echo of the dogs' screams as they plunged to their deaths on the rocks below. Shuddering, sick, he forced himself back to full alertness.

On the other side of the chasm, Cuffie gathered himself to make the return leap. For a fraction of a second that seemed to be in slow motion, his body was suspended in the air, and then he was across. Simon stifled the cry of triumph that rose in his throat.

But something was wrong. Cuffie staggered and went down on one knee, and when he rose again and tried to walk his leg went out from under him. He had injured it when he had landed, and there was no time to go to his aid. The chasseurs were in sight, running as though they had not made a climb that would exhaust any ordinary man, running as though all the additional terrain they had covered to come up with their quarry had been no more than a short sprint.

His forehead covered with sweat, his muscles almost in spasm from the strain of his suspense, Simon nocked the one arrow he would have time to use, and drew back the bowstring.

The arrow found its mark, the chasseur who was in the lead, but there was no force behind it, the drawstring bowstring had not the elasticity and strength to make it effective. It did no more than draw a little blood as it glanced off the chasseur's open-shirted chest before it fell to the ground. The chasseur stopped only for an instant to look at it with uncomprehending eyes and then to smile a smile of inner amusement as he kicked it aside.

Simon leapt to meet the second chasseur, Elisha's knife in his hand. It was much larger than the knife the chasseur held, but the chasseur was an experienced knife fighter, and Simon was not. Simon took the only chance he would have, knowing he could not last for long against such an adversary. Gripping the heavy hilt of his knife with both hands, he brought it down with all the strength he possessed on the chasseur's darting wrist.

It took the chasseur unaware. His smaller knife dropped from a hand that had gone numb to his elbow, and Simon had Elisha's knife at his throat, commanding him to surrender, wondering, incongruously, if the man understood English. Not that it mattered. The chasseur would grasp the meaning of his words, the knife made the meaning clear.

His victory was short-lived. The second chasseur was almost upon him, and Cuffie, running as fast as he could with a leg that kept buckling under him, could not possibly reach him in time. It was possible that Cuffie would be able to disable or kill the man once he reached them, but by that time Simon might well be dead, and Cuffie would be left to face the other, uninjured man alone. Still Simon stayed his hand, unable to bring himself to kill the one he had in his power until he was certain that killing him would be the only way to save both himself and Cuffie.

The figure came out of nowhere, short and stocky, immensely powerful. It landed on the second chasseur's back, hands with incredible strength closed around his throat. And now another figure was there, and another.

Uncomprehending, Simon could do nothing but stare. And as comprehension flooded over him, he lost his last shred of hope.

These men were Maroons, and while it was almost

certain that they would kill both of the chasseurs, whom
they had reason to hate with a hatred beyond the understanding of any man who had never been hunted and
dragged back to a life of captivity, it was equally certain
that they would also kill Simon. They would not leave a
white man alive to tell of what they had done.

Chapter Twelve

"DON'T KILL 'EM! HANG ONTO 'EM, DON'T LET 'EM GET away, but don't you go akilling 'em! We're going to need 'em!"

The stocky man gave Cuffie a withering look, and his voice was guttural, emanating from deep within his powerful chest.

"You don't give us no orders, *slave!* Won't kill you if you join us. Won't kill the white man or the white woman, don't want no militia to come hunting us. Won't kill the black girl nohow. She's mine."

Cuffie's face hardened. "No. Dicey's my woman. And I ain't going to join you, I got to stay with my mistress. And we got to take these chasseurs back with us, 'cause we got to make 'em tell how they was sent to hunt us down and kill us."

"Not to kill you." The chasseur who was within a

hair's-breadth of death at the hands of the man who held him down, his hands still on his throat, spoke calmly. "Only to find you and bring you back. We were not instructed to kill, and we would not, in any case."

"Kill us yourselves, or turn us over to Mistress Vanessa and that Chloe to be killed, what's the difference?" Cuffie demanded.

"We know nothing of that. We were told that you were fugitives, and that we were to take you. You certainly are fugitives, or you would not have made such an effort to escape us."

The stocky man, who was patently the leader of this small group of Maroons, spat full in the chasseur's face. "Shut up. Nobody told you you can talk." His eyes returned to Cuffie. "Why this Mistress Vanessa want to kill you, slave? And kill the white ones?"

A horrified witness to the scene that had just taken place, but too far away to hear what was being said, Noelle ran to join them, with Dicey outstripping her because she could not run as fast in her boots as the other girl. Noelle threw herself into Simon's arms, with Dicey already standing beside Cuffie, her face filled with apprehension.

"Mistress Vanessa, there at Maynard Penn, she killed her brother, this white mistress's brother. She had Chloe do it for her. And we knows about it, and so she has to kill us too."

The stocky man's eyes narrowed as he continued to study Cuffie's face. "Maynard Penn," he said. "We done heard stories 'bout Chloe. Stories that slaves have died when she put curses on 'em. That true?"

"That's true," Cuffie said. "And she killed Hector, Chloe did, 'cause he and Elisha didn't kill Captain Spencer and Mistress Noelle here in the mountains like they was told to. I seed Chloe kill Hector. She killed him with his own knife, and she buried him, but the other mistress stood and watched her, she's the one told her to do it."

"Elisha is the one we found and buried?"

"He's the one. Captain Spencer had to kill him, to save his life and these others. But Hector got away, and when he come back and told what happened, Mistress Vanessa said kill him, and Chloe did." Cuffie tried to face the other man down. "You got our mules. That had ought to be enough for you."

"The mules were there for the taking. We take what we find."

Simon finally found his voice, after a few moments of conviction that this entire scene was so unreal that he must be imagining it in some delirium.

"You're welcome to the mules. All we want in return is freedom to get down out of the mountains. We've never done you any harm. Mistress Noelle's father was always a kind master to his slaves, but now he too is in danger from his other daughter. It is essential that we get back, in order to save his life."

"Maybe Master Maynard kind, but what that matter to us?"

"He has the welfare of all of your people at heart. Before he was stricken down by his daughter Vanessa and the woman Chloe, he was working to make sure that no black person would suffer when the emancipation comes."

"And it's coming?"

"Yes, it is coming. There is no doubt about that. You will be free to go on living here in the Blue Mountains if that is what you wish, and no man can come hunting you. Or you will be able to come out of the mountains and live wherever you choose."

"He speaks the truth," Noelle said. "My father is a good man, a compassionate man. No slave we ever owned was ever abused before he was stricken down. But if we don't get back, if we can't find a way to save him, he will die, and there will be one less white man working in your behalf."

"Still don't see no reason we shouldn't kill these chasseurs. If they say they was only going to take you back, they ain't going to be no help to you."

"Our story is true," the second chasseur said. He still showed no trace of fear. If he and his companion were going to die here, it was the will of God. They would die with honor, as they had lived.

Cuffie's eyes were filled with a sudden hope. At least these Maroons were listening to them, and they seemed impressed by Simon's and Noelle's statements that it would serve the interests of all the blacks on the island if Daniel Maynard could be rescued.

"You could come with us. There's enough of you in these mountains to storm the plantation house, no matter how Chloe sics the slaves on us. They're scairt of her, but they couldn't fight all of you, they wouldn't even try."

Noelle's breath caught in her throat, and she couldn't breathe. If the Maroons would help, their chances of success would be more than doubled. Could this nightmare really be coming to an end, would she soon have her father safe, where he could recover his health, would both she and her father soon be free of the threat of death?

"No." The word was definite. "We got no part in white folks' quarrels. We're free now, free as we'll ever be, ain't nothing in it for us if we helped you. And if we got cotched, then we wouldn't be free no more."

The disappointment he felt at the Maroons' refusal to help them hit Simon almost as hard as it did Noelle, whose shoulders sagged as she drew in a ragged breath that was close to tears. But he refused to lose all hope. They were still alive. The chasseurs had not been successful in capturing them and returning them to Vanessa's mercies, and apparently the Maroons weren't going to kill them, even if they refused to help them.

"But you will let us go? And the chasseurs, as our prisoners?"

"Tell you what." The leader crossed his arms, his jaw thrust out. "We got your mules, and we keep 'em. Don' want to kill you an' have these mountains crawling with militia. Would have liked to keep the girl . . ." his eyes flicked briefly at Dicey, who stood straight and proud under his glance and glared at him ". . . but if she's this man's woman, won't make her stay. Wouldn't be able to trust her, might wake up some night with a knife in my back.''

"You'd better believe it!" Dicey said, heedless of the danger of talking back to this man who now held them in his power. Cuffie squeezed her arm to caution her, but she would not be silenced. "Maybe not in your back, neither. Maybe I'd get you face to face!''

The Maroon's eyes left her and rested on Cuffie. He was grinning. "If I was you, I'd be careful not to make that one mad at me. This is what we will do, and no more. You'll have to rest for a spell, not neither of you men fit to get down the mountains now. But once you can make it on your own feet, without having to be toted, we'll show you the quickest way down and take you as far as it'll be safe for us. Ain't made up my mind about the chasseurs yet. We'll make camp here. We got us a boar a while back, reckon you're hungry, know I am.''

So they would get down out of the mountains, but the obstacles they would still face were enough to make Simon quail. Storming Maynard Penn, just the four of them, and two of them mere slips of girls, was out of the question. Getting inside by stealth and getting Daniel out the same way was just as impossible.

But there had to be a way, and he'd find it. Looking at Noelle, so exhausted, so frightened, so scratched and bruised and bedraggled in her petticoat and camisole after an ordeal that was more than any girl should have been forced to endure, he knew that he had to find a way, or he would never be able to live with himself no matter how safe and free he was, even on the high seas or at home in Boston.

Right at the moment, his strength had come to an end. It was luxury to be able to sit down and know that he wouldn't have to get up again in a moment and start climbing, running for his life. It was luxury to see other men start a fire, and butcher out the old boar they had killed, and set pieces of it to roasting, the aroma making his mouth water. He smiled when one of the other

Maroons told the girls where there was a stream close by, so that they could wash.

The girls came back looking a good deal better than they had such a short time before. Dicey knelt and wrapped a strip of the linen around Cuffie's ankle, taking care to strap it tight but not tight enough to cut off his circulation.

"That feels good," Cuffie said. He reached for Dicey's hand.

Simon held out his hand to Noelle, and she came to him. He took her hand and pulled her down beside him, and still held it. He only wished that he would never have to let it go.

Two days later, in Kingston, Aaron Godbehere sat in Ian Macintyre's livingroom-cum-bedroom-cum-kitchen, his callused hand holding the tot of rum that Ian had pressed on him in the name of hospitality. His sailor's eye for neatness approved the order that Ian had achieved even in such cramped quarters, but he was not here to judge the man's housekeeping, but on a much more serious matter.

"It isn't like the cap'n," Aaron said. "I expected him to come in from that plantation where he's visiting, and see for himself the extent of the fire damage and how the repairs are coming along, before this. Now we're ship-shape to sail any time, and he must know it, and seeing that we're already so far behind schedule, he should have shown up.

"So I sent our second mate to Maynard Penn to tell him the repairs have been completed and we can sail as soon as he puts in an appearance. But Jake came back with word that the captain wasn't there, he was off somewhere gallivanting around with the mistress's sister. Now that might be true, but it doesn't set well with me. If the cap'n had been off gallivanting anywhere, it would have been here to Kingston, where he could see how near we're ready to sail."

Ian's eyes were dark with speculation. He didn't like it. He was glad that the first mate, knowing of his friendship with Simon, had come to him. Like the first mate, this whole thing didn't set well with Ian, either.

"I'm sure that Simon can take care of himself, but all the same, it's strange," Ian said. "I've made the journey to Maynard Penn twice, myself, and Simon wasn't there at either time. I believe I will make a third visit tomorrow, and this time I intend to come back with more than evasions as to his whereabouts."

"This Mistress Vanessa, there's no way I can come up with any idea that she might be holding something back," Aaron said. "Everybody on the island holds her in the highest regard." The rum slid down his throat with a satisfying bite. Ordinarily he wasn't a drinking man, but his concern about Simon made the potion welcome. "A beautiful woman, she is. I never thought to see a woman that beautiful, when the cap'n brought her to see the ship."

"She's beautiful, I agree. And reputed to be no less than a living saint," Ian conceded. "Nevertheless, we haven't been able to locate Simon. Yes, I will definitely call at Maynard Penn tomorrow, and if Simon is there I'll impress on him that the ship is ready to sail and bring him back with me. If he isn't there, this time I'm damned well going to find out where he is."

Aaron's chin squared, a sure sign to all of the *Maid of Boston*'s crew that he was not to be trifled with. "If he isn't there, and there isn't any answer as to where he is that sets well with me, I'm going to the authorities. An American citizen can't just flat up and disappear on an island this size. It ain't reasonable."

"I don't think it is, either. I think it is definitely time that we had some answers."

Aaron declined a second drink. With Simon away, he was in command of the ship, and his hard and fast rule about not becoming incapacitated by alcohol while on duty held as true for himself as it did for any member of the crew. "I'll be waiting to hear from you, then. God willing, the cap'n will be at the plantation this time."

Everything seemed to be normal when Ian approached

Maynard Penn on the following day. The slaves were working in the fields under a sky so blue that it hurt his eyes to look directly at it, the sun was hot but not unbearable, birdsong filled the air and the myriad butterflies of the island wafted on ethereal wings among vines and flowers.

The air in the house, when he was admitted, was spicy with the orange scent of freshly polished floors. Oranges, such a luxury in Scotland, were used here for that utilitarian purpose, their cut halves rubbed on the intricate parquet and then polished by the housegirls with cloths held between their toes.

No speck of dust marred the surfaces of the furniture, vases filled with flowers lent exotic splashes of color wherever he looked. Noelle had lived all of her life amid this luxury, luxury such as Ian would not be able to provide for her for years, if he would ever be able to provide it at all. His own needs were simple, he cared nothing for the trappings of wealth for himself, but there was no way he could ask Noelle to leave surroundings like this to share a spartan life with him.

Vanessa was a vision in palest green, her golden hair beautifully dressed, with tendrils of curls framing her face in a manner calculated to enslave every man upon whom she smiled.

She smiled at Ian now, holding out her hand, a hand so soft and white that he was almost afraid to take it for fear of crushing it. Noelle's hands were as unmarked by menial work as her sister's, but they were not as fragile. Small and square, they were much more to Ian's liking. Vanessa seemed to him to be not quite real, but Noelle was warm flesh and blood, the flesh and blood that could stir his heart until he knew that she was the only girl he would ever want.

"Mr. Macintyre! There, I've done it again! Doctor Macintyre, what a delightful surprise!"

Ian was amused. He had a very good idea that Vanessa's slip was caused by her total disregard for him, penniless and of no social importance as he was.

"I had not thought to see you so soon after your last visit, but you are more than welcome. It's lonesome, with my sister and Captain Spencer away visiting friends on another plantation."

So they were not here again today. Odder and odder, Ian thought. Three times in a row, they had not been here, and they hadn't been here yesterday either, when Aaron Godbehere had sent his second mate with a message for Simon.

"I'm sorry to have missed them, but I would have made the journey in any case. What a beautiful place you have here! It draws me back time and again, just to admire it." And its mistress, his tone implied. Blatant flattery, and he did not mean a word of it, but now that he was here he was determined to make one more bid to see Daniel Maynard. "And it's a beautiful day, I have seldom seen one more beautiful. On such a day as this, your father must be feeling well enough so that I could pay him my compliments."

Vanessa's expression gave no hint of her perturbation. How persistent this Scotsman was! She had already fended him off twice, to do so a third time might rouse his suspicions, something that she could not risk. After all, what could he detect in the moment or two she would allow him, with her father so heavily drugged that he could speak no more than a word or two at a time?

"I'm sure that he is," she said. "I'll go and prepare him, and come back for you, but you must remember that you can only stay with him for a few moments."

"Of course." Ian inclined his head.

Chloe looked up from her place beside Daniel's bed when her mistress entered the room. "That man is here again!" Vanessa said. "And this time I can't put him off, he's determined to see my father. Are you certain that his dose this morning has made him sufficiently befuddled?"

"Ain't I always sure?" Chloe rose and went to the windows, adjusting the slats so that the room was plunged into almost total darkness. "He won't be saying anything that makes sense, and you tell him that the room has to be kept dark because the light hurts his eyes. We'll be shut of him in no time, and this time he ought to be satisfied."

Even with the room as dark as it was, Ian was shocked by the condition of the man who lay on the bed with his head propped up on a pillow. Daniel seemed already to be a corpse, and he a man who should have been in his prime.

"Mr. Maynard? I'm Ian Macintyre. I've called before, but you were too ill to see me."

The hand that lay skeletonlike on the sheet twitched, and Daniel's eyebrows drew together. "Macintyre? I don't believe . . ."

"No, sir, we have never met before today. I'm sorry that you aren't well. Everyone on the island speaks well of you, and we all hope that you will recover your strength soon."

"Ill," Daniel said. His hand twitched again. "Is Noelle here? I can't see . . ."

Vanessa moved to place herself between the sick man and Ian. Her fingers stroked her father's forehead, and her face in the gloom was filled with tenderness and pity.

"I'll send her to you immediately she returns, Father. She's gone out with Captain Spencer, don't you remember?"

"Spencer." Daniel was making a tremendous effort to think, to remember. "A sea captain. He visited me? I'm not certain. So weak . . ."

Vanessa cast a stricken glance at Ian. "I'm sorry, but my father is already tired. Seeing visitors is a strain on him, but I know that he's glad that you stopped in to see him."

Almost before he had entered the room, Ian was eased out again, with Vanessa's hand on his arm.

"If only he would take a turn for the better!" Vanessa said. "Doctor Eastlake still holds out hope, but it's been so long, and I'm beginning to fear that he will never recover." Her lips trembled, tears glistened in her eyes, enough to make any man want to protect and comfort her, to shield her from any more grief and care.

If only he had had a chance to make a thorough

examination! The suspicions Noelle had voiced to him were like warning flags in his mind. It was possible that this was a natural illness, but without an examination there was no way Ian could be sure. Surely Daniel's voice had been slurred, even beyond a natural slurring from weakness? Slurred as though he had been dosed with something. If Ian had been the attending physician, he would not have allowed opiates of any kind. Opiates were debilitating, they not only fogged the mind but weakened the body. Nature itself was the best healer, as long as nothing was done to interfere with it. Specific illnesses responded to certain drugs, but an illness supposedly brought on by grief alone should have healed itself long before now.

Vanessa's annoyance because Ian had insisted on seeing her father was gone. It was probably to her advantage that Ian Macintyre, a doctor, had seen how weak Daniel was, how close already to death. With him to testify to that, his actual death could cause no least flutter of suspicion, when news of Noelle's having been slain by Maroons reached him. Still, Vanessa wished that this whole nerve-destroying period of waiting was over. It was taking its toll on her; if the chasseurs did not return soon, with Noelle and Simon and Dicey in tow, she would have to ask Chloe for something to calm her nerves.

Ian was speaking to her. "Do you know where Simon and your sister went, Miss Maynard? If they're visiting some place not too far out of my way I might try to catch them there."

A little frown puckered Vanessa's forehead, making her look distracted and apologetic, as though she were doing her best to remember.

"I'm sorry. I'm sure they told me before they left, but some domestic snag came up and I wasn't giving them my full attention. Was it the Cartwrights? Or it could have been the Carlysles? What a bother! They live in opposite directions, I'm afraid, and for the life of me I can't remember which family it was."

"Don't distress yourself," Ian told her. "It doesn't

matter. Actually, I should be getting back to Kingston, and I shouldn't spare the time in any case. I'm certain to see Simon before he sails, he wouldn't leave without saying good-bye to me, and your sister will still be here at Maynard Penn in case I might be welcome to visit her.''

So it was as Vanessa had suspected, this upstart young doctor was smitten with Noelle. Vanessa controlled her smile of derision as she thought how futile his interest in her sister was fated to be. It had turned out to be a good thing after all that she had had to push her plans ahead and get rid of Noelle now, before their father died. If Noelle had been given time to return Ian's affections, she might have told him more than Vanessa would like for him to know. Now there was no chance that his suspicions would be aroused. Noelle would be dead, and Ian would be out of the picture.

"Of course you will be welcome, Doctor Macintyre! Noelle will be lonesome once the captain has sailed, your company will be a distraction for her, and you know that I will be happy to see you, as well.''

Ian accepted only a cup of coffee before he took his leave, asking no more about where Simon and Noelle might be visiting. But once out of sight of Maynard Penn, he stopped the first traveler he encountered, a black man dressed in the colorful pink and white trousers of the island, with a yellow shirt and his head shaded by an enormous straw hat as he led a donkey along, with a black girl as colorfully dressed perched sideways on the animal's back.

"Do you know where Cartwright Penn is? Which direction?'' Ian asked.

Both smiles were dazzling white in the dark faces, both faces beamed at the privilege of being able to help. "Certainly, suh. It's that way, take the first branch to your left and you cannot miss it. Have a pleasant journey, suh.''

"And a pleasant journey to you.'' Ian extracted a coin from his pocket and handed it to the man, not tossing it as other white men would, to see the black scramble for it, but according him the dignity of being paid for a service, one man to another. "Thank you for your help."

"Thank you, suh." The grin widened, and as Ian touched his heel to Explorer's side, he saw the girl reach out her hand and the man place the coin in it, his smile indulgent.

In another moment Ian had forgotten them both. He had only one thing in mind, and that was to track down Simon and Noelle. Enough was enough. It was time that he knew where they were; Aaron Godbehere was waiting in Kingston for news of them and Ian had no intention going back to town as ignorant as he had left.

The distance to Cartwright Penn was farther than he had supposed, but his welcome when he arrived there could not have been more warm. His host and hostess insisted that he take advantage of a room where he could wash the dust of the road from his hands and face, they pressed refreshments on him, and invited him to stay for the evening meal, indeed to stay for the night as the afternoon was already growing late. But Simon and Noelle were not there, nor had the Cartwrights seen them.

"I must have got the names twisted in my mind," Ian apologized. "I wasn't sure whether it was you or the Carlysles they were visiting."

"They wouldn't be at Carlysle Penn," Mr. Cartwright told him, his face filled with consternation. "The Carlysles are not at home, they have been in Spanish Town for this past week."

Odder and odder, Ian thought, and his sense of uneasiness grew. Aaron Godbehere was right. It didn't set well.

It was far too late at night to see Aaron when Ian got back to Kingston, but he would see him the first thing in the morning.

At Maynard Penn, Miranda worked among the rows of cane, her eyes hot and hard. This morning they had taken her father away. Her father was old, and he was sick, and his days of useful work were over.

They had carried him away on a litter, and Miranda

193

knew where they had taken him. They had taken him to a deep gorge to be thrown down upon the rocks, either to die from the fall or to die slowly and in agony from his injuries, alone and with no one to hear his feeble cries for help.

This had always been the custom among certain planters of Jamaica. When a man could no longer work, he must be disposed of. A prosperous plantation had no room for idle slaves. But it had never been done at Maynard Penn until the master had been stricken down, Daniel Maynard abhorred the practice, and had spoken against it, trying to have laws enacted to forbid it. At Maynard Penn, a slave was allowed to die with dignity, among his loved ones, his passing made as comfortable as it was possible to make it.

But since the evil mistress had taken over the running of the plantation, two slaves before Miranda's father had been disposed of in this manner. It was Chloe who gave the orders, and the slaves delegated to carry them out did not dare to disobey her. And now it was Miranda's father who had fallen ill, worn out by his years of labor. Still he needn't have died. Under the master's rule, he would have been allowed to rest and recover. Under Vanessa's rule, no such rest was allowed.

Miranda had seen the two strong slaves, tears running down their faces, carry her father away. And she had seen them carry the litter back, along with the clothing that her father had worn. The clothing was still useful, another slave could wear it.

Hatred battled with grief in Miranda's heart. She had loved her father, he had been a good man. He had never lifted his hand to her, or to her mother before she had died. Miranda's only consolation had been that her father had lived to see his granddaughter born, and to know that the child would not grow up a slave. Before the infant was old enough to understand, slavery in Jamaica would be a thing of the past.

But her father was dead, murdered in cold blood, brutally, and Miranda wanted to take the whole world in her own hands and shake it until all the evil people in it plummeted into the fires of hell.

Not only was her father dead by now, or she fervently hoped that he was dead, and not still suffering, but Elisha had not come back from the mountains where he had gone to guide and protect the good mistress and Captain Spencer. None of them had come back, and Miranda's heart was filled with dread. Something had happened, she was sure of it. If the Maroons had set upon the small party, Elisha would have fought to protect them, and he would have been killed too, just like the young mistress, the good mistress, and Captain Spencer.

Miranda worked automatically. Not to do your work well, these days, meant feeling the lash on your back. It didn't matter if the black overseers wept when they wielded it, and begged for forgiveness, they had to do it, or Chloe would put a curse on them.

Miranda did not weep as she worked. She was beyond weeping. But the fires of hatred raged in her, and she yearned for revenge. Revenge against the evil mistress, and most of all, revenge against Chloe, because without Chloe even the evil that possessed the evil mistress would be powerless.

Elisha, she thought, where are you? But in her heart she was convinced that she would never see him again.

Chapter Thirteen

THE MAROONS WERE IN POSSESSION NOT ONLY OF THE three mules that they had stolen from the fugitives, but of horses that they had taken on their lightning raids on outlying plantations. Cuffie was allowed to ride one of the mules because his ankle was twisted, Noelle and Dicey were allowed to ride double on the second, and Simon was allowed the use of the third because of his weakness from his wound. The chasseurs were forced to walk, leading the pack mule.

The offer of the mules was not tendered out of generosity, but rather to expedite their traveling. Two girls and two men who were in less than perfect physical condition would slow the party down, and the leader was anxious to find a better base for a hunting camp.

Simon's chagrin when he learned that the Maroons had reached the spot where they had come to their rescue by using another, much less precipitous route, made him grit

196

his teeth. But Cuffie had chosen the only way he had known, and they had hoped that the chasseurs' dogs would not be able to scale the cliff to run them down all the sooner. If that had turned out to be true, they would still have had a long lead on the chasseurs, and a better chance of escaping them. As it had happened, it had turned out for the best. It was the derision of the Maroon leader that was hard to bear.

"I 'spect Cuffie didn't know no better, being nothing but a slave. We know that the chasseurs was after you, and we knowed that they'd get them dogs up that cliff. Wasn't going to mix in it at all, only wanted to watch and see what happened. But that was smart, the way you built that trap and made them dogs kill theirselves. Thought that if you was that smart, mebby we should give you a hand and get ourselves a couple of chasseurs at the same time. And another strong man, and a girl. Now it looks like we went to all that work for nothing. Ought to leave you where you are and not take you with us at all."

"Won't hurt you none to take us," Cuffie pointed out. "We won't be stayin' with you for long."

"Won't do us no good, neither. Mebby we should have let them chasseurs take you. Only then we wouldn't have got to kill 'em. Killing us a couple of chasseurs would make helping you worth the trouble."

"You gave your word that you wouldn't kill them!" Simon pointed out angrily.

"White men all the time lie. Why shouldn't I lie?" The thickset leader glared at Simon, his expression ferocious.

"But they weren't after you, they were after us! You have no reason to kill them!" Simon shuddered at the thought of the Spaniards being massacred in front of Noelle and Dicey. Noelle had already been through so much, seeing these men slaughtered might cause her to have a complete collapse, to say nothing of the fact that Simon was against the taking of human life unless it was essential as a matter of self-defense.

"We'll do what we want, not what you want. You ain't a boss-man here, white man! Now you shut your mouth,

I'm tired of listening to you. And you don't open your mouth, neither." This remark was directed at Cuffie, with a scowl calculated to make Cuffie obey.

The frustration of this entire adventure was getting to Simon. While it was true that they were still alive and no longer in danger from the chasseurs, who wisely kept out of the argument, they were no better off than before regarding getting down out of the mountains and rescuing Daniel Maynard. They were completely at the mercy of this man who refused to tell them his name. The man might let them go, as he had given them to understand he would directly after their rescue from the chasseurs, but he might change his mind at any moment.

And so, as much as it galled him, Simon kept his mouth shut, as the chasseurs had had the sense to do from the start. Angering this Maroon could only worsen their situation and make it that much more dangerous.

The Maroons had their own towns, two of them, in the mountains, but these men showed no inclination to take them to either of them. The leader was a loner, wanting only his own small band of followers among whom he was the absolute monarch. If they had been taken to one of the towns, it might have been possible to persuade some man to make his way down to Kingston and to the *Maid of Boston*, where a message from Simon would bring Aaron Godbehere and his own party of mounted and armed men to get them out of these mountains and go with them to make an assault against Maynard Penn. But no promise of reward would stir this Maroon leader to order one of his men to carry a message.

"Look, white man. You got trouble, that's your problem, ain't none of ours. We feed you, we let you rest, and that's all we do. Don't go pushing your luck."

They had slept the first night at the spot where the Maroons had rescued them, and ridden all of today, with the chasseurs trotting on foot without complaint and without giving any indication that they could not walk for the rest of their lives without tiring. Simon was forced into granting them a grudging admiration. Hunters of men that they were, they were still possessed of a strength and courage that commanded respect.

Now, late in the afternoon, they had come to a spot almost as idyllically beautiful as the place where Simon and Noelle had gone for what should have been nothing more than an enjoyable picnic, and the Maroon leader said that they would camp here for several days. It was difficult for Simon to judge whether they had climbed higher into the mountains, or gone a little lower, because the way had been both up and down, with no discernible track or trail.

Noelle had suffered the daylong ride with remarkable endurance, never uttering a word of complaint. Her courage amazed Simon. He knew that she must be terrified, but she gave no outward indication of it. Only the paleness of her face and the way she pressed her lips together to keep them from trembling betrayed her. She was as aware of the precariousness of their situation as Simon was.

There was nothing to stop the Maroon leader from changing his mind, as he had taunted them that he might, and kill not only the chasseurs but Simon and Cuffie as well. And then he would more than likely kill Noelle, so as not to take any chance of being discovered with her as his prisoner, but before he killed her, he would be free to use her in any way he chose.

Noelle had heard enough stories of the atrocities perpetrated against the owners of plantations where the slaves had rebelled, as well as what had been done by marauding Maroons, to have an all too clear picture of what might be in store for her.

Neither her fears nor Simon's were alleviated when the first thing the Maroons did when they chose the campsite was to truss up the chasseurs so that there would be no possibility that they could escape. Simon fully expected that he and Cuffie would be next, and possibly even the girls, but no such thing happened. If the chasseurs managed to escape, they would have a good chance of getting away, as mountain-wise and strong and tireless as they were, but there was no way that the four fugitives, two of them tender girls and the other two men who were incapacitated by injuries, could elude their captors and get very far before they were caught and dragged back. Being left with freedom of movement was not a sign of respect or compassion, but of contempt.

As on the night before, a small fire was built, so that chunks of the wild boar could be roasted over it. The Maroons had flint and steel, bringing back to mind the difficulty that Simon had had in his attempts to kindle a fire without them. Simon and Cuffie, and Noelle and Dicey, were given their share of the meat, but as on the night before the chasseurs were given nothing.

The two Spaniards did not complain, or even look with hungry eyes at the meat that the others were consuming. Even though they ordinarily refused meat in any form, Simon knew that by now their hunger must be a living, tearing agony.

This was beyond humanity! Simon could not and would not stand for it. He rose and went to where the chasseurs were trussed up in sitting positions against the trunks of small trees, and began to feed them.

"You give them what you got, you don't get no more." The Maroon leader warned him.

"Then I'll do without. I ate last night, and they did not." Simon said curtly. Only a short while ago he had been intent on killing both of these men if he could, and now he was giving them his food. The irony of the situation was not lost on him, but he could not have acted in any other way.

Noelle came to kneel beside him, also sharing her food. Dicey and Cuffie followed. The Maroons watched impassively, but made no move to stop them. All four of the fugitives had enough to quell their hunger, and the chasseurs more than enough.

For the first time, the bound men showed some emotion, although it was well controlled. "Gracias, Señoritas," they said, their voices cultivated. "Gracias, Señors."

Simon managed a wry smile. "I hope that you would do as much for us, if our situations were reversed."

"You may be assured that we would," he was told. Strangely, Simon believed them.

They went back to where the Maroons were sitting around the fire, warming themselves by its blaze and finishing their meal. They sat down, close together, a short distance away, aching with exhaustion and fearful of what tomorrow would bring.

But a danger much closer than tomorrow was already here. The Maroon leader kept his eyes fastened on Dicey, eyes that were filled with speculation. It was apparent that he had had time to reconsider his original intention of leaving Dicey alone because Cuffie had claimed that she was his woman. Dicey moved uncomfortably under his gaze and edged closer to Cuffie, who put his arm around her and tried to stare the leader down.

"You sure she's your woman?"

"She's my woman," Cuffie said.

"Maybe I'll just see if she is. She don't have the look of anybody's woman. If she ain't been broke in, then she ain't your woman, she's anybody's for the taking."

"You'll have to kill me first," Cuffie said.

"That won't take no time at all, slave. No more'n killing a fly. I got me a notion to see if she's your woman or not."

Cuffie stood up and drew Dicey with him. "She's my woman," he said again. He turned his back on the Maroons and walked away, with Dicey pressed close to his side. They walked for a good distance, and then sank out of sight behind a growth of bushes that shielded them from sight.

The Maroon leader laughed. "Hell with it. Plenty women if I wants 'em." He looked at Noelle, and she felt her flesh shrink and pressed close to Simon, trembling.

"Get to sleep," the leader said. He spat in the fire, and lay down himself, and his followers followed suit.

In the coldness of the mountain night, Noelle had put

her riding habit back on, and she was thankful that she wasn't still only in her camisole and petticoat, so that every curve of her body was revealed.

Simon drew her down onto the ground close to him, a good distance from the others. When he put his arms around her he could feel her trembling.

"I was so frightened!" she confessed. "I was terrified that that man was going to take Dicey! And Cuffie would have been killed, because he would have fought him."

"That makes two of us," Simon told her. "I would have had to try to help Cuffie, so we'd better be forever thankful that the man changed his mind."

"Do you think they'll ever let us go? Maybe they're just toying with us, like a cat toys with a mouse!" The fear in Noelle's voice wrenched at Simon's heart.

"They have no reason to keep us prisoner, and no reason for killing us. I'm not so sure about the chasseurs, but I'll do my best to talk them into letting them go free as well, after the four of us have had plenty of time to get down out of the mountains so that there will be no danger of them overtaking us. Not that I think that they would do that now, but there's no use taking chances."

Holding Noelle like this put a strain on Simon's self-control that taxed every ounce of his willpower. There was no assurance that they would still be alive when the sun rose again. The Maroons might decide to kill them all in their sleep. They had already angered them by feeding the chasseurs, and Cuffie and Dicey had angered them by refusing to join them. If the Maroons should fall upon them, Simon would have no chance at all to defend Noelle, much less himself. They would kill him first, and then all he could wish for Noelle was a death as swift.

As exhausted as they were, sleep eluded them. Noelle still trembled in Simon's arms, and he knew that she was putting up a gallant effort not to cry. He traced the curve of her cheek with his fingers, he pressed his lips against her forehead, and then he kissed her.

All the pent-up fire of his passion for this girl raged in him. Here, in these hostile mountains, held prisoner by a band of men who might decide to kill them at any moment, the driving urge to go on living, to love and to mate while there was still time, was all-consuming.

In his arms, Noelle fought her own battle against the same emotions. All they could be sure of having was now, this moment. She had never dreamed that her body could be wracked by such a rage to be possessed by the man she loved, to give herself to him and to take him as fiercely as he would take her.

The fact that it was impossible for them to assuage their need for each other, within sight and hearing of the Maroons, who lay sprawled around the fire, only made it harder.

"I love you, Noelle," Simon said. His voice was harsh with urgency. "Tell me that you'll marry me when all this is over, tell me that even if I've been the worst fool who ever walked the earth, you've forgiven me and you'll marry me!"

"I love you," Noelle said. "I love you, Simon."

The Maroons slept. If one or two of them remained alert, there was no sign of it. They were confident that their captives would not attempt to escape, and they knew that the chasseurs could not escape. But in the silence of the mountain night, Simon and Noelle could hear Dicey and Cuffie, and the realization of what they were hearing made it all the harder on them.

"They had to," Simon told Noelle. "They had no choice. It's the only way Cuffie can protect her. If he hadn't proved that Dicey was his woman, the leader would have taken her for himself."

Apparently, these renegades had respect for a man's right to keep his woman for himself, but any woman who was not already claimed was fair game. One thought was in both their minds. What if Simon were forced to protect Noelle in the same way?

They fell silent, still holding each other, neither of them knowing what the future might hold, their need for and yearning for each other all but unbearable. But as incredible as it was, they finally fell asleep. Simon had heard men tell of their overwhelming desire to sleep when they had been in extreme danger, but this was his first experience of the phenomenon. It was as if the mind, unable to bear the strain, sought release in oblivion in order to preserve its sanity.

Daylight found them still alive and unharmed, a fact that filled them with an even keener appreciation of life. Sometime during the night, Cuffie and Dicey had come to lie in a spot near to them. Cuffie met Simon's eyes, a little shamefaced.

"Thought if we was to be jumped during the night, we might have a better chance if we was together. Not that there'd be any chance nohow."

At first Dicey was embarrassed to meet Noelle's eyes, but there was a glow in her own, and on her face, that made Noelle envy her with all her heart. Dicey held her head proudly, and the looks she and Cuffie gave each other were filled with adoration. The Maroon leader gave them a dour look, filled with bile.

"We're going hunting. You come with us." He pointed to Cuffie. "If you can't walk good enough yet, you can take a mule. You going to eat, you going to help us hunt."

Dicey's eyes filled with a terror that twisted Noelle's and Simon's hearts. What assurance did they have that Cuffie would come back, that the Maroon leader wouldn't kill him in order to have him out of the way so that he would have a legitimate claim on Dicey?

Cuffie did not flinch, although that same knowledge was on his face. "Don't worry, Dicey. Was he going kill me, he could do it here as well as out hunting. I'll come back."

"He will if a boar don't chop him to ribbons," the leader said. "I bet he ain't never hunted no boar before."

"I ain't never hunted nothing. I'm a field slave."

"Then it's time you learned. That emancipation comes, you'll hev to fend for yourself, same as us."

The two Maroons who were left to guard the prisoners made no objection when Noelle and Dicey walked to the stream close by to wash themselves. Simon went with them, and stood with his back to them so that they could remove their outer clothing, making sure that their guards did not take it into their heads to take advantage of the situation. But the Maroons only sat talking quietly, without as much as looking their way. Until their leader gave the word, they would make no move.

"Mistress?"

The word was spoken softly, with tentativeness, but Dicey's eyes were steady. "You know what me and Cuffie did last night. We had to, but I ain't sorry, not a bit. I was always Cuffie's woman, but now I really belong to him. And when the time comes for you, don't you be afraid. It only hurts a little, right at first, and then it's wonderful and nothing to be afraid of. If you love your man the way I love Cuffie, then the pain won't mean nothing, only the glory."

Noelle took Dicey into her arms and kissed her cheek. "Thank you, Dicey. I'm glad that you and Cuffie belong to each other, even if it had to happen in circumstances like this. And you needn't worry about having children born into slavery. As soon as all of this is over, I'll see that you are both set free. Only don't leave me, even then! I don't know what I'd do without you, you're the truest friend I have."

"Won't ever leave you!" Dicey said, her eyes glittering with tears. "Not ever. It's like that place in the Bible you read to me, about Ruth and Naomi. You ain't my mother-in-law, but it's just the same."

The two girls smiled into each other's eyes. Friendship, Noelle thought, true friendship such as existed between her and Dicey, was the most precious thing in the world. If they were to die today, at least they would not die alone, and somehow, that would make it easier.

The Maroons were armed with guns, but Cuffie was not. He wouldn't have known how to use one even if they had supplied him with one. But they gave him a sort of crude javelin that they had made themselves, knowing that even if he thought of taking a fool's risk, he could not get close enough to any of them to use it before he would be shot down.

"Didn't have me no gun when first I run," the leader told him. "Didn't have nothing but my hands. Made me a spear out of a branch, and killed my first boar with that. Not afore it 'most got me first." He rolled up his ragged pant leg, and Cuffie saw a crisscrossing of deep, twisted scars. "Thought that boar was going take my leg right off afore it finally decided it was dead."

He grinned at the expression on Cuffie's face. "After I killed the boar, and got the bleedin' stopped, I found one of the Maroon villages, and they took me in. Stayed till my leg healed good, and then I took off. Don't like no villages nohow. Like it out in the open, with nobody but me to boss, me and the men I let join me, who don't like no village neither. You changed your mind about joining us? You'd be free now, 'thout waiting for no emancipation. You and your woman."

"We stay with our mistress," Cuffie said, meeting the man's gaze without flinching. "The mistress be a good mistress, always she be good and kind to all the slaves, same as the master, her father. It be the other mistress, this one's sister, who be bad. She real bad, evil, she and Chloe. Got to get rid of them two evil ones, got to help the young mistress get shut of 'em."

The leader studied Cuffie's face, speculation in his eyes, but he made no comment.

After three miles of riding, the leader signaled a halt. He pointed to a clump of thick brush. "In there," he said. "I see the signs. There's a boar in there. Git off that mule, Cuffie, and go in there and flush him out."

Cuffie's mouth tightened. This was a game to the Maroon leader, who was watching to see Cuffie show signs of fear. And Cuffie was afraid, so afraid that his gut seemed to shrivel, but his pride wouldn't let him refuse to obey the order.

Pouring with sweat, limping on his bad ankle, Cuffie grasped the crude javelin with both hands and pushed his way into the brush. The prospect of coming face to face with a wild boar that would cut him to ribbons filled him with terror. He didn't even know how to use the weapon he held, he would have to rely on his agility and his instinct. His agility was impaired, and so he prayed that his instinct, his natural reflexes, would be enough to swing the balance in his favor.

There was no boar in the brush. Cuffie searched it thoroughly, crashing around to flush it out if it had been there, but there was nothing. Weak with relief so intense that it threatened to loosen his bowels, he made his way out again.

"Nothing in there," he said.

Still mounted on his horse, the leader grinned. "I knowed that. Wanted to see would you go in."

Cuffie's lips tightened again. He'd been made a fool of, and he had to fight against his impulse to drag the man off his horse and beat him to a pulp. But any such move would bring instant death. These men wouldn't hesitate to shoot him at the first hostile move.

"Look out! Look there!" one of the Maroons shouted, his voice filled with startled alarm.

The boar came from the opposite direction, and Cuffie, on foot, was the one it charged. He had barely time to leap aside and whirl to face it before it was on him, slashing at him with its razor-sharp tusks, its evil little eyes filled with murderous rage.

One of the tusks caught Cuffie's bad leg. Pain blinded him, red flashes swirled in front of his eyes. Still he lifted the javelin and thrust it with all the strength he possessed. He caught the maddened animal in its left eye, penetrating deep into the brain. The boar screamed, a sound that sent the fear of Satan all through Cuffie's body.

The leader had sat unmoving on his horse, his lifted hand stopping his followers from interfering on Cuffie's behalf.

"How you knowed to do that? How'd you manage to get it right smack in the eye?" he demanded.

Cuffie could see again now, and he looked at the man without a trace of a flinch, and he lied.

"I just knowed to do it," he said. The fact was that the javelin had penetrated the boar's eye by complete accident, but that was a fact that he was not about to admit to this man. "Seemed like the likeliest place."

"We'll get back to camp. That leg got to be tended. One of you tie it up so it'll do till we get there."

Dicey cried out in alarm when they rode in and she saw the crude bandage, torn from Cuffie's shirt. She ran to meet him, panic-stricken fear on her face.

Cuffie slid down off the mule and gathered her into his arms. "Got me a boar," he said. "Pretty good, for my first hunt."

"Fix his leg," the leader ordered Dicey. "You his woman or ain't you?"

Noelle helped her. The bandage took the last of the tablecloth. This wound would heal, as far as they could tell it had not torn any essential muscles or severed any blood vessels. But they hoped and prayed that there would be no more need for bandages.

Once again, when the freshly roasted boar was divided, Simon and Noelle, and Dicey and Cuffie, gave part of their shares to the chasseurs. No one made any move to prevent them, but no one offered them any more to make up for what they gave away, either.

Again that night, Dicey and Cuffie made their bed away from the camp. And again that night, Noelle and Simon slept in each other's arms, their bodies in agony because of their wanting, envying Dicey and Cuffie. If God so chose, they would live to wake up again in the morning.

Chapter Fourteen

SIMON HAD MADE UP HIS MIND. TIME WAS BEING WASTED which could not be afforded. He must get to the *Maid of Boston,* and he must do it now. His enforced rest had renewed his strength, and he must go today.

He faced the Maroon leader, trying to talk him into letting him take one of the horses, but so far he had gotten nowhere. Money meant nothing to the man, where would he spend it? In any case, Simon hadn't brought enough with him to constitute a reasonable bribe.

"What else you got?" the leader demanded, scowling at him. "Your boots won't fit me, I'd never get my feet in 'em, and your clothes might be fancy but they're too small for me, too. If you ain't got something I want, no horse."

Simon was at a loss. Without a horse, it would take him far too long to get down out of the mountains and make his way to Kingston for the help he had to have if he was to rescue Daniel Maynard from Maynard Penn.

"I'll send you anything you want, from Kingston," he said, desperate enough to promise anything. "I have a friend who knows Papa Emile, a gangan, and the gangan will know some man who will bring you what I buy for you."

"Ain't nothing I want, ain't nothing I need. Got everything I want and need right here. Could use me a woman, but Papa Emile wouldn't send me one of those, and she'd be a nuisance, anyhow. And no place for me to show off fancy clothes. Got plenty to eat, I ain't never gone hungry in the mountains. White man, there ain't but one thing you got that I might want."

"Then tell me what it is!" It was going to be hard enough to leave Noelle and Cuffie and Dicey behind while he rode for help, but this suspense was killing him.

"You got a watch. I'll take that."

The watch Simon's father had given him on his eighteenth birthday, the one material possession that Simon valued above all else! But he had no choice. He took the watch from his pocket and handed it over.

The leader looked at it, shook it, held it to his ear and shook it again.

"It has to be wound. Gently, so as not to break the spring. A broken spring can be repaired, but not here in the mountains." Simon wound the watch and set it at what he judged to be the approximate time, according to the position of the sun.

The Maroon leader accepted it back, his grin wider than before. "It be a good watch. It's gold," he said. "Not no other Maroon in these mountains got a finer watch, even the ones they stole on their raids. You can have the horse. You can have the chasseurs too. I don't want to feed 'em any more. Maybe they'll help you get to Kingston in one piece. They can take horses too. I can always get more horses."

"We will be pleased to guard you on your journey, Señor," one of the chasseurs said. Simon thought that this one was Ramon, the other one was Luis, but he couldn't be sure, they were as alike as two peas in a pod. "We owe you our lives, it is the least we can do."

Simon's heart leapt with exultation. He had never expected such generosity from the Maroon leader. With the chasseurs, he would have a real chance of reaching Kingston and his ship.

"You will help Noelle and Dicey and Cuffie get down?"

"You got a real nerve, man! Ain't we done enough, not killing you and now letting you have a horse?"

"Simon, we'll be all right! We can make our way down by ourselves, Cuffie will be able to find the way." Noelle came to stand beside Simon, her eyes imploring him not to push the Maroon leader too far.

The leader regarded her, frowning again before another glance at the watch made him grin again.

"We'll bring 'em down, far enough so's they won't have no trouble finding the rest of the way. Bring 'em on horses, first part of the trip, so's they won't have to walk too far. Be glad to get shut of the lot of you. This one"—he scowled at Dicey—"would be trouble, mens would be fighting over her. Don't want the white mistress nohow, don't want nobody to come alooking for her. You take them chasseurs and you get. The others'll be along."

Simon took the chasseurs, and he got. The horses were good ones, taken on raids. It was good to be in the saddle again, to have a strong horse under him that would cover the distance between the mountains and Kingston in record time. It was even better to have the chasseurs with him. In spite of their fearsome reputations, he trusted them. They had given their word, they were grateful that he had talked the Maroon leader out of killing them, and he knew that they would keep their word.

It was the middle of the night before they left the last of the mountains behind them. On the road they would make faster time, but they had had to go slowly up until now so as not to risk injury to the horses.

Half an hour along the road to Kingston, two stalwart

slaves loomed up in front of them, Vanessa's guards, sent to prevent him from reaching town. If Simon had been alone, they might have managed to pull him from his horse and capture him. But at the sight of the two chasseurs, they shrank back, and made to run.

"Stay where you are!" Luis, or was it Ramon, commanded them. "Do not go back to your mistress and tell her that you have seen us. If you do, we will learn of it, and you are dead men."

There was no doubt that the slaves believed him. They stood rooted to the spot, afraid to move, and Simon was sure that they would stay where they were.

"Gracias," Simon said.

"De nada. It is we who are in your debt. Let us be going. You understand that when we reach Kingston, we will be leaving you? We will have fulfilled our obligation to you, your quarrel is not our quarrel."

"I understand. I'd be happier if you would testify that Vanessa sent you to capture us, but you must do as you see fit."

"Our testimony would be of no avail. The lady only sent us to bring you in, she would say that she thought you were lost. That is all we could testify to, for fear of danger to our souls."

The sun was just rising by the time they reached Kingston and the chasseurs melted away as if they had never been with him at all. Simon wished them well. He believed them when they said that they would not have killed them, and they had saved him from capture by Vanessa's guards.

The only place that Simon knew he could get the help he needed was his own ship, where a crew of men who were loyal to him would do his bidding without question. Going to the governor or any other authorities would only be to waste time, and they would not believe a word against Vanessa in any case. For Simon, a foreigner, a stranger among them to bring such charges against Vanessa would be an exercise in futility. They would think that he was mad, they would probably lock him up for his own safety. Certainly he must look like a madman, unshaven, ragged and bedraggled as he was.

The few people stirring on the streets, most of them free blacks or slaves, looked at him curiously, but they did not accost him. Like the authorities would have if he had gone to them, they probably thought that he was mad.

Perhaps he was mad to attempt a plan so audacious that he shuddered to think of all that depended on it. But it was the only plan that had any hope of succeeding, and he was committed to it.

"Cap'n!" the man on watch exclaimed, when he reached his destination. "Is that you? Lord, Cap'n, what's happened to you? You look a sight!"

"I feel a sight. Never mind that now. Is Aaron on board?"

"Certain sure he is. Shall I fetch him?" The watch's mouth still hung open, his eyes bugging out at the apparition that had loomed up in front of him. For the captain to have been missing all this time, and then return in such a state, boggled the young man's mind. He could hardly leave off staring to obey the order he had just been given.

The thing that Simon had always liked the most about his first mate was that you never had to repeat yourself to him. Aaron only told him, tersely and angrily, that neither he nor Ian had been able to persuade the authorities to make a thorough search for the missing party, because Vanessa had not reported them missing.

Simon chose four crewmen and saw that they were armed. With Aaron and himself, that made six. Six determined men with guns could hold any number of slaves at bay, no matter what forces Vanessa and Chloe might try to set against them.

Simon did not wish to dwell upon the consequences of this unlawful act if Daniel Maynard should not show improvement after he had been taken from Maynard Penn. He and every member of the crew that he took with him might find themselves languishing in prison for an unknown number of years. He simply had to have faith that Daniel would improve, and go ahead with his plan.

The next step was the procuring of horses to carry his raiding party to Maynard Penn, and the quickest way to get them was to ask Bertram Cottswood for them. The Cottswoods kept saddle horses as well as coach horses, they would have no trouble supplying them. The only problem would be in persuading Bertram to let him have them without offering the man any explanation.

The Cottswood family was just sitting down to their breakfast when Simon arrived and demanded admittance from a servant who was not inclined to admit him in his present state. There being no time for niceties, Simon pushed the man aside and strode into the dining room, where his appearance threw his erstwhile hosts into a state of horrified consternation. They stared at him, struck speechless.

Brenda was the first to recover the use of her tongue. Nothing could silence Brenda for long, her spate of words seemed to spring from a never-failing font somewhere deep inside herself.

"Captain Spencer! My lands, whatever has happened to you? You look simply frightful! And you've been hurt, your shoulder is bandaged! Mama, Papa, we must have a bed prepared for the captain immediately! Claude, go and fetch Doctor Eastlake! If he isn't up yet, drag him out of bed and bring him here without a moment's delay! Poor Captain Spencer, does it hurt just dreadfully? Let me help you to your room. Henry, come and help me help him. Mama, have hot water sent to his room, and Joshua to bathe him, and a clean nightshirt sent in. Are you hungry, Captain Spencer? Do you think you could eat something? We'll have a tray fetched to you, you must get to bed at once, you look ready to drop in your tracks. Claude, for goodness sake, don't just sit there with your mouth hanging open, go and fetch the doctor!"

Simon despaired of getting a word in edgeways, but

Brenda ran down at last, as Claude finally collected himself enough to rise from his chair and do as his sister had bidden him. If Brenda had been a man, she would have made an admirable first mate, or better yet, a sergeant in the army. Throwing orders around came naturally to her, and she fully expected to be obeyed, a trait that was to be desired in a first mate or a sergeant, because when a man expects to be obeyed, he usually is.

"I have no need of a bed, Miss Brenda, but I could do with a little food while five of your horses are being saddled. I am afraid that I am going to have to borrow them. If you don't have enough saddle horses, coach horses will do. I'm sorry to break in on you at such an hour with such a request, but I assure you that it is of the utmost importance. I must have the horses at once."

"May I inquire why you must have them, and why you are in such a state?" Bertram Cottswood had finally remembered that he was the head of this household, and now he moved to exert his authority. "As my daughter has so tactlessly pointed out, you look frightful. I can't fathom what has happened to you. Brenda is right, you should be put to bed at once and attended by a doctor. As for the horses, of course you are welcome to them if the matter is all that urgent, but I believe that I have the right to know why you want them."

"I have to get to Maynard Penn. Things are afoot there that make it essential for me to remove Daniel Maynard from the plantation and bring him here to Kingston for his own safety."

Bertram pushed his chair back from the table and rose to his feet, his heavy face quivering.

"An uprising! The Maynards' slaves have revolted! This is a matter for the militia, Captain Spencer, not for you and a handful of men to try to quell! I've advised Vanessa over and over that it wasn't safe for Maynard Penn to be without white overseers, and now this is the result! A force must be sent at once, we must on no account let the revolt spread to other plantations! The entire island might be set ablaze before this is over unless we can bring it under control at once!''

"Noelle! Vanessa!" Brenda cried, her eyes wide with terror. "Have they been killed, have they already been slaughtered?''

"Noelle is not at the plantation, and I promise you that Vanessa is in no danger. There has been no uprising that I know of and I am quite certain that one has not taken place.''

"Then why, in the name of God, is it so essential that you get there in such a rush to bring Daniel away?'' Bertram Cottswood demanded.

"It's too long a story to go into now. Even if I had the time to tell it, I doubt that you would credit it. Only have the horses made ready, if you will. They will be returned to you at the earliest opportunity. Noelle knows what I am doing, and it has her full approval, if that will relieve your anxieties.''

Bertram Cottswood wavered, clearly at a loss whether to comply with Simon's request, or refuse out of hand unless more explanations were forthcoming. Once again, it was Brenda who took charge.

"Papa, for goodness' sake do as Captain Spencer asks! I can't wait to find out what all of this is about, and it's obvious that none of us will find out until he gets back. If Noelle knows about it, it must be all right, and the captain must bring Mr. Maynard straight here, and we'll have Doctor Eastlake waiting to attend him to make sure that he suffers no ill effects from being moved. Henry, don't just stand there, go and see to the horses! And where is a plate for Captain Spencer, and food? Do hurry, all of you, the suspense is killing me! Captain Spencer, may I go with you? I promise you that I can ride quite well, I won't hold you up, or I could follow in the curricle.''

"You may not," Simon said. "I'm sorry, Miss Brenda, but it's out of the question. I have no idea of what we might run into once we arrive, there may be danger, and you are to stay safely here in Kingston.''

"Well, I should certainly hope so!" Faith Cottswood spoke for the first time, her voice holding a distinct quaver. Faith's life had always been a placid one, the most excitement she experienced in the course of a year was a successful party or a fruitful shopping trip. "You shall stay at home, Brenda, and we will bar all the doors! How do we know that there has not actually been an uprising? Bertram, do something before we're all murdered in our beds!"

"Mana, we aren't in bed, and Captain Spencer has already told us that there is no uprising. Do drink your coffee, and try to calm yourself. Captain, have you finished eating? The horses must be saddled by now, unless Henry stubbed his toe on the way to the stables, the clumsy thing. I should have gone myself!" Brenda was fairly jumping up and down in her excitement, but that was natural to her, she was always agog about something, and the events that were taking place at the moment only afforded her the opportunity to be more excited than usual.

Simon could have done with more breakfast, but Brenda was right. It was time to get moving.

"You'll never know how much I appreciate this, but I'll try to make you understand my gratitude when everything has been resolved. I'll be forever in your debt, sir," he said to his host before he strode out of the room.

A groom was cinching up the last saddle when Simon arrived at the stables, and even as he checked the cinch to make sure that the saddle would not slip, Aaron and the four crewmen arrived. The sailors looked at the horses doubtfully, but loyalty to their captain made them climb onto their backs no matter how much they distrusted four-legged beasts.

To Simon's consternation, there was a complication that he had not foreseen. Six horses had been saddled, not five, and Henry was already astride one of them.

"I am going with you, of course," Henry said. "If there is trouble at my fiancée's home, then I must be there to set things to rights. With Mr. Maynard ill, I am the closest to being the man of the Maynard family, and I intend to see to it myself that everything is done that should be done."

There would be no shaking the arrogant young man from his purpose, and Simon groaned inwardly. It would be a disaster for Henry to accompany them, considering the second stage of Simon's plan, to abduct Vanessa as well as Daniel, and place her aboard his own ship for safekeeping. Henry would have every authority on the island down around their heads, he would ruin the entire plan.

Brenda stood on the steps that led into the house as the seven grim-faced men rode out. "Hurry, for goodness' sake, do hurry!" she cried. "I'll have perished from the suspense before you get back as it is!"

What the devil was he going to do about Henry, Simon wondered. He could scarcely overpower him and tie him up somewhere along the road, he'd be sure to be found and released, and then there'd be the devil to pay. But if Henry went with them, he would believe anything Vanessa said, and take her part, and try to prevent Simon from carrying out his plan, and as much as he disliked the man, he certainly didn't want to have to shoot him.

He was still pondering the problem, seeking for a solution and finding none, when Ian joined them, mounted on Explorer.

"Aaron sent word to me," Ian said. "I'm coming along."

"You're more than welcome. I hope that you're armed."

"I'm armed, although I don't know if I could hit the broad side of a barn. But would you mind giving me some hint of why you've mounted this expedition? Just in case I did hit someone, I'd like to know the reason why I killed him."

Simon nodded toward Henry, who had taken the lead, his air of self-importance proclaiming that he was very much the leader of this foray. Mouthing his words, hoping that Ian would understand, he said, "I don't want Henry along! I'll explain why we're going to Maynard Penn, but Henry will ruin everything!''

To Simon's gratification, Ian understood at once. He pulled up his horse and made an exclamation of annoyance.

"I told you that I'm not a very good marksman! It's even worse than that, I'm afraid. Would you believe that I forgot to load my pistol? However, it will take only a moment to stop by my house so I can remedy the situation.''

"I can't believe that even a doctor could be so absentminded!" Henry said, scorn in every word. Henry was only too aware that Ian was interested in Noelle, and Noelle's liking for Ian was a thorn in Henry's side, one that chafed and pricked him more than he would have admitted. When he told Noelle what an ass Ian had been to start out with an unloaded pistol, it would lower her estimation of the young doctor a peg or two, and that thought pleased Henry so that he didn't grumble too much as they stopped outside Ian's mean little house.

"Mr. Cottswood, would you dismount for a moment, and come inside? I've been experimenting at making my own wine. I think that the results are quite good, but then I'm no connoisseur, as you are, and I'd appreciate your opinion.''

"What nonsense! How could you possibly hope to make a potable wine?" Henry derided him. "If you insist, I'll sample it, but I know what my opinion will be even before I taste it.''

Inside the house, where Henry looked around with a distaste that he made no attempt to keep from showing, Ian brought him a glass of the cheap wine that was all he kept, for medicinal purposes only. Looking at Ian's pitiful collection of rough, native-made furniture, Henry did not see the quick movement of Ian's hand as he introduced something into the glass. As Henry drank the small potion, Ian made a pretense of searching for powder and ball and loading his pistol.

"This is without any doubt the worst wine I have ever

tasted!'' Henry said. "I don't see how even you could have come up with something so vile!''

"Is it that bad?'' Ian gave every appearance of being crushed. "Well, perhaps I'll have better luck with the next batch. Practice makes perfect, as they always say.''

"My palate will be ruined for days!'' Henry complained. "Are you ready, or are we going to dally here while you bumble around?''

Henry's face turned green almost before the words were out of his mouth. He doubled over, holding his stomach. "Oh, my God, you've poisoned me with that stuff!'' he managed.

Ian caught him and led him to his cot. "Here, lie down! I assure you that you aren't poisoned. Now what in the world could I have done to make the wine have such an effect on you? I don't understand it, I tasted it myself only yesterday and it had no such effect on me at all!''

A moment later Ian emerged from his house, alone. Looking properly concerned, he said, "I'm afraid that young Mr. Cottswood will not be able to go on with us. He has suddenly become a bit under the weather.''

Simon looked at him with appreciative suspicion. "And how long do you expect that his indisposition will last? Will he recover sufficiently in a short time to be able to catch up with us?''

"Oh, I shouldn't think so! In fact, I'm quite sure that after his initial nausea has passed, he will sleep for the rest of the day. He's quite all right where he is, I put him on my bed and removed his boots so he'll be comfortable enough. But we'd better go on without him, Simon. There's no telling how long he'll sleep.''

Papa Emile had not let Ian in on all his secrets, by any means, but he had instructed him in the method to keep someone out of things for several hours, without any suspicion of foul play, should the need arise. It was a useful bit of information, never more useful than now. Ian determined to see that Papa Emile was suitably recompensed for having been of so much help, even though the gangan had had no idea on whom his concoction would be used. Papa Emile was fond of rum, and as a black man he seldom had the wherewithal to purchase as much as he would like. Tomorrow he would have a whole keg. If the gangan overindulged, Ian at least knew several prime remedies for hangovers.

Chapter Fifteen

MIRANDA WAS IN THE GARDEN OUTSIDE THE HUT THAT she shared with Elisha, the hut where their girl-baby was sleeping right now. Miranda had come back to the hut for the noon meal, as did all of the slaves, but she had not been hungry, she had not been able to force down more than two or three mouthfuls. Her mind was still filled with grief and anger over her father's death. Her father had served Maynard Penn all of his life, he had been put to work in the cane fields when he was only six, and now, after his lifetime of service, he had been rewarded by being thrown alive down into a deep gully, to die on the rocks below. Miranda had no idea whether he had died instantly from the fall, or whether he had lived for hours to suffer. The slaves who had thrown him into the gully did not know, or they would not tell her. They had been ordered to be silent by Chloe, and they dared not disobey the obeah woman's commands.

Miranda had nursed her baby. It had sucked at her breast greedily, it was a strong baby and it was thriving. When it had been satisfied, Miranda had left it for the crone to watch, a woman too old to be good for anything but tending infants and toddlers. She tended Adele's baby, too, both of them in Miranda's hut while Adele worked in the fields, miraculously cured of the fever she had never had so that she could go back to work.

Soon it would be the crone's turn to be carried to the gully and thrown in, still alive. The old woman knew this, and her hands and her chin shook as she watched the infants, and there was nothing that Miranda or any other slave could say to her to comfort her. As long as Mistress Vanessa ruled Maynard Penn, with Chloe to give the commands, the practice would go on being carried out although most of the other plantations in Jamaica had abandoned it years ago.

Elisha and Hector and the picnic party still had not come back. Miranda knew that something had happened to them. The slaves whispered among themselves that the Maroons had got them, that they were dead, slain in the mountains, and that their bodies would never be found. They knew, because they knew everything that went on at Maynard Penn, that Vanessa had sent chasseurs to find them. And they knew that Cuffie had run away, and that he had run away to search for Dicey. Cuffie had better never come back, whether he found Dicey or not. Chloe's fury because he had run would make sure that he would suffer as few slaves had ever suffered, if he dared to return.

Word that seven white men, on horses and armed, were approaching Maynard Penn swept through the slave village as though it were carried by the wind. Five of the white men were strangers, but two of them were known. One of them was the young doctor from Kingston, who had called at the plantation three times in recent days, and the other was Captain Simon Spencer himself, who had been a guest at Maynard Penn and who had set off on a picnic in the Blue Mountains with Mistress Noelle and

Dicey, and Elisha and Hector to act as guides and bodyguards for them.

The party had ridden away from Maynard Penn, Elisha and Hector and Dicey on mules, Mistress Noelle and the captain on horses. The captain and Mistress Noelle had been in high spirits, but Dicey had been subdued, not at all as she should have been at the prospect of a day in the mountains with her mistress, and Elisha and Hector had been equally subdued although they too should have been happy to escape from the fields for a day. They should have returned that same afternoon, all five of them.

But now here was Captain Spencer and six other men, but no sign of Elisha and Hector and no sign of Dicey and Mistress Noelle.

Miranda left her garden, still carrying the hoe she had been using simply because she forgot to put it down. From her hut five huts away, Arla, Hector's woman, did the same. Other slaves fell in behind them. One of the black overseers shouted at them to come back, but they paid no heed to him. They walked silently, their eyes straight ahead, with Miranda in the lead and Arla only a step behind her. Arla also carried her hoe, although others who had been spending a few moments cultivating their vegetables had left theirs behind.

If the overseer had been white, he might have been obeyed, but he was black, the same as they. When the man ran and caught up with her and grasped her arm, she shook him off.

"Going find out where's Elisha," Miranda said. "Arla, she's going find out where's Hector. Get out of our way."

The overseer was angry, but there was no way he could stop this determined march toward the plantation house. The slaves skirted the palisade fence that had been designed to keep them at bay, and came to the gate, which was locked. Miranda lifted her hoe and attacked the lock. She was a tall woman, and strong, and after half a dozen blows it gave way and the gate swung open. The overseer covered his eyes with his hand. He would have to face

Chloe's wrath, and it was not a thing that he contemplated with pleasure. Chloe would punish Miranda and Arla as well, Miranda and Arla more than those who simply followed them, but the brunt of her wrath would fall on him.

The slaves poured through the gate, with Miranda and Arla still in the lead. They came to a stop in the area in front of the plantation house just as Simon and his party were drawing rein.

There was still no air of menace by the slaves who simply stood there, waiting and watching and listening. Some of them were afraid and ready to turn tail and run at the first sight of their mistress, and especially at the first sight of Chloe, but all of them were curious, and they hoped that Chloe would overlook them, that she would not remember who had been there except for Miranda and Arla, who still stood apart from them and several paces in front of them.

"Captain, sir, where is Elisha?" Miranda called. "Where is Hector?"

Inside the house, Vanessa had been apprised that the body of horsemen was approaching, with Simon and Ian Macintyre in the lead. She stepped out of the house, controlling her sudden panic. This was no time to lose her head, she needed all of her wits about her! With Chloe standing directly behind her, she stopped at the top of the stairs that led up to the living quarters of the house.

"Captain Spencer! Where on earth have you been all this while? I've been frantic about you, I even sent men to find you after I became convinced that you were lost in the mountains!"

Simon dismounted and took the steps two at a time, with Ian on his heels. Simon stood looming over the beautiful woman, his face like granite.

"The men you sent found us," he said.

"If they found you, then where is Noelle, where are the three slaves?" Simon thought that he had never seen a better actress, even on the stage. Vanessa's hand was at

225

her breast, her eyes were beseeching, her air so anxious that she would have deceived anyone who didn't know her as well as Simon knew her.

"Your sister is safe, and so is Dicey and Cuffie. Hector escaped after he and Elisha failed to kill us as you had ordered, and I surmised that he returned to Maynard Penn. Elisha, I am sorry to say, is dead. I had to kill him, or be killed and see Noelle and Dicey killed as well."

Miranda's body turned to stone.

"Dead? How can he be dead?" Vanessa's voice rose, filled with bewilderment. "I don't know what you're talking about!"

"I believe that I made myself plain. You understand English, do you not? Elisha and Hector tried to kill us. Hector escaped, but I killed Elisha in defense of all of us. But Elisha lived long enough to tell us that it was by Chloe's orders that he and Hector tried to slay us. You will be called to account for your actions, Vanessa, in good time. At the moment we are here to remove your father from this house and take him to Kingston. I have good reason to believe that you and Chloe have been keeping him drugged, that you have been slowly killing him. I only hope that we have arrived in time, and that he is not already dead."

"You're mad! You must be stark, raving mad! My father isn't going anywhere, he's much too ill to be moved, much less suffer the long journey to Kingston! Everything you have said is a pack of lies! Elisha and Hector might have tried to kill you so that they could escape to the Maroons, but I had nothing to do with it!"

"Not only do I believe that you have consistently kept your father drugged for months, I believe that your brother's death was not a natural one. I believe that Chloe, under your instigation, poisoned him with some undetectable poison that would make it appear that he had died of an infection." Simon's voice was hard, and his eyes, which did not waver from Vanessa's face, were just as hard.

"Chloe!" Vanessa's voice was a shriek. "Chloe, do

you hear what this man is saying? Tell him that it's a lie, tell them all that it's nothing but a pack of lies! Noelle has put him up to this, it's Noelle who put these insane notions in his head! Everybody knows how much she hates me, how jealous she is of me, she'd do anything to hurt me! Doctor Macintyre, you are aware of Noelle's mad jealousy of me, have you no influence over this man who has apparently believed all of her lies?''

Ian's eyes, and his voice, were as cold as Simon's.

"I know who has lied, consistently lied, these days just past. Each time I came here to your plantation, you told me that Simon and Noelle were off jaunting around the countryside. There was never a word about their being lost in the mountains, about their being missing. You gave me to understand that they had been home, in each case, the evening before, and that you expected them again that evening. I was not allowed a close look at your father; the few moments I saw him, the room was darkened and you urged me out of his presence almost before I had spoken with him. If anyone is lying, Miss Maynard, I believe that it is you.''

Vanessa saw all of her plans, all of her dreams, come crashing down around her. Her back was to the wall, and only violent action could save her.

"Chloe! Do something! Kill these men, kill them all!'' She could say, after all of them were dead, that there had been a slave uprising, that she and Chloe alone had escaped. Her father must be killed as well, slain in his bed, so that he could not be questioned.

With no living witnesses against her, Vanessa knew that her story would be believed. There were no white overseers at Maynard Penn, no one to stop the slaves if they rose against their masters as so many slaves had done during these troubled times. No one would give Noelle's story any credence, much less take stock in anything that Dicey and Cuffie had to say; as blacks and slaves, they would not even be allowed to testify.

Simon and Ian and the men they had brought with them were armed. Some of the slaves would be killed, but that did not matter. There were enough of them to overwhelm the white men after their bullets had been spent.

Chloe stepped forward. Her eyes raked over the group of slaves who were standing close together. "Kill them!" Chloe ordered. "Kill them all!"

Terrified, knowing Chloe's powers, they took a step forward, but the men with Simon held their pistols leveled at them, and their faces said that they would shoot without a moment's compunction.

"I'll put a curse on you, I'll put spells on all your families!" Chloe shouted at them. "You know how you will die, you, and your children, your sisters and your brothers! I will spare no one you love, no one who is close to you! I will curse the children first, even the babies in arms. I see you, I know who you are, and who your children are, and not one will escape!" All that mattered was to protect Vanessa and herself, and preserve the dreams of glory that they would share once all of the Maynard fortune was in Vanessa's hands.

In France, in Paris, they would be as equals, she and Vanessa. She would no longer be a slave, she would bow to no one's will but her own. This was something that Chloe was not willing to lose, and she did not intend to lose it.

Standing frozen, Miranda comprehended nothing of what was going on around her. Only the fact that Elisha was dead mattered to her, and the fact that it had been Chloe who had ordered him to murder Captain Spencer and the young mistress, and that he had been killed in attempting to carry out those orders.

A scream of rage burst from Miranda's throat, and she leaped forward, covering the ground that separated her from the massive obeah woman in a few rushing strides. Chloe had descended most of the steps, and Miranda scaled the few that remained. She lifted her hoe, with it's sharp cutting edge, and raised it above her head, and brought it down in a chopping motion, directly into Chloe's throat.

A look of astonishment crossed Chloe's face as she fell,

her life's blood gushing from the gaping wound. She clutched at her throat, trying to stem its flow, but she knew that she was mortally wounded. She could make no sound, not even to mutter a curse against her murderer.

She staggered, and dropped to her knees, her eyes fastened on Miranda's face, her eyes cursing her as her voice could not. Miranda raised her hoe again, and then there were two hoes slashing and chopping at the woman who went completely down before their assault, as Arla joined Miranda, because Arla knew, in her heart, with every ounce of her instinct, that Hector was also dead, that he had returned to Maynard Penn and that Chloe had killed him for failing in his mission.

The hoes rose and fell, rose and fell, even though Chloe was already dead.

For a moment, it seemed that the twenty or so other slaves who were watching were paralyzed, as paralyzed as Simon and Ian and the seamen felt. And then the slaves surged forward, intent on tearing what was left of Chloe's body apart. This was the woman who had held them terrorized, the woman who had caused sickness and agony and death. Now their hatred exploded, their intentions clear on their hate-twisted faces.

Ian was the first to collect his wits. Stepping forward, he shouted, "No! Papa Emile would not want you to do this!" It was the only name he could think of that would carry enough influence to stop the hate-ridden mob. "Papa Emile would not want you to do anything that would bring punishment down on your heads! The obeah woman is dead, she can never hurt you again. Go back to your huts, go back to the fields. Let us take care of everything for you. We will see that you are not punished, nothing will happen to you if you will do as Papa Emile would tell you!"

The slaves wavered, and then they fell back. "You know Papa Emile?" one of them called.

"Papa Emile is my friend. I know him well and I know what he would tell you to do." Ian's voice carried conviction.

Now Simon added his voice to Ian's. "Mistress Noelle would want you to do as Papa Emile would want. You all know that the young mistress is good and kind. It will be she who is in charge of Maynard Penn now, not Mistress Vanessa. And soon your master will be well, Master Daniel who never treated you with anything but kindness.

"We are going to take your evil mistress away so that she can never hurt you again. But you must do nothing that would let her accuse you of an uprising. Do as the doctor says, he speaks the truth when he tells you that Papa Emile is his friend. Go now, without lifting a hand. You can trust us. We wish you nothing but well."

Aaron Godbehere was the first of the *Maid of Boston's* crew to recover his wits. Born and bred in New England, the first mate had been stunned by the violence that had erupted before his eyes. This was something that was entirely outside of his experience, but he knew what he must do now. He grasped Miranda's arm and pulled her away from Chloe's body, ordering his crewmen to help him subdue her and Arla as well.

"Back off, that's enough! The woman is already dead! Chopping her into little bits isn't going to make her any more dead!"

He and his crewmen dragged the two women away, and now Chloe's mutilated body was in full sight. Still standing at the top of the steps, Vanessa looked at her and began to scream.

Ian slapped her, the slap so hard that it left an ugly red mark on her cheek. "Come into the house," he commanded her. "I'll find you some brandy."

Vanessa's screams broke off, and Ian knew that he had never seen eyes filled with such virulent hatred.

"You'll hang for this! Every one of you will hang! You came here to my plantation with the intention of taking my father away by force, you incited my slaves to rise against me, you incited them to kill Chloe! You will be charged with murder, and you will be tried and convicted and I will watch you hang! Do you think that anyone in Kingston, anyone in Jamaica, will believe a word you say? Do you think that even if you managed to have charges brought against me, any jury would convict me?''

Damn her, Ian thought! She's more than likely right about that. What jury, comprised of men, would look at this woman and convict her? Where could twelve men be found on this island who would not believe every word she said, who would not convict him and Simon instead? But they were committed now, and there was no way they could turn back. Come what may, they had to take Daniel away, and see if he would regain his health once he was no longer drugged, they had to do everything in their power to see that Vanessa's rule of evil came to an end.

Simon's eyes met Aaron's, both of them sick. ''That was ugly for a while,'' Simon said. ''I didn't think to let you in for anything like this, Aaron, when I asked you to help me. And those poor slaves! The two women who killed Chloe will be certain to be punished for her death, they'll pay for it with their own lives.''

Aaron did not flinch. In his dry, New England voice, he said, ''Far as I could see, nobody knows which slaves killed the woman. I can't tell one slave from another, and neither can any of our crew, and there were a passel of them, all milling around. They can't execute all of them for what only two did, and who's to say which two? If that one there''—he nodded toward Vanessa—''claims that she knows, we'll claim that she's mistaken, that it couldn't have been those two at all. We'll be able to cast at least a reasonable doubt.''

Simon was stunned. He would never have believed that Aaron, with his New England conscience, would lie under oath. But Aaron's eyes held his, without wavering.

''By the time those two mix in with all the others, we won't honestly be able to swear which ones they are. Not me, and not our men. That only leaves you and the doctor. Do you think that you could recollect which ones were guilty, Cap'n?''

Simon swallowed. If Aaron could stretch a point when it came to the truth, so could he. He was determined that Miranda and Arla shouldn't suffer for what they had done.

"The trouble is, it will be our word against that of Mistress Vanessa," Aaron said, his eyes bleak. "But we can only do our best. I'm not looking forward to going back to town with that one in tow, Cap'n, and I'll admit it freely. I'd hoped to end my days in my own parlor, living over my life on the quarter-deck, not swinging at the end of a rope. Seems to me that we've got ourselves in a mess of trouble that ain't going to be easy to get ourselves out of. We've been in Jamaica long enough to know how folks hereabouts regard Vanessa Maynard. Making any kind of charges against her stick is going to be nigh impossible. They'll let her go the minute she opens her mouth, and we'll find ourselves behind bars."

Simon clapped the older man on his shoulder. "I have a trick or two up my sleeve. You probably won't like them, but I hope you'll go along with them. It will be our only hope, so bear that in mind when I ask you to do something you aren't going to want to do."

"What in tarnation you could ask me to do that I haven't already done beats me!" Aaron said. His tone was grumpy, but Simon knew that he could count on him.

The slaves were drifting away, looking over their shoulders uneasily, afraid of being ordered to stop, afraid that these white men would change their minds and they would be rounded up and sent off to be hanged. Simon went to speak to them.

"I promise you that my men and I, and Doctor Macintyre, will swear that there was no uprising here. No one but the woman Chloe was hurt, and we know that that was because she had done harm to you. A good attorney will be able to keep the women who killed her from being punished for it, and I will see to it that they get the best."

Miranda lifted her head proudly. "If they hang me, at least Chloe's dead. If her spirit come back from the grave looking for revenge, maybe it will be only me she gets, 'cause I'm the one that killed her. Maybe her spirit will be satisfied with me, and leave the others alone."

Miranda's eyes were dark and brooding, filled not with fear for herself but fear for her child. "If she leave Arla be, Arla will see to my little one. If she gets Arla like she gets me, Adele will see to our babies. But if she revenge herself on our babies, then killing her didn't do no good.''

Simon's heart twisted for her. ''There are no such things as spells and evil spirits. Any evil that Chloe brought about on this plantation came from her own hand, not from magic.''

Miranda's eyes rested on his, dark with the knowledge that had been handed down through countless generations.

''We know things no white man knows. We know that Chloe's spirit can come back and do more evil. Might be that Papa Emile could cast spells to stop her. If you would ask the white doctor to ask him to come, might be he would. Maybe then we'd have a chance, Arla and me. Maybe Chloe will come back to put curses on every slave on this plantation 'cause of what I did, but maybe Papa Emile could stop her. Will you ask him, Captain Spencer?''

Helplessly, Simon nodded. He realized that it would be impossible for him to wipe out the superstitions of generations in the short time he had, that in all probability it would be impossible in any case.

''I'll ask him,'' he said. If it would relieve this woman's mind, and alleviate the fears of the others, it would do no harm. He would be glad to pay the gangan for his services out of his own pocket, anything that Papa Emile asked.

He must also make sure that Miranda and the other woman had legal representation if they should need it, that there would be someone with the best legal training to speak for all these people if Vanessa proved so vindictive that she brought charges of having rebelled against her to bear on them.

He only hoped that if the worst came to the worst, his own legal representative would do as good a job for him and for Ian and for Aaron Godbehere as Miranda's would do for her. His crewmen had done nothing wrong, they had only followed orders, and so they should have nothing to fear.

Right at the moment, everything hinged on Daniel Maynard's recovery, a recovery that would have to take place before Vanessa had a chance to talk to anyone.

What his desperate plan to rescue Daniel Maynard might do to Ian was something that he did not want to face. Ian was a free agent, he had not been compelled to take part in this scheme, and any jury would take that into consideration when it passed sentence on him. To have ruined another man's life, perhaps to have cost him that life itself, was a burden that Simon prayed that he would not be called upon to bear.

He turned back to Aaron as Miranda and the other slaves started to drift back toward the fields. He hoped to heaven that they would stay there, and harbor no thoughts of a genuine uprising. They faced enough trouble without that.

"Aaron, if I were to ask you to keep someone in close custody, on the ship, under guard, what would your reaction be?" Captain or not, Simon would be hard put to demand that Aaron do this thing if the first mate disagreed. The act would implicate him so deeply that he would be certain to have to face the full penalties of the law if Simon's scheme failed.

"The person being the lady in there?" Aaron nodded toward the house.

"Yes. It might be necessary for you to lay out to sea for a few days, without me, and with her on board. It is essential to keep her from seeing or talking to anyone for a few days. After that, things will have resolved themselves one way or another." And pray God that they would have resolved themselves as Simon hoped, or all of their gooses would be cooked!

"So you propose to add kidnapping the lady and her unlawful restraint to the kidnapping and unlawful restraint of her father, and to fomenting a slave uprising, to your crimes!" Aaron's eyes were like flint. For a moment Simon wondered if he were going to refuse outright. Because Aaron was right, they were crimes. Without a shred of real proof against Vanessa, Simon was proposing to take the law into his own hands.

If Daniel Maynard were to die from the trauma of being removed from his bed and the exhaustion from the journey into Kingston, murder would be added to the charges of kidnapping. And this was a foreign country, and it would go hard on aliens who had dared to abuse Jamaica's hospitality in such a highhanded manner. Asking Aaron to involve himself even more deeply than he had already done was asking too much of him, but still Simon hoped that he would agree.

"I expect that it wouldn't do to let the lady talk to anyone, until you've been able to prove something one way or the other," Aaron conceded. "Amity will be disgraced if I'm thrown into a Jamaican prison, she'll never let me hear the last of it." Amity was Aaron's wife; the two had been married for almost twenty-five years, and on the whole they got along admirably well, but Amity had a strong sense of what was decent and fitting and what was not. For Aaron to be arrested would put a strong strain on their relationship, even if he were to be exonerated later.

Aaron considered Simon's proposal for only a moment longer.

"I expect that we'd better do it. If Mr. Maynard gets well, maybe we'll be allowed to sail away from this place instead of being hanged out of hand."

"I can offer you no guarantee that things will turn out as we hope." Simon's throat felt tight. "We may be jumping from the frying pan into the fire."

"As long as we're already hopping around on a hot frying pan, we might as well jump, and hope we miss the fire," Aaron said laconically. "Although what your father is going to say about all of this is something I'd druther not think about. He has a sharp tongue, your father. I won't be the only one never to hear the last of it."

"At least his sharp tongue won't fall on you. I'll make him understand that I gave you direct orders."

"On land, not at sea." Aaron's voice was dry. "There's a difference there, Cap'n, and your father isn't one to overlook it. Between him and Amity, I might wish they'd hanged me after all."

Simon granted him that, but there was no help for it.

"Send one of the men to have the curricle hitched up. No, you'd better make that two men, and have them keep their pistols drawn. The slaves at Maynard Penn have suffered too much at the hands of white people, and although I hope they took my advice to heart it wouldn't do to count on it. I have to go and see about restraining Vanessa, and getting her father out of the house."

Aaron nodded, and Simon strode up the outside staircase and through the wide door. Vanessa was pacing up and down in the drawing room, her face ashen with fury, and Ian was keeping a wary eye on her.

"Vanessa, I'm afraid that I have to insist that you come with us," Simon told her. It was an effort to keep his voice even reasonably courteous. What he would like to do was to throttle her where she stood. This woman had made a fool of him, she'd used him in the most shameful manner, and his pride was smarting. Add to that Noelle's suffering at her hands, and Simon would have as soon see her drop dead. "We will treat you as gently as you will allow us, but if you struggle, we will have to use severe measures to keep you under control."

Vanessa stared at him, her eyes dilating. "You wouldn't dare! If you lay a hand on me, I'll have you prosecuted to the full extent of the law! You will be prosecuted in any case for invading my home with an armed force, for causing the murder of my servant, for interfering with the care and well-being of my father.

"You must be mad, Simon! There is no other way to account for your actions. If you aren't hanged for your crimes, I'll make sure that you are put away in an institution for the criminally insane for the rest of your life! And Noelle will be committed as well, for having incited you to do these things! It will be either prison or an asylum for her, and I will see to it that she never has another day of freedom!''

''I don't happen to believe that Noelle lied to me,'' Simon told her. ''What I am doing now is gathering proof that she did not lie.''

''Simon, think! You know that you can't get away with this, you know that nobody in Jamaica will believe you, or anything that Noelle tries to make them believe! For the sake of what was between us before this madness overtook you, I will give you a chance to get away without being placed under arrest. Your ship is ready to sail, all you have to do is take your men and return to it and weigh anchor. I shouldn't make you such a generous offer, but I was fond of you, I loved you, and I hope that once you have got away from Jamaica your senses will return to you. I can still put Chloe's death down to a rebellion among the slaves, one that I was able to quell.''

It was a generous offer indeed. The flaw in it was that Simon could see the desperation that lay behind it. Vanessa wanted no investigation, for fear of what might be found. And what was to happen to Noelle if Simon were to take advantage of her offer?

As if she could read his thoughts, Vanessa played her last card.

''I'll let you take Noelle with you. Only see that she never returns to Jamaica, and I will never call her to account for what she has done! She will be safe, and you will be safe, and you can forget everything that has happened.''

For a moment, Simon was tempted. He had no assurance that Vanessa would not win against them if he persevered in the course he was taking. Not only he and Ian and Aaron would suffer the consequences, but Noelle as well.

The temptation only lasted for a moment.

''Ian, go and see to Daniel. One of the crew will help you carry him to the curricle. I'll take care of Vanessa.''

''Get away from me!'' Vanessa stood her ground as Simon advanced on her. ''Don't come one step closer!''

Simon not only came a step closer, but he grasped her waist in a grip that even her frantic struggles couldn't break. Pulling her along after him to the doorway, he called to one of his tars.

"Ned, will you come here? I want you to find something to bind this lady's hands and feet, and to stop her mouth. I'm afraid I can't let loose of her long enough to find anything myself."

His eyes starting out of his head, stunned by Vanessa's beauty and her anger, Ned Campbell obeyed. The seaman was only nineteen years old, and in all of his nineteen years he had never laid his hand on a woman. But his captain had given an order, and he jumped to obey it.

A sheet was ripped into strips, one of which was used to bind Vanessa's hands and another her feet. A third strip made an effective gag. Ned Campbell, his face a fiery red, backed off when the trussing up was finished.

"Will that be all, Cap'n?"

"I think it will be sufficient. Go and find Ian Macintyre, and help him with the sick man. We will be leaving directly."

Ned Campbell was glad of that. He needed fresh salt air from the ocean to wipe the stink of violence and death from his nostrils, he needed the familiar surroundings of shipboard to wipe what he had seen at this plantation from his mind's eye. When the cap'n said that they would be leaving directly, Ned hoped fervently that he had meant that they would be setting sail and that they would never come back to Jamaica.

Chapter Sixteen

IAN REAPPEARED IN THE ENTRANCE TO THE DRAWING room, a bottle of Daniel's tonic in his hand. "Mr. Maynard is asleep, and if I have any claim at all to being a doctor, it's a drugged sleep. But his heart is reasonably steady, I think he'll be able to endure the trip to Kingston. I'm going to take this along with me to see if I can figure out what's in it, and if you can wait for a few more minutes, I'd like to gather up any other potions and powders that Chloe might have in her hut. Where the devil is that girl Julie? She'll be able to direct me. For that matter, where are any of the house servants? I haven't had a glimpse of one since I came in!"

Simon raised his voice, using every ounce of his best quarter-deck authority. "Julie! Come here at once!" His shout seemed to make the walls of the house tremble, and he congratulated himself that even Aaron couldn't have done better.

Julie, trembling in every limb, came creeping into the room, her eyes wide with terror. She and the other house servants had taken refuge in Noelle's room when the trouble had started, and Julie's hair was disheveled because she had crawled under the bed seeking additional safety.

"Julie, you are to take Doctor Macintyre to Chloe's hut. I know that you know which one it is."

Julie's eyes rolled, showing white all around.

"No, sir, please sir, I can't go in there! Not nobody can go in there, the spirits'll get us if we does! The duppies'll reach right down and get us!"

Ian spoke sternly. "Duppies never hurt anyone, Julie. They're benign spirits, Papa Emile told me that. And you won't have to go inside, all you have to do is lead me there."

Chloe's hut was set apart from the others in the slave village, for the simple reason that all of the slaves were too terrified of her to have her as a close neighbor. Their fear of her was so great that, before Vanessa had ordered another hut, larger and more comfortable, built for her at some distance from the others, their work had suffered.

The air in the hut had a peculiar odor that made Ian wrinkle his nose when he entered, but he noted that the place was furnished with a real bed, with an upholstered chair and a table, and there were curtains at the slatted windows, luxuries that none of the other slaves enjoyed. There was a rug on the floor, and pictures on the walls, and real china and glassware in the open cupboard.

Ian had no interest in these trappings of special favor. His eyes went immediately to two open shelves where jars and vials were lined up in a row, as well as containers that held feathers and bones and other matter that looked like dried viscera of various animals, along with things so unidentifiable that he did not care to think about them.

Making sure that every container was securely sealed, he swept them into a pillow sham from Chloe's bed and left the hut. He would be interested in Papa Emile's reaction to these materials. He had a very good idea that the gangan would be able to tell him what they were, if he so chose. Whether or not he would choose to do so was another matter. In that case, Ian would find out for himself, although it would take a good deal longer.

Daniel Maynard was still sleeping when he was carried outside and lifted into the curricle, but it was a good deal more trouble to get Vanessa inside. Bound and gagged as she was, she still struggled, so that it took two men to handle her.

Simon called the house servants together. They stood in a line in front of him, their faces showing their terror.

"You have nothing to fear," Simon told them. "The obeah woman is dead, and Doctor Macintyre will send Papa Emile to Maynard Penn to counteract any evil that she might have left behind." Ian suppressed a grin, wondering what his prosaic father, back in Edinburgh, would have to say about his son having anything to do with such heathen goings-on. For that matter, he wondered what Simon's father would have to say! It was as well that their sires could not see across the hundreds of miles of ocean, and know what their scions were up to.

"I am leaving you in charge of the house. I expect you to take the same care of it that you did under Vanessa's rule. Only this time, you will be caring for it for your master, and for Mistress Noelle. You are to admit no one, and you are to talk to no one. If anyone should call, you are to tell them that no one is at home. Do you understand that?"

Simon waited. There were tentative nods, but it was plain that these people were not sure that they would be able to fend off questions asked by white people if they should come. Simon groped for something to ensure their silence, and came up with it.

"Papa Emile will call you to account, when he comes," he said. Ian all but choked. "If you have obeyed my orders, he will smile upon you. If you have not, you will have to answer to him."

A sudden courage appeared in Julie's eyes. She had always hated Chloe as well as feared her, and been jealous of her authority as well. "Will I be in charge? Will I be the boss?"

"You will be the boss," Simon told her. "When your master is well, which will be very soon, he will put you in charge of all the house servants, on a permanent basis. For now, I give you full authority."

A gleam came into Julie's eyes. She turned to the other servants and clapped her hands. "What you just standing here for, doing nothing? Get to work! I don't want to see one speck of dust in this house, you hear me? Polish them floors, do it now!" It didn't matter that the floors were already polished to such a sheen that faces were mirrored in them, they would be polished again. Julie would see to that. She was the boss woman, she was in charge.

Lying in a trussed-up bundle on the floor of the curricle, where she would be out of sight of anyone they might meet on the road, Vanessa had given up struggling as hopeless, but her eyes still spat hate. Simon spared her only a glance before he swung into the driver's seat and took up the lines. At least he could drive better than he could ride, and it was easier on his posterior.

He had accomplished what he had set out to do, he had Daniel out of Vanessa's and Chloe's power, and he had made sure that Vanessa could cause no more mischief until he chose to set her free. He had a burning hope that everything would work out as he had planned, but still his mind was dark with worry.

Leaving Noelle in the mountains under the doubtful protection of the Maroons had been the hardest thing he had ever had to do. With only Cuffie to guard them, both girls were at the mercy of a man whose moods were unpredictable, to say the least. The leader might have already regretted his generosity in letting Simon take one of the horses, and letting the chasseurs go as well when he would much rather have killed them. What was to prevent him from taking out his frustration on the girls and on Cuffie?

But time had been the most important factor, and the

Maroon leader had flatly refused to spare any more horses. Noelle had begged him to go, the torment in her eyes showing her worry for her father. Still, Simon would not draw an easy breath until he had seen her again, until he could hold her safe in his arms. If the leader did not keep his promise and bring the three remaining refugees down out of the mountains, Simon would find him, no matter where he tried to hide, and this time he would be armed.

His relief when he saw Cuffie sitting on the verge of the road, his arms wrapped around his knees, only eight miles from Maynard Penn, was so great that he felt weak. He drew the curricle to a halt, and the rest of the entourage reined in.

"Cuffie! You made it down! But where is Noelle, and Dicey?"

"There," Cuffie pointed. "Thought it best they keep hid. I got something for you, Captain. The Maroon told me to give it back to you. He wound it too tight and it broke. Said it weren't no good, and don't you never come back in his mountains or he'll kill you for giving him something that weren't no good."

Simon held out his hand, and his fingers closed over the watch that his father had given him.

"I warned him not to wind it too tight. I wonder what made him do it."

"Don' know that, Captain. But I knows his name now. His name is Simon, same as yours."

So the man had a sense of humor, after all! No doubt he was chuckling right now, thinking of Simon's reaction when he found out that they had the same name. And Simon had a sudden suspicion that the other Simon had wound the watch too tight on purpose. The man wasn't stupid. Having the mainspring broken had given him the excuse to send it back to him. The man had not only kept his word about bringing Cuffie and the girls down, but he had gone one step more.

Simon wished the other Simon well. He was sure of one thing, and that was that he would never forget him.

Now Noelle and Dicey were running toward them.

They had done the best they could about their appearance before they had started down out of the mountains, but still Noelle looked exhausted and bedraggled. Simon leaped out of the curricle and ran to meet her, sweeping her into his arms and holding her close, feeling her heart beat against his.

"You have my father? Is he still alive, is he all right?"

"He's still alive, and Ian thinks that he will be all right. He's certainly heavily drugged, Ian is sure of that, but that will wear off when he is not administered any more."

"And my sister? Where is she?"

"She's in the curricle, trussed up like a chicken ready for market. We are going to take very good care of your sister, you can be sure of that. She will have no opportunity to see or talk to anyone until we have your father well on the road to recovery, so that his testimony can be used against her. You'd better get in the curricle now, darling. It will be dark long before we reach Kingston, which is what we want, but you need a place to rest and recover."

"I'm all right. As long as my father is safe, I'll always be all right. But I am not going to get into the curricle with my sister, I'd walk all the way to Kingston before I'll share a carriage with her even if she is tied up!"

"I'm afraid that you're going to have to bear her company for a few days, no matter how much you dislike it," Simon told her. "I'm going to put her on the *Maid of Boston,* and I'm going to put you in the same place. Aaron is going to take the ship out to sea, until it's safe for you to be brought back. If the worst should happen, if it turns out that we'll be charged with kidnapping and even more serious things, I want you safe. Aaron will have orders to set sail for Boston, taking you out of any danger of being prosecuted. As for Vanessa, he can set her ashore at the nearest port, with money enough to buy passage back to Jamaica, although I'd as soon tell him to throw her overboard!"

"I won't stay on the ship with Vanessa! I want to stay with my father! How can there be any danger of being charged with kidnapping or anything else, if my father is going to get well?''

"Unfortunately, Henry Cottswood knows something of what has been going on. He insisted on starting out with us when we went to Maynard Penn to rescue your father, but Ian managed to put him out of action and leave him behind. However, knowing Henry, he'll make it his business to discover exactly what we've done, and also knowing Henry, he'll insist on being self-important and calling in the authorities in short order if your father does not recover sufficiently to talk, in a short enough time. And if Ian should be wrong, if your father should not recover . . .''

"Don't say that! Don't ever say that! He's going to get well, he has to get well! And I won't leave him, you can't make me, and I won't ride in the curricle with Vanessa either!" Noelle's little fists pounded on Simon's chest, and tears of fury were coursing down her cheeks.

Ian thought that it was time to intervene. Dismounting, he came to put his arms around Noelle. She clung to him, pressing her face into his shoulder, and Simon felt an unreasonable surge of jealousy.

"She can ride double with me, Simon. I don't blame her for not wanting to ride with Vanessa. She'll be all right, I'll take care of her. Let Cuffie and Dicey ride in the curricle, Dicey can watch Daniel and let me know if she thinks he needs me.''

There was infinite tenderness in the way Ian lifted Noelle onto his horse, and Simon felt his face muscles stiffen. The way Noelle was looking at him as if he were her savior was enough to make him grit his teeth. There was no mistaking Ian's feelings for Noelle, the man was in love with her, and now in spite of the nights that he and Noelle had spent wrapped in each other's arms against the chill of the mountain air and for comfort during the dangers they had had to endure at the hands of the Maroons, Noelle was turning to Ian because she was angry with Simon.

He set the horses into motion again. He had no moral right to be jealous, and there was no time for it now, anyway. There were still many miles to cover and many things that had to be done before the sun rose again. By that time, Noelle would be safely on board the *Maid of Boston*, if he had to tie her up and carry her just as Vanessa would be carried! She would forgive him when all of this was over, or she wouldn't.

If Noelle didn't forgive him, if she chose Ian instead, at least he had the consolation that Ian was a better man than Henry Cottswood. Simon wouldn't be able to live with the knowledge that Noelle had married Henry, but Ian would make her a good husband, he would love and cherish her as she deserved to be loved and cherished.

If that should happen, if Noelle should actually choose to marry Ian, Simon should bow out of the picture with good grace, and wish them happiness. But would he be able to do it? Right at the moment he wasn't at all sure that he would.

What a fool he'd been, what a blind, fatuous fool, to let Vanessa Maynard blind him with her beauty, to be taken in by the saintly façade that covered the evil that was her true nature! If he'd lost Noelle, it served him no more than right. But he knew that he would spend the rest of his life wanting her, and castigating himself for having thrown away his only chance for happiness with the girl he had been stupid enough to betray and lose.

His heart was filled with foreboding as they continued their journey. The few other travelers they met on the road looked at them with open curiosity. Fortunately, they saw no white face, and the natives, the slaves and the mustees and the free blacks, did not presume to question them, but only smiled and bobbed their heads and wished them a pleasant journey. Still they must have wondered at the presence of the party of grim-faced, armed men who were escorting a curricle that seemed to contain only Simon, and two blacks who should by rights either be mounted on mules or donkeys, or walking.

Simon slowed their pace, but even so they had to stop

and wait for the hour to become sufficiently late so that they could risk driving through the streets of town and then carrying Vanessa aboard the *Maid of Boston*. If Noelle would not board the ship willingly, the danger would be all the greater.

Noelle boarded the ship, reluctantly, and refusing to look at Simon. Simon did not know how Ian had persuaded her, but he was thankful that he had. If everything caved in around them, at least Noelle would be safe. Aaron would take her to his family in Boston, and they would care for her as tenderly as though she were the daughter-in-law to them that Simon had hoped, even if Simon himself never returned.

In time, she would forget him. In time, she would fall in love with and marry some upstanding New England man, possibly a sea-faring man, but certainly one who would make her happy. His mother and father would make sure that her choice was the right one, Simon could trust them for that.

It was a noble thought, but all the same Simon had a sudden, fierce wish that when Noelle was in her marriage bed, images of him would return to haunt her. So much for nobility of spirit! He was no saint, and he had never been one, and Noelle was his, and even if he was dead at the end of the rope Vanessa would use to hang him with, he didn't want Noelle to belong to anyone else.

"I'm sorry that you will have to share my cabin with your sister," Simon apologized to Noelle. "It's the only one on board that's large enough to accommodate both of you. This isn't a passenger ship, it's a cargo ship. Aaron has a cabin, as first mate, but it's very small. I expect that if Vanessa gives you too much trouble, you can stay in there when Aaron isn't using it. If I could, I'd order that Vanessa be kept tied up and gagged, but that isn't possible, as you will be aboard for three days."

"I expect I'll live through it, but don't expect me to like it!" Noelle said tartly. "If I tear every hair out of Vanessa's head before I'm allowed off this boat, don't be surprised!" She looked down at her hands, ruefully, and

Simon wanted to take them in his own and kiss every one of her fingers.

But he couldn't do that in front of Aaron and Ian, even if Noelle would have allowed it, in her present mood. He settled for trying to kiss her cheek, but she jerked her head away from him.

Ian was keeping a close watch on Vanessa. From the malice in her eyes, he judged that she was not going to give her sister an easy time.

"You'd best keep Miss Maynard gagged until you've put out to sea. If you were to remove the gag now, I've no doubt that she'd scream the ship down and alert every soul on shore for a mile around. I'll take one of the crewmen with me when I take Daniel Maynard to my place, and send back a potion you might be able to force down her that will keep her quiet until you can set sail. It won't hurt her, but it will make her sleep the sleep of the innocent who haven't a guilty deed to haunt them."

"Thank you, Ian." Noelle's smile was brilliant as she smiled at the young doctor. "At least you have some regard for my feelings, if Simon doesn't!"

"Noelle, you know that that isn't true! I have every regard for your feelings, it's simply necessary that we do things my way. Aaron, this is how we will manage things. You know that high hill a mile from the city? Keep a watch on it every night. If it's necessary for you to up anchor and sail for Boston, I'll see that a bonfire is lighted at the top of it. If no bonfire is lighted after the third night, you are to bring the girls back to Kingston, because things will have turned in our favor."

"I'll do that, Cap'n. But heaven help me, if I have to sail for Boston without you! Luke Spencer will have my hide for leaving you behind."

"My father will understand, when you and Noelle explain everything to him."

"If you think that I'm going to Boston, you're very much mistaken! I can swim, Simon, and I'll swim back here if I have to!"

"Through shark-infested waters, for several miles?

Don't even suggest such an idiotic thing! Aaron is going to have enough trouble with Vanessa without having to keep a close eye on you! Don't make things harder on any of us than they have to be, Noelle. I'm doing the best I can, what I think is right. If you don't approve, I'm sorry, but that's still the way it has to be.''

Back at the curricle, where two of the sailors were guarding Daniel Maynard, Simon slammed one of his fists into the palm of his other hand.

"Damn it, Ian, while we were still in the mountains, Noelle gave every indication that she loved me, she even told me that she did! I thought that everything was right between us, but now I don't know what to think!''

"There's no accounting for women, Simon. You'd be wise not to try. Noelle will get over it, even if she's miffed with you now. Let's get along, I want to get Daniel to bed, and then take a good look at those jars and bottles I collected from Chloe's hut. I wish Papa Emile were around, but I haven't the foggiest notion of where he lives. The man came to me, to check me out, I suppose, when he heard that a new white doctor was in town. He's always come to me, choosing his own times, never with any advance notice. I expect that there's no use in hoping that he might choose tonight for one of his visits!''

"You can put word about, tomorrow, that you want to see him. Word spreads through the native population like wildfire. Just tell some lad that you need Papa Emile, and the chances are that the old man will show up,'' Simon told him. "As soon as we get Daniel to bed, I'll take the curricle to the Cottswoods'. I'd as soon it wasn't seen outside your place, someone would be bound to ask questions. I have to see to the return of the Cottswoods' horses, as well, although how they'll take being awakened at this hour of the night I have no idea. If there was any way of sneaking the curricle and the horses into their stable without arousing them, I'd do it, and put off having to face them and their questions until tomorrow.''

Ian sympathized with him, but that was Simon's problem. His own was to make sure that Daniel was all right, and to try to ascertain exactly what dangerous and lethal substances Chloe had had at her disposal.

Simon was right about not being able to leave the curricle and the horses at the Cottswood stables without rousing the family. The stables were locked tight, and the slave who tended them would not have accommodated him without permission even if he had been able to. As the slave was not entrusted with the keys, but had to rouse a house slave to rouse the master to get them, Simon had no alternative but to face Bertram Cottswood that night.

Not only Bertram, but the entire family. And as he had dreaded, it was Henry he had to answer to first.

Henry was not only angry, he was beside himself with indignation.

"I know perfectly well that that upstart young physician put something into that abominable wine he pressed on me to put me out of action! No wine in the world would have made me that ill, let alone put me to sleep for several hours, no matter how poor it was! It was done to keep me from accompanying you to Maynard Penn, and there's no use in your trying to deny it! I intend to have some answers, and I intend to have them now!"

"Henry, for goodness sake be quiet! How can poor Captain Spencer explain anything if you won't let him get a word in edgeways? I never knew anyone who runs on the way you do, you're always talking, nobody else ever has a chance! And just look at poor Captain Spencer! He's absolutely exhausted, he's still unshaven, and he must be famished! I don't care how late it is, have Esther fix him some supper right now, a lot of supper! Claude, don't just stand there, fetch Captain Spencer something to drink! Father, have water heated so that he can bathe. If he has to tell a long, involved story, the least we can do is see that he's comfortable while he's telling it! Yes, Mama, I know I'm in my nightgown and robe, but I am not going to go to my room and get dressed because I have no intention of missing one word of Captain Spencer's story! I'm quite decent as I am, and certainly well enough chaperoned, with my entire family around me, and don't you dare go swooning, you're in your nightrobes too, and nobody's ordering you to go and get dressed!''

As always, Brenda stopped talking only because she had run out of breath. If the situation hadn't been so serious Simon would have had to laugh.

"You can go and dress, Miss Cottswood. It will make your mother feel better, and I promise that I won't say a word until you get back."

"Well, I should certainly hope that you wouldn't! I'm Noelle's best friend, after all, I have a right to know everything that concerns her, and this certainly concerns her because you've been to Maynard Penn! Where is she, does she know what's going on? Does Vanessa know? Henry, stop glaring at me, I have as much right to ask questions as you do! You'll get your turn later. Remember, Captain Spencer, not one word, even one, before I get back!"

"You have my solemn promise," Simon assured her. Satisfied with that, Brenda left them to make herself decent, her mother scuttling along with her to do the same.

"Now, sir, I want those answers!" Henry exploded, as soon as his sister had left the room.

"I'm sorry, but you'll have to wait until your sister returns. I gave my word as a gentleman, and I have no intention of breaking it," Simon told him blandly, and he was gratified to see Henry's face turn a bright red and hear the sputtering that was all his indignant state would let him get out.

The story, when he told it, was received with all of the incredulity that Simon had expected. Not only incredulity, but indignation and righteous anger.

"Do you mean to tell me, Captain Spencer, that you removed Daniel Maynard from Maynard Penn by *force?* That you invaded the plantation with armed men, and took him away without a by-your-leave?"

"As there was no other way to get him away, that is

251

exactly what we did. But as I told you when I asked you to lend me your horses, Noelle not only knows, but approves, of my actions.''

''Noelle! Noelle has no authority, it is Vanessa who is in charge of Maynard Penn now that her father is too ill to manage the place! Surely Vanessa must have been there, and I cannot conceive that she would allow you to take her father away, as ill as he is!''

''Vanessa is fully aware that we have taken her father.'' Simon felt perspiration gathering on his forehead. This was becoming even more difficult than he had thought it would be.

''I am afraid that I will have to make sure of that!'' Bertram Cottswood told him. ''Henry, you are to ride to Maynard Penn at first light, to confirm what Captain Spencer has told us. Otherwise, this is a matter for the authorities. Kidnapping, sir! If you have actually kidnapped the man, against Vanessa's wishes, you will find that Jamaica does not deal lightly with such criminal acts!''

Without any doubt Henry would burn up the road between Kingston and Maynard Penn, but his journey would be for nothing. He would not find Vanessa at home, and Simon had confidence that neither Julie nor any of the other slaves would tell him a thing. Right at the moment, Simon was not about to tell these people that not only Daniel Maynard had been kidnapped, but Vanessa as well. If that fact were divulged, both he and Ian would be behind bars before another hour had passed! It was time they needed, two or three days' time, and he would somehow have to find a means of holding Bertram Cottswood off until Ian could tell them, with assurance, that Daniel was on the road to recovery.

''Mr. Cottswood, I have good reason to believe that Daniel Maynard was being drugged, that the woman Chloe was systematically introducing some substance into the medicine that Doctor Eastlake left for him. Dicey, Noelle's girl, saw the woman put something into Daniel's bottle of tonic. That is why we took him away from Maynard Penn, to see if his condition will improve now that we can make sure that no drugs are administered to him.''

"Chloe is an obeah woman! Everybody in Kingston knows that!'' Brenda's excitement was blazing in her cheeks. "Papa, maybe she did drug Mr. Maynard! I wouldn't put anything past that woman, I never liked her, she always gave me the chills! And I know Dicey well, I'm absolutely positive that she wouldn't have lied! And I'm just as positive that Vanessa wouldn't believe anything against Chloe, Chloe has been her nursemaid and then her personal maid since Vanessa was just a little girl. No wonder Noelle wanted you to take her father away, Captain Spencer! In her place I'd have done the same thing!''

"Brenda, be quiet!'' Henry was bristling, his face red with anger. "If I ever have a daughter, I'll make sure that she's trained to speak only when she's spoken to! As I see it, no matter the reason Mr. Maynard was taken from his home, it should be Doctor Eastlake who was called in to attend him here in Kingston! The man should have been brought here, we were given to understand that you would bring him here, Captain Spencer! Instead he's under the care of an upstart young doctor about whom we know nothing, whose credentials are sadly lacking! I shall not only ride to Maynard Penn to confirm what you have told me, but Doctor Eastlake must be sent for the first thing in the morning, and Mr. Maynard must be brought here to our house so that we can make sure that he is receiving every care!''

"It is Noelle's express wish that Ian Macintyre care for her father.'' Simon faced the irate young man down. "And Vanessa is fully aware that Ian is now in charge of her father's case. For the moment, Mr. Maynard is all right where he is, where Ian can keep a constant eye on him. Later, when he has improved, he can be brought here where he will be more comfortable.''

"Captain Spencer, this is all highly irregular! I am of a mind to call in the authorities immediately," Bertram Cottswood said.

"As long as both Noelle and Vanessa know that we have their father, and that Ian is caring for him, surely you can wait a day or two? You will be able to see Daniel for yourself tomorrow, and make sure that he is all right."

"Of course we must wait!" Brenda said. "My goodness gracious, think of the embarrassment it would cause Noelle and Vanessa if you were to go chasing off after the authorities and have poor Captain Spencer, and poor Doctor Macintyre, put to all that trouble! Why, Captain Spencer would be perfectly within his rights to place countercharges against you for false arrest! Where is Noelle, Captain? I should have thought that she would have come with you, to be close to her father!"

Somehow, Simon managed to meet her eyes. "Noelle is with Vanessa. You will see both of them in good time. I'm afraid that I must leave you now. Ian McIntyre might need my help in attending his patient. Just bear in mind that Doctor Eastlake is off Mr. Maynard's case; Noelle is not satisfied with him and she has complete trust in Ian."

He left the Cottswood house quickly, before he could be asked any more questions that he would be hard put to answer. Thank God for Brenda! As scatterbrained as the girl appeared to be on the surface, she was proving a godsend to him and Ian now. As long as she was on their side, it was possible that they might be granted the time they needed.

There was no turning back now. They had set their course, and they must follow it. If it led them into a storm that would destroy them, then it couldn't be helped.

At least Noelle was safe. She and Dicey and Cuffie were aboard the *Maid of Boston,* to be taken to Simon's parents if things went against them here. The thought that he himself might be hanged, knowing that Vanessa would go scot-free, was something that made him flinch, but knowing that Noelle was safe in Boston might make it a little easier, if not much.

Chapter Seventeen

In any other circumstances, Noelle would have been enthralled to be on board the *Maid of Boston*, laying well off the shoreline of Jamaica. She had never been on a sailing ship before, except for her two tours to inspect the craft with Simon, the second one ruined by Vanessa's presence.

The weather could not have been more perfect. Although the day was hot, there was a breeze, and the ship rocked in the gentle swells, but not enough to cause Noelle discomfort. A few fleecy, white clouds broke the monotony of a sky that was dazzling blue, and all around her the ocean seemed to stretch into infinity.

Vanessa had just begun to stir when Noelle had left the captain's cabin that they were forced to share. Simon's cabin, where everything it contained belonged to him, had been handled by him. Its appointments impressed Noelle with their neatness and utility, not an inch of space was wasted. The table where he spread out his charts and took his meals was bolted down, as were the chairs and the cabinets and the narrow bed. Overhead, a lamp hung from the beams, swinging with every swell of the waves. Every surface in the cabin was immaculately clean and polished to a high gloss.

As it had been necessary for Vanessa to be given the bed because of the potion that Aaron Godbehere had forced down her throat, sending her into a deep sleep, a hammock had been rigged for Noelle. At first she had marveled that the sailors could sleep in such contraptions, which seemed to turn completely over with every movement to throw the occupant out, but after a while she had got the hang of it, and after a few more moments the gentle swaying had served to lull her to sleep.

She had roused three or four times during the night, not understanding why her bed was moving, not knowing where she was. And then she had remembered, and worry about her father had held her rigid, with her hands clenched tightly and tears gathering in her eyes.

Ian had told her that her father was all right, and she had to trust him. But the last time she had seen Daniel, he had seemed so close to death that a breath might carry him away. She remembered the man he had been before he had been stricken with the illness that seemed determined to kill him long before his natural time. He wasn't a particularly tall man—Kenneth, at sixteen, had already been taller than his father—but he had been strongly built, with broad shoulders and muscular arms and legs, and always in perfect health. When Noelle had been a child, it had never occurred to her that he wasn't indestructible, that, like God, he would not live forever.

But it had never occurred to her that her brother would die, either. Kenneth had seemed as indestructible as her father, as impossible to destroy. Kenneth had been the second half of herself, and then one day he'd been gone, and the world had trembled under her feet and there had been no safety anywhere, nothing to cling to and believe in with a belief that could not be shaken.

First Kenneth, and then her father. And Vanessa's face had remained serene, her calm unshaken, her eyes clear and guileless, and Chloe had looked at Noelle with her inscrutable eyes, and smiled, and smiled, and smiled, while Noelle's world had crumbled around her and there had been no happiness anywhere.

Until Simon had come to Jamaica, astride the deck of this beautiful ship that he had brought limping into port, and she had dared to believe, just for a little while, that the world would right itself again.

But there had been Vanessa, just as there had always been Vanessa. And Vanessa had taken Simon, and Vanessa and Chloe had been poisoning her father, but nobody would believe her and there had been nothing she could do about it.

The adventure in the mountains, when she and Simon and Dicey and Cuffie had escaped death by so narrow a margin that even now she could scarcely believe that they were still alive, was beginning to seem like a dream to her, a nightmare from which she was only just awakening. Her terror that Simon would die, her terror as they had fled from the chasseurs, her terror when the Maroon leader Simon had threatened to take Dicey, was already beginning to fade, and someday it would fade away entirely.

Now that she had had a chance to rest, to sleep without fear of being murdered before she woke, Noelle was ashamed of her outburst against Simon last night, when he had forced her to board the *Maid of Boston* against her wishes. She had wanted to stay with her father, it had seemed totally unreasonable to her that he would not allow it. The exhaustion that had resulted from her days and nights of brutal physical effort and of the fear that had never left her had left her in a state near hysteria.

What must Simon think of her! She'd acted like an unreasonable child, she had even struck him! She had turned her face away when he'd tried to kiss her, she had clung to Ian instead, like a spoiled child who was having a tantrum would cling to the one person she knew would take her side. Simon had been hurt, it had been clear on his face in the half-twilight of the Jamaica night.

How could she have behaved in such an unreasonable manner? Simon was risking imprisonment for her sake, risking his life itself! The thought that she might never see him again, that Aaron Godbehere would see a bonfire blazing on the shoreline and up anchor and turn the ship's prow toward Boston as Simon had ordered him, was more than she could bear. What use would her life be to her if Simon were imprisoned or dead, and her father was dead as well? It wouldn't matter how kind Simon's family would be to her, how warmly they would welcome her and cherish her, she would be as dead as Simon and her father even though she still walked and talked and breathed.

Simon had told Aaron to put Vanessa off at the nearest port, if the bonfire were sighted, but Noelle wondered if she would be able to see her half sister walk away free without trying to kill her and send her plunging into the hell she had earned by her actions here on earth. She wouldn't be able to bear knowing that Vanessa was to go unscathed, they would have to restrain her or she would find a way to plunge a knife into Vanessa's heart, or to cast her overboard to drown.

Dicey, with sleep still in her eyes, joined Noelle at the rail. The girl smiled, and reached out to smooth a tendril of Noelle's hair from her face where the breeze had blown it.

"Cuffie's still asleep," she said. "He was sick last night. The up and down of this ship made him throw up his insides. I wasn't sick, it didn't bother me none at all. He'll be all right, I think. Did you sleep, mistress?"

"Yes, I did. I wasn't sick either."

"Can't believe that Chloe's dead. Just can't believe it, even if the young doctor and Captain Spencer saw her get killed. It was Miranda done it. They didn't know her name, but I know it was Miranda. Don't blame her, she had the right 'cause Elisha's dead, but I don't see how she dared. Only maybe I do. If it was Cuffie that was dead 'cause of her, I think I'd have been able to kill her no matter how scared of her I was.''

Chloe, at least, had died for her crimes, and Noelle didn't blame Miranda either. When she got back to Maynard Penn, she'd make sure that Miranda wasn't made to suffer for what she had done. The young woman would be set free, she and her baby, although they would always have a home at the plantation if that was what Miranda wished.

If she ever got back to Maynard Penn! There was no certainty of that. It might be Vanessa who returned, not Noelle, and then Miranda's fate would be so dreadful that her only escape would be death, both for her and her child.

"Dicey, do you think my father will be all right, do you think he'll get well?'' The question made her throat constrict, so that it was hard to force the words out.

"'Course I do! Doctor Macintyre is a good doctor, a fine doctor, you told me so yourself. Captain Spencer trusts him and so we can trust him, too. Chloe can't go on hurting the master, Chloe's dead. And Mistress Vanessa is right here on this boat, so she can't hurt him neither. You just trust the doctor and Captain Spencer, and everything's going to be all right.''

Dicey's face lighted up as Cuffie appeared beside them. "You awake, you lazy man? Ain't this boat just beautiful? I never saw nothing so pretty. Never thought I'd get to be on a ship like this! Wish the sails was spread, with the wind blowing them and making them billow, like this morning when Mr. Godbehere put out to sea. You done missed that, Cuffie, you was fast asleep. I most missed it too, after you kept me awake most all of the night, but I woke up just in time.''

"It's pretty, but I likes solid ground under my feet,'' Cuffie said sheepishly. "Be glad to get back on shore.''

"Me, I'd like to go sailing for miles and miles and miles. Sailing like a bird, and feeling just as free!'' Dicey said, longing in her eyes.

But not now, not to Boston, leaving Simon behind, Noelle prayed! Simon imprisoned, her father dead!

Dicey reached out to steady her. "Mistress? You all right? You went as white as them sails, all of a sudden! You ain't been taken seasick, like Cuffie?"

"I'm all right." Noelle managed a smile, even though it was a wan attempt at one. She changed the subject, needing something to distract her mind. "Where did you and Cuffie sleep last night? Did you sleep in hammocks, like I did?"

"Mercy, no! Cuffie would have died of his sickness for sure in one of them things! We curled up in one of them little boats, 'cept for the time I was holding his head while he leaned over the railing. But tonight I'm going to sleep in a hammock, that'll be something! Got to try one of those, for sure, whilst I got the chance!"

"Then you'll sleep alone, girl!" Cuffie told her rather sourly.

Dicey looked demure. "Got to sleep alone anyhow. We ain't in the mountains now, don't have to sleep with you to keep that Maroon from taking me! And we ain't married yet, Cuffie."

Cuffie looked so stricken that Noelle felt sorry for him. And then she thought of something, and she hurried to find Aaron Godbehere.

Aaron was on the quarter-deck, surveying the sky with keen and narrowed eyes, his feet planted far apart as he swayed with the gentle roll of the ship, apparently not even noticing it.

"Miss Maynard! I trust that you slept well? I'll have some breakfast served up to you in short order, and for your servants, too."

"I'm not sure that Cuffie will want any breakfast. He was seasick last night." A dimple appeared at the corner of Noelle's mouth, and Aaron thought how much better he liked the appearance of this small girl, with her dark hair and brown eyes, than he liked Vanessa's fair beauty. "Dicey will appreciate some food, and so will I, but there's something we would like even better. Is it true that without the actual captain on board, you are the acting captain?''

"It is," Aaron told her, wondering what she could be getting at.

"And a captain can marry people, can't he? I've always heard that that was true."

"And which one of my crew are you thinking of marrying, Miss Maynard?" Amusement smiled in Aaron's eyes. "Providing that I thought it would be legal for me to perform such an act."

"But it must be legal, because you're the acting captain! And you know perfectly well that I don't want to marry anyone among your crew! I might be tempted to ask for your hand, but I understand that you're already taken."

"Very much so, or so my Amity would have me believe. If not you, there's only Dicey and Cuffie."

"Yes! It would mean so much to Dicey! Will you do it, Mr. Godbehere?"

Aaron considered for what seemed to Noelle to be an unreasonable length of time.

"Seeing that I'm the acting captain, and seeing that we're at sea even if we aren't moving, I expect that it would be legal enough. They might want to have it done over again later, just to make sure, but it would serve for now."

Noelle was already off and running. "Stay right where you are! I'll bring them!" she called over her shoulder.

It was probably the strangest wedding ever performed on shipboard. Both the bride and the groom were ragged and tattered, their clothing was far from clean even though Dicey had washed their garments in a mountain stream. Cold water, with no soap, had not done a good job, and they were wrinkled as well as ragged.

The bride's attendant was in almost as bad a case. Dicey had done what she could with Noelle's hair, but her riding habit was the worse for wear, torn and stained, her boots were scuffed, and her hands and face were scratched and her fingernails were torn down to the quick. Of the four people who stood in front of Aaron while he faltered his way through the wedding service, the seaman Ned Campbell, who had volunteered to stand up with Cuffie, was by far the most presentable. Ned's honest young face was beaming almost as broadly as Cuffie's. He was always ready to do his duty for his captain and his first mate, but today's duty was a deal more agreeable than the one he had been called upon to perform at Maynard Penn, the binding up of a furiously struggling woman who had screamed vitriolic obscenities at him until he had stopped her mouth with a gag.

The entire ship's assemblage had gathered to watch this momentous event. None of them had ever witnessed the marriage of black slaves before, but all of them agreed that the bride was beautiful and the bridegroom was handsome, and all of them wished the couple a long and happy life together.

There was only one slight hitch in the proceedings. When it came time for Cuffie to say "With this ring I thee wed" there was no ring. Noelle would have given hers for the purpose, but she had worn no jewelry when she had started out for a day's picnic.

Aaron paused, his brow knit with perplexity. And then the shy, diffident cabin boy, Josh Perkins, who had been bug-eyed when this strange group of people had been brought on board, stepped forward, his face a brilliant red, and stammering with embarrassment.

"I got a ring, Mr. Godbehere, sir. I made it myself, just afore we sailed, for luck, a talisman like." The twelve-year-old boy removed his ring, which he had made by pounding out a horseshoe nail, and held it out. "I'd be proud if it'll do. I got enough luck, sailing my first voyage under Cap'n Spencer and you. Haven't been knocked around at all, or cursed at, like my ma feared I would."

"You'll get it back," Noelle promised him, bestowing such a brilliant smile on him that the boy shuffled his feet and turned redder than ever, even his protuberant ears turning scarlet. "I'll see that Dicey has a proper wedding ring as soon as we set foot on land again. In the meantime, we're very grateful to you for lending yours."

After one false try, Cuffie got the ring on the correct finger. It was almost a perfect fit.

When the last words had been spoken, when Aaron pronounced that Dicey and Cuffie were man and wife, instead of kissing the bride as he was supposed to do, Cuffie let out a triumphant whoop and began to scramble up the rigging. Up and up he went, while those below watched open-mouthed, and Dicey screamed for him to come down again before he broke his neck. High above them, Cuffie stopped at last, and waved one arm while he held on with the other.

"I'm going to sail this here ship all the way to Boston, Massachusetts!" Cuffie shouted, his voice filled with exultation. "Me and Dicey, we're going to be free! Cap'n Spencer said so! Ain't going to be seasick no more, going to help sail this ship all the way to the land of freedom!"

"You ain't never going to live to get there 'less you come down, you great fool, you!" Dicey screamed at him. "An' you ain't even kissed me yet! The marriage ain't legal till you've kissed me!"

The crew, and Noelle along with them, burst into laughter as Cuffie scrambled down again, consternation written all over his face. The kiss he bestowed on Dicey satisfied the most exacting of them.

The moment was spoiled for Noelle when a shadow fell across her, and she turned to find Vanessa at her side. Her sister's hair was down around her shoulders, a glory of gold, glowing where the sun touched it and set it on fire. In spite of the rough handling she had undergone the night before, she was so beautiful that the crewmen drew in their breaths in awe.

"Very touching!" Vanessa said. She kept her voice so low that only Noelle could hear her. "Your pet married, quite as though she were a white person, an actual person, not a mere slave! You're as stupidly sentimental as our father, spoiling the slaves rotten, coddling them until not enough work can be got out of them to make it worthwhile keeping them! What good will this farce of a marriage do them, when they're hanging by their necks? And they will hang, little sister, you can be sure of that! They'll hang for their part in abducting me and Father, just as you will hang, and Simon, and that upstart doctor!''

Noelle faced her, blazing with fury. ''Be quiet! I don't want you to speak to me, I don't want you to as much as look at me! Keep away from me, or I swear I'll make you sorry!''

Vanessa laughed. ''And what exactly do you think you could do to me? No, little sister, there's nothing you can do, not one thing! I'm the one who will do something to you, as soon as we're on land again!''

''You'll do nothing! You'll be in prison, unless you're the one to hang! Simon and Ian are proving that you drugged our father right at this moment, and you'll be charged with ordering Elisha and Hector to murder Simon and Dicey and me!''

Noelle turned and walked away from her, not trusting herself not to attack her sister physically. She wanted to slash at Vanessa's face with her fingernails, except that she didn't have any left, she wanted to punish her with her hands. But Mr. Godbehere would stop her before she'd be able to accomplish enough damage to satisfy her, and so there would be no use in it.

She avoided Vanessa all the rest of that day. Whenever her sister approached her, she hurried to stand beside either Aaron or one of the seamen, knowing that the image Vanessa wanted to project of herself in front of even these common men would not allow her to taunt her with verbal abuse where they could overhear her. She kept Dicey at her side as much as she could, although that was no easy task, because now that Cuffie had thrown off his seasickness he was all over the ship, poking and prying into everything, asking so many questions that the sailors could hardly keep up with their answers, and every so often scrambling up into the rigging again, to wave his arms and shout his exultation to the skies. Dicey ran after him wherever he went, and stood on deck screaming at him when he went aloft, predicting that he was going to fall and break his neck and kill himself and swearing that she would never speak to him again if he did.

"I'll make a sailor out of that one, given the chance," Aaron told Noelle, watching Cuffie's antics with a benevolent smile. "And the way that little wife of his runs after him and nags him, he'll be glad to get away from her when we set sail for foreign ports! She'll have her babies to occupy her time, and you to take care of while Simon is away, so she won't suffer from his absence, and you'll be company for each other."

"Are you able to look into the future, Mr. Godbehere? Do you think that all of that will really happen?"

"Only God knows that, young lady, and He isn't inclined to divulge His secrets ahead of time. But this I do know. God smiles on those who help themselves. I wouldn't fret overmuch if I were you. If I were a wagering man, I'd wager that we'll never see that signal bonfire on the hill, telling us to set sail without the cap'n. Your father will be getting well, and everything will be fine."

Noelle was comforted by Aaron's down-to-earth wisdom, but when night fell and once again she had to share Simon's cabin with Vanessa, it was as though she had stepped through the gates of hell.

"For the sake of argument, let us say that what you and Simon are planning meets with success," Vanessa taunted her. "For the sake of argument, let us suppose that I will be disposed of, never to cross your path again. That would make you happy, would it not?"

"Of course it will make me happy!" Noelle told her.

"But that is where you are mistaken! Do you honestly believe, even for one moment, that Simon will ever be satisfied with you, after he's had me? Can you honestly believe that every time he holds you in his arms, every time he makes love to you, he won't be comparing you with me?

"I gave him glory, Noelle! I lifted him to heights that you can never scale! My beauty, my body, my fire, are those things that he will forget? Let me tell you how it was between us, little sister! Let me tell you how he held me, how he caressed me, how he kissed me with a passion that no man had ever known before!''

Noelle clapped her hands over her ears, but she could not drown out Vanessa's voice. Vanessa told her, in mocking, taunting detail everything that Simon had done to her, everything that she had done to Simon.

"I am skilled in love in ways you could never conceive! I know how to get a man's body quivering, how to make him moan and beg for more and yet more and more! His every nerve ending vibrates and throbs, his blood runs faster and faster, until he is consumed in an agony of sensation that is nearer to pain than bliss! And still he comes back, again and again, he can't get enough of me, only I can satisfy him!

"He loved me with a passion that he will never feel again. I was everything to him! He told me that he'd never been alive before he met me, that without me, he might as well be dead. Could you . . .'' Vanessa went into graphic detail of the lovemaking that had passed between her and Simon, words that made Noelle writhe and agonies of shame flood her body. Vanessa went on and on, sparing her nothing.

"He loves me, Noelle, me! He may have turned against me now, but he will never forget me, not if he lives to be an old, old man with a long gray beard! And every day of every year he lives, he will remember me, and regret that he lost me, and long to hold me in his arms again. You may think that he is making love to you, but it will be only the husk of the man, the real man will be with me in his mind, in his thoughts, in his longings!''

"Stop it, stop it, be quiet!'' Noelle screamed. But still Vanessa went on, as if she hadn't heard her.

"I have known many men, I have had many lovers, but I never had one like Simon. Until Simon, I never knew the ultimate in physical love, the glory that such a man can bring to a woman like me! But it took two to achieve that glory, little sister, Simon and me! I was the catalyst that set his body aflame, just as he was the catalyst that set my body aflame! When you go into his arms, it will not be the same at all. And he will remember me, and feel cheated, and turn from you, wanting only me! He may make love to you, but soon it will be only from a feeling of duty. Once a man has known what only I can give him, no one else will ever satisfy him, no one else ever could!''

Vanessa's face took on a look of wild exultation. ''He swore to me that his love for me would never die, and he spoke truer than he thought! His mind might reject me, but his body will burn with longing for me as he relives every moment we spent in each other's arms! His love for me was without bounds, we were not mere humans then, but a god and a goddess! We enjoyed what no mere mortals could ever enjoy, or will ever be able to enjoy again!''

Noelle could bear no more. She bolted from the cabin and went on deck, to lean against the rail, tears streaming down her face. She was shaking, she felt ill to her very soul. She wanted to cry out that every word Vanessa had taunted her with had been a lie, but she knew that her sister had not been lying. Simon had done those things, Simon had said those things, Simon had loved Vanessa with every ounce of love and passion that he possessed!

Beautiful, beautiful Vanessa! Golden, glowing Vanessa! And Noelle was small, and dark, and not beautiful at all, she was only moderately pretty, she had never been able to compete with Vanessa. And now she knew, with a certainty that was like death, that she would never be able to compete with her even though Vanessa herself were dead. Knowledge of the hours that Simon had spent in Vanessa's arms would haunt her all her life, the words that Simon had spoken to Vanessa would echo in her ears.

''Has she been bedeviling you, lass?'' Aaron was beside her, his hand on her shoulder trying to comfort her. ''Pay no heed to her. All of this will be over soon, and then you can forget that you ever had a sister.''

But Noelle would never be able to forget. And she knew that she would never be able to marry Simon, knowing that she could never be to him what Vanessa had been. She would not be second choice, a pale imitation of what Simon had known with her sister! She would rather go to her grave never having known love at all.

She did not return to the cabin that night. Shaking his head, Aaron finally let her have her way, and he had a pallet brought into his own tiny cabin, and made her take his narrow bed. It might not seem decent to the large part of upright society if they ever found out, but the lass was safe with him, and as long as he was with her, guarding her, that other one could not reach her to torment her.

Simon, or anyone else, Aaron could face down if it ever became known. He only hoped that his Amity would never get wind of it. If any man in his crew had noticed Noelle going into his cabin, and dared to open his mouth about it, that would be the first man Aaron had ever lashed to the mast and whipped.

Vanessa was all sweetness and light when she appeared on deck the next morning. Her smile at Aaron was brilliant, and filled with such wistfulness that any other man's heart would have melted.

"Mr. Godbehere, surely you can see the pitiful state I'm in! I was brought to your ship by force, with nothing but the clothing I'm wearing! Would you believe that I was actually gagged before I could ask, very reasonably, if I could not have a few things packed for me? I am not only without fresh wearing apparel, but even the most basic of toilet articles! I don't believe it's asking too much for you to put back to shore and have one of your crew go into town and purchase a few things for me! I can make out a list, and you will be reimbursed as soon as I am released from this prison."

"I'm sorry if you're inconvenienced, ma'am," Aaron told her. "But you are in no worse case than your sister. Her clothing is in a much worse state than yours, after her

ordeal in the mountains, and she isn't complaining. I can
supply you with a comb, and fresh water for washing, but
that is all. You will just have to make do."

"This is outrageous!" Vanessa's charm melted away,
and her eyes glittered. "As soon as I'm rescued from my
enforced stay on this ship as your prisoner, I will take
particular pains to see that you are called to account for
your inhuman treatment of me as well as for your
participation in all the other crimes you have committed
against me! The fact that you will claim that you were only
following your captain's orders will not mitigate your
punishment, I assure you!"

Aaron had never in his life heard such pure vituperation
pour from a woman's lips as the tirade he was subjected to
as Vanessa faced him with blazing eyes, her face drained
of every trace of color by her fury.

"Your duty is patent! The moment you were aware that
your captain was launched on the committing of crimes,
you should not only have refused to aid and abet him, but
you should have informed the authorities and taken over
the command of this ship! Your guilt is equal to his, and it
will give me the greatest pleasure to stand in a court of law
and charge you with an armed invasion of my home, of
inciting an uprising among my slaves, of kidnapping me at
pistol point and bringing me here to hold me prisoner on
this ship! I have been subjected not only to bodily harm,
but to every indignity that it is possible to inflict on a
human being! And I will see that you pay for it, that you
will pay dearly for every moment I have suffered at your
hands!"

"Miss Maynard!" Aaron's voice rose to his full quarterdeck roar. "That will be enough! As far as I can see,
your body has suffered no harm whatsoever! No man has
laid a hand on you since you were brought to this ship, but
as God is my witness, if you don't belay that blather
instantly, hands will be laid on you! I am in command
here, and I can order you bound again and confined to
your cabin until such time as the captain sees fit to release

you! I will thank you to get off my quarter-deck immediately! If you do not do it in all haste, I will have you carried off!''

Vanessa took a step backward, her eyes dilating. No man had ever dared to speak to her in that tone of voice. Aaron took a step forward, and she retreated another.

"One more thing, Miss Maynard! You are not to bedevil your sister in any manner, or I will hold true to my promise to have you locked in your cabin. I hope that I have made myself clear!''

If things went against the captain, Aaron had no doubt that Vanessa's bile against him would weigh heavily on him. She would turn heaven and earth to gain revenge on him for daring to speak to her as he had. But the risk was worth it to see the woman retreat, and he felt a surge of satisfaction that brought laughter to his eyes as he watched her retreating back. His Amity was no beauty, as this woman was, but after Aaron's experiences with Vanessa Maynard, he doubted that he would ever trust a truly beautiful woman again.

In Simon's cabin, Vanessa paced, quivering like an outraged tigress. The fact that the cabin was so small that she could pace for only a few steps in any direction only increased her anger. How dare that man, that common seaman, refuse her request? She had been confident that he would do as she asked. And she had had supreme confidence that she would be able to persuade whichever man Aaron had sent ashore to make her purchases to divulge her plight to the authorities, her very beauty would sway him to come to her aid, even without the promise of a lavish reward as soon as she was rescued.

No one came near her except the cabin boy, Josh Perkins of the ridiculous horseshoe-nail ring, and that was only to bring her her breakfast and later something at noon, and carry away the slops. Josh did not speak to her nor she to him, Josh because Mr. Godbehere had ordered him not to speak to her, and Vanessa because he was beneath her notice.

Her agitation grew as the hours wore on. She knew that

she was in the greatest danger, and that the danger increased with every hour that passed. If her father were to recover under Ian's care, everything would be lost. Always before, she had been able to manipulate him however she wished. Because she looked so much like her mother, the wife Daniel had worshiped, he had worshiped her in turn.

But Noelle was also his daughter, and her testimony would be so damaging that Vanessa dared not risk it. Dicey and Cuffie could be discounted. No matter what Dicey said, Vanessa could claim that she was lying because of her loyalty to Noelle, and her testimony would not be allowed in court in any case. It was Noelle she must do something about, and she had to do it before the *Maid of Boston* put back to port.

Drawing a deep breath of resolution, she went out on deck. She breathed a sigh of satisfaction when she saw that Noelle was alone, leaning against the rail and gazing toward the direction of shore. No member of the crew was near enough to overhear, and once again Cuffie was high in the rigging, with Dicey railing at him to come down, and the seamen's eyes were all on Cuffie as they grinned and urged him on.

Vanessa put a doleful expression on her face, and went to stand beside her sister. "Noelle, I feel so ill!" she said. "Let me stand here with you for a while, I'm in need of air to settle my stomach. Everything is going against me, I don't know what to do or where to turn!"

Her lying words distracted Noelle, and she was taken completely unaware when Vanessa lunged at her and toppled her over the rail. But Noelle's hand reached out and grasped Vanessa's dress, and Vanessa screamed a scream of pure terror as she too plunged into the waves.

On deck, pandemonium broke out, as shouts of "Man overboard!" rent the air, the crew so stunned that they failed to stipulate that it was two women, not a man, who had plunged into the ocean. Cuffie came scrambling down from the rigging many times faster than he had gone up, and Dicey ran to lean over the rail, wailing Noelle's name.

In the water, Noelle had kicked her way to the surface and was drawing in deep lungsful of air. She knew how to swim, Kenneth had taught her when they'd been children, but she had never been in the ocean, only in placid mountain pools where there were no waves to swamp her and where she had been wearing nothing but the barest essentials of underclothing, not a heavy riding habit and boots to drag her down.

Noelle kicked, and flailed with her arms, fighting against being dragged under again. Beside her, Vanessa's head broke the surface. She too was flailing out with her arms, but she did not possess the barest rudiments of swimming. Her eyes were wild, her mouth was open, but no sound came out as a wave caught her full in the face and strangled her, and she started to go under again.

Noelle acted out of pure reflex. She grabbed at Vanessa's hair, and caught it and held on with all her strength, while she still struggled to keep her own head above water. But it was a losing battle. Dressed as she was, and with Vanessa's struggling weight working against her, she was sure to go under and drown.

A body arced through the air, and Ned Campbell's strong arms cut the waves until he was beside them.

"Not me! Take my sister!" Noelle managed to gasp.

Now another man was in the water, and a boat was being lowered, while on deck Dicey went on wailing, and Cuffie, his hands clenched into fists at his sides, cursed himself because he didn't know how to swim.

In a matter of moments both girls were on the deck of the *Maid of Boston* again, Vanessa doubled over and retching, her face green and her hair in sodden tangles around her face, as she threw up unbelievable amounts of the sea water she had swallowed.

"She pushed the mistress, I saw her!" Cuffie shouted, his face contorted with fury. "From way up there, I saw her do it!"

The face of every man who looked at Vanessa was turned against her. Her beauty meant nothing now. She had tried to kill Noelle.

Dicey, holding Noelle's head in her lap, cried out in anguished anger.

"Mistress, why didn't you let her drown! Why did you have to go and save her!"

"I don't know," Noelle said, before she began to cry. "I just don't know."

Chapter Eighteen

IAN CHECKED ONCE MORE TO MAKE SURE THAT DANIEL was resting comfortably. Daniel's breathing and heart had strengthened, and his sleep now seemed to be natural. During the moments when he was awake, his voice was no longer slurred, and he seemed to understand where he was and that Ian was helping him. Satisfied, Ian turned away from the bed.

"Call me if he wakes, or even stirs," he told the little black ragamuffin who had spread the word for him that he wanted Papa Emile to come to him. There had been no response, Papa Emile had not put in an appearance, but the lad had appointed himself as Ian's servant, asking no wages, but only the chance to stay with him, and food and the right to curl up in a corner at night to sleep. Ian didn't have the heart to send the boy away. Free blacks were hard put to survive in Jamaica, there was little work for them, and the lad had been all but starving when Ian had charged him with his errand.

Ian had spent most of his time since he and Simon had brought Daniel to his house sniffing at, tasting, and stirring around the contents of the jars and vials he had collected from Chloe's hut, but the investigations had told him little. If Papa Emile were here, he would know, but Papa Emile was not here. It was as if the man had disappeared from the face of the earth.

Now he picked up the bottle of tonic that he had taken from Daniel's room at Maynard Penn. He had smelled it and tasted it, a little on the tip of his tongue, several times, but what could be in it eluded him. More drastic measures were called for, and right away, because there wasn't all the time in the world; this wasn't a problem set in front of him by his instructors in Edinburgh, to test what he had learned from them and how much he still had to learn.

Simon lay on an improvised pallet in the corner, sound asleep. Ian looked at him with a tinge of envy, and at Beggar, who had elected to curl up at Simon's feet, although the dog's eyes were reproachful as they regarded his master, who had little time for him now, and who had not taken him for romps in the yard for far too long a time.

Ian looked at Beggar, a rather shamefaced expression in his eyes. He snapped his fingers, and Beggar got up reluctantly, stretching and yawning, before he padded over to him. Ian ruffled his ears, and scratched behind them, and Beggar wriggled with pleasure.

"I'm sorry about this," Ian told him. "But you see there isn't anybody else, so you're elected."

He poured out half a teaspoon of the tonic, and then, reflecting, poured half of that amount back into the bottle. Beggar had only a fraction of Daniel's weight and size. It was no easy task to pry Beggar's mouth open and insert the spoon, turning it upside down so that the liquid ran down his throat. When he was released, Beggar shook his head in violent protest, and sneezed, and, giving his master a dirty look, he padded back to lie down at Simon's feet again.

Ian settled himself in a straight-backed chair and waited. In spite of himself, his eyes kept closing, and once he jerked awake convinced that a snore had escaped his throat and brought him back to awareness. Getting up, he shook the sleep from his head, and went to kneel beside the dog, and then he began to curse in a low but steady and venomous tone.

He had given Beggar too much. The dog was unconscious. Ian scrambled for an emetic, he got the animal on his four legs, which persisted in spreading out until his stomach dragged the floor. He slapped the sides of the dog's face, he shook him, and eventually Beggar's eyes fluttered, but when he looked at his master they seemed to be crossed, for all the world as if he were dead drunk.

Beggar was in no condition to struggle against being given the emetic. Ian carried him into the yard, and hoped that once his stomach had been emptied he would recover. If he didn't, Ian would go all through the rest of his life feeling like a murderer.

To his relief, Beggar was soon able to stand up without being supported, and his eyes straightened out, although the look he gave his master was so accusatory that Ian winced.

"Sorry," Ian said, stroking and fondling him. "I'm afraid I overdid it, but you're going to be all right now. You'll have to forgive me for treating you in such a beastly manner, but it was in a good cause."

There was no doubt about it. The tonic contained a powerful opiate. Now, there remained the rest of the concoctions.

Ian was in the yard again, feeding his goat a slice of bread that had been sprinkled with powder from one of the vials, when Simon appeared in the doorway several hours later, supporting himself with both hands against the lintels.

"What the devil are you doing?" Simon demanded. "Bread, for a goat?"

"Goats will eat anything. This is the third slice so far,"

Ian said cheerfully. "No results from the first, and an extremely amorous disposition after the second. If I'd been a ram, she would have raped me! I had to wait for that to wear off before I tried this bit. But the tonic was drugged. I tried it on Beggar, and the poor fellow almost died."

"Daniel's stirring," Simon told him.

Ian left the rest of the slice of bread for the goat to finish by herself, and sprinted into the house. The lad was leaning over Daniel, patting his face.

Ian pushed him aside. "Mr. Maynard," he said. And then more sharply, "Mr. Maynard, wake up! Do you know who I am?"

Daniel's eyebrows drew together. "Why, yes. You're Doctor Macintyre. Am I still in your house in Kingston? I seem to recall that you brought me here, and were here when I was awake some time ago."

"Yes, yes, that's right! You're doing fine! There isn't a thing to worry about. Do you remember this man? He was a guest in your house only recently and he talked to you, if only briefly."

Daniel's eyes focused on Simon. "A sea captain," he said. "Out of Boston, I believe."

Ian's smile lighted up his entire homely face. "That's enough talking for now. You are to have something to eat, we must build up your strength. We'll explain everything to you as soon as you're stronger."

The lad supported Daniel's head while Ian spooned soup into his mouth, filled with self-importance at so responsible a task. Ian didn't pretend to be the best cook in the world, but the soup was nourishing.

At last Daniel turned his head away, indicating that he could take no more.

"My daughters. Vanessa and Noelle. Do they know I am here?"

"Yes, they both know you are here. It's all right. You must rest again now. You've been very ill."

"Yes, I've been very ill. It's hard to remember,"

Daniel frowned. "Everything is hazy. And I feel so damnably weak!"

"That's only to be expected, and nothing to worry about. You'll be yourself in no time at all, now." Ian assured him.

Daniel was satisfied with that, and closed his eyes again. Ian's expression was triumphant as he turned to Simon.

"He's over the worst of it, there's no doubt at all that he'll make a complete recovery. Now I'm going to get some rest. I'm sick of seeing you snore away while I do all the work! Keep your eye on Daniel, and wake me when he wakes up, so I can check him again, will you? You haven't anything else to do anyway, so you might as well make yourself useful."

Not having anything to do was wearing on Simon's nerves. He paced up and down, sat down only to get up again, looked at Daniel to make sure that he was sleeping comfortably, and paced again. The little lad watched him, not understanding why this white master was so disturbed, but content that the man's anger was not directed at him.

What peace there was in the little house was disrupted by Henry Cottswood's arrival. Henry was in a towering rage.

"I have been to Maynard Penn again, and I was turned away again! Those impudent servants refused to admit me to the house, even to let me refresh myself with a glass of wine before my return journey! It's apparent that neither Vanessa nor Noelle are at home, so where the devil can they be?

"And not only that, but something's going on there that I don't like a bit! The slaves are overexcited, and one of the slave huts has been burned to the ground, and some kind of ceremony was going on, all mumbo-jumbo that no sane man could understand. There was an old man there, they called him Papa Emile, and he just looked at me as if he were mocking me, and told me that what they were doing was no affair of mine, and to go away so they could get on with it, that my presence would contaminate whatever it was they were doing! It's intolerable, and I don't intend to stand for it!''

So that was where Papa Emile was! How the devil had the man known that he was wanted at Maynard Penn? But there was no doubt that he had found out somehow, and Simon had no doubt that what they were up to was some kind of magic to counteract any magic that Chloe might have left behind. They'd burned her hut, and Papa Emile was purifying the place. Miranda's mind would be set at rest now, she would no longer live in terror that Chloe's spirit would return and wreak revenge on her, and Simon was glad of that.

"I intend to have some answers!" Henry glared at Simon, who had edged him back outside so that his shouting wouldn't disturb either Daniel or Ian. "I will not be put off any longer!"

"I promise you that it won't be much longer, everything will be explained to you very shortly now," Simon assured him. "Mr. Maynard has improved tremendously. I'll let you know as soon as it's possible to give you every detail of what has been going on. If you will just go home and wait, Ian and I will send for you very soon."

Henry left, making no effort to conceal how disgruntled he was. "If I don't hear from you soon, I will take matters into my own hands and call in the authorities, and then we'll get to the bottom of this matter in short order!" was his parting shot as he remounted his horse and reined it around.

Ian slept for five hours. Once during that time Daniel roused again, but he seemed to be still improving, so Simon and the lad fed him again and let Ian go on sleeping, in spite of Ian's request to be roused. He needed his sleep, he'd been staggering on his feet when he had taken Simon's place on the pallet.

Now Simon shook Ian's shoulder, and he came awake at once, fully alert.

"Your goat is dead," Simon told him.

Simon had not been mistaken. The goat was dead. Poor creature, it was Ian's fault, he shouldn't have given her so large a dose, but he'd been even more afraid of not giving her enough so that he could be sure of the effects of the powder he had sprinkled on the bread.

"No more goat's milk," he told Beggar. "Not until I buy another goat." He looked at Simon. "Here's our proof. Not proof that Chloe poisoned Kenneth, I'm afraid, but proof that she possessed the poison that could have done it. With Daniel's improvement, we should be able to present our case as soon as your first mate brings your ship back. The hardest part is going to be to make Mr. Maynard believe that Vanessa would try to harm him, but he's an intelligent man, and he'll have to accept the facts. His own rapid recovery once he was removed from his plantation will go far to convince him, and what Noelle will tell him will make him certain."

A sudden, boyish grin lighted up his face. "I can't wait to see Eastlake's face when his nose is rubbed in the fact that his patient has been systematically drugged and it escaped his notice! He'll try to bluster his way out of it, of course, that man wouldn't believe that he was dead if he heard the clods falling on the lid of his own coffin! But as long as Daniel Maynard believes it, that will be all that's necessary."

Bertram Cottswood had sent his curricle to carry Daniel Maynard to his home when the little lad had run to his house with the message. Now Daniel was in bed in the Cottswoods' most comfortable guest room, and an angry Doctor Eastlake had already examined him and had to concede that his former patient was much improved, although he still maintained that the improvement was a natural event that would have taken place even if Daniel had not been removed from Vanessa's and Chloe's care. He had threatened to bring action against Ian for interfering with a case not his own, and left the house red-faced and indignant when Bertram Cottswood advised him to hold off on any such action in case it might prove to be more of an embarrassment to him than to Ian.

But although Bertram, impressed by Daniel's improved

condition, had taken their part in that matter, he was still far from convinced of anything else that he was now being told.

"I concede that the goat is dead," Bertram said. "I even concede that it died because of some concoction that had belonged to the woman Chloe. But that does not mean that Vanessa Maynard was involved in her father's illness in any way!"

"Mr. Cottswood, with all due respect, there is no mere supposition about the fact that Noelle and Dicey and I were almost murdered in the Blue Mountains where we went to picnic. Vanessa made an excuse not to accompany us, and it could only have been by her orders that Elisha and Hector tried to kill us!"

"Slaves turn against their masters every day. Those two could easily have taken advantage that they were already in the mountains, where they could find the renegade Maroons quite easily and take shelter with them with little chance that they would be recaptured. As for Daniel being drugged, I concede that that is more than likely, but Chloe might have had a grudge against him, and Vanessa would have known nothing of what the woman was about."

He placed his half-finished glass on a table, looking at Simon and Ian from underneath beetled brows. "Indeed, sirrahs, I cannot see that you have a leg to stand on! There will be the most grave of repercussions from this business. Vanessa Maynard a murderess? I never heard such nonsense! You will never make me believe it, nor any other man on this island! I am sure that both of my sons agree with me entirely."

Henry stood with his legs spread apart, his arms folded behind his back in that belligerent manner he had that Simon found so irritating.

"No, I do not agree with you, Father. I think that I know Vanessa Maynard better than you do, and certainly better than Claude has ever known her. I am an astute observer of human nature, it is one of my hobbies, and there is a coldness and ruthlessness in Vanessa that only someone as observant as I am would discern. I believe that she is capable of doing just what these men have told us, and I am convinced that what they have told us is true. Even as a child, Vanessa considered herself better than anyone else, and that she was above being called to account for her actions. I admit that I myself fell under her spell briefly, but I was disillusioned soon enough, and that was the end of it.''

He had been disillusioned, Simon knew, because Vanessa had sent him packing, Henry not being the type of man who would appeal to her. But unlike the other men who had allowed her to send them away without a murmur of protest, Henry had not taken it kindly. His pride, his insufferable ego, had resented her treatment of him, and he had held onto his resentment to this day.

Still, although he had a personal motive for not liking Vanessa, he had been discerning enough to realize that she was not the saint she was reputed to be. As much as Simon disliked the young man personally, it was a good thing to have him on their side.

"When will that ship of yours put back into port?" Bertram demanded. "I still cannot bring myself to believe that you had the temerity to kidnap Vanessa, to have her held prisoner on your ship! To invade Maynard Penn with an armed force, to stand by and watch the woman Chloe be murdered, to remove both Daniel and Vanessa from their own home at gunpoint! I begin to doubt your sanity, Captain Spencer, in spite of anything my son has to say!''

In spite of his bluster, Simon could see that Bertram was shaken. He knew that his younger son was as astute as he claimed to be. Claude was a good and steady worker, but Henry had been given more than his share of the intelligence that had been divided between the two brothers.

"Aaron will be bringing the *Maid of Boston* in at any time now. The time for the signal that we arranged for him to sail to Boston instead has passed, and he will already be on his way back to Kingston. All I ask is that you listen to what Noelle will tell you with an open mind.''

"Certainly I will listen to her with an open mind! But I

owe as much to Vanessa, as well. I will listen to both of them, and then I will draw my own conclusions.'' Bertram reached for his glass again. Simon had already noted, and Ian had confirmed his observation, that men in warm climates tended to drink more than was good for them. In all of his life, Simon had not seen his father overindulge, nor any other respected older man of his acquaintance.

Jamaica was a beautiful place, but Simon would as soon never have to spend any great deal of time here. Massachusetts was much more to his liking. There, at least, the beauties of nature, although not as brilliant and overwhelming as those of this island, were natural, with no underlying rot, and its climate did not persuade men to ease their discomfort in a bottle.

Fortunately, Brenda had decided that she was the only one in her house who could see to Daniel Maynard's comfort, and she had been in his room during most of this discussion, else they would have been interrupted so many times that they would have gotten nowhere. But now she came bustling into the drawing room, agog with excitement.

''Someone is coming! I saw them from the window! I'm sure that Vanessa is with them, no one could mistake that golden hair of hers, but I don't think that Noelle is with them, I didn't see her at all! Whatever could have happened to her? And you've been talking, I can see it on your faces, and you weren't supposed to be talking at all until I could be here to hear everything, it's just too annoying of you! Now you'll have to tell everything all over again, because I'm certainly going to know everything there is to know! They're here!''

Brenda lifted her skirts and ran toward the front of the house, and a few seconds later they heard her scream.

''My lands! Noelle, is that you? Goodness gracious sakes, just look at you! Why ever are you wearing those outlandish clothes, you look for all the world like a boy! And you aren't even wearing shoes! It isn't even decent! Come inside at once before anyone sees you or your reputation will be demolished! Hello, Vanessa. My goodness, you look just simply dreadful, too! You look as if . . . you look as if you'd been all wet, clothes and all, but that isn't possible, is it? Why are you just standing there without saying a word?''

Brenda shooed them into the house like a mother hen shooing a batch of chicks, her tongue still clacking. ''I don't have a single, solitary thing that will fit you, Noelle, you're so disgustingly slender! And there's nothing here that will fit Vanessa either, Mama's even shorter and fatter than I am! Wouldn't you know that even Captain Spencer would be so stupid that he wouldn't think to have us send to Maynard Penn to have some of your things sent in! Men! If they didn't have us women to think for them, I declare I don't know what would become of them! I'll send someone right away, just tell me what you want, our servants are really good at remembering what they're told, as they very well ought to be, because goodness knows I've spent enough time training them to be responsible! Dicey, go and find my Lucie, her things will fit you till something of your own gets here. Cuffie doesn't look all that bad, but I expect one of our men will have something he can borrow. Noelle, I declare, you still haven't said a word! Am I to wait until I'm an old woman before I find out what's been going on?''

Simon started forward to meet Noelle, his arms held out, as soon as she crossed the threshold. She started to run, and his face lighted up. He had no idea why she was wearing what were certainly Josh Perkins's clothes, but to him she was the loveliest sight in the world, even dressed as a boy and with her feet bare.

Noelle bypassed him and kept right on going, and in another instant she was clinging to Ian. Ian looked first completely bewildered, and then delighted. Simon's face showed not only bewilderment, but pain. What the devil! Could Noelle possibly still be angry with him because he'd forced her to go aboard the *Maid of Boston?* He'd been certain that she would have gotten over her pique by now, but she didn't even look at him, she just went on clinging to Ian.

"My father? Is he better, is he all right? I want to see him, Ian! Is he here?"

"He's much better, and he's here," Ian told her. "I only hope that the sight of you dressed like a street gamin won't send him into a relapse! Not that you don't make an uncommonly attractive boy, but he's expecting a daughter, not a cabinboy!"

Daniel Maynard himself put that notion to rest. Still so weak that he could scarcely stand, he had gotten out of bed when he had heard the commotion of the arrival, and now he appeared in the archway to the drawing room. Cuffie's reaction came before any of the others'. He leaped across the space between them to support his master, yelping for Dicey to find a chair.

"Shouldn't be up on your feet! Just look at you, all white and shaking!" Cuffie scolded. "Land sakes, ain't I had 'nough things to worry me, 'thout you falling down right at my feet? Let me help you, Dicey, fetch a cushion for the master's back! You ought to be in bed, Massa Daniel!"

Daniel remained standing for a moment, his only concession being to let Cuffie support him.

"Noelle, may I ask why you are dressed as you are?" Daniel asked.

"Vanessa tried to drown me." Noelle's answer was simple. "She pushed me overboard, but I took her with me and she almost drowned, herself, for her pains!"

"And you should have let her drown!" Dicey spoke up, her indignation so great that she forgot her usual diffidence in the presence of white people whom she did not know well. She looked at her master, pride intermingling with her indignation as she added, "She saved that one from drowning, she did. Might have drowned her ownself, saving her, but she latched onto Mistress Vanessa's hair and wouldn't let go. Could have let her drown, not nobody would of blamed her, but she didn't!"

"So you have added yet another crime to the long list of crimes that you had already committed!" Daniel's eyes fixed on his elder daughter, and they were cold and without mercy. He had already gone through his private hell of grief and horror after he had learned all the things that this worshiped daughter of his had done. Ian and Simon had told him everything that he had to know, as gently as they could, but there had been no way to spare him. Both of their hearts had ached for him when they'd seen how shattered he had been. Ian had said, and Simon agreed with him, that to learn the sort of person Vanessa was must be fully as bad as Kenneth's death had been.

"Lies, all lies!" Vanessa threw herself at her father, reaching out her arms. "You won't believe them! You can't! You know that Noelle would say anything to discredit me, she's always hated me, nothing that she says is true! Father, I've had such a dreadful time, I was kidnapped, held prisoner, subjected to every discomfort and indignity! But you're better now, you'll put a stop to all this, and then we'll go home, we'll be together just as we always were!"

"I do not wish to hear any more from you, Vanessa." Daniel forced her clinging arms from around his neck, finding a strength that Simon and Ian would not have thought that he had. "You are guilty of every charge that has been brought against you, and you will pay the price."

Vanessa's face changed, it became cold and hard and vindictive. As she always did when she was furious, she began to pace.

"Nothing can be proven against me, there is no proof at all! To have me brought up on charges will only disgrace you, and nothing will be accomplished because I will be vindicated! No jury in Jamaica will ever convict me!"

"That remains to be seen," her father told her. "If you are acquitted, you will have to find another home, another means of support. You are no longer my daughter. I have already disowned you in my heart, and I will make it legal within a matter of days. You will receive nothing from me, Vanessa. Not money, not even the clothing that I have

286

bought for you, except for one dress to replace the ruined one you are wearing. You will not be allowed to keep your mother's jewels. I see that you are wearing a necklace and two rings that belonged to her. Remove them now, hand them to Dicey.

"A jury may acquit you, but you will still be held guilty in the eyes of everyone in Jamaica. When it becomes known that I have repudiated you, you will find that your friends have melted away. You are never to approach me again, for any reason.

"That is all I have to say to you. Cuffie, help me back to bed. I am very glad that you and Dicey, as well as my only remaining daughter, escaped death at this she-devil's hands. You will be rewarded for all your help to Noelle, you may be sure of that."

"Don't want no reward. Me, I got reward 'nough, just knowing that Mistress Noelle is all right now, and being married to my Dicey. Ain't nothing else in the world I could want, 'cepting to go to Boston, Massachusetts, with Cap'n Spencer like he said we could, when all this was over."

"Then that is what you shall have. I will set you free, both you and Dicey, immediately."

"And Dicey must have a proper wedding ring!" Noelle said. "A gold wedding ring. She had to borrow Josh Perkins's horseshoe-nail ring to get married, but I promised her a real one."

Dicey covered the horseshoe-nail ring with her right hand, her face falling, and she looked as if she were going to cry.

"Like this one," Dicey whispered, her voice anguished. "This the one I was married with, want to keep this one. Couldn't you give Josh another ring, instead? Don't reckon he'd ask for gold."

For the first time, Daniel smiled. "But gold is what he shall have. I will tell him that it is a present from you, as it actually will be. Cuffie, I am ready. It's the room on the right, at the end of the hall."

Noelle went to him, and his arms closed around her,

and he held her close. "Welcome home, Noelle. Somehow, although I don't yet know how, I will make all you have suffered up to you."

"Vanessa is right, you know," Henry said. He stood in his usual stance, legs apart, his arms folded behind his back, his jaw thrust out. "There is no way we will ever get a conviction. All the blame will be thrown on Chloe.

"However, I have an alternative that will serve us all as well. With the island's economy in its present state and sure to worsen once the emancipation goes through, I will not be needed here in Jamaica to assist my father and brother in running our business affairs. I propose to take my share of the family fortune and make my home in England. I have long toyed with the idea of becoming a country squire, with reasonable but solid holdings, nothing grand, but it will be enough to suit me."

Simon's eyes pierced him. "What are you getting at, Henry? Aren't you straying from the point?"

"I am not. It is very much to the point. I propose to marry Vanessa and take her to England with me. As my wife, on our country estate, she will find no opportunity for mischief. Indeed, she will be much too busy. I intend to have a large family. Our social life will be moderate, supervising my tenant farms and my estate, and riding to hounds, will satisfy me. We may go in to London a very few times during a year, as I will wish to show my wife off. But our friends will be solid country people, there will be few glittering affairs even if Vanessa would have time for them between bearing and rearing our children."

Vanessa's shock turned her face as white as parchment. Her gaze traveled around the room, resting on first one and then another of its occupants. Every face was hard, every hand was turned against her.

For a moment, her shoulders sagged. And then she straightened them again, and turned to Bertram Cottswood.

"I trust that I will be welcome as a guest in your house until this marriage takes place?" she asked.

Bertram inclined his head. "As you have no other place to go, we will have to extend you our hospitality."

"And a suitable wardrobe will be provided for me?"

"I shall see to that," Henry said. "I can hardly have my future wife going around in the rag you're wearing."

Ian found his voice, after having come near to strangling at Henry's proposal. "Aren't you afraid that she'll poison you, or find some other way to do away with you?"

"I shall take the greatest care that she has no opportunity. Just in case the idea might cross her mind, I intend to write a full account of these events, and leave it in safekeeping with a reputable barrister, to be opened and read in the event of my death. I will state that my untimely death, even if it seemed natural or an accident, must be probed into in every detail, as I have good and sufficient reason to believe that my wife will kill me if she can find the means."

"But why in the name of all that's holy do you want to marry her, knowing what she is?" Simon burst out, still not crediting that Henry could be serious.

Henry smiled, a humorless smile, but there was a flicker of amusement in his eyes.

"Look at her," he said. "She is a beautiful woman, the most beautiful woman in Jamaica. She will undoubtedly be one of the most beautiful women in England. And I will possess her, and be the envy of every man I meet. We will be married here in Kingston, at the earliest possible date. It will be a large wedding, the event of the year if not of the decade.

"Vanessa spurned me once. Now we shall see who will have the upper hand, who will call the tune. Now everyone will see that it is I she chose, above all of the other suitors who clamored for her hand!"

He looked at Vanessa, waiting. "I will have your answer now. If it is yes, you will be provided with a wardrobe suitable to your high estate, you will be provided with adequate jewels, if not as many and as costly as those you have lost. If your answer, on sober reflection, is no, then I promise you that I will move heaven and earth to see that you are convicted and hanged!''

Vanessa's gaze met his without flinching. ''My answer is yes,'' she said. And then she turned and left the room, her head held high, pride in every line of her, although she had been brought so low.

Simon sat down, feeling limp. He looked at Ian.

''What do you think of all this as a solution? In Henry's place, I wouldn't care to take Vanessa as a wife. She'll be up to some trickery, I'll be bound!''

Ian grinned. ''I'll put my money on Henry,'' he said. ''If I'm not mistaken, he'll be more than a match for her. I wouldn't worry about him, Simon. Henry Cottswood can take care of himself. And for all that Vanessa deserves every moment of misery that Henry will inflict on her, I don't envy her her life. I have an idea that being Henry's wife, with no prospect of escape, will be a more fitting punishment for her than hanging by the neck until she's dead.''

Ian left to go home. Beggar and the little lad would be waiting for him. It seemed that his household had increased by one, as the lad resisted every suggestion that he should return to his family.

Simon also left, to spend the night aboard the *Maid of Boston*. It would be good to be aboard again. He had to leave without having a chance to speak to Noelle alone. Brenda had swept Noelle off to her room before Henry had made his startling proposal, to see that Noelle had a bath, and had a tray brought to her, and was tucked up in bed for as good a night's sleep as Brenda's chatter and her dozens of questions would allow her.

It irked Simon that Noelle had ignored him ever since she had come on shore. Tomorrow she would not elude him, he would have it out with her, and whatever it was that was bothering her would be settled. One thing was sure, he had no intention of sailing without her. If he couldn't reason her anger at him away, he would kiss it away.

All around Vanessa, the Cottswood house was silent,

everyone had been in bed and asleep hours ago. But Vanessa lay awake in the room that had been given her, her mind racing.

To be married to Henry, to have to suffer his caresses, his lovemaking! That gross, overbearing clod! To be held a virtual prisoner on some dreary country estate in England, far from neighbors of her social standing, going to London only a few times a year and even then to have Henry's eye constantly on her, Henry always close at her side!

Her body, her beautiful body that had set every man she had ever known on fire with desire for her, would thicken again and again as she was forced to bear Henry's children. She would become old before her time, her beauty would fade.

There was no escape for her on this island. Even if she were acquitted, if she chose to stand trial rather than marry Henry, no man of any standing would marry her. And there was no man she would wish to marry, because every man she knew would be all but ruined once the emancipation was enacted.

Her dreams of wealth and glory, of a title, of bringing all of Europe to her feet, were shattered. Without Chloe, she would have no means of ensuring that Henry would die in a manner that could not possibly implicate her. Without Chloe, she would have no way of avoiding the pregnancies that Henry would inflict on her.

She sat up and swung her legs over the side of the bed. In the long nightgown, several sizes too large for her, that she had been forced to borrow from Brenda, she moved like a sleepwalking ghost. She left the bedroom on silent feet.

She had seen where Bertram Cottswood had locked up the powders and potions that Ian had entrusted to his care. They were in his study, in a locked, glass-fronted case, for safekeeping.

She lifted the hem of the nightgown and wrapped it around her hand. She wanted no cuts, no flaws, on her body when she was found. She doubled her fist and broke

the glass. Freeing her hand, it went unerringly to the vial
that she wanted. She knew these pots and vials well, even
though Chloe had never allowed her to touch them.

It took time for the other occupants of the house to
rouse after the shattering of the glass had disturbed their
sleep, and even longer for them to orient themselves and
place where the sound had come from.

Henry was the first to reach her. When the others
gathered in the study, he was kneeling beside her, his head
on her breast as he listened for a heartbeat.

"She's still alive! Send for Ian Macintyre!"

Claude was the one to scramble into his clothing and
go, actually mounting a horse bareback to save time. But
by the time Ian arrived, Vanessa was dead. She had made
her choice.

Chapter Nineteen

SIMON'S FACE WAS WHITE TO THE LIPS, BUT NO WHITER than Noelle's. He wanted to take Noelle by her shoulders and shake her, he wanted to crush her in his arms and kiss her into submission. If both of those things failed, he wanted to pick her up bodily and take her aboard the *Maid of Boston* and lock her in his cabin and not release her until they were far at sea.

He did none of those things. The resolution in her eyes told him that none of them would be of any use. Noelle had made up her mind, and nothing would change it. She was not going to marry him.

"But why? In the name of God, will you tell me why?"

That was one question that Noelle was not going to answer. She could not answer it, without breaking up entirely and dying of shame. The things that Vanessa had said to her, while they'd been on the ship waiting to learn whether they should sail without Simon or put back to port, still burned in her mind, every word like a blow that had left bruises that penetrated to her heart and that would never heal.

Vanessa's death by suicide had swept the island like wildfire. Speculation and rumor ran rife, but no one except the Cottswoods knew anything of the true story. The favored explanation was that Vanessa had killed herself out of remorse because her own trusted slave, the woman Chloe, had taken it on herself to administer cures of her own to her ailing master, and that the supposed cures had all but killed him. An ignorant, superstition-ridden slave, an obeah woman, no white person on the island would put it past her to believe that she knew more than the white doctor.

That, some people said, nodding sagely, might be part of the truth, but what about the Captain from Massachusetts? They were certain that Vanessa had given her heart at last, that she had fallen desperately in love with Simon, but for some unexplainable and all but unbelievable reason, the captain had decided that it was Noelle he loved and wanted. Tragic, saintly Vanessa, whom so many men had loved, to be spurned herself, as incredible as it was!

Simon was convinced that the true story would leak out, little by little. It was impossible that it would not, because Brenda knew, and what Brenda knew, Brenda told. Not with malice, not with any intention of causing mischief, but simply because she could not keep her tongue from wagging. She would confide in one dear, close friend, with the admonition for her not to breathe a word of it, and the friend would pass it along to another friend with the same admonition. The story would grow as it was told and retold, and become garbled, but enough of the truth would be known so Vanessa's reputation as a latter-day angel would be tarnished, and those who had believed in her saintliness would feel the very foundations of their faith shattered.

It was going to be hard on Daniel, and Simon's heart ached for him. But right at the moment everything except the fact that Noelle had told him that she would never marry him was swept from his mind.

"I simply changed my mind," Noelle told him. "I believe that I have that right. As I recall, I am not the first person to change my mind, without giving a reason or any explanation whatever."

Simon winced. He knew that he had that coming, after he had given Noelle every reason to believe that he was serious about her and then turned to Vanessa. But in the mountains, Noelle had told him that she had forgiven him, she had told him that she loved him, she had kissed him and clung to him and promised him that she would marry him.

"That isn't good enough! I won't accept it, Noelle. There must be some other reason, you could not have changed in so short a time!"

"You will have to accept it. If it will salve your pride, one of my most pressing reasons is that I will not leave my father. I know that I can never fill Vanessa's place in his heart, but at least I will be here so that he won't be alone."

"Your father would understand. If you feel that you can't leave him now, so soon after Vanessa's death and before he's regained his full strength, I will be content to wait, no matter how I dislike the idea. I'll come back to Jamaica, and we can be married then. You know that your father is welcome to make his home in Boston with us, as soon as he feels that he can leave the plantation, and so you wouldn't be apart for very long."

"No, Simon. It will be of no use for you to come back. I'm sorry if I've hurt you, but I don't doubt that you'll get over it shortly." That last was not meant as a gibe, although it had come out that way, and Noelle flushed. Still, she turned aside, indicating that this last meeting was over. "I have to go to my father now, so this is good-bye."

She didn't even hold out her hand, much less give Simon a chance to kiss her. He had no way of knowing that she was being as torn apart as he was, no more than he had any notion as to the true reason for her change of heart.

He retraced his steps to the *Maid of Boston*, and spent all the rest of the day making sure that everything was ready for an early sailing. Aaron didn't have to caution the crew to step softly around him: his grim, unsmiling face was warning enough. Even Josh Perkins, who ran to show him the ring that had been delivered to him that morning, took one look at him and backed away. The ring was an exact replica of his own handmade, horseshoe-nail ring, except that Kingston's leading goldsmith had fashioned it from gold. Josh would treasure it for a lifetime, it would always be his proudest possession.

By early afternoon, Simon could find nothing more to do. In spite of all the time that had been lost, his voyage would not be without a tidy profit. He had managed to dispose of a good share of the cargo he had carried, and now the holds were bulging with rum and coffee and indigo, all bought through Bertram Cottswood at a price lower than he could have hoped. Planters were disposing of their crops, gathering together all the cash they could against the coming debacle. Simon's father would be pleased at the bargain he had struck.

With an exclamation, Simon pushed aside a bill of lading that Aaron was showing him, item by item.

"You can check it, Aaron. There's no need for me to go over it, I know that you won't have made any mistakes." Purposefully, he changed into fresh clothing, and set out for the second time that day for the Cottswoods' house. He was going to make one more try to make Noelle see reason, and this time he didn't intend to take no for an answer. Early that morning, he had been too shocked to gather his forces, but now he was certain that he could argue her down. At the very least, they would visit the goldsmith, and Noelle would be wearing his betrothal ring before he sailed.

Neither Noelle nor her father were there. They had set out for Maynard Penn almost immediately after Simon had left that morning. Damn the girl, she hadn't been taking any chances that he'd come back and force her to bend to his will!

"I shouldn't have thought that Daniel Maynard was well enough to return home!" he burst out, his voice filled with all the anger and frustration he felt.

"It will be all right. Ian Macintyre went with them. He'll stay for several days, to make sure that Mr. Maynard is progressing as he should," Brenda told him. "Although I must say that Noelle was in a tearing hurry to leave, you'd have thought that the devil was on her tail! I suppose that she and her father thought that the plantation will fall to wrack and ruin if they didn't get back, but it does seem to me that they could have waited for a few more days! Why, I hardly got to see Noelle at all, what with all that business of Vanessa killing herself, and the funeral, and all! There are dozens of things I still want to ask her—"

For once in her eighteen years, Brenda was cut short. "Miss Brenda, may I borrow a saddle horse?"

"Of course you may, it goes without asking . . ."

Brenda had no time to say any more, in spite of the spate of words and questions that were churning around inside of her fighting to get out, because Simon was already striding toward the stables.

In a matter of minutes he was on the road that led to Maynard Penn. Only his regard for good horseflesh kept him from pushing his borrowed mount at full speed. This was getting to be positively ridiculous! In the mood he was in, Noelle would be lucky if he didn't shake her until her teeth rattled, once he laid hands on her! What kind of a game was she playing, how could she have changed so much in a period of only a few days?

The answer, he was afraid, was staring him full in the face. Ian Macintyre! Noelle had fallen in love with Ian, there could be no other reason for her change of heart. And Ian had gone with her and her father to the plantation, no doubt at Noelle's insistence.

As much as Simon liked Ian, and he considered Ian the

finest friend he had ever known, still all was fair in love
and war. He would never forgive himself if he didn't make
one last, all-out effort to win Noelle back before he left
Jamaica, else the next time he came to the island he would
find that Noelle and Ian were already married and her loss
would be irreversible. He had never dreamed that one
small, dark-haired girl could take such a hold on his heart
that he could not conceive of life without her, but that was
the way it was, and he was going to fight for her with
every atom of strength that he possessed.

Beggar was the first to greet Simon when he arrived,
jumping all over him when he dismounted from his horse.
Next, the little lad came running to take the reins and lead
the horse away, but not before he had set Simon straight
on one important matter.

"Ain't no stableboy, Massa Cap'n," the lad said.
"Only doing it to keep me busy till Massa Ian and me gets
back home. I'se Massa Ian's *assistant!*"

In spite of his black mood, the lad's self-importance
made Simon smile. He was a bright boy, there was no
doubt of that.

A wizened old man rose from where he had been
squatting in a shady spot near the stable, where he had
been talking to the lad. The man's face was so wrinkled
that he had a mummylike appearance, but his eyes were
sharp and intelligent.

"That's Papa Emile. He's teaching me things," the lad
informed Simon. "He lives here now. They built him a
hut, right on top of the spot where that Chloe's was
burned down. That way, with Papa Emile there to guard,
ain't no way that ole obeah woman can come back to
haunt us."

Simon's curiosity got the better of the tearing hurry he
was in to confront Noelle and have it out with her. He
approached the old man and asked, "Papa Emile, how did
you know that you were wanted here at Maynard Penn,
before Ian had a chance to tell you? When he tried to find
you in Kingston, you were already here."

The old man's face wrinkled still more in a toothless smile.

"I'll tell you what I told him. If I told you, you still wouldn't understand. Some things are for you to know, some things are not. I knew, and I came, and I was made welcome. Before I came, there was much fear here. Now there is no fear."

"And Miranda? How is she?"

"Miranda is fine. Not afraid no more, for her or her child. Didn't want to be set free, wants to stay here long's she can. She cooks for me, and does for me, doesn't have to work in the canefield 'less she wants to, but she works anyway. You got no worry about Miranda, she'll be fine."

"I'm glad that you're here, even if I will never understand how you knew to come," Simon told him, offering his hand.

Papa Emile took it, without embarrassment, meeting Simon's eyes man to man. "Do you need me, I'll be here," he said.

The front door was standing open to admit what breeze there was. Simon did not knock. He wanted Noelle to have no chance to evade him. She and Ian were both in the drawing room when Simon shouldered his way past Julie, whose face turned petulant because she was being denied her right, in her new capacity of ruling the house slaves, of announcing him.

Noelle rose to her feet, her face draining of color, but her eyes did not waver as they met his.

"You've come to say good-bye to Ian. I'll find Julie, and have refreshments brought in."

Before Simon could say a word, she was gone, and she did not come back even after Julie had brought in a tray with glasses and bottles.

"That must have been a thumping great quarrel you and Noelle had!" Ian said, raising his eyebrows. "I'm surprised that you even came to Maynard Penn to say good-bye to me. That is why you've come, isn't it?"

"You know damned well that that isn't why I've come!

I want to see Noelle! Unless, of course, I'm already too late. For all I know you've already asked her to marry you, and she's accepted. From the look of things, you've moved in bag and baggage, prepared to stay, your dog, your horse, and the little lad included!"

"She's turned to me, yes. And I don't doubt that she'll accept me in time. Young lasses have a habit of turning to someone else on the rebound. And although a week ago this wouldn't have been true, now it looks as though I may be in a position to ask her sooner than I thought. Everybody in Kingston knows that Daniel Maynard dismissed Eastlake from his case because he wasn't satisfied with the care he gave him, and a good many of Eastlake's patients are sure to come to me as a result. It looks as though I might find myself in comfortable circumstances quite soon now. If you're fool enough to let her get away, I will most certainly ask her to be my wife."

"Not until I've talked to her, you won't!" Simon glared at him. "No, I do not want a drink. What I want just walked out of this room, and I'm going to find her, and if you love her, I'm sorry, but I'm not going to hand her over to you without a fight!"

Noelle had taken refuge in her father's room, hoping that even Simon would not have the temerity to follow her there and renew the quarrel they'd had this morning. But Simon walked in without as much as knocking.

"Simon! My father is napping, the journey from Kingston tired him. And we have nothing to say to each other, it was all said this morning."

Simon's hand closed over her wrist. "We have a good deal to say to each other, and if we can't say it here, then we'll say it in the garden!" He pulled her along behind him, his grip so firm that struggling was of no use. Unless she wanted to scream for help, and disturb and upset her father, she had to go along with him.

In the garden, she turned to face him, her face blazing with anger. "This is pointless, Simon! I am not going to change my mind! I will not marry you, now or ever! Now please leave this plantation! I never want to set eyes on you again as long as I live!''

Simon's answer was to crush her in his arms and kiss her, a kiss that seared and bruised her lips and took the last bit of breath and strength from her body. She stiffened in his arms, pushing against him, refusing to respond. If she responded, if she relaxed her guard even for an instant, everything would be lost. She wouldn't be able to hold out against him, and she would let herself in for a lifetime of heartbreak and humiliation, trying to battle against his memories of Vanessa.

You'll never satisfy him! He'll never forget me, little sister! Do you honestly believe that you could ever satisfy him, after he's had me? When he holds you in his arms, when he makes love to you, it will be me he's thinking of!

Vanessa's words came back to her in all their stinging, taunting force. Noelle made one last effort and broke free.

"Now that you've demonstrated that you're stronger than I am, I hope you're satisfied! But nothing has changed. I still will not marry you.''

"It's Ian, then!'' Now Simon's face was as white as her own, white to the lips. "You've fallen in love with him!''

Noelle took a deep breath and forced her voice to be steady.

"Yes, it is!'' she cried out at him. "I love Ian, not you, and nothing can ever change it!''

Their eyes held for a moment, and then Noelle turned and left him, running back into the house and calling Ian's name. Simon stood where he was for only a second or two longer, before he started to stride toward the stables. He had wanted to make sure, and now he was sure. He had lost and Ian had won. Right at the moment, he had no inclination to see Ian again to congratulate him. All he wanted was the deck of the *Maid of Boston* rolling under his feet, and the open sea.

Papa Emile met him before he reached his destination, leading Pilot. "Your borrowed horse be tired, and you'll be riding fast. You can leave this one with the Cottswoods, and they'll be traded back later," Papa Emile told him.

"That was thoughtful of you, Papa Emile," Simon managed to say, the effort of speaking all but choking him.

"Be it that someone might should ask me, I would tell him that all white men are fools, but some are bigger fools than others," Papa Emile told him.

But Simon was already in the saddle, setting Pilot into a gallop, and Papa Emile's words were all but lost on him, having no meaning. As far as Simon was concerned, very little in life would ever have meaning for him again.

Simon stood by the wheel, where Ned Campbell was keeping the *Maid of Boston* on a steady course. Ned hadn't ventured to speak to his captain, nobody but Aaron Godbehere had dared to speak to him since he had reboarded the ship last night, and ordered that full sail be set at first outgoing tide. And even Aaron had spoken to him in the fewest possible words, and only when it had been absolutely necessary.

At Maynard Penn, Noelle sat disconsolate in the garden, her eyes seeing nothing of the beauty around her. Her father was up, sitting in a chair at the top of the steps leading into the house, going over plantation accounts, and Ian had gone to the fields to tell the overseers that Daniel wanted to speak to them, one at a time. Although grief for what Vanessa had done still showed plainly on his face, he was already picking up the reins of his life, and soon he would be in full control.

A shadow fell across Noelle's face, and she looked up. It was Papa Emile, who dared to come here without being bidden, as no other slave on the plantation would dare to come.

"The mistress is sad because she has been foolish," Papa Emile said.

"I wasn't foolish, Papa Emile. I only did what I had to do. I had no choice."

"Always there is a choice. If one person does not fight

for what he wants, then he is a fool because he will have no chance of getting it."

"There was no way I could fight Vanessa! There is no way I could ever fight her!" Noelle cried, agony in her voice.

"Your sister is dead, and her evil is dead with her. But you are alive. Those who live can fight. You let your sister fool you with her wicked lies. They were lies, Mistress Noelle, all lies. This I know. The one who went away loves only you, and he has only disgust for the memory of that other one."

"He'd go on remembering her, he'd never forget her!"

"It would be for you to make him forget, if that is what you think. But there would have been no need. His memory of her now is nothing but hatred, and soon even that would fade and go away and he would not remember her at all. If someone should have asked me, this is what I would have told her."

"How do you know so much? How do you know how it was between Simon and me, between Vanessa and me?" Noelle looked at the old man out of tear-dimmed eyes.

Papa Emile knew what Dicey and Cuffie knew, but there was no need to tell the young mistress this.

"And even if what you say is true, it's too late! Simon is gone, and he will never come back!"

"Are you an obeah woman, that you know such things?" The voice was gentle, but with a little laughter in it.

"Of course I'm not! I don't have to be an obeah woman to know that he won't come back! I made sure that he wouldn't, when I told him that I loved Ian!"

"Were he to come back, would you be a fool again?" Papa Emile wanted to know.

"Yes . . . no . . . I don't know!" Noelle cried. She rose from the wrought-iron bench and gathered up her skirts and ran toward the house, to throw herself across her bed and weep as she had not allowed herself to weep before. All of the slaves on the plantation said that Papa Emile was wise, that he was the wisest man who had ever lived. Dicey and Cuffie both swore that this was true. If they were right, then she had been the biggest fool who had ever lived!

She knew that Ian loved her. She knew that eventually he would ask her to marry him. She knew that she was so fond of him that they would be able to have a happy and successful marriage, except for one thing. She would be cheating him, because when he held her in his arms and made love to her, it would be Simon she was thinking about, Simon for whom she was longing.

She would never marry. She would stay with her father, and devote her life to trying to make him as happy as it would be possible to make him. But no matter how well she succeeded in erasing his bitter memories, her life would be sterile.

And so she wept, and wondered if she would ever be able to stop.

In the garden, Dicey and Cuffie looked at Papa Emile.

"How you know he'll come back?" Dicey demanded. "How you know that for sure?"

"Did I tell you, you wouldn't understand. Say I made a spell," Papa Emile said. And smiling, he walked away.

On the deck of the *Maid of Boston,* Simon's face turned even more grim than it had been ever since he had come aboard.

"Come about!" he barked at Ned Campbell. "Put back for Jamaica!"

"Cap'n?" Ned asked, his face blank with surprise.

"You heard the captain's order! Put about!" Aaron Godbehere barked at him. Giving his captain only one look, Aaron left him standing by the wheel and found some other business to occupy him. It had taken Simon longer than Aaron had thought it would, but now that the order had been given, Aaron's faith in his own intuition was vindicated.

It was midmorning of the following day when Simon arrived back at Maynard Penn. Once again the little lad ran to take his horse. At the Cottswoods' house in

Kingston, Brenda was still flabbergasted, but far from speechless.

"Mama, I must have a new gown! A fabulous gown! If I'm to be Noelle's bridesmaid, then I must do her credit! Claude will stand up with Simon, I'm sure that Henry would refuse and I can't really blame him, even if Noelle did tell him all along that she wouldn't marry him! Noelle and Simon won't have much time to make plans, so we must make them for them! Have Papa arrange for the church at a moment's notice, and you'll have to help me spread the word so everybody will be prepared when they're bidden to attend a wedding. We'll have to have at least three seamstresses to get my dress ready on time, but that's no matter. I shall want blue because that's my best color, that new bolt of silk in Papa's warehouse will do very nicely, and you shall have the mauve, if he's already sold them I'll never forgive him!"

"Brenda, how can you be talking about a wedding, when all Captain Spencer did was ask to borrow a horse?"

"Oh, Mama, don't be so obtuse! Of course they're going to be married, didn't you see his face? And it's just about time things were settled between them, the suspense was beginning to wear me down to a shadow!" Brenda patted her plump waist, quite unaware that she hadn't lost an ounce. "Come, come, don't just sit there, we've a hundred things to do!"

"Brenda, there cannot be a large wedding! It would be flying in the face of all decency, with Vanessa only just in her grave!" Faith Cottswood finally managed to remind her daughter.

"Bother! Then I suppose that we will be the only ones to attend, and no doubt the crew of the *Maid of Boston*, they will want to see their captain married, surely. And we'll have the wedding breakfast or dinner or whatever right here, as fancy as if all of Kingston were coming. Esther must bake the most fabulous wedding cake ever, except for mine when the time comes, of course. Do get up out of that chair, Mama, and start helping me arrange things, we haven't all that much time you know, and everything must be perfect for Noelle. I'm so excited I can't even think!'' Which was probably true, but that didn't keep Brenda from talking, and that was the only important thing.

Once again Simon entered the plantation house without knocking to give advance warning of his arrival. He found Noelle and her father in Daniel's study, where Daniel was dictating a letter to the governor, and Noelle was copying it down in her neat, precise hand.

Simon placed himself directly in front of the desk, his legs spread as though he were on his own quarter-deck. Noelle's escape was cut off, she would have no chance to run away from him this time.

''Mr. Maynard, I am going to marry your daughter,'' he said.

Daniel's mouth quirked at the corners in a slight smile. ''So young Ian has apprised me, he having learned it from Papa Emile.''

The quill had dropped from Noelle's hand, leaving a series of blots across the paper. ''Simon! I thought that you had left Jamaica!'' Her heart was beating like a kettle drum, and her breath stilled in her throat.

''Ships sail both ways. It was only a matter of turning around and coming back. I remembered what Papa Emile said to me as I was leaving Maynard Penn the last time. He said that all white men are fools, but some are greater fools than others. I've been a fool, but I decided not to be a greater fool than I've already been. Your change toward me was too sudden, Noelle. There's something behind it, and I would be the greatest fool ever born if I didn't get to the bottom of it! I'm not going to stand for any more nonsense from you. I want the truth, and I want it now!''

Noelle had started to tremble, and Simon couldn't bear it. He reached for her, and drew her to her feet and into his arms, holding her close, swearing that he would never let her go.

''Vanessa said things to me, terrible things.'' Noelle's

voice was faint. "She said that you would never forget
her, that all of your life you would remember her, and the
g-g-glory you had with her, g-g-glory that I could never
give you! She told me everything, Simon, and I couldn't
bear it, there was no way I could bear it. She was so
b-b-beautiful, every man who ever saw her loved her, and
I'm just me, n-n-not beautiful at all, and I don't know how
to compete with her, I could never be like her . . ."

"And you believed her! You're as great a fool as I am,
Noelle! How could you believe her lies, how could you
have doubted that it's you I love? Vanessa bewitched me,
but she had to have Chloe's help to do it! Don't you
remember Chloe's potions, the things she could do with
them? They drugged me, Noelle, they gave me something
to make my blood run hot and my mind become befuddled, else it would never have happened! And I thought
that you had cooled toward me, you changed toward me as
soon as Vanessa came to Kingston and I met her, you
acted as though you couldn't care less about those moments we shared, as though you'd only been enjoying a
flirtation, but now your interest had waned.

"I'm only a man, I'm not a gangan like Papa Emile!
Men make mistakes, but they don't have to go on making
them, any more than women have to go on making them!
You're going to marry me, and sail to Boston with me,
and all of this will be behind us and we'll never think of it
again!"

Noelle's trembling became even more pronounced.
There was nothing that she wanted more in the world!
Papa Emile was right. It was for her to make Simon forget
Vanessa, it was for her to fight for him and for her own
happiness, and his. But there was her father, how could
she leave him now, when he needed her as he had never
needed her before?

"My father . . ." she said, her breath catching in a
heartbroken sob.

Daniel Maynard looked at her, this younger daughter
whom he had always loved, but who had always been

forced to take second place to Vanessa. He bore a burden of guilt about that, and he was not going to add to it by asking her to stay with him now, as much as he dreaded her leaving him.

"I want you to marry Simon, Noelle, and go with him. You love him and he loves you. You have suffered enough. The scandal of Vanessa's actions is already spreading throughout Jamaica, and I do not want you to be here to have to bear the curious stares, the curious questions that will come as people begin to seek us out, determined to rake it all up and learn every detail at firsthand. I want you well out of it, safe with Simon where you belong. It will not trouble me overmuch, I have a great deal of work to do, helping the governor and other men of good will prepare for the emancipation and its consequences. I will be far too busy to let it bother me."

Simon gave Daniel a look of gratitude. "Thank you, sir."

"We will go to Kingston at once, and arrange for your marriage." Daniel gathered some papers together and placed a paper weight on them, and rose from his chair. "There is no need to look so stricken. I will visit you in Boston from time to time, especially when there is a new grandchild for me to see." He would have grandsons, boys who could never take Kenneth's place but who would fill his heart and make his grieving for his son fade. And granddaughters, who would fill his heart with tenderness as he dandled them on his knee.

Dicey poked her head into the room. "Cuffie and me already ready. Not that much to pack, and what we got, it's packed," she said. "I'll get Mistress Noelle's things packed right now."

"I suppose that Papa Emile told you that I'd be back, and take you to Massachusetts with me?" Simon's left eyebrow rose, and Noelle's heart turned over. She wished that he wouldn't do that! How could she kiss him the way it made her want to kiss him, with a passion that was positively shameful, right here in front of her father?

"He told us true," Dicey said, smiling a starry-eyed smile. "And he told us that we going to be happy, all of us, and I know that true, too. We better hurry, that Mistress Brenda, she's getting everything ready there in Kingston for you to get married."

Ian loomed up behind her. "And I suppose Papa Emile has seen through all the miles between here and Kingston, to know that Brenda is being her usual busy, bossy self and arranging everything! Now how do you suppose he knows such things, Dicey? No, don't answer. If he were to tell us, we still wouldn't understand."

If Papa Emile had told them, he would have lost a great deal of his mystery and supposed magic powers. The antics of white people amused the gangan, and like Henry Cottswood, he was a keen observer of human nature. Because of his friendship with Ian and Ian's friendship with the Cottswoods, Papa Emile had observed the Cottswoods closely, and he had recognized not only Brenda's bossiness and proclivity to run everything, but her intuition. Simon had stopped at the Cottswoods' to borrow a horse, so Brenda knew where he was coming, and the gangan did not doubt for a moment that Brenda's intuition had told her that this time Simon would not take no for an answer. Therefore, a wedding was in the offing, and of course Brenda would insist on managing it.

"Ian!" Noelle's voice was stricken. Ian was being hurt, and she hated for him to be hurt.

Ian grinned. "Don't give it a thought, Noelle. I'd have made a poor husband, my nose forever in some medical tome, or I'd be off searching for all those plants and herbs I'm determined to wrest secrets from! Or trying to wring Papa Emile's secrets from him, with a great deal less success. But I'm working on the wily old boy, and I'll wring him dry before I'm through! I won't languish from loneliness, I have quite a household now, you know. The little lad, and Beggar, and Explorer, and the new goat I'll acquire as soon as I'm settled back at home.

"By the way, did you know that I have a new and

important patient? Not that I'll be keeping him long. Henry Cottswood had me give him a going over, and prescribe something to alleviate his seasickness when he sails for England. I made sure not to tell him that the concoction came from Papa Emile! For all that Vanessa's death left Henry shaken, he seems to have landed on his feet. He told me that no doubt he'll find another woman in England who will suit him as well, and one who will be a deal less expensive to keep and no end less trouble.''

"Good for Henry. I half hope that he ends up with a battle-ax, but on the other hand he's behaved quite well these last few days. Ian, how long are you going to go on calling the boy 'the little lad'? Isn't it about time he had a name?''

"He's named himself. He calls himself Little Lad.'' Ian's grin became even wider. "When he isn't little any more, I'll see what I can do to change it to just plain Lad. Go on, you two. Have yourselves a few minutes alone. Once you get to Kingston, you won't be able to shake Brenda off until you're man and wife and locked in your cabin on the *Maid of Boston*. I'll see that no one disturbs you until the curricle is ready. I just hope that Noelle doesn't take enough luggage to sink the ship!''

In the drawing room, Simon held Noelle close, chafing at every moment that he would have to endure before they actually were alone in his cabin, with no man in his crew daring to disturb him unless the *Maid of Boston* were actually about to sink. Noelle still trembled in his arms, but her cheeks were flaming as she thought of the cabin door closing behind them, and the gentle swell of the waves that would rock Simon's narrow bed, a bed that had never been designed for two but that would be more than wide enough.

A new world was opening up before her, a world of such glory that even Vanessa could never have dreamed of it. Her world, and Simon's, and the glory would be of their own making, because they had had the courage to fight for it.

Here in Simon's arms, she vowed that she would never look back, and as Simon's lips closed over hers and she felt the long hardness of his body press against her, she knew that it was a vow that would be easy to keep.

Jamaica was said to be a paradise, but she was not leaving paradise, she was just entering it.

Tapestry
HISTORICAL ROMANCES

POCKET BOOKS.

GOLDEN DESTINY
Jean Saunders
61744/$3.50

SWEET REVENGE
Patricia Pellicane
61761/$3.50

MY REBEL, MY LOVE
Willo Davis Roberts
61448/$3.50

AN UNFORGOTTEN LOVE
Jacqueline Marten
62346/$2.95

SILVER MOON
Monica Barrie
62843/$2.95

BELOVED ENEMY
Cynthia Sinclair
63017/$2.95

WHISPERS IN THE WIND
Patricia Pellicane
63015/$2.95

MIDWINTER'S NIGHT
Jean Canavan
64686/$2.95

SHADOWS OF DESIRE
Catherine Lyndell
64397/$2.95

FOX HUNT
Carol Jerina
64640/$2.95

TENDER LONGING
Rebecca George
61449/$2.95

BRIGHT DESIRE
Erica Mitchell
64395/$2.95

___ FIERY HEARTS
Julia Grice
61709/$3.50

___ ENCHANTED DESIRE
Marylye Rogers
54430/$2.95

___ JOURNEY TO LOVE
Cynthia Sinclair
54605/$2.95

___ GENTLE WARRIOR
Julie Garwood
54746/$2.95

___ THE GOLDEN LILY
Jan McGowan
54388/$2.95

___ RIVER TO RAPTURE
Louisa Gillette
52364/$2.95

___ A LOVING ENCHANTMENT
Cynthia Sinclair
60356/$2.95

___ SEPTEMBER'S DREAM
Ruth Ryan Langan
60453/$2.95

___ LOVING LONGEST
Jacqueline Marten
54608/$2.95

___ A MINSTREL'S SONG
Marylyle Rogers
54604/$2.95

___ HIGHLAND TRYST
Jean Canavan
61742/$3.50

___ SWEET POSSESSION
Elizabeth Turner
61447/$3.50

Tapestry

886